The Secret of Goldenrod

The Secret of Goldenrod

JANE O'REILLY

CAROLRHODA BOOKS
MINNEAPOLIS

Carolrhoda Books
A division of Lerner Publishing Group, Inc.
241 First Avenue North
Minneapolis, MN 55401 USA

For reading levels and more information, look up this title at www.lernerbooks.com.

Illustrations by Elly MacKay.

Additional images: © Shtonado/Shutterstock.com (title font); © Oleg Golovnev/Shutterstock.com (border); © Le Chernina/Shutterstock.com (texture).

Main body text set in Bembo Std 12/16.5.
Typeface provided by Monotype.

Library of Congress Cataloging-in-Publication Data

Names: O'Reilly, Jane H.
Title: The secret of Goldenrod / by Jane O'Reilly.
Description: Minneapolis : Carolrhoda Books, [2016] | Summary: "Fifth-grader Trina, who has never lived anywhere long enough to call home, is excited about moving into Goldenrod, an abandoned mansion, with her dad. But soon Goldenrod brings its secrets to her attention, including a forgotten doll, leaving Trina wondering what the old house wants from her." —Provided by publisher
Identifiers: LCCN 2015038098| ISBN 9781512401356 (th : alk. paper) | ISBN 9781512408942 (eb pdf)
Subjects: | CYAC: Dwellings—Fiction. | Moving, Household—Fiction. | Dolls—Fiction. | Friendship—Fiction. | Mothers and daughters—Fiction. | Fathers and daughters—Fiction.
Classification: LCC PZ7.1.O7 Se 2016 | DDC [Fic]—dc23

LC record available at http://lccn.loc.gov/2015038098

Manufactured in the United States of America
1-38945-20974-4/4/2016

For Jack, Hudson, and Ella Jane

Chapter One

Trina pushed up the brim of her baseball cap and strained against her seat belt to look through the dusty, bug-smeared windshield. "Do you see it yet, Poppo?"

Her dad shook his head, yawning. The two full days of driving since they left New Mexico were nothing compared to the eternity of the last twenty minutes on a narrow two-lane road flanked by nothing but cornfields.

The ball game on the radio turned to garbled voices and then to static. "Read me the directions again," her dad said, turning off the radio. "The part after we exit the highway."

Trina reached for the letter. The smudged and crumpled letter she had read a million times. *"Go east until you come to the big red barn with three silos. Then turn left onto the dirt road. After the double bump, cross the creek and turn right."*

"That's it? That's all it says?"

"Yup," Trina said, and then she continued to read the letter out loud with brand-new excitement. *"The house is a Queen Anne with six bedrooms, four fireplaces, a library, a parlor, a butler's pantry . . ."* Wait a minute. How could she have missed it all these times? "Poppo, it doesn't say anything about bathrooms. It better have indoor plumbing."

"There's always . . . you know." He pointed at the cornfields.

"No way," Trina said, grimacing. Then she rushed to her favorite part of the letter. *"The Harlan M. Roy family is giving you one year to restore the house to marketable condition."* No matter how many times she read that line, she couldn't believe it. One whole year was almost like having a real home. And now she couldn't wait to get there. "Please hurry, Poppo."

"Hurry? Any faster and I might miss the turn."

"Please," Trina insisted, knowing her dad was often too calm about important things.

"How about you read and I drive?" he said.

Trina scrunched up her face at him and turned back to the letter. *"Mechanical systems are functional but not up to code. A credit account has been established at Hank's Tool and Lumber on Main Street for all your supplies. The key to the front door will be under the mat. At your service, Mr. Gerald Shegstad."* Trina sighed. "Six bedrooms and four fireplaces."

"Biggest house we've ever fixed up," her dad said.

"But what's a Queen Anne?"

"The fancy kind. With gingerbread and wraparound porches."

"Gingerbread?" Trina asked.

"You know, all that frilly trim they used to put around the eaves of the roof." Her dad drew curlicues in the air as he spoke. "It'll probably look like a wedding cake."

Trina imagined the house as big and as fancy as a palace, and herself as the princess with a grand bedroom and servants. "But what's marketable condition?"

"So it can be sold. It's been in the same family for over a hundred years but nobody's lived there for a really long time. Some great-great-nephew in New York inherited it and he's decided he'd rather have the money than the house."

Trina looked out her window, watching row after row after row of corn, corn, corn, thinking about what her dad had said. "That's sad. If I had a house that had been in my family for a hundred years, I'd keep it forever, wouldn't you?"

Her dad shook his head. "People always want what they don't have. If they have big, they want small. If they have the country, they want the city. If they stay too long in one place, they want to get moving."

"And if they're always moving, sometimes they want to stay put," Trina added, looking forward to calling New Royal, Iowa, home. At least for a year, anyway.

Her dad reached over and tugged on the bill of her baseball cap. "Until they catch the traveling bug all over again, like you and me."

Trina didn't actually have the traveling bug. Her dad did. And her mother had it worst of all. Her mother was exactly the restless person her dad was talking about. He always said she was trying to find herself. Luckily her postcards, which came from all over the world, had no problem finding Trina wherever she was. The last one had come from Tanzania in East Africa. "Sounds just like Mom," she said.

"I guess," her dad said.

Trina was used to the silence that followed any mention of her mother. She figured her dad missed her so much he couldn't talk about her. But the more postcards she got, the more curious about her mother Trina became. She hadn't seen her mother in nearly eight years and she had no idea what her mother looked like now, or how she dressed and wore her hair. And if she liked sports. Someday her mother would have to run out of places to visit and then she'd come home.

As the truck crested a hill, Trina could see a big red barn in the shallow valley below. "There's a red barn," she said. "With silos!" She leaned forward in her seat. "One . . . two . . . three!" And when they reached the bottom of the hill, there was the dirt road. They took a left-hand turn and bounced off the main road onto nothing more than a rutted dirt path that cut through a field of cornstalks taller than the truck.

They were almost there now. Trina could feel it. With an urge to jump out of the truck and run the rest of the way, she rolled down her window and stuck her head into the steamy August air, watching for any sign of a house at the end of the tunnel of dirt road and corn.

The truck bounced over a large bump with a loud *ca-thunk* and Trina bounced with the truck. The old cargo trailer heaved behind them, sounding like it was ready to snap off.

Ca-thunk. The truck jolted again.

"I guess that's the double bump," her dad said. Trina checked the trailer in the rearview mirror, glad to see it was still attached.

"Look!" Trina cried. "Up there! I see the bridge!"

The truck shuddered over the wooden bridge and headed straight for a wall of corn. "That was the creek! Turn right, Poppo! Turn right!"

Her dad placed one big, calm hand over the other and turned the wheel. "What else would we do but turn right?"

All of a sudden, Trina had a funny feeling the house was waiting for them and they were running late. She kept her eyes glued to the windshield as the truck rolled on and on through the cornfield. Her dad's cell phone rang, just once, before it went silent. He glanced at its blank screen. "So much for cell service way out here."

At that moment, the cornfields gave way to a meadow of tall yellow flowers, and then a big gray house with gables and chimneys emerged as if it were growing straight out of the ground. Her dad put his foot on the brake and let the truck inch its way to a tall black wrought iron gate. Trina could feel her mouth hanging open as she stared through the bars of the gate at the enormous house.

The house was not what she had expected. It didn't need to be fixed up. It needed to be torn down. Boards covered all the windows, and the few shutters that remained dangled from their hinges. Pillars that would have held up a porch roof, if the porch had still been there, lay in the weeds like fallen trees.

Trina blinked and blinked, hoping she would open her eyes to the palace she had imagined. But with each blink the house just looked worse. There wasn't a fleck of paint on the wind-beaten siding or a crumb of gingerbread anywhere. If the house was supposed to look like a wedding cake, the bride had to be an evil witch.

"Poppo—"

"I know what you're thinking," he said, shifting the truck into park just before he let out a sweeping whistle. "Isn't she a beauty?"

No, their next project wasn't a beauty. It was a hopeless old house, sitting in the middle of a yellow sea like a dried-up island. "We aren't really going to live here, are we?" Trina asked.

"Trina," her dad said in surprise. "You know I signed a contract. Besides, I think it's going to be a lot of fun working on this place."

Fun. Fun was playing softball. Fun was going to the movies. Fun was not fixing up a decrepit old house in the middle of nowhere. Trina sat helplessly in the truck as her dad got out and waded through the sea of yellow flowers. He pushed open one side of the big black gate, which squealed in protest, and then the other side, which was just as rusty. He hopped back into the driver's seat without closing the door and let his foot drag through the snapping overgrowth as they crawled to a stop beneath a gnarled arm of a giant oak tree. "What if I make you a swing and hang it from that big branch?"

Trina sighed, disappointed by the house and even more disappointed by her dad for still thinking of her as a little girl. He should know that almost fifth graders were too old for swings.

Reluctantly, Trina got out of the truck. She felt as limp

as the tall flowers all around her until the eerie feeling that someone was watching her from the highest window—a window that was all boarded up—snapped her to attention. She shivered, despite the heat.

"Poppo, do you think it's haunted?"

"You and your imagination," he said, shaking his head. "If I've said it once, I've said it a million times. There's no such thing as a haunted house." He hooked his thumbs in his belt loops and looked up at the house. "Try seeing her for the masterpiece she really is." Pointing up at the roof, he said, "See the fancy corbels under the eaves?"

Trina had no idea what a corbel was, but she knew she saw nothing but gray, weathered wood. "Sure," she said.

"And just think about sitting on the porch and sipping lemonade all afternoon. Or sliding down the porch railing into the front yard."

Almost fifth graders were also too old for sliding down railings, and there was no porch, and the front yard was an overgrown mass of weeds, but Trina nodded anyway. Arguing with Poppo at a time like this would be as hopeless as the old house.

"And that turret?"

"The what?" Trina said, feeling her voice getting sadder and sadder.

"That little tower with the pointed roof." He cupped his hands around his mouth and shouted, "Rapunzel! Rapunzel!"

Right then, as if answering his call, a small bird darted from its nest in the eaves, which made Trina wonder what else might be living in the big, abandoned house.

"That turret is fit for a princess just like you. Windows on all sides for a view of your own country gardens." Then he yanked one of the tall yellow flowers from the ground, roots and all. "Look at all these weeds. No wonder they call her Goldenrod."

"Who?"

"The house."

"The house has a name?"

"Sure she does. And isn't she amazing? She's what you call a grande dame." He bowed to the house as if it were royalty. "I am honored to make your acquaintance, Madam Goldenrod."

Trina looked up at Madam Goldenrod, but the only amazing thing about her was that she was still standing. Even so, she tried to play along with her dad's giant dream. She even tried to imagine the house with a coat of paint. "She's such a beautiful . . ." But there was nothing at all beautiful about the house. Trina's eyes shifted from the drab clapboard house to the sparkling meadow of yellow goldenrod. "Yellow," she said, trying to sound excited. After all, yellow was her mother's favorite color.

"Then yellow she'll be!" her dad said. He took the steps—nothing but stacked bricks and rotten planks—two at a time and playfully knocked on the faded *No Trespassing* sign tacked to the door.

"The key is under the mat," Trina reminded him, but that didn't matter. One of the big wooden double doors creaked open on its own, and he stepped inside.

Trina slowly went up the makeshift steps and paused at

the open door. She lifted a corner of the ragged doormat, which was anything but welcoming. No key. She peeled away the doormat completely, revealing a rectangle of dark wood where the doormat had sat forever, but still no key.

"Trina?" her dad's distant voice called.

"Coming," she said. But with her first step across the threshold into the pitch-black house, she felt like she was barging in where she didn't belong. As if the darkness was a suspicious old lady, her white cobweb hair tied up in a bun, standing with her dusty hands on her hips, blocking Trina's way. Trina stopped dead in her tracks, wishing she had stayed in the truck.

"Power must be off," her dad called from somewhere deep in the darkness. "Shoot," he said as Trina heard him slap his pockets. "No flashlight. Lucky I still have my lighter." A tiny dot of flame appeared like a lightning bug. The creaks of his footsteps moved farther away, taking the dot of light with him, and then something squealed like a mad cat.

"Poppo?" Trina yelled, scared that the house had gotten him.

"Just a squeaky door," he hollered back.

More doors squeaked and boots clomped down hollow steps. He must have been heading to the basement to turn on the electricity—if a house this old even had electricity.

The air inside the house was thick, and somehow it even smelled forgotten. The odor tickled her nose and she sneezed so hard the noise echoed around her, making her feel very small and very alone.

Except for that strange feeling she wasn't.

A light came on in a distant room. It was dim and flickering, but Trina could see enough to know she was standing in a foyer as big as a hotel lobby.

In front of her was a grand staircase that reached into the blackness of the second floor while the rest of the house stretched off forever and ever into the shadows.

"Man, is our work cut out for us," her dad said, his voice bouncing in the emptiness. "But she has steam heat, and someone delivered us a brand-new refrigerator, washer, and dryer. And lucky for you, I passed a bathroom on my way to the basement. Right by the servants' stairs." He pushed the top button of an odd-looking light switch on the wall, and a few dusty bulbs of a fancy chandelier with beads and prisms lit up high above Trina's head.

The speckled light revealed pale wood floors, but the banister, doors, and archways were made of dark wood. "Look at this place," he said. "The whole house is trimmed in mahogany."

Mahogany schmogany. The house was dark and creepy and it smelled like a cellar. "Is steam heat a good thing?"

"Steam heat is amazing," he said, standing on the tips of his boots to examine a tarnished brass sconce mounted on the wall. "Watch this," he said as he turned a valve on the bottom of the sconce and flicked his lighter. A flame shot out of the top of the sconce at the same time an electric light bulb glowed beneath it. "They didn't trust electricity back then, so the fixtures used gas, too."

Then, without a word, he sprinted past the staircase, pushed open two fancily carved sliding doors and pulled them shut again, leaving Trina by herself in the foyer. "Pocket doors," he shouted, his voice muffled. "I think I'm in the library. There are built-in bookcases everywhere." Before Trina had a chance to be scared, he slid the doors back open.

Trina was actually curious about the library. Maybe books had been left behind. She'd be happy for any sign that people had really once lived there. But one look around the big dreary room made her heart sink. The library shelves, a forest's worth of mahogany, were completely empty.

Trina stayed close to her dad as he walked past a deep, blackened fireplace, toward another pair of pocket doors. These doors led to the darkest of rooms. "Ah, the smoking room," her dad said, inhaling deeply. "You can still smell the burning pipe tobacco."

Even with a light on, the room was really dark. Her dad spotted a doorknob, nearly invisible in the heavy paneling, and turned it. "Look, a secret passageway." Trina was afraid he'd leave her alone again, so she grabbed hold of his T-shirt and followed him.

"Where are we, Poppo?" Trina asked as they walked down the passageway in the darkness.

"Under the stairs," he said. "And if I'm right, this room will be . . ." He paused to open a second door to another disappointingly empty room with another dusty chandelier. "The dining room. Just as I suspected." Trina let go of his T-shirt.

"Man, look at that buffet," her dad said, pointing at a long cupboard with a big mirror above it. "And those

French doors must lead outside," he added, glancing at a wall of boards as he kept going, passing under a spindled archway into a room as big as a school gym, which had a huge fireplace and another elaborate chandelier. From there Trina could see the archway that led back to the foyer. Trina sensed that whoever, or *whatever*, had met her at the front door was still standing there. Waiting. Trina quickly turned her back on the foyer. "Is this the living room?"

"Yup. But I think they were called parlors back then."

His voice was muffled again. This time he was reaching up inside the chimney. Metal clanked against metal as he forced open the flue. When he crawled back out, a look of deep concern crossed his face. "She's got good bones, but . . ."

Trina waited for his next word, wondering if he felt the presence of someone in the house the way she did. She held her breath as he looked from the boarded-up bay window to the curling wallpaper and the cracked plaster on the ceiling.

"She has good bones, but what?"

He kicked at a bit of fallen plaster. "She's suffered from being empty."

The hair on Trina's arms prickled. "What do you mean?"

"A house goes downhill when no one lives in it. It needs people. People who love it." He wiped his sooty hands on his pants. "I guess I'm saying she needs us."

Trina didn't like thinking of the house as something that needed her. "I think it's too much work, Poppo."

"Nah, nothing stops us," he said with a big grin. And then he put his hand on her shoulder. "I bet some lunch will perk you up. The kitchen is back that way," he said, pointing through the dining room. "I'll get the cooler."

At the far end of the dining room was a swinging door that screeched as Trina pushed through it into what had to be the butler's pantry because it was full of a million empty cabinets with leaded glass doors. She pushed through another swinging door and finally arrived at a kitchen big enough for ten cooks. The walls were covered in white tiles and the sink was nearly as big as a bathtub. Above the sink was a boarded-up window, and between the sink and a big black stove was a doorway to a small bathroom, a boarded-up back door and a plain, narrow staircase that led both up and down. The servants' stairway.

As Trina ran her hand along the long marble counter-top, she found a bill:

SPOT-RITE HOUSE CLEANING
DAVENPORT, IA

General	$1500.00
Travel	$125.00
Total	$1625.00

PAID IN FULL

Knowing she wouldn't have to do the cleaning was the first good thing about Goldenrod, and then she realized the kitchen floor was filthy, which meant the cleaners hadn't done a very good job.

A loud *SCREECH* made Trina jump, but she quickly recognized the sound of nails being ripped from wood. More screeches were followed by a bang as a board fell off the kitchen window and sunlight poured in over the sink. Standing outside was her dad, waving at Trina with his hammer, his sweaty face as red as the bandana he held in his other hand.

Trina leaned across the sink and shouted at the closed window. "What about the cooler?"

Her dad frowned, which meant he had forgotten all about lunch. He held up his finger and mouthed the words, "One minute."

One minute, right. One minute to Poppo was like an hour to everyone else. Whenever he started a project he'd lose track of time. Sometimes he even forgot what day it was.

Sighing for at least the hundredth time that day, Trina turned on the cold water faucet and was promptly splashed with rusty brown water that smelled like a swamp. "Yuck!" she said out loud. She left the faucet on, just like her dad had taught her, hoping the dirty water would eventually run clear.

CREAK!

Trina jumped again, as annoyed by her jumpiness as she was by the noises.

"Better oil this door," her dad said, coming through the swinging door. He set the cooler, topped with two bags of groceries, on the kitchen counter. "How about I make you a peanut butter sandwich?"

"I'm old enough to make lunch, Poppo."

"You bet," he said. Then he spotted the bill on the counter. "Davenport! That's a long way to drive to clean a house. I would have cleaned it myself for that much. How about you?"

Trina shook her head. "No way." Even if the cleaners hadn't done a very good job, she had to give them credit for cleaning up the cobwebs and bugs and whatever else that must have been living in the house for a hundred years. And then she put two and two together. She imagined the cleaners washing and sweeping, working hard until they heard a noise and the hairs on their necks prickled and they felt sure someone was watching them. Scared to death, they raced out of the house before they finished—too frightened to put the key back under the mat.

"Water looks pretty good," her dad said as he turned off the faucet. Then he pulled out a little notepad and his contractor's pencil. The pages were already filling with lists and calculations. "I need to trim that oak tree before it rips any more slate off the roof. Lucky it's slate. Should last another hundred years."

As he talked and made notes, Trina unloaded paper plates, plastic cups, plastic silverware, and a big roll of paper towels—all the luxuries of living out of the truck—followed by the basics: peanut butter, grapes, spaghetti, pickles, milk, bread, butter, instant coffee, and dish soap.

"First real order of business will be putting in the new septic system before the ground freezes," her dad said.

Trina's hand stopped on the jar of dill pickles. "A *new* septic system? Does that mean we can't use the bathroom?"

He laughed. "We might get a few surprises, but yes, we can use the bathroom."

"What kinds of surprises?" Trina asked, slathering peanut butter on two pieces of bread and layering the pickles between them—just the way he liked it. And then she made her own sandwich—no pickles.

"You never know what can happen with these old houses," he said, just as the ceiling light flickered.

Trina raised her eyebrows. "Was that one of the surprises?"

"Nah," he said without looking up. "That's just a bulb that's loose in its socket."

Trina poured milk into the plastic cups and set the peanut butter sandwiches on paper plates. Her dad slipped his pencil over his ear and grabbed half his sandwich, downing it in two bites. "I'm going into town to get lumber for the new porch. I'll need every inch of room in the truck. You stay here, okay?" He grabbed the other half of his sandwich. "Maybe unpack the trailer."

"All by myself?" she squeaked.

"Not everything," he said as he crumpled his paper plate and stuffed it into an empty grocery bag. "I'll help with the big stuff. Should be back in a couple hours."

Unpacking the trailer by herself was not what Trina had meant, but the last thing she wanted was for her dad to think she was afraid to be alone. *There's no such thing as a haunted house. There's no such thing as a haunted house.* If there was ever a chance to prove she was growing up, this was it. Trying to sound brave, she said, "I'll pick out my room while you're gone."

Chapter Two

Trina finished her sandwich alone, leaning over the sink and looking out through the ancient rippled glass, beyond an overgrown field, to a grove of trees acres away. No neighbors, no roads, no nothing.

Even when they lived on the outskirts of Santa Fe, they had neighbors. Neighbors she could wave at. Neighbors with friendly dogs. And when they lived up in the hills in Portland, she could see the city lights glimmering like stars when she walked outside at night.

But from the kitchen window at Goldenrod, all Trina could see was an endless ocean of yellow weeds. Not even flowers. Weeds. At least she could look forward to school. For the first time in her life she'd get to stay in one place long enough to make friends. "One friend. That's all I ask," Trina said to the window.

The ceiling light flickered, and Trina whirled around and looked up. If Poppo were home he'd just tell her it was a loose bulb, but Trina wondered if the house was somehow listening to her. But now she was scaring herself. And she didn't want to be scared if she was going to be alone in the biggest, darkest, creepiest house she'd ever set foot in.

She wanted to be strong and grown-up. "There's no such thing as a haunted house," she said out loud to the kitchen.

The light flickered again.

Ignoring the light, she stomped straight through the house and outside. She found a branch beneath the oak tree, wedged open the front door with it, and fought through the goldenrod to get to the trailer.

She set up the card table in the dining room, followed by the folding chairs. By the time she made the trip for the fourth chair, she had flattened the weeds into a thick, yellow-green path. Next was the laundry basket full of pillows, sheets, and towels, and then a box with their spaghetti pot, two saucepans, a frying pan, and a bunch of other cooking stuff. Everything fit into a single cupboard.

She was down to their bags of clothes.

The time had come to pick out her room.

Trina slung her backpack over one shoulder and grabbed her duffel bag. She looked up at Goldenrod's second-floor windows, convinced herself she had only imagined someone watching her, and trudged forward. With dull, heavy thuds, she dragged the duffel bag up the plank steps and slid it across the foyer to the bottom of the stairs. She turned on the light, hoping it would brighten the dark stairwell, but instead it cast elongated shadows of the railings and spindles like a scene in an old black-and-white horror movie.

I can do this, she told herself. She was almost eleven. She was going into fifth grade. She wasn't a little girl anymore. "I'm moving in," she announced to the house. "Whether you like it or not."

She bumped her way up to the landing and forced herself to keep going up the mountain of stairs. The air got hotter and hotter and thicker and thicker. Panting by the time she got to the top, she let her backpack slide down her sweaty arm to the floor, sat on her duffel bag, and leaned against the railing, overwhelmed by the heat and the loneliness and the size of the house.

She was sitting in a gloomy hallway surrounded by doors. A lot of doors. She decided to start at one end of the hall and work her way around the circle, but the first thing she did after she pushed herself up was to peer over the railing. She could see all the way down to the foyer. "Hello," she said. "Hello, oh, oh, oh," her distorted voice answered. She was glad to hear only her own voice come back to her, but when it seemed the echoes might never stop, she wished she hadn't said anything at all.

She opened the door nearest the stairs to a very large room with three boarded-up windows and a window seat that ran beneath them. When she turned on the light, a small crystal chandelier did its best to sparkle, and Trina could see that the woodwork was painted white. It was a pretty room, even if the paint was peeling, and it was perfect for the woman of the house. Perfect for her mother, maybe. Someday.

The next room—a huge room with a fireplace—also had three boarded-up windows, but it was paneled with a very dark wood just like the smoking room. It was perfect for the man of the house. Perfect for her dad.

Opposite the stairwell was an ordinary room that

didn't feel at all like a room she would want to live in for a whole year, so she crossed the hall and opened two doors right in a row to identical small square rooms. "They sure must have had a lot of kids," she said, quietly enough to avoid an echo.

Then the hall narrowed, leading to two boarded-up windows with another window seat. Trina walked softly toward the windows, listening carefully, making sure the only footsteps she heard were her own. To her relief she came upon the servants' staircase again. She liked knowing there was another way out of the house, just in case.

Next to the servants' stairs was a door, but when Trina turned the doorknob, the door wouldn't budge. She pushed and pulled and finally yanked it open, only to be met with a blast of hot dust that swirled around her, and another dark, narrow staircase. She knew attic stairs when she saw them. "I'm never going up there," she said out loud. The door creaked when she slammed it shut. The next door opened to nothing but a big closet.

But the door across from the closet opened to an enormous bathroom with a fancy white tub on a raised platform, a sink with curved legs, and a toilet with a tank that was mounted so high on the wall it nearly touched the ceiling. A chain hung from the tank. As soon as Trina pulled it she wished she hadn't.

The walls rattled as water squealed through the pipes, and Trina watched with dread as the water in the toilet churned with the force of an opened fire hydrant. She crossed her fingers that she hadn't broken the plumbing, and closed the door, certain she had just encountered one of the surprises her dad was talking about.

Now there was only one room left to go.

Trina turned the knob and opened the door. In the faint light from the hall, she could tell this room was not too big and not too small. She eagerly stepped in, and immediately, from the corner of her eye, she saw something move. She froze in place and kept her breaths soft and shallow. Waiting. Listening.

Nothing.

Nothing except her own pulse pounding against her eardrums as her heart raced.

Maybe she was seeing things.

"I'm not afraid of you," she said to the silence.

She took another step in, and it—whatever it was—moved again.

Her heart beat harder and faster. She backed up slowly, only to bump into the door. Stumbling, she watched as the thing kept moving, faster now, frantically. Trina was frantic too, trying to get away until she realized that whatever it was moved when she did. She covered her mouth with her hand and watched herself cover her mouth. The scary creature was not a ghost or a monster; it was her own reflection in a mirror.

When she finally found the light switch, and the sconce glowed, she discovered that the walls were covered with pale pink wallpaper and the woodwork was painted white. Even the fireplace was painted white. Toward the far end of the room, mounted on the wall, was the mirror. It rose from the floor to the ceiling and was wider than the window. Its white frame was carved with fine little animals—ducklings and kittens, birds and horses—linked together with the clusters of delicate flowers. Goldenrod, of course. And it was rimmed with at least a dozen tarnished curlicue hooks she could hang things on.

Feeling a little like Goldilocks, she decided that this room *felt just right,* so she went out to the hall and grabbed her duffel bag and backpack.

The first thing she unpacked was the stack of postcards from her mother. She piled them on the fireplace mantel, and then she set her snow globe of skiers in the Rocky Mountains next to them. In front of the snow globe, she lined up the pieces of sea glass she'd found on the shore of Lake Superior.

Her softball glove was next, followed by her collection of baseball caps. She hung them one by one on the hooks around the big mirror—Minnesota Twins, Seattle Mariners, Milwaukee Brewers, Colorado Rockies—wondering who she'd be rooting for while she lived in New Royal.

The last thing she took out was her new leather tool belt. Poppo had said he would fill it with tools as soon as they got to their next project. Trina buckled it around her waist and looked at herself in the mirror.

Standing there in her jean shorts and blue T-shirt, with a bruise on her knee and her Diamondbacks baseball cap covering her short brown hair, she didn't look like the princess who must have lived in this pretty room. Instead, she looked like the skinny tomboy she'd always been. She took off her tool belt and hung it on one of the hooks. With all the work to do at Goldenrod, she would need to keep it handy.

Ah-zuh-zah. Ah-zuh-zah.

Trina stood still and listened. The noise had sounded like a sputter. Or like a saw. Or like someone sighing.

"Poppo?" she hollered.

No answer.

Trina crept into the hall and leaned over the railing. "Poppo?" she called a second time. Only her echo answered, but then she heard the noise again.

Ah-zuh-zah. Ah-zuh-zah.

"Poppo!" she screamed as she raced down the stairs. When she got to the bottom step, she could see her dad's truck coming to a stop in the yard. She dashed through the front door and down the plank steps into the sunshine, right up to her dad, who was climbing out of the truck.

"Poppo!" she shouted.

But he didn't seem to notice she was so scared she could hardly breathe. "You won't believe Hank's Tool and Lumber," he said. "Straight out of an old movie, with a tin ceiling and all these big, wooden barrels full of who-knows-what and buckets of nails and screws. It's a mess, but Hank knows where everything is." He put on his work gloves and started pulling out long boards from the back of the truck, stacking them on the ground. *Cedar.* Trina could smell the sweet wood from where she stood. "Hey . . ." He checked his pockets one by one. "I got you something from Hank's." Finally he fished out a sucker.

Trina grimaced. The sucker had a loop on one end. "Poppo, this kind of sucker is for babies." She pulled at the wrapper, but the plastic and the candy had melted together. "And it's a million years old."

"Mine tasted okay," he said.

Trina did her best to smile, twirling the baby sucker between her fingers, and decided not to breathe a word about scaring herself silly—or about the noises. "I picked out our rooms. We both get fireplaces. We just need to bring in the mattresses."

"Fireplace, huh? Just what I need on a scorcher like today." He ducked into the cargo trailer and pushed the mattresses to the door. "Grab an end," he called. "I'm running out of energy in this heat."

They carried in Trina's mattress first. As they crossed the foyer, headed for the staircase, Trina let go and the mattress fell to the floor. "I can't make it another step, Poppo. Besides, we'll boil to death if we sleep upstairs."

"Then we'll sleep in the parlor until I can get the boards off the windows and the screens on," he said. They pushed Trina's mattress into the parlor and made a second trip for his mattress. Just as they let it fall to the floor, there was a loud clang from the parlor fireplace, followed by a billowing black cloud.

"What's that?" Trina squawked, jumping next to her dad.

"Soot," he said. "The flue must have fallen closed."

"But how does a flue close by itself?"

Her dad wiped his brow. "Well, it's either a negative

pressure, or . . ." With a sly grin, he scooped her up and twirled her in the air. "Tiny flue fairies live in the chimney, and when they get too hot . . ."

"Poppo, put me down," she said, but for the moment she liked being safe in his arms.

When he set her on the floor, the front door blew shut and the house was dark again.

And Trina went back to being scared.

Her dad walked quickly to the door and Trina followed close behind. He twisted the knob and fiddled with the lock, but it wouldn't open. "Great, one more thing I have to fix."

"Let me try," Trina said. She turned the knob and the door opened easily.

"Looks like you have the magic touch," her dad said. "Maybe we should just prop it open."

"I did prop it open," Trina muttered, a little frightened by the idea that she had a magic touch. She looked out at the cornstalks and the goldenrod. Everything was as still as could be. And then she spotted her handy tree branch lying on the bottom step. "How in the world does a door blow shut when it's not even windy?"

Her dad folded his arms and thought for a moment. "Imagine if you hadn't opened your mouth in a hundred years. You might get used to keeping it shut," he said.

"If I hadn't opened my mouth for a hundred years, I think I'd have a lot to say."

"So, you think Goldenrod's trying to tell us something, do you?"

She sure did. Goldenrod was telling them she was a haunted house. But Trina knew better than to say that out loud to her dad, so she just shrugged.

Trina spent the next couple of hours helping her dad. They unloaded the rest of the wood and set up the power tools—mostly in the parlor. "This is the fanciest work-room I've ever had," her dad said. And then she held the tape measure as he mapped out the porch and made more notes.

When it was dinnertime, she lit one of the giant burners on the big black stove. It popped and smoked with burning dust before the flame settled into a perfect blue ring beneath the spaghetti pot.

"What's for dinner?" her dad said, coming into the kitchen, carrying his oilcan and a screwdriver. "Let me guess. Sushi."

"Yup," Trina said. "And chocolate mousse for dessert."

He worked on the squeaky swinging doors while the spaghetti boiled. When it was done, Trina heaped two piles of sticky spaghetti onto paper plates and carried them one at a time to the card table in the dining room. "Oops, I forgot the chopsticks." She hurried back to the kitchen and returned with a pair of forks and a jar of spaghetti sauce, which she poured cold onto each steaming mound of spaghetti.

With a mouth full of spaghetti and a twinkle in his eye,

her dad announced, "First dinner on a new project. You know what that means. It's time to play . . ."

"*Don't Remind Me!*" Trina spluttered with her mouth so full of spaghetti her dad beat her to the first question.

"Worst dinner. Go!"

Trina swallowed fast. "The barbecued snake in the desert. Worst motel. Go!"

"The pink one in Wisconsin where our key unlocked all the doors. Funniest moment. Go!" He slurped up a few strands of spaghetti.

This one took Trina a minute. Poppo worked so hard there hadn't been a lot of funny moments. At least not lately. She put a big forkful of spaghetti in her mouth, thinking. "Umm . . ."

"Ding, ding, ding!" he said, tapping his plastic cup with his plastic fork. "Five seconds remain. Five, four, three—"

"When we went to the beach in Oregon and you, you . . ." Trina started to laugh. "You ran and got the lifeguard to rescue a dog that was swimming too deep in the waves and . . . and it turned out to be a sea lion." Now Trina was laughing so hard she was afraid spaghetti would shoot out her nose.

"And who told me to run for the lifeguard?"

"I did, but I already knew it wasn't a dog." She batted her eyes at him.

He stopped twisting his spaghetti around his fork and looked up. "You what?"

"Worst night," Trina said, quickly resuming the game *and* changing the subject. "Go!"

Her dad answered this one a little sadly. "When we got snowed in up in Minnesota. I thought they'd never dig us out. Best night. Go!"

"When we got snowed in up in Minnesota." Trina smiled, watching her dad eat, waiting for him to respond.

He looked up, confused.

"It was the best night, Poppo, because we had popcorn and cocoa for dinner and played Crazy Eights by the lantern in front of the fire. It was the best night ever." And it really had been the best night, waiting out the storm together.

"Ding, ding, ding," her dad said, tapping his plastic cup again. "Trina wins by a landslide." Then he pushed his plate to the center of the card table and it left a trail of tomato sauce.

"You know, Poppo, if we're going to be here a whole year, maybe we should get a few real plates and stop wasting paper."

"Good idea," he said. He pulled out his notebook and scribbled as he talked. "I'll put it on the list for tomorrow. Along with building a new porch, rewiring the house— you should see the attic; it looks like Frankenstein's lab up there—and then I'll put in a new septic system." He tapped the pencil against his chin. "Oh, yeah, and I need to get the screens on the windows." With a heavy sigh he said, "There's only one way to cope with all that work."

"How?" Trina asked.

"With a good night's sleep. It's time for me to hit the hay. I'll get the sleeping bags from the truck if you wash all the dishes," he said with a smile.

Sleeping in the parlor was like sleeping in an enormous cavern. The tiniest noises sounded as if they were blown through bullhorns. And if the impossible heat didn't wake Trina up every little while, her dad's snoring did. When he started to sound like his chain saw, she stopped trying to sleep at all.

She lay there, blearily staring up at the ceiling. Enough moonlight trickled in between cracks of the boards covering the bay window to make the chandelier twinkle like a handful of stars in a black sky. It made her homesick for Portland. *Worst project, go,* she thought to herself. Goldenrod, hands down. Six bedrooms, four fireplaces, and a library. So what? It would be nothing but work. And loneliness. Six bedrooms and one turret room.

Trina sat up, alert and wide-awake now. Where *was* the door to the turret room?

Ssss . . .

"What, Poppo?" She looked over at him, but he wasn't talking. He wasn't even snoring.

Ssss-konk. Ssss-konk. Ssss—

"Poppo!" she shouted. "Poppo, there's someone in the house!"

All he did was roll over.

Konk.

Trina's heart sputtered. What if the noise was coming from the turret room?

"Poppo," she hollered, crawling off her mattress to tug on his arm.

This time he sat bolt upright. "What? What is it?"

"There's someone in the house!"

They sat there in silence. Listening.

"I don't hear anything," he finally said. He was right. All Trina could hear now was her own pounding heart. "What did it sound like?"

"Like someone whispering. Or breathing. I don't know."

"I'm sure it's just the tree scraping against the roof," he said, lying back on his pillow. "Go back to sleep. Long day ahead."

Just the tree. Just the tree, Trina repeated silently to herself, trying to calm down. And then, all of a sudden, a squeal came from the back of the house, followed by a rumbling in the walls. "You heard *that*, didn't you, Poppo?"

"Yes," he said, sounding frustrated. "It's the toilet flushing."

"By . . . itself?" Trina squeaked.

"Probably a leaky valve."

"Can you check? Please?" She wanted to believe her dad but she couldn't. Not if she would be lying awake listening for strange noises while he snored the night away. He turned on his flashlight and dragged himself sleepily out of the room, his footsteps gradually fading away. She waited, alone in the dark, hugging her pillow as tightly as she could.

Minutes went by. Or maybe hours. Maybe she should have followed him. What if something had happened? Just when she couldn't take another second of waiting, she heard his footsteps padding back through the dining room and into the parlor. "It's a slow leak in a valve, just like I thought," he said. "Likely to happen again when it fills up." He crawled back into bed. "I'll look into it in the morning."

Trina lay back down.

Ssss—

She pulled her pillow over her head and whispered, "There is no such thing as a haunted house. There is no such thing as a haunted house." She repeated her dad's words over and over until she eventually fell asleep.

The next thing Trina knew, she was wide awake again, but this time the air smelled like burned toast and she could hardly breathe. She sat up quickly. A smoky haze swirled around her. "Poppo," she choked. "Something's burning!" She jumped to her feet. "Poppo, wake up! The house is on fire!"

Her dad was awake in an instant. "Get out! Hurry!"

He flung open the front door and Trina raced down the steps into the sunshine, but when she turned around, her dad wasn't there. "Poppo?" she hollered. He didn't answer, but as she ran back into the house, she could hear him laughing. "Poppo?"

"Nothing's burning," he called. "It's just steam."

"Steam?" Trina asked, following her dad's voice across the hazy foyer one shaky step at a time.

"Yup," he said, coming out of the library. "Someone must have bumped the thermostat and the furnace kicked on. Any open valve on a radiator will steam like a sauna. I'd say you found your ghost."

"My ghost?" Trina's skin crawled. "Poppo, what do you mean?"

"All I'm saying is the furnace probably caused the noise you heard in the night. C'mon. Let's get cleaned up and go get breakfast in town."

"Okay," Trina said, but she was still a little wary as she headed upstairs. Every other time something scary happened, her dad had an ordinary explanation, but who bumped the thermostat? She brushed her teeth in record time and then chose her purple Santa Fe T-shirt and her Diamondbacks cap to wear into town.

As she headed back downstairs, she remembered the turret room. She paused to count the doors to the rooms on her fingers. Five on one hand, four on the other. Nine doors. And she had opened every one of them.

What if Poppo was right? What if there was a ghost? And what if the ghost lived in the turret room? Wherever it was.

Chapter Three

"Is it a long way into town?" Trina asked as they hit rut after rut on the dirt road that cut through the cornfield.

"Six point four miles. I clocked it," her dad said as they stopped across from the big red barn. "Of course, that's once you get to this point." He looked in both directions before taking a left-hand turn onto the two-lane road toward town.

As Trina twisted in her seat, watching for a stir of dust that meant they weren't the only people left on Earth, a terrible thought struck her. "Poppo, do you think the school bus comes way out here?"

"Maybe," he said, turning on the radio to nothing but static. "But I can drive you if it doesn't."

"You sent the school my records, right?" Trina said. After too long a pause, Trina turned to stare at her dad. "Poppo, did you forget to register me?" *Again,* she wanted to say, only this time it would be a lot worse if he forgot because this was the one chance she had to be there for the first day of school, just like all the other kids.

"Of course not," he said, switching off the radio. "I just figured we'd take care of it when we got here."

Trina folded her arms and scowled. "No you didn't. You forgot. You always forget everything." She stamped the floor with both feet and turned her head to the window.

"I tell you what," he said calmly, as if she hadn't just acted like a baby. "After breakfast we'll get you registered and then we'll go buy school supplies at Hank's. And if you're a really good girl, I'll get you another sucker."

He was trying to make her smile, but it wasn't working this time. "I'm not a little girl," she said. "You have to take me seriously. You have to think about *my* feelings sometimes."

He didn't say anything, but Trina wasn't surprised. He was really good at not talking about things that made him feel bad. She looked out the window again, just as they passed a large green sign that read:

Welcome to New Royal
Population 397

Trina would have slipped off her seat if it hadn't been for her seat belt. "Three hundred ninety-seven people? That's it? Poppo, my last school was bigger than that!" Why hadn't he warned her that the town was so small? "Do they even have a school?"

"Of course they have a school," he said, fiddling with the radio again.

They turned off the road, following a handmade sign with an arrow that said, "Main Street This Way," and drove toward a little park in the center of town. The park had a bandstand and ornate benches and drinking fountains, but there wasn't a single person in sight. "It looks like a ghost town," Trina said.

"Nah. It's a cute little town," her dad said. "I'll give you a tour."

Her dad turned right, driving past Al's Antiques and Vacuum Repair that shared the block with Shegstad's Funeral Home, *Three Generations Taking Care of Your Loved Ones, Gerald Shegstad, Director.*

Shegstad. The name was familiar. "Hey," Trina said. "Isn't it kind of weird that the funeral director is the one who wrote you the letter about Goldenrod?"

Her dad shrugged. "I don't know. Sometimes funeral directors have a lot of family records."

"I think it's weird," she said. They turned another corner of the square and passed the surprisingly majestic First National Bank of New Royal and an elegant post office. Hank's Tool and Lumber took up most of the next block. One more turn put them in front of the red brick New Royal Public Library with white columns and lots of steps. It sat on a block all by itself.

"Sure are a lot of big buildings for such a small town," Trina said. "That's weird, too."

"I'm guessing New Royal was an important town in its day. Probably the only town for miles."

They pulled up in front of the Cat's Meow Diner, a low, white building badly in need of paint. It sat in the middle of a block with the New Royal City Hall on one side and an old-fashioned gas station with one pump on the other. Bolted to the window frame above a flower box filled with dried-up flowers was a rusty dinner bell. *Homemade Breakfast Served All Day* was painted on the window in peeling blue paint, surrounded by blinking white lights. Most of the lights had burned out.

"How about this place?" her dad said cheerfully.

"I hear it's the best place in town," Trina said, certain it was the *only* place in town.

Dangling tin cat cutouts clinked overhead as Trina pushed open the café door. She counted six stools, five tables, four booths, and one jukebox in the whole restaurant, and the jukebox was out of order. Except for two men in a corner booth and a plump gray-haired waitress carrying a dirty dish in each hand, the place was empty.

"Seat yourselves," the waitress said in a hoarse voice, her ponytail bobbing as she went by. "I need a chance to clean up some after the rush." Then she disappeared behind a set of swinging doors.

Rush? Trina wondered. When her dad rolled his eyes she knew he was thinking the same thing. They both squelched giggles as they sat down at the counter on stools covered with cracked black plastic.

The menu was an old school chalkboard mounted above an enormous griddle: eggs every which way, waffles, and mile-high pancakes with real maple syrup. On the end of the counter was a plastic dessert case with chocolate chip cookies and mammoth brownies for fifty cents each. The place was run-down, but the food sounded delicious.

Dishes clattered somewhere in a sink, and then the waitress pushed back through the swinging doors. She gave them the once-over. "You folks just passing through?"

"Nope," her dad said.

"We live here," Trina chimed in, making out the name Miss Kitty on her waitress badge.

"Live here? Then you must be brand-spanking new because I know everybody in town." Miss Kitty grabbed a coffeepot from a hot plate next to the griddle and filled Trina's dad's cup with steaming black coffee. When Trina held up her cup, Miss Kitty pursed her lips and shook her head.

"We're living out at Goldenrod," Trina's dad said.

Trina swore that Miss Kitty's pink cheeks paled by several shades.

"You didn't say Goldenrod, did you?" Miss Kitty said, squinting suspiciously.

"Sure did." Her dad poured sugar into his teaspoon until it spilled over its rim and into his coffee.

Trina nodded.

"Hear that, boys?" Miss Kitty's hand trembled as she set the coffeepot down with a clank. "They say they're living in Goldenrod."

Both men snorted. "That's a good one," the older man scoffed.

"Not for long," the younger one said, and they snorted again.

"That's right," said Miss Kitty. "Nobody can live out there. The old place is haunted."

Trina felt every hair on her body stand straight up.

But her dad laughed. "Anyone who believes in haunted houses needs to have their head examined."

"So you're one of those," Miss Kitty said, slipping paper place mats in front of them. "Believe you can explain everything away with a fact."

This time he shook his head. "All I'm saying is old houses shift and creak with the weather and suddenly everyone thinks they're haunted."

"Town council voted to tear down that eyesore—" Miss Kitty stopped midsentence and stared at them with eyes like red-hot laser beams. "Now I know who you are. You folks are the whole reason that place is still standing. Come here to fix it up. Well, good luck with that."

Miss Kitty slapped a fork wrapped in a paper napkin on each place mat, making it clear she wanted to get on with her business. "So what do two newcomers like yourselves want for breakfast?"

"Two eggs with bacon," Trina's dad said. "Sunny-side up."

"Mile-high pancakes for me," Trina said. Miss Kitty waited. "Please," Trina added.

Miss Kitty didn't write down the order; she just stepped up to the griddle and started cooking. She cracked the eggs with one hand as she whipped up the pancake batter with the other, shouting the whole time above the sizzling bacon and the rattling roar of the fan. "That house has caused nothing but trouble since it was built. Crops and businesses have been drying up around here for generations."

Trina's dad set down his coffee. "You can say that about any small town in the Midwest. Blame it on the interstate. It's simple American history."

Trina winced. Sometimes she wished her dad wouldn't sound like he thought he knew everything—and this was one of those times. "Poppo, shh," she whispered, but it was too late.

Miss Kitty whirled around. Her eyes were glossy and for a second Trina wondered if she had seen a tear in one of them, until Miss Kitty pointed the spatula at her dad and poked the air with it as she talked. "Unless you've lived in this town your whole life and can tell me something I don't know about it, you can just zip your lip."

Trina's dad took a sip of his coffee.

Miss Kitty was still fuming. "You just wait until you set foot in that house."

"We spent last night there and we're still standing," he said in his usual playful way.

"You spent a night there?" whispered Miss Kitty. The hand squeezing the spatula dropped to her side. "Did anything strange happen?"

Trina's ears pricked up. *Strange?* How about lights that flickered as if they heard what you said, and a chimney flue and a front door that shut when they felt like it, a furnace that turned on by itself, and a toilet that flushed on its own—not to mention the strange feeling that someone else was there with them? But Trina kept her mouth shut. She didn't need to add any more fuel to Miss Kitty's fire.

"Nope. Nada. Zip," said her dad.

"Well, that's pretty strange all by itself," Miss Kitty said, turning back to her cooking. "When I was a kid, we used to play a game we called *The Dare*. We placed our bets and then whoever spent the whole night at Goldenrod would win the money. Hash browns?"

"Sure," Trina's dad said.

"No, thank you," said Trina.

Miss Kitty slapped a slab of frozen potatoes on the griddle. "We put all the money in a coffee can and that prize just kept getting bigger and bigger 'til it was up over $300, which was a lot of money when I was a kid. Still is," she said, giving the hash browns a hefty flip. "I'll bet every kid in town tried to spend the night there. But nobody ever made it through the whole night."

Trina thought back to the bill on the kitchen counter. No wonder the cleaners came all the way from Davenport. Anyone who lived in New Royal would be afraid to enter the house.

"What happened?" Trina whispered.

"What happened?" Miss Kitty said. "What didn't happen?"

With that, two eggs, sunny-side up, slipped from Miss Kitty's spatula onto a plain white plate, followed by a pile of bacon and the hash browns. Then she stacked up Trina's pancakes. "If you want my advice," she said, setting the plates down in front of them so hard the silverware clattered, "don't take anything for granted out there. Whatever you think that house isn't, it is."

When Miss Kitty stared into Trina's eyes and Trina

stared back, she wondered if Miss Kitty could tell Trina believed every word she said.

"Funny there's no sign of vandalism with all those kids breaking in," Trina's dad said, winking at Trina while he poured ketchup all over his fried eggs.

Miss Kitty refilled his coffee cup. "You mean to tell me you don't know why?"

Trina felt bold enough to speak up. After all, she and Miss Kitty had something in common: fear of Goldenrod. "Because the house scared them away before they could do anything?" *Or the real truth, which she kept to herself: the invisible old lady wouldn't let them stay.*

"Smart girl," Miss Kitty said, nodding. Then she paused. "Hey, if you're so smart, how come you're not in school today?"

Trina gagged on her bite of pancake. "School? Already?"

Miss Kitty nodded. "It started last week. My granddaughter, Charlotte, is in the fifth grade, so I know when school starts and when it doesn't."

Last week? Trina slumped on her stool. "But it's not even Labor Day yet," she said, as welling tears stung her eyes. She blinked hard. She didn't want to cry about school. She didn't want to cry about anything, but there was nothing she hated more than being the new kid in class, and now she was going to be a whole week late, which made it ten times worse.

"Where is the school?" her dad asked.

Miss Kitty switched off the fan and started scraping the griddle with her spatula. "Straight up Main. East side."

She pointed in the opposite direction of the way they came into town. "Past Millie's Grocery Store and up the hill. By the cemetery. You can't miss it."

Trina set her fork down at the side of her plate. "Come on, Poppo," she said, tugging on his arm. "You have to take me to school. Right now."

Miss Kitty shook her head. "Not so fast, there, young lady. You're going to eat those pancakes first."

Chapter Four

Trina couldn't sit still on the way up Main Street. She rolled down her window and leaned out of the truck. "There's Millie's," she said, pointing to a little store on the corner, the last corner of the last block of New Royal businesses.

Without a word, her dad shifted into low gear and proceeded up the steep hill. "Royal Hill Cemetery," Trina read out loud as they drove past a wrought iron gate exactly like the gate at Goldenrod.

As soon as they passed the cemetery, there was the school. Miss Kitty was right; you couldn't miss it. It was another red brick building way too big for the 397 people who lived in New Royal.

They drove past the front of the school: three stories with broad steps and shiny brass doors. When they turned the corner, the school seemed to get bigger and bigger. "Not exactly the one-room schoolhouse I was expecting," her dad said as they came to a small parking lot next to an overgrown field with bleachers and swings. "It looks more like a college."

Trina was barely listening to him. All she could think about was what she was wearing—why had she picked this stupid T-shirt? and cutoffs?—and how she didn't have any school supplies. What if she was already behind on her homework? Worse yet, what if the kids laughed at her for being late?

Her dad didn't show an ounce of urgency as he pulled in next to one of the three cars parked in the lot, but Trina didn't want to miss another second of school. She hopped out of the truck before he shut off the engine and ran to the front entrance.

Trina dragged open the big brass door to a long, dark hallway. And, just like everything else in New Royal, it was empty. It didn't even have any kids in it. She kept walking down the hall until she came to a room with a big glass window and an open door. It had to be the office, so she walked in.

A prim woman with gray hair rolled tightly into a bun on top her head sat at a big wooden desk behind the nameplate, *Miss Lincoln, Secretary*. A loose-leaf notebook was opened to a page labeled KINDERGARTEN in big black letters, and a stack of plain white envelopes was next to it. The woman was carefully addressing the envelopes with perfect handwriting and placing the finished ones in a neat pile next to another nameplate, which read *Principal*.

Trina was confused. Was Miss Lincoln the secretary, the principal, or both? She had never seen a principal address envelopes before, but there was no one else in the office.

"Excuse me?" Trina eked out in a tiny voice. She tried again, a little louder this time. "Miss Lincoln?"

Miss Lincoln held up her index finger, indicating that she was concentrating and Trina should wait until she was done. After she placed another finished envelope in the pile, Miss Lincoln peered at Trina above her bifocals. "May I help you?"

Trina tried to sound grown-up. "My name is Trina Maxwell. I'm in fifth grade and I'm new."

"I can see that you are new," Miss Lincoln said. She licked her thumb and turned the pages in the notebook until she came to one labeled FIFTH GRADE. "Is Trina your given name or a nickname?"

No one had ever asked Trina that question before. She wondered why it mattered but she wasn't about to question Miss Lincoln. "My real name is Citrine, but everyone calls me—"

"Capital C," Miss Lincoln said as if she were vying for first place in a spelling bee, "-i-t-r-i-n-e," she continued, spelling Trina's name as she wrote it down at the bottom of a very short list. "Maxwell, is that correct?"

"Yes, but everyone calls me—"

"Fifth grade is with Miss Dale. Room 216." Trina was too anxious to get started to worry about her name. She turned for the door, all set to find room 216 when Miss Lincoln said, "I'm afraid you will need to register before you can go to class."

Trina felt her face flush with embarrassment. Where was her dad? Why wasn't he ever there when she really needed him?

Miss Lincoln pulled a form from a drawer that was as perfectly organized as her desk. "Now tell me your address, please."

"Um," Trina said, watching the doorway for her dad. What was taking him so long anyway? "I don't know the address. We're living at Goldenrod, the big mansion out—"

"Goldenrod!" Miss Lincoln dropped her pen. "No one lives out there."

Trina couldn't tell if Miss Lincoln was scared of Goldenrod or accusing her of lying, so she kept her eyes on the office window and didn't say anything. "Ahem," Miss Lincoln said, but in the nick of time Trina saw her dad hurrying toward the office. She relaxed until she saw a woman in a flowered skirt approaching the door from the other direction. Trina squeezed her eyes shut, thinking her dad would run right into the woman.

"Whoa," he said, grabbing onto the door frame to slow down. "Sorry about that. I forgot. There's no running in school." The woman, who was young and pretty, with long dark hair, smiled. Miss Lincoln frowned and Trina rolled her eyes. Why couldn't Poppo be serious just once in his life?

"We do make a few exceptions on occasion," the pretty woman said with a twinkle in her eye. "It's still early in the year."

"I'm Mike. Mike Maxwell," he said, holding out his hand.

"I'm Carrie Dale," she said, shaking his hand.

"Miss Dale?" Trina exclaimed, picking out the most important part of this silly conversation. "Then you're my new teacher."

"And what is your name?" Miss Dale said, looking at Trina with the kindest green eyes Trina had ever seen.

"That would be Citrine," Miss Lincoln interjected before Trina could open her mouth. "Citrine Maxwell."

"No," said her dad. "Her name is—"

Trina glared at him and shook her head. She didn't want him to correct Miss Lincoln and start the year off on the wrong foot when she was already late. Her dad shut his mouth, startled.

"Citrine," Miss Dale repeated. "What a lovely name."

A lovely name. Trina felt a swoop of confidence, maybe even excitement. Being called Citrine made her want to stand taller. It made her feel more grown-up.

"She's my daughter," he said. "And she loves school."

"That's wonderful," Miss Dale said.

Trina did love school, but her dad was getting more embarrassing by the second. Now she wished he had stayed in the truck.

Miss Dale reached out and took Trina's hand in hers, a beautiful, smooth hand with perfect half-moon shaped fingernails the color of watermelon. And she smelled like springtime. With her other hand she lifted Trina's baseball hat from her head and handed it to her dad. "We don't allow hats in school." And finally she said, "You can come with me, Citrine. We'll get you settled."

Trina sighed with relief as all of her first-day jitters melted away.

"Hold your horses," Miss Lincoln said sternly. "We're still waiting on the paperwork."

Trina turned and stared at her dad. "My dad will bring it this afternoon. Won't you, Poppo?"

"Sure, Trina," he said, but Trina glared at him again. "I mean, Citrine," he said, quickly correcting himself. "I thought it was in the truck. That's why I was so late—"

"School lets out at three thirty, Mr. Maxwell," Miss Lincoln interrupted. "I go home at three forty-five. Sharp."

"I'm sure he'll be here in plenty of time, Miss Lincoln," Miss Dale said in her soothing voice. "And could you please let Mr. Bert know I need a couple mousetraps set in my classroom? It's that time of year again." Then she smiled at Trina. "My classroom is upstairs."

Halfway down the hall, Trina looked over her shoulder and saw her dad standing there, twirling her baseball cap in his hands. What was he doing? Was he waiting for her to wave? Didn't he know that fifth graders didn't wave at their dads? She gave a quick nod and turned around again.

Walking next to Miss Dale, Trina felt as if she floated up the marble stairs and down the hall, all the way to the threshold of room 216. A dark-haired boy was doing jumping jacks at the front of the room. Everyone was laughing, but when the kids saw Miss Dale, they took their seats. "Fifth graders, you have a new classmate," said Miss Dale.

Eons seemed to pass while Trina stood there with all the kids staring at her. She was trying to take in everything at once. Miss Dale's old desk looked like it belonged at Goldenrod. A long chalkboard ran the whole width of the classroom at the front, and the alphabet, with both uppercase and lowercase letters in a swirly script, was painted on the back wall. There was a big white sink in one corner and some cabinets and dark wood bookcases in the other, but there wasn't a single computer in the room. Trina had no idea that moving up a grade would mean going back in time.

The desks were in neat rows, but the kids were scattered around the room and at least half the desks were empty. Trina counted eleven new faces, excited to think she would soon make new friends. But twelve kids total meant there weren't enough girls for a softball team. And even if the boys and girls played together on one team, who would they play against?

"Everyone, please welcome Citrine," Miss Dale said.

"Welcome, Citrine," they said in unison, and Trina instantly felt like she was in kindergarten.

Miss Dale pointed at an empty desk behind a prissy-looking girl. Her shiny brown hair was in a perfect pony-tail, her hands were perfectly crossed on top of the desk, and she was the only girl in the classroom wearing a dress. She looked like a little-girl version of Miss Lincoln. "Please sit behind Missy, Citrine."

Trina smiled at Missy, but Missy didn't smile back, which meant Missy didn't just look like Miss Lincoln; she acted like her too. As Trina walked to her desk, she noticed the girl who would be sitting behind her, a very tall girl with long red braids, two pink barrettes holding back her overgrown bangs, and a mass of freckles on her face. She didn't smile either. Looking down, Trina slipped into the empty desk between Prissy Missy and the tall girl, who immediately leaned over and whispered.

"Welcome, Latrine."

Latrine? Did the tall girl really say *Latrine?* Maybe she had misunderstood. Maybe she didn't know that a latrine was an outhouse they used on construction sites when there wasn't any plumbing. Trina turned around, trying to be friendly. "It's *Ci*-trine, not *La*—"

The tall girl smiled and slowly mouthed the word again: LA-TRINE. A terrible taste bubbled in Trina's mouth. She swallowed and swallowed, trying to make it go away. Being the new girl was awful, but throwing up in front of everyone would be a lot worse.

"Charlotte, Citrine, is everything okay?" Miss Dale asked.

Charlotte? Scary old Miss Kitty's granddaughter? No wonder. Sawdust didn't fall far from the wood, as Poppo liked to say.

"It's just fine, Miss Dale," Charlotte said, using the same smile to be nice that she had used to be mean. "I was just telling Citrine how wonderful it is to have a new girl in class."

Trina also smiled as if nothing had happened. "Everything's just perfect," she said.

Perfect? Right. Why couldn't she sit in one of the other desks? Why did her name have to sound like an outhouse? Why didn't she tell Miss Lincoln her real name was Trina when she had the chance?

"Citrine, most of your classmates have been in school together since kindergarten, so they all know each other. It's very rare that we get a new student."

"Nu-uh," said the jumping-jacks boy. "We moved here from Cedar Rapids when I was seven."

"No wonder you think you're so special," Charlotte sneered, prompting a round of snickers.

"Edward, please raise your hand to speak. Charlotte, I expect you to mind your manners."

Prissy Missy raised her hand and waved it until Miss Dale nodded at her. "Maybe we should introduce ourselves, Miss Dale."

"Good idea, Missy. Why don't you go first?"

Prissy Missy stood up. "My name is Missy. It's short for Melissa. And my favorite subject is spelling." After Missy, all the introductions blurred together because Trina wasn't listening. She was too nervous knowing she'd soon have to stand up and talk in front of her new classmates.

"Citrine," Miss Dale smiled at her. "Why don't you tell us a little about yourself?" Miss Dale sat down on the edge of her desk. "Maybe start by telling us where you're from."

From? As Trina stood up, her stomach swelled with the mile-high pancakes. She wasn't *from* anywhere. She could tell them about every place she'd ever lived, but she wasn't from any one of those places.

One by one, the kids turned in their seats to stare at her, except for Charlotte who hissed behind her back, "Cat got your tongue, Latrine?"

Trina pretended she didn't hear Charlotte. She stared at the front of the classroom, hoping Miss Dale would move on to another question. Any question except where she was from.

"Do you have any brothers or sisters?" Miss Dale asked sweetly.

"I have five brothers and sisters," Edward shouted from his desk.

"Thank you, Edward," Miss Dale said. "But you already had your turn."

Trina shook her head. No brothers. No sisters. No mother. "I live with my dad. He's a master carpenter and we—"

"Ooo, *master carpenter*," Charlotte sneered, sending a ripple of chuckles up and down the rows.

"Charlotte, please," Miss Dale said with a stern look.

"What? I mean it," Charlotte said. "A master carpenter is really cool."

Trina ignored Charlotte's fake compliment. "We move a lot so my dad can remodel houses. We just moved here from Santa Fe." There. Done. As usual, she had told her life story in two simple sentences.

"Ooo. *Santa Fe. Grand Canyon.* Cool." Another fake comment from Charlotte.

But Trina was too good at geography to let that one go by. She turned around and said, "The Grand Canyon is in Arizona, not New Mexico." And then she smiled, pleased with herself.

Edward laughed, but the rest of the class was silent, eyes wide and focused on Charlotte, who squinted spitefully at Trina.

"That's correct," Miss Dale said. "And now you're living here in town?"

Trina shook her head, wondering what the reaction of the class was going to be to her next bit of news, but at this point she wasn't sure she cared. "We're living at Goldenrod." Eleven kids and Miss Dale uttered one big gasp.

"Goldenrod is haunted," Charlotte said.

"My dad says there's no such thing as a haunted house," Trina snapped back.

Charlotte got louder. "My grandma says—"

"I know that house," Miss Dale interrupted. "We all do. It must be very interesting to live there."

"It is very interesting," Trina said, keeping the details to herself as she sat down.

"*It is very interesting,*" Charlotte mimicked.

"Charlotte," Miss Dale said firmly, pointing at an empty desk in front of her. "Enough. Please sit up here by me."

Charlotte didn't move. Miss Dale didn't either. Not even her eyes, which she kept straight and steady on Charlotte. At last, Charlotte huffed, slid out of her desk, and shuffled to the desk at the front of the room.

"That house is a historic treasure," Miss Dale continued. "As you know, my great-grandparents—your own great-great-aunt and great-great-uncle, Charlotte—were gardeners there."

Did that mean Miss Dale and Charlotte were related? Trina was dumbfounded that someone so mean and nasty could be related to the wonderful Miss Dale.

A blond boy raised his hand. "Yes, Ben," Miss Dale said.

"My grandpa says the whole reason this town is so small is because people are afraid to live anywhere near it. So everyone keeps moving away."

"Yeah," Edward said as he shot a rubber band that hit Ben's head. "My dad says Mr. Shegstad has the only successful business in town."

Shegstad. Shegstad's Funeral Home. A funeral home was the most successful business in this dying town. Trina laughed out loud at her own thought, making everyone stare at her again—including Charlotte, who turned her head and stuck her tongue out.

At this point, Trina would have given anything to undo the entire morning. If the radiators hadn't filled Goldenrod with steam, they wouldn't have gone to Miss Kitty's diner. If they hadn't gone to Miss Kitty's, she wouldn't know school had started. If she hadn't known school had started, she'd be back at Goldenrod and never would have had to meet Charlotte and the other kids. If only the radiators hadn't gone crazy, then she wouldn't be sitting here with everyone staring at her. It was all Goldenrod's fault.

Miss Dale hopped off her desk. "As you can see, Citrine, there are lots of stories about Goldenrod. We look forward to hearing yours as the year goes on." Then she picked up a silver whistle and blew it so loudly Trina thought the windows might break. "Please line up for gym. Dodgeball today."

Dodgeball! Trina loved dodgeball so much she stopped fretting. The game would be the first good thing to happen so far in New Royal. Just in case, though, she put herself at the end of the line so she wouldn't have to stand next to Charlotte, who barged her way up to the front.

She ended up on the same team with Edward and Prissy Missy and a few other kids, playing opposite Charlotte, who had declared herself the captain of the other team. Every time the ball came anywhere near Missy, Missy screamed and turned her back. And then Edward was out when Ben smacked him in the back with the ball.

One by one Trina's teammates ended up on the sidelines and pretty soon it was just Charlotte and Trina left on the court. And Charlotte had the ball. Charlotte made an angry face at Trina, wound up, and threw the ball as hard as she could right at her. Poor Charlotte, Trina thought for a moment, but only for a moment. She caught the ball with both hands as easily as she would catch a pop fly. In a second, Charlotte was out and the game was over.

Edward started jumping up and down, shouting, "We won! We won! We're the champs!"

Miss Dale blew her whistle. "Edward. Sportsmanship," she said. "And please get in line with your team."

"Good game. Good game. Good game," all the kids said, slapping hands in passing until Charlotte paused in front of Trina. Instead of high-fiving her, Charlotte gave her hand a burning squeeze. "This'll teach you to butt in where you don't belong, Latrine," she whispered.

"What will?" Trina said, refusing to buckle, pretending her fingers didn't feel as if every one of them was being held to Miss Kitty's hot griddle. She wasn't going to give Charlotte an iota of satisfaction, so she smiled. Charlotte sneered. When she released Trina's hand, Trina made a beeline for the drinking fountain. Charlotte followed her.

"Hey, Latrine," Charlotte called as the rest of the kids headed back to the classroom.

Trina ignored her and got an extra-long drink.

"Latrine, I'm talking to you." Charlotte tapped her big foot. "Are you deaf or something?"

What would you say that's worth listening to? Trina thought. She wished she was bold enough to say it out loud, but she knew she was no match for Charlotte—at least not off the dodgeball court. Finally turning around, Trina said, "I can hear you just fine."

Charlotte squinted her eyes. "That's good, because I'm going to tell you a little secret."

Trina stood as tall as she could, but Charlotte, with her mean, freckled face, still loomed over her. She clenched her teeth so her lips wouldn't quiver.

"Just because you lived in Santa Fe and have traveled around a lot, you're no better than anyone else, Latrine. You understand? And just so you know, these are *my* friends." Charlotte made a huge fist with her big right hand and waved it in Trina's face. "If you ever have trouble remembering . . ." She slugged her fist into the open palm of her big left hand. "I'll remind you."

Trina didn't need a big fist to remind her that she wasn't better than anyone else. She already knew it. No friends, no real home, no mother. "Thank you, Charlotte, I'm sure I won't forget." As she gave Charlotte her biggest fake smile possible, she made up her mind right then and there she would simply keep to herself for the rest of the day and never again set foot in New Royal Public School.

When the bell rang at three thirty, Trina was the first one out of her seat. She left her books on her desk and ran from the classroom, down the stairs, out the door, and all the way to the parking lot.

Her dad's truck was nowhere in sight.

And then it started to rain.

Trina wrapped her arms around her shoulders, hopping from one foot to the other, staring down the road for her dad. "Hurry, hurry, hurry," she whispered to herself. When he finally turned into the parking lot, she ran for the truck. As soon as it stopped, she opened the door and climbed in, out of breath. "You're late," she said.

"A minute, maybe, but don't worry. We still have plenty of time. I have all the papers right here." He picked up the tattered green folder that contained Trina's records. Birth certificate. Shots. Grades. Everything. Her whole life fit into one measly file folder.

She yanked her seat belt across herself and clicked the buckle. "It doesn't matter. I'm never coming back. I hate New Royal."

"Now wait a minute, Trina. I mean, Citrine—"

Citrine. Her own name made her sick. "Don't call me that. Don't call me Citrine ever again."

"Oh, o . . . kay." Her dad slipped the green folder between their seats. "Can you tell me what's going on?"

"No."

"But you love school."

"You always say that, but it's not true. Why would I love school? Everybody knows everybody else and I'm always the new kid." She folded her arms across her chest and looked at her feet. "Just take me home," she said, doing everything she could do to keep from crying at that meaningless word: *home.*

Her dad flicked on the windshield wipers and they sat silently in the idling truck for what seemed like forever until he slid her baseball cap from the gear shift and placed it cockeyed on her head—as if that made everything okay—and drove out of the parking lot.

Trina pulled down the brim of her cap, put her feet on the dashboard, and stared straight between the tips of her tennis shoes at the gray world. She could feel her dad watching her, but she didn't look at him, and he didn't say anything until they were halfway to Goldenrod.

"I stopped by the post office today." He pulled a postcard of a yellow hot-air balloon from his shirt pocket and waved it in the air. "Maybe this'll cheer you up."

Trina felt a flicker of hope. Maybe her mother would invite her along on an adventure and she could leave this terrible place for good. "Where is she now?" She grabbed the postcard from her dad and turned it over, eager to read the note.

Dear Citrine,

I am an official, certified hot-air balloonist tour guide here in New Zealand. I hope you like your new school. Someday I will show you what the world looks like from way up here. Remember, the sky's the limit.

Love, Mom

"Wow. She's in New Zealand," Trina said.

"I saw that. Pretty amazing," her dad said, cranking up the windshield wipers. "Man, these prairie storms roll through as fast as semitrucks on a highway."

Raindrops the size of grapes plinked against the truck as Trina read the note again, holding onto that word, *someday*, as tightly as she held onto the postcard. Someday. Someday her mother would come for her. And then her hope flickered out. New Zealand was on the other side of the world. Her mother wouldn't be coming home anytime soon.

Trina pulled off her cap and twirled it in her fingers, thinking of Miss Dale's perfume and wondering what kind of perfume her mother wore. And if her mother ever wore nail polish. She bit down on her lip and let the scrub and swipe of the windshield wipers fill the silence the rest of the way to Goldenrod. By the time they pulled through the black gate, the rain had stopped and the sun was peeking through the clouds.

"What do you think?" her dad said as they got out of the truck. "Took me forever to get the boards off the turret."

Trina glanced up. Extension ladders and scaffolding leaned against the front of the house. The boards were gone from the big bay window in the parlor. Gone from the turret and the rest of the upstairs windows, too. The ancient glass shimmered.

Goldenrod was changing, beginning to come to life, but Trina was stuck in the middle of nowhere. And she was never going back to school.

"Looks nice," she said only because her dad was waiting for her to say something.

He bent down and picked up a long squeegee from the ground. "Think maybe you could help me out a little?

Maybe wash the inside of the windows and let me keep going on the outside? There's an extra bucket in the basement. Or maybe you could tackle the laundry."

Trina waved the hot-air balloon postcard in the air as she headed in the front door. "Just let me put this away first," she said.

Clutching the postcard, Trina went into the kitchen, grabbed a piece of bread, and ate it on the way upstairs to her room. So what if sunshine poured through the stained glass windows in the stairwell, casting a rainbow of colors across the walls? So what if the hall was filled with light? What difference would it really make that the windows were open, letting fresh air into the house for the first time in a hundred years?

She was still motherless. And friendless.

She flopped on her mattress, grateful her dad had brought it upstairs so she had somewhere to go to feel sorry for herself, and read the postcard again. But she had no idea when someday would come and she was too antsy to wait. She got up and put the postcard on the mantel with the others and then she took off her Diamondbacks cap and hung it on one of the curlicue hooks on the big mirror. The hook was loose and her first thought was to grab a screwdriver and tighten it, but when she wiggled the hook, it clicked. Like a latch.

The hook was not an ordinary hook.

And the mirror was not an ordinary mirror.

The mirror was a door.

Chapter Five

Trina's heart fluttered in her chest.

She pushed on the mirror and felt it give way, slowly opening inward.

The turret room!

Trina gasped, but for some reason, she wasn't afraid. Even though secret rooms were notorious for scary and mysterious things, Trina could see that this little room was different. It had pink shutters on the windows and it was ringed with deep shelves as tall as she was, and each shelf was painted a different color. Frayed yellow fabric was tacked to the edge of the shelves, which made the room look like an old-fashioned circus wagon.

The shelves were empty except for one lonesome book—a copy of *Grimm's Fairy Tales*. Trina blew dust off its cover and set it back in its outline on the dusty shelf.

A nursery rhyme was painted on the walls above the shelves, each line a banner floating through the air, carried by little blue birds.

What are little girls made of, made of?
What are little girls made of?

"Sugar and spice and all that's nice.
That's what little girls are made of."

A playroom. That's what this room had been. A room full of toys for the little girl who slept in the bedroom next door. A hundred years ago the shelves were probably filled with puzzles and dolls and books. Now it was a room full of loneliness, and it made Trina feel sad, so sad she wanted to leave the room and forget all about it.

When she put her hand on the doorknob, she heard a tiny *ping*—the sound of something very small hitting the floor—and it rolled toward her shoe. *A nail?* She took it to the windows and opened the shutters to see it better in the sunlight. It couldn't be a nail because it was bumpy and had four little balls on one end and a pinhole at the other. Trina still wasn't sure what it was, so she stuck it in her pocket for safekeeping. This time, when she turned to leave, the mirrored door swung shut in front of her, creaking as if to say, "Take another look!"

Trina took another look.

There, hidden in the shadows, recessed beneath a deep shelf like a puzzle piece in a puzzle, was a dollhouse—a two-story dollhouse whose rooftop, complete with a chimney and weather vane—reached to her waist.

The tiny curtains hung in tatters, wallpaper curled just like in the parlor downstairs, and everything was covered in a layer of fine dust. But Trina could tell in an instant, *the house had good bones.*

Very carefully, she pulled the dollhouse forward. It slid

smoothly across the wooden floor, as if it had traveled the same path many times and knew the way. When Trina reached the center of the room, the yellow dollhouse filled with sunshine through its own rippled glass windows.

Sunlight glinted off tiny brass sconces and silver mirrors, illuminating a parlor with a fireplace, a dining room, and a kitchen with its own little swinging door. Trina gave the swinging door a nudge and it swung with a tiny squeak. "The first thing I'll do is oil that door," she whispered.

Miniature books were stacked on shelves in the parlor, paintings the size of postage stamps adorned the papered walls, petite fringed rugs were scattered across its wooden floors, and the dining table was set for three with little white dishes—and one tarnished candlestick in the center of the table, identical to the mysterious object in Trina's pocket. She pulled out the bit of silver and stood it next to the other candlestick. The dining table was now ready for company.

The dollhouse didn't have a bay window or a turret, but it had a very large balcony, and beneath the balcony was a stable with four stalls. An old-fashioned carriage was in one of the stalls and a little black horse lay on its side in front of the carriage, still wearing its bridle and saddle.

The upstairs had a bathroom with a claw-foot tub, and two bedrooms, one green and one pink, each with a four-poster bed. Most extraordinary of all was the tiny doll lying in the bed in the pink room. Her face, no bigger than a dime, peeked from beneath the covers.

"Do you live here all alone?" Trina whispered.

She pulled back the doll's covers, shook the dust from the quilt made of little squares of flowered fabric, and wiped the doll's delicate little face with its corner. The doll was made of white porcelain, and when Trina sat her up, her sparkling blue eyes opened. She had long blonde hair and wore a frilly white dress with short sleeves. Her little black boots had hooks and ties and were made of real leather. Trina was impressed with the tiny stitches and the detail of the doll's face and clothing, but she didn't think much of dolls. In fact, she'd never owned one, so she was quick to put this one back to bed.

But she loved the dollhouse.

Maybe it could be her project. Maybe she could show her dad how much she could do all by herself.

Trina was crouching, sitting on her heels, trying to stand up the little black horse and straighten his bridle at the same time, when she heard something rustle. She held the horse as still as could be in midair and listened.

Nothing.

She wondered if mice lived in this hidden room, or if maybe even a bat had made its home in the walls. She held her breath, waiting for another rustle, a hiss, a squeak. Any sound at all.

Nothing.

And then—something.

Trina cocked her head, trying to place the faint noise. If it hadn't been for the silence of the secret room, in a corner of a great empty house, sitting all by itself in the middle of a cornfield, miles from anywhere, she wouldn't have heard the tiniest voice imaginable ask, "Are you my prince?"

The tiny porcelain doll was sitting up in her tiny four-poster bed.

And her tiny blue eyes were open.

Trina dropped the horse and fell backward, but she didn't scream. She opened her mouth and tried, but she couldn't make a single sound.

As the doll got out of bed, Trina scooted away. When the doll leaned out her bedroom window, Trina plastered herself against the closed door.

"If you are my prince, the first thing I would like you to do is build me a fire so I can warm myself by the hearth. Can you not see that I am shivering with cold and fear?"

No, she couldn't. As far as Trina was concerned, *she* was the one shivering with cold and fear. Trina shook her head. Then, thinking logic might be her only weapon, she said in her own small voice, "A fire is too dangerous." But just in case she needed to be kind to the doll, she said, "Would you like a sweater?"

"A sweater?"

The doll cocked her head, confused. Trina realized the doll didn't know what a sweater was, which somehow made her much less frightening. "Would you like me to find you some warmer clothes?"

The doll clasped her hands together happily, making a little tinkling sound. "Oh, so you are my maid. Why did you not say so?"

"No, I'm not your maid. Or your prince," Trina said emphatically, thinking she should stay in control of the situation. "I am the girl who discovered you, but that's beside the point. You're a doll and dolls don't talk, not for real. On top of that, I am too old to play with dolls. And I have no interest in playing with you, so this shouldn't be happening."

The doll looked at Trina curiously. "Then why are you here?"

"I live here," Trina said.

"Here? In my house?" the doll said incredulously. "But you are much too large."

Trina shook her head. "No, not in your house. I live in the house that your house is in." Trina knew she wasn't sounding very logical anymore. "I am a person and you are just a doll."

The doll looked taken aback. She descended the stairs from her second floor and disappeared, but Trina could hear her dainty footsteps getting closer. And then the doll stepped out her front door and started walking toward Trina.

"You stay right there," Trina said.

"There is no reason to be afraid of me," the doll said, "for you are very large and I am very small. I should think it would be the other way around."

The doll had made a good point. Still, there was every reason to be afraid of a doll that talked.

"And, by the by, where I come from, dolls *do* talk." The doll rose up on her tiptoes, looking at Trina as if she were some kind of mountain in the distance. "You do not look like a girl. Your hair is too short. Maidens have long, beautiful hair, like mine." She twisted her hair at her shoulder and stroked it with both hands. "And furthermore, if anyone has reason to complain, it would be me. Suddenly the sun is shining in my face and I am wide awake. And I am cold." The doll shook enough for her little porcelain joints to rattle. "Perhaps you would be kind enough to at least tell me your name."

"Trina," Trina answered quickly, surprised to be scolded by someone, or *something,* so small.

The doll made a face as if she had bitten into a lemon. "I have never heard of such a name."

Being insulted about her name twice in one day was too much. "My given name is Citrine," said Trina stiffly, "but my mother is the only one who ever called me that. Everyone else calls me Trina."

"I much prefer the name Citrine," the doll said brightly, lingering on the last syllable. "It sounds like the name of a beautiful princess, so that is what I will call you."

"It does?" Trina asked.

"Yes, it does, and I know all about princesses."

Ci-tree-een. Ci-tree-een. If she said her name the way the doll said it, her name sounded like a song. Charlotte or no Charlotte, Trina fell in love with her name. "What's your name?" she asked. She couldn't believe she was having a conversation with a doll, but it seemed polite to return the question.

A sad look came over the doll's face. She took a deep breath and sighed, which made the ruffles of her dress rise and fall. She sat down on the threshold of her house with a little clink. "I do not know. I do not believe I ever had a name. How did you come by yours?"

"My mother named me. Citrine is my birthstone. It's yellow and it means kindness. It's supposed to protect me from negative energy."

"Negative energy," the doll repeated. "What is negative energy?"

"Bad things," Trina said.

"Ah, yes. Bad things. I know of many bad things." The doll raised one little eyebrow and whispered, "Does it work?"

Trina considered this question. A lot of bad things had happened to her. Her mother had left home to travel the world. She had no friends. And now she lived in New Royal. And then there was Charlotte. And, of course, a scary house to live in. Trina eyed the doll, still uncertain what to make of her. "I'm not sure."

The little doll put her finger to her temple. "Now that I think of it, I had one of those."

"A name?"

"No, a mother. And a father." Scrutinizing Trina's face, she added, "I think I also had one of you."

"One of me? What do you mean?" Trina shifted to her stomach and leaned in on her elbows to hear the doll more clearly.

"A girl who played with me and put me places. But often I grew annoyed. Sometimes I wanted to sit in the parlor and she put me in the dining room. And sometimes she put me to bed when I was perfectly happy riding my pony. The worst of it was when she left me on the floor and forgot about me." The doll sighed again. "I have not seen my little girl for ages and ages, nor have I seen my mother. One day she was here and the next day she was nowhere to be seen."

"Sounds like my mother," Trina said. "My mother joined a dance troupe in Paris when I was three and never came home. She travels all over the world, from one adventure to another."

The little doll's eyes widened. "A life full of travel and adventure sounds wonderful to me."

Trina shook her head, thinking of all the places she and her dad had been, from Wisconsin to New Mexico and Oregon, and everything in between. "Not to me. I just want to live in one normal place. Forever."

"Such as Paris, France," the doll said wistfully. "My dress and my shoes are from Paris, France." The little doll sat up straight and tall. "Why, I believe *I* am from Paris, France." She brushed her hair from her face with her thin porcelain fingers and continued. "My father is also from Paris, France, but I am quite certain my beautiful mother is from Italy. Is your mother very beautiful?"

"I don't remember," said Trina. "Her name is Caroline and that's about all I know. My father doesn't like to talk about her. But I understand why. Talking about her makes me sad, too."

"Ah, then you must tell me all your woes, because I am a doll. Dolls are very good at listening and keeping secrets." The little doll stood up and straightened her dress. "Is your father also traveling all over the world?"

Trina shook her head. "No, he's outside. Working."

The doll nodded, staring into the sunlight. "Do tell me, do you think we could find me one?"

"A father?" Trina asked, confused.

"No, a name."

Trina shrugged. "Sure. But why don't you just pick one?"

The little doll's face beamed. "Is that truly possible?"

"Yes, but you should think about it carefully. Your name should have meaning," Trina said.

"Such as Gretel?"

Of all the names in the world, Trina was surprised the doll would come up with Gretel. "Of course," she said, trying to be supportive, "unless you want it to sound more like a princess."

"Oh, I do, I do. And you are correct, my dear Citrine. Gretel is not the name of a princess." The little doll lowered her head and looked up at Trina, batting her eyelashes. "Should I call myself Beauty?"

"Um," Trina hesitated. "That sounds a little conceited." Trina thought about her own name and its significance. "I know. When is your birthday?"

"My birthday?" The doll's face furrowed. "Please, tell me. What is a birthday?"

"It's the day you're . . ." Trina paused. She was about to say "born" but dolls weren't born; they were manufactured. "Maybe we could just name you for the month we're in right now. August. Except I don't know the birthstone for August."

"How about Augus-*tine*," the doll said, putting her hands behind her head and leaning against the front door of her house with a very satisfied look on her face. "What do you think of that? *Au-gus-tine*," the doll said slowly, practicing.

"I think it's perfect. You look like an Augustine. Like a warm summer day," Trina said, beginning to like the fussy little doll.

"I think a prince would find it very beautiful."

"TRINA!" her dad bellowed up the stairwell.

The little doll ran inside her house and peeked out from behind the door. "What was that dreadful roar?"

"That's my father. I have to go now. I have chores to do before it gets too late."

Standing up, Trina opened the turret room door and hollered, "COMING!" and then she turned back to see Augustine with her hands covering her ears and her mouth in the shape of an O as if something had hurt her. "I'm sorry, Augustine. I had to yell so he would hear me," she said. "I have to go."

"My dear Citrine, before you go, would you be so kind as to move my house into the big room? I much prefer the big room and I am afraid my prince will not find me if I am tucked in here away from everything."

Tucked away from everything was exactly how Trina felt, so it made complete sense to move the dollhouse into her room, especially if fixing up the house was going to be her project. Trina picked up Augustine and set her on her tiny four-poster bed. Moments earlier she had been terrified—or at least unsure—of the little doll, but now she was acting like she talked to dolls all the time. Slowly she pushed the dollhouse from the turret room into her room.

"You're lucky to have such a beautiful house," Trina said. "It needs a good cleaning and a few things are broken, but I can fix them for you." Augustine beamed and held onto one of the posts of her four-poster bed as if she were sailing on a ship across the ocean.

"Are you really waiting for a prince?" Trina asked.

"Indeed," Augustine said. "My prince should be along any minute, because I was asleep for a very long time and now I have awakened. Are you not expecting yours?"

"No," Trina said, embarrassed at the thought. "I'm too young to have a boyfr—I mean, prince. I'd be happy just to have a friend. Girl or boy."

Trina pulled the mirrored door to the turret room shut and paused to look at herself again, getting used to herself as Citrine instead of Trina.

"Citrine, will I see you again tomorrow?"

If Trina could figure out a way to avoid going to school and stay home, she'd be able to spend the whole day with Augustine. "Of course," she said as she crossed the room. "You'll see me later tonight." She had her hand on her bedroom door when Augustine stopped her again.

"Citrine?"

"Yes?"

"Is it nearly evening?"

Trina glanced at the window and shook her head. "Not for a few more hours, but the sky is cloudy, so it's darker than usual."

"Even so," the doll said, "would you mind helping me change into my bedclothes?"

Augustine faced away from Trina and held her hands over her head, waiting. Trina felt as if she were wearing her dad's big work gloves trying to unbutton the little dress.

Once the dress was off, Augustine told Trina to open a dresser drawer where Trina found a white nightgown trimmed in lace. Trina hurried to dress Augustine, sensing the doll's embarrassment at standing there half naked.

Augustine picked up her dress and handed it to Trina. "I understand you are not my maid, but perhaps you could wash my dress for me. It is quite dusty and I have been wearing it a very long time. I should like to be properly dressed when my prince comes for me."

"TRINA!" her dad's voice boomed again, and Augustine's little hands shot to her ears.

Trina looked down at the rumpled dress in her hand, wondering how she'd gotten herself into this situation, and started out the door.

"Citrine?"

Trina turned around, a little exasperated. "What?"

Augustine was sitting on her bed, swinging her legs, brushing her hair with a brush so small Trina could barely see it. She smiled at Trina and said, "I shall be waiting for you right here."

Trina wondered whether having a doll waiting for her was a good thing. She had just stepped out the door when she heard the little voice again. "Citrine?"

"Yes?" She tried to sound less impatient this time.

"I believe we are going to be great friends."

Chapter Six

With Augustine's little dress cupped in her hand like a rescued butterfly, Trina crossed the hall to the stairway. This time she was struck by how pretty the light was coming through the stained glass windows—pictures of goldenrod, exactly like the ones carved in the woodwork in her new room. She had the funny feeling the house was showing off, saying, "Look at me! Look at me!"

She washed Augustine's dress in the kitchen sink as gently as she could, afraid it might disintegrate in her hands. She hung the dress on a plastic fork and was wedging the fork under the window lock, so the dress could dry in the warm breeze, when her dad came into the kitchen.

"Man, am I ever thirsty," he said.

Trina reached into the cupboard to get him a plastic cup, but she was too late. He was already drinking from the faucet, eye-level with Augustine's dress. "A doll dress?" He gave the ruffle a little nudge. "Since when do you play with dolls?"

"It belongs to Augus—" Trina caught herself and faked a cough through the rest of Augustine's name. She motioned her dad out of the way and took a swig of water from the faucet too. The truth was, Trina was as perplexed as her

dad. She had never played with dolls. And now was *talking*
to a doll who lived upstairs in her room. "You won't believe
what I found, Poppo. The turret room has a secret door and
I found a dollhouse in there. Do you want to see it?"

He shook his head. "Maybe later. I need to finish the
upstairs windows before it gets dark." He looked out the
window at the graying sky. "Or before it storms." After
one more drink of water, he was out the door.

Trina gave a sigh of relief that her dad was too busy to
see the dollhouse. For a millisecond she had wanted to tell
him everything about Augustine, but what could she say? To
him the idea of a talking doll would sound crazier than saying Goldenrod was a haunted house. Besides, she could never
show Augustine to her dad unless she could be sure the doll
would keep quiet, or who knew what would happen next.

A doll? Really? Was she really worrying about a doll?
And what was she doing washing its silly little dress when
there was so much work to be done?

Trina started her chores in the basement by doing the
real laundry. Except for the furnace that was as big as a
train engine, the basement wasn't as scary as she thought
it would be—until the wash cycle kicked in and the water
pipes shook so ferociously she expected the whole house to
come crashing down around her. She grabbed the bucket
and ran upstairs.

Feeling like Cinderella left alone to clean while her
stepsisters went to a party, Trina washed the parlor windows. And then, because the cleaners had done such a
poor job, she scrubbed the kitchen floor on her hands and

knees. If Augustine asked her if she were the maid now, she'd have to say yes.

Just as she finished, it started to rain. A moment later she heard her dad calling as he came through the front door. "Trina! How about hot dogs for dinner? I'll do the cooking."

Trina stopped him at the kitchen door. "Hot dogs sound good, but you have to take your boots off. I just washed the floor."

"Yes, ma'am," he said as he left.

When he came back he had clean socks on, and his face was freshly shaved. He held out his hands for her to inspect. "You may be seated," she said, trying not to grin. She had already boiled the hot dogs—three for him and one for her—*and* she had already set the card table with paper plates, ketchup, relish, a bowl of barbecue-flavored potato chips, and the last of the grapes.

"Poppo," she said as she carried the plate of steaming hot dogs into the dining room and put them on the card table. "I've been thinking." She stood up straight and tall and cleared her throat. She wanted to sound as grown-up as possible.

He raised one eyebrow, concerned. "What is it?"

"I've made the decision to go by my real name from now on, so please call me Citrine."

"Ci-*trine*?" he said, sounding out her name softly as he went into the kitchen. "Ci-*trine*," he said again, coming back with the buns. "But this afternoon you said—"

"I know, but I've changed my mind." She knew she had already changed her mind once, and now she was changing it again, but she trusted elegant little Augustine's opinion more than she trusted mean old Charlotte's.

Poppo scratched the back of his neck as he looked around the dining room, the way he did when he was assessing a new building project. "But I've always called you Trina."

"But Trina is a nickname. And it sounds like it belongs to a little girl. I'm not a little girl anymore."

"I'm beginning to see that," he said, finally pulling his chair away from the card table to sit down. "That'll take some getting used to, unless . . ." Instead of sitting down, he looked at Trina with a serious face.

"Unless what?"

His serious look broke into a smile. "Unless my real daughter has been abducted by aliens. WAH-HA-HA!" he roared in his monster voice. He picked her up and spun her around. "You tell those aliens I won't let you go without a fight."

The room swirled around Trina, but she didn't giggle the way she did when she was little. "This is what I mean, Poppo. Put me down. Please."

She said it so seriously that her dad instantly placed her on her feet. He acted dizzy as he sat down, and then he grabbed the ketchup bottle and pretended he was going to squirt her with it before he smothered his hot dogs with ketchup. "Okay, then," he said. "Citrine it is."

Trina knew he was trying to make a joke out of something that hurt his feelings, but she was pleased to be making a little progress with her dad in the growing-up department.

Outside, the wind picked up. When lightning lit up the eastern sky, they both turned their heads to the French doors. "Lucky I finished my work when I did. But you're right. There is something very strange about this house." He took a bite of hot dog and chewed it very slowly.

"Really, Poppo?" Trina wondered if he had been keeping scary things he knew about the house to himself, too. "Like what?"

"Like I haven't found a single piece of rotten wood on this whole house. I keep thinking, if they'd brought in a wrecking ball to tear it down, I don't think the house would have budged. I've never seen anything built as rock-solid as this place."

Right then a big gust of wind hit the house and the French doors, screeching on their hinges, swung open into the yard. Trina grabbed the paper plates as they slid across the table. Her dad hurried to close the doors. "I take it back," he said. "Looks like I'll have to replace the lock, but . . ." He turned the lock handle over and over again with a puzzled look on his face. "Now it works fine. Maybe the doors weren't locked. Or maybe they're just fickle."

Fickle. Fickle meant you changed your mind a lot. What decision could a door lock be trying to make? The front doors, too, for that matter. But Poppo didn't seem the least bit concerned.

He sat back down at the table and they finished eating without talking, watching the storm roll in as if it were a movie on a big screen. Then, out of the blue, he said, "About school."

Trina was silent for a moment, reliving her awful day at school. "I told you, I'm never going back." Although she was full, she took another potato chip and nibbled it, looking down at her plate.

Her dad leaned forward, trying to make eye contact. "You've always liked school."

She had liked school, but she had never liked being the new kid. And she had never expected anything like New Royal. Even if some of the kids were nice, like Edward, there weren't enough for a softball team. And to top it off, there was the humiliation of Charlotte calling her an outhouse.

"It's different here, Poppo. All the kids know each other. And they all think this house is haunted."

Lightning cracked the sky, closer this time, but her dad talked right through the rumble of thunder. "You have to give it time."

Time. That was the problem. Too much time. Going to school meant she would be miserable for a whole year. This was certainly a woe she could tell to Augustine. Trina set down her half-eaten potato chip. "May I please be excused?"

She didn't give him a chance to speak. She didn't even look at him because she knew he would have that faraway look in his eyes. The one that meant it was hard being a dad sometimes. But it was hard being a kid, too. She put her paper plate in the garbage and went upstairs, feeling a little less lonesome now that Augustine was sharing her room.

Trina opened her bedroom door and whispered, "Augustine, I'm back," but the little doll didn't answer.

Trina got down on her hands and knees and crawled up to Augustine's dollhouse and peered into her bedroom. The little doll lay peacefully in bed with her eyes closed.

"Augustine, wake up." Trina nudged the little doll, but she didn't move. Frightened now by a doll that *didn't* talk, Trina picked her up. Augustine's eyes opened when Trina tilted her, but she remained silent, just like an ordinary doll.

Trina put her cheek to the doll's cool little head and wondered if she had imagined the doll waking up and speaking to her. Was a talking doll just another strange thing about the house to add to the list? Or did she want a friend so badly she made one up?

Confused, Trina put Augustine back in her bed. She picked up her tiny silver hairbrush and brushed the doll's golden hair until it fanned out in a fine yellow spray against her pillow.

"You look just like a princess now," said Trina, thinking that might wake up the doll.

Augustine didn't utter a sound.

Sighing, Trina tore up one of her old T-shirts and started cleaning the dollhouse. She dusted the furniture and the pictures and the tiny books. She took down the tattered curtains, thinking she could learn to make new ones. She shook the rugs in the air and washed the dinner plates and the tea set in the bathroom sink. She was sitting on the floor by the dollhouse, making a list of the work to be done, when her dad knocked on her door.

"How about a game of Crazy Eights?"

"Not tonight, Poppo. I'm busy."

There was a long pause before he said, "Can I come in? I have an idea."

Trina glanced at Augustine, this time making sure she was still an ordinary doll, and was both sad and relieved that she was. She got up and opened her door to her dad, who was standing there with a plate of vanilla wafers in one hand and Augustine's dress in the other. Trina recognized a peace offering when she saw one. Her dad always brought her a treat when something went wrong. Tonight cookies weren't enough to make things better, but she didn't want to seem ungrateful either. She took the dress and helped herself to a vanilla wafer. "So what's your idea?"

"Is everything okay? I mean . . ." The window flashed bright with lightning, barely a second before thunder clapped, interrupting her dad in midsentence. Trina hoped he'd lose his train of thought, but he didn't. "I mean changing your name. And not wanting to go back to school. Are you sure everything's okay? Is this some kind of girl thing I don't understand?"

Trina had never thought much about girl things, but the idea of using girl things as an excuse sounded like a good idea. Maybe girl things were a way to get what she wanted. She shrugged and took a bite of the wafer.

"Listen, I know it's hard getting used to a new place. So I was thinking, what if you took a few days off? A little R & R. And then you can start school again next week."

Trina gave the idea a bite's worth of thought, figuring out that a few days off would buy her time to think of a permanent way to avoid New Royal Public School. "Okay," she said.

"That's great," her dad said, sounding relieved. Then he looked past Trina to the dollhouse. "Wow. Sure is a beauty. Where did you say you found it?"

Trina led her dad to the mirrored door, glad to be off the hook about school. "In here," she said, pushing down on the latch. "It's a secret door to the turret room. I think it was a playroom."

Her dad peered into the room over her shoulder as lightning magically lit up the colorful shelves. "Makes sense. Back then children were meant to be seen and not heard. Must be why they call them the good old days," he said, winking as soon as he caught Trina's eye.

He started to go in, but Trina pulled him toward the dollhouse. "Come and see it."

She crouched down and hung Augustine's dress on her four-poster bed. When her dad crouched next to her, Trina gushed with excitement. "Look at the dining room table, Poppo. It's set for three people. See the little dishes and the tiny silverware? And the newspapers on the side table? And there's the doll. In bed. The dress belongs to her." Trina knew better than to introduce her to him as Augustine—as if she were real.

"This little doll?" He picked up Augustine and her eyes popped open with a vacant stare. "She's pretty fancy," he said. When he flicked her arms and legs, they kicked and waved as if yanked by a marionette's string. Trina watched in horror, imagining what Augustine might say if she were awake. "Please don't, Poppo. She wants you to take her more seriously."

"She does? Oh, of course she does," he said sheepishly, putting her back in her bed. "I don't know much about dolls," he said. "But I know houses and this is one of the finest I've ever seen. Even the doorknobs work." He opened and shut the front door. "Better than Goldenrod's." He sat back and put his hands on his knees. "You know, I bet a hundred years ago, on a stormy night just like this one, some little girl was playing with this dollhouse."

In the next gust of wind, the room went dark. Even the hum of electricity stopped. Trina sat still and listened as the storm raged outside. But this time the house didn't feel scary; it just felt empty and sad. No wonder Augustine was eager to make friends. She had been lying in darkness this lonesome for a hundred years without anyone to play with her.

With a click of his lighter, her dad found his way to the gas sconce. When he lit it, the room glowed golden. "I guess I wasn't kidding. Some little girl would have played with the dollhouse exactly like this. By gaslight."

The flame of the gaslight emitted a little puff, like a tiny gasp, and so did Trina. Poppo was talking about Augustine's little girl and he didn't even know it. A little girl who was now long gone.

"Look at that. It even has a stable." He sat down next to Trina and set the horse in one of the stalls. "That means this dollhouse is a carriage house. Every mansion had a carriage house back then. It was kind of like a garage. And that's where the caretakers lived." He picked up the carriage and turned its wooden wheels. "Makes me wonder what happened to the carriage house for Goldenrod. People wealthy enough to build this place would have had a lot of carriages."

"Maybe they ran out of money," Trina suggested.

"Could be," he said, gently picking up a little blue velvet chair with three legs and the splinter of a fourth. "A little glue and this chair will withstand Goldilocks." It was funny to watch her dad's big hands touch the small things. If Augustine woke up now, she'd be terrified.

He set down the chair in Augustine's room and pressed a piece of curling wallpaper back into place, but it let go as soon as he moved his finger. "Sure needs a lot of work," he said.

"It's definitely a fixer-upper," Trina said, "but I know it's all doable."

"I don't know, Princess. I've got a lot on my plate with Goldenrod. Every wall. Every system. The painting. Winter will be here before you know it and—"

"No, Poppo. I want the dollhouse to be *my* project. You said I get my own tools, remember? And I want to learn how to sew, so I can make new curtains for it and fix the quilts and—"

"You know you're on your own there, right?" Her dad stood up and put his hands in his pockets. "I was always going to build your mother a dollhouse." His voice was low and distant. And he had that faraway look in his eyes.

"Really?"

He nodded. "I would have, too, especially if I'd known you'd end up playing with one."

Now Trina had something new to think about: her mother liked dollhouses. "Why didn't you?" she asked.

He flexed his fingers. "With these clunkers? Just imagine." And then he got quiet again. "You know you can't keep it," he said. "Nothing here belongs to us."

Every time Trina got her hopes up her dad seemed to knock them down. "I know I can't keep it. We never keep any of the houses we fix up." Trina glanced at Augustine. Only Augustine knew how badly she wanted to live in one normal place forever. Someday things would be different. Someday.

POUND! POUND! POUND!

Trina jumped. "Someone's at the door, Poppo!"

Her dad shook his head in disbelief. "Who would come all the way out here on a night like this?"

Trina pulled Augustine's quilt to the doll's tiny chin before she followed her dad out of her room. The hallway and stairwell were blacker than the sky, but downstairs the parlor was filled with the bright beams of headlights.

POUND! POUND! POUND!

Her dad opened the door to a short man with a big black mustache wearing a long raincoat that nearly brushed the ground. He was bouncing from one foot to the other on the top plank step, rain dripping down from his soaked head.

"Hank!" Trina's dad said, shaking his hand. "Tr—I mean Citrine, this is Mr. Hank from the hardware store."

"Nice to make the acquaintance." Mr. Hank tipped his wet head and raindrops flew. "Got a dining room table for you, Mr. Mike. Heh-heh," he said. "Used to belong to this old place. High time she came home."

"Thanks, but are you sure? In this weather?" Trina's dad sounded bewildered.

"Just take a quick jiffy," Mr. Hank said, glancing back and forth between the foyer and his idling truck, acting like it might drive off without him. "If you give me a hand."

"Sure, I guess," Trina's dad said. "Power's out. Come in while I get a light on."

With a quick shake of his head, Mr. Hank hobbled backward through the door, turned to go down the steps, and sloshed through the puddles to his truck.

Her dad lit the parlor and dining room sconces and went outside. As he and Mr. Hank carried a long table covered in plastic through the front door, Trina hurried into the dining room to move the card table and the folding chairs out of the way.

They centered the table in front of the French doors, and Mr. Hank pulled off the plastic in a single swoop. As if a master switch had been flipped, the lights came on and the chandelier brightened the table's dark wood with a red shimmer.

"Wow," Trina gasped. "I've never seen a table like this before."

The lights of the chandelier blinked off and then on again, in a sort of happy little wink, and Trina had a funny feeling someone was tapping her on her shoulder, trying to get her attention. She placed her hand on the table's shiny, smooth top, and all at once she saw it set with white dishes, sparkling glasses, and a big bouquet of yellow flowers. She swore she could hear people, all dressed up and sitting around the table, talking with each other and laughing.

Goldenrod, the sad house, now had one happy room.

"She's a beaut, all right. Finally back where she belongs." Mr. Hank bounced on the tips of his toes as he quickly bundled up the wet plastic in his arms. "Don't have the chairs, though. Nope, sure don't. Wish I did, heh-heh," he said, bouncing himself backward out of the dining room, across the parlor, all the way to the foyer as if he couldn't wait to get out of the house.

"Do I owe you any money?" Trina's dad said, running to keep up with Mr. Hank. "I'm sure the Roy estate could buy it back from—"

"Nope. She was stole in the first place," Mr. Hank said without slowing down.

"Stolen?" Trina blurted, trotting behind her dad. "Who stole it?"

"Heh-heh," was all Mr. Hank said as he disappeared out the front door into the wet, gray night. "The spindles for your porch should be in tomorrow," he called over his shoulder. "Banister too."

"Great, I'll stop by," her dad called back just as Mr. Hank ducked into his truck, plastic and all, and rattled away.

Trina stood in the doorway with her dad, watching the red taillights of Mr. Hank's truck recede into the corn-field as the rain poured down in sheets. "Stolen!" Trina repeated. "Why was it stolen?"

"Why not?" he said. "People steal all kinds of things." He imitated Mr. Hank walking backward, bouncing from one foot to the other, all jumpy and jittery, until they both burst out laughing. "He sure was scared to come in."

"See what I mean, Poppo? Everyone thinks this house is haunted."

"And you know what I have to say about that," he said as the electric lights in the chandelier flickered like candles and dots of light danced on the new dining room table.

Trina gave the ceiling a distrustful glance.

"Don't worry," her dad said. "Even if we lose power again, we'll still have the gas lights."

Losing power didn't worry Trina. But the idea that the house could somehow be listening did. A storm could make the lights flicker, but a storm wouldn't know how to make the lights flicker as though winking at her, or when to shut a door, or how to blow French doors open if the locks worked properly. And most of all, what could possibly explain Augustine, except for something in the house itself?

Trina knew she was right when she said everything was Goldenrod's fault. She could blame everything on the old house, even how the kids at school treated her, except . . . except nothing had gotten her yet, so it was more like the house had cried wolf. And she knew that people who cried wolf wanted attention.

That was it.

Goldenrod wanted her attention.

Goldenrod was trying to tell her something.

But what would a house want her to know?

Chapter Seven

Ci-tree-een! Ci-tree-een! Trina was dreaming she was running through a sunny field of yellow flowers. Petals were tickling her face and someone was calling her name. She opened her eyes to a dreary morning, squeezed them shut, and rolled over.

A flower tickled her face again.

"Good morning, Citrine," a little voice said.

Trina's eyes flew open. She recognized that tiny voice. Augustine was standing on the edge of her pillow, brushing her cheek.

"It's you!" Trina felt a rush of gratitude that the little doll was alive again, if "alive" was even the right word.

Augustine extended her delicate hand and brushed Trina's bangs from her eyes. "I have already had the greatest adventure in your world, Citrine. I climbed this mountain to look for you and here you are."

Without another word, the little doll threw her arms in the air and slid down a wrinkle in Trina's bedsheet all the way to the floor. Awake now, Trina watched the doll skip into her house and up her steps to her own bedroom. "Thank you," she said, pointing at her dress hanging from her bedpost. "You have washed my dress for me." Augustine turned around, fought to pull her nightgown over her head, and finally succeeded. "Do not look," she said. Trina closed her eyes dutifully, giving in to sleep, only to be startled a few seconds later by tiny thumps. Augustine was hopping around on one leg, trying to pull the sleeve of her dress over her foot.

"Do you want some help?" Trina asked.

"No," the doll said. "I assure you, I can do it by myself."

Trying to hide the grin on her face, Trina watched Augustine hop some more. "That part goes over your arm," Trina finally said. Augustine looked confused. When Trina got off her mattress and reached into Augustine's bedroom to help, Augustine ducked behind the broken blue chair.

"No, Citrine. If I am to live in your world and have many adventures, then I must learn to do this task myself." Augustine righted her dress, figured out how to put her arms through the sleeves, and finally poked her head through the collar. She struggled with her buttons, smoothed her skirt, and turned to Trina expectantly. "Now, what adventures have you planned for us today?"

Trina stretched out on the floor with her hands under her head. "I haven't planned any adventures. I have planned relaxation and recreation because I don't have to go to school."

"Ah, School." Now Augustine was sitting on the edge of her little bed, swinging her legs and brushing her hair. "I have heard of School. It is a land far, far away."

"It's more of a building," Trina corrected her. "It's full of teachers and books. Children go there to learn."

"Oh, yes, now I remember. The children go there for many, many hours and read books. I love books. They are full of stories. The Land of School must be wonderful!"

Trina sat up to be eye-level with Augustine. "No, it isn't wonderful. And I don't want to go back. Ever. The children there are mean. One of them is really mean."

"Is he an ogre?"

"It's a she, and she's more of a witch. I told them my name is Citrine . . ." Augustine smiled, nodding her approval. "But the witch made fun of it."

Augustine dropped her brush in her lap and clasped her hands over her ears. "Oh, Citrine, tell me it is not so. Not your beautiful name. You must avenge this indignity."

"She says she'll beat me up if—"

Augustine waved her hands wildly. "Stop! I have heard enough. There is only one thing you can do with a witch who wants to eat you up. You must push her into the oven."

Trina leaned her head toward Augustine's bedroom. "Did you say *eat you up?*"

"Yes, but you are awfully skinny. You would not make much of a meal for anyone. Not even for the wolf in the wood."

"The wolf in the wood?" Trina said. Now it all made sense: the witch and the oven, the wolf in the wood, the prince, the names Gretel and Beauty. "Wait a minute." Trina went into the turret room and came back with the old copy of *Grimm's Fairy Tales*. "Do you know this book?" Trina asked. But before she could hold it up for Augustine to see, the little doll was already hurrying down her stairs.

"Book? Did you say book?"

Trina nodded and set it on the floor. "It's called *Grimm's Fairy Tales*. Do you remember it?"

Augustine's face glowed like a dewdrop. She climbed onto the cover of the book, hurried to the title, and twirled in a circle on the big, gold capital G. "I do remember, I do! I do! The mother read this book to my little girl as she lay in bed. The mother sat next to her in a big chair and the room was very, very still. Only that lamp glowed." Augustine pointed to the brass sconce above Trina's mattress.

"It must have been wonderful for the girl to have her mother read to her," Trina said. She couldn't remember if her own mother had ever read to her.

"Oh, yes, it was," Augustine said. "The mother read from many books, but this one—" Augustine knelt down and placed her hand in the dot of the *i*. "—was my favorite. Sometimes I listened from the parlor, and sometimes while sitting on my pony. But the best place to hear the stories was in bed with the quilt pulled up to my chin, just like my little girl."

Augustine stared into the empty, dark fireplace for a long time. Trina could sense her sadness. "Augustine, what is it?"

"I have longed for stories, Citrine. Do you think you might read one to me now?" Augustine climbed down from the book, sat on the floor, and carefully covered her knobby little knees with her dress. "Please?"

Trina felt honored to be asked to read. Augustine was looking up to her, which made Trina feel like a big sister. But she also felt like Augustine's new little girl. Like they belonged together. Happily she opened *Grimm's Fairy Tales* and ran her finger down the table of contents, past "The Frog Prince," "Hansel and Gretel," and "Snow White." "Here's one just for you," she whispered excitedly, turning to page fifty-seven of the ancient book, to the story of "Briar Rose."

"Once upon a time," Trina began, *"there lived in a distant kingdom a very lonesome king and queen. 'If only we had a child,' they wished, but for many years they remained alone."*

Heavy clouds rolled across the morning sky and thunder rumbled in the distance as Trina read aloud the story of the young princess who, at the fate of a wicked spell, pricked her finger on a spindle and fell into a deep sleep for a hundred years. Trina held up the page with the picture of Briar Rose in her long blue gown and pointed cap and showed it to Augustine, and then, feeling as if someone was looking over her shoulder, hanging on her every word, and expecting to see the pictures too, she held the book up in the air.

"What are you doing?" asked Augustine, puzzled and indignant.

Maybe Poppo was right. Maybe the real Trina *had* been captured by aliens. What else could explain her reading a story to a talking doll and showing pictures to the walls of her room? Still she felt compelled to continue reading in a loud voice about how the princess was finally awakened by a kiss from a handsome prince. *"Then the marriage of the prince and Briar Rose was celebrated with extreme grandness and they lived happily ever after. The end."*

Augustine put her hands to her mouth and looked as if she might cry. "What a wonderful story. It is exactly how I remember it. You must read it again. Please."

"Again?"

"Of course, again. Good stories are meant to be read over and over and over—"

"Okay, okay, Augustine. I'll read it again." Trina didn't really mind reading it again. She loved the part where the prince kissed the sleeping beauty and the kingdom woke up and the fire crackled in the hearth, and even the flies began to buzz again, and everybody danced with joy. *"The end,"* she said finally as the storm rolled off to the horizon and a ray of sun pierced the thinning clouds.

Augustine leaped to her feet. "I know what we shall do today. But it shall remain a surprise until you get dressed," she said. "You are still in your bedclothes."

Trina pulled off her pajama bottoms and green T-shirt and pulled on her denim shorts and a light blue T-shirt. She grabbed her Brewers cap because it matched her shirt. "Ready," Trina said.

"We shall look for my prince. I have awakened twice and still he is not here. Perhaps he is lost. We must search hill and dale for him."

"Now?" Trina asked.

"Of course now. What else do you have to do with your many hours if you are never returning to the Land of School?" Augustine ran into her little house and looked at herself in the hallway mirror. She turned this way and that, tucked a few strands of her yellow hair behind her porcelain ear, and batted her pale eyelashes at herself.

"But your prince . . ." Trina slipped her feet into her flip-flops.

"Yes?"

Augustine looked at Trina so earnestly, Trina didn't know how to tell her that waking up and finding a prince waiting to marry you only happened in fairy tales. Still, Augustine deserved to know the truth. She sat down on the floor and held Augustine's little hand between her thumb and her forefinger. "I'm afraid your prince isn't coming," she said.

Augustine clutched at Trina's finger, her eyes fluttering as if she might faint. Trina now wished she hadn't said anything. True friends didn't trick you, but they didn't steal all your hope away either. "I mean . . . *yet*," Trina said quickly. "He isn't here *yet*. He could be outside. Maybe he's trapped in the briar."

"Trapped in the briar?" Augustine's eyes flashed with distress. "We must go to him at once."

"We'll do our best to find him," Trina said, but then she had the awful thought that when they left her room, they might run into her dad. What if Augustine spoke to him? What would happen then? "Augustine, you must promise me that if we see my father, you won't move or say a word."

"Will he be frightened of me?"

Trina shook her head. "No, it will be worse than that. If word gets out about you, you'll be famous. And then they'll put you on, I mean *in*, the Land of TV. Your life will never be the same."

Augustine's brow furrowed with great concern. "You must tell me of this Land of TV. It does not sound like a pleasant kingdom."

"The Land of TV is like a prison. They would never let you out."

Augustine looked horrified. "Is it worse than being trapped in a tower forever and ever?"

"Much worse than a tower, Augustine. It's would be like being trapped in a cage. People would watch you and—"

Augustine held up her hand to stop Trina. "You need speak no more of this horrible land, Citrine, for I understand its grave danger. Still, we must set forth to find my prince. Sometimes we must take great risks for those we love. Should we encounter another person, I will say not a word and move not a finger." Then she climbed into Trina's hand, ready to be carried off on their first adventure together.

With all the rain it was too wet for her dad to work outside, so Trina expected him to be working inside the house somewhere. But the house was quiet—there was no whine of a saw or thunk of a nail gun anywhere.

They walked through the foyer and parlor, Augustine gazing about with her mouth in a little O, and into the dining room. Despite four beat-up metal folding chairs, the dining room looked regal. Trina set Augustine on the gleaming table next to a bowl of oatmeal sitting on a paper plate and read a note her dad had left for her:

F. C. I'm out walking the grounds, trying to plan the
new septic system. I left you some oatmeal. —P

The oatmeal was covered with cinnamon sugar, just the
way she liked it, and the bowl was warm so Trina knew
her dad hadn't been gone long. She sat down and picked
up her spoon. "I'll hurry and eat my oatmeal," she said to
Augustine. She knew dolls didn't eat real food, but even so,
she felt strange eating in front of Augustine.

Augustine grasped the rim of Trina's bowl, stood on
her tiptoes, and peered at Trina's breakfast. "Tell me, what
is oatmeal?"

Trina tilted her bowl to give Augustine a better view.
"I think you would call it porridge."

"Ah, yes, porridge," Augustine said seriously. "I have
heard of porridge. Is it too hot or too cold?"

Trina shook her head with her mouth full. It was hard
to eat when she was trying not to laugh.

"Then it is just right," Augustine said with certainty.

Trina swallowed her last bite of oatmeal, gently curled
her fingers around Augustine, and opened the French
doors to the muggy morning air. As soon as she stepped
onto the massive stone stoop, Augustine clutched Trina's
thumb with both hands. "Oh, Citrine, what land is this?"

Trina racked her brain. Goldenrod sat on land that
belonged to the Roy family, but the Land of Roy sounded
silly. "This is the Land of Goldenrod," she finally said.

"I remember this land," Augustine said in a shaky little voice. "I was here once with my father. Please, hold me tight or I will become lost to you."

Trina closed her fingers more tightly around Augustine, making sure Augustine's head still peeked above her thumb and forefinger. "I'll hold you tight, but you have to keep your eyes open for toads."

"Toads?" Augustine yelped.

"Yes, toads. Your prince. Maybe he's under a wicked spell and has been turned into a toad."

Augustine shuddered in Trina's hand. "Citrine, toads are often quite ugly. If my prince is going to be under a spell, I would much prefer a frog."

Trina rolled her eyes. "Okay, we'll look for frogs."

A haze covered the Land of Goldenrod between the house and the grove of trees in the distance. And new wooden stakes dotted the field. Trina pushed through the long, tangled stems of goldenrod, making sure to hold Augustine high above the weeds. She didn't notice any toads or frogs hopping in puddles, but she did find daisies and chrysanthemums and some flowers she didn't recognize growing among the goldenrod. She also discovered a long section of wrought iron fence lying on its side and figured it must have marked the boundary of an ancient garden.

"Look," she said, holding Augustine's face close to a yellow chrysanthemum. "The old flowers are still coming up. Isn't that amazing? I think we should pick some flowers for the dining room table."

Trina felt Augustine nod her head, but she could also tell the doll had curled up in her hand, frightened. "Don't worry, Augustine, I've got you."

Across the field, Trina saw her dad coming from the grove of trees. "Poppo," she called, plucking daisies by the handful as she ran toward him, eager to show him her discovery. Then her flip-flop caught on something hard. Her arms shot straight out and she soared through the air before belly-flopping into the deep weeds. Her Brewers cap and her bouquet of daisies flew sky-high—along with Augustine.

"Trina!" her dad hollered and came running.

Trina tried to get up, but pain stabbed her rib cage and all she could do was roll over and sink back into the weeds.

"Are you okay?" he asked, leaning over her.

Trina nodded, but she was dizzy with worry. Knowing his next step could shatter Augustine, she tried to say, *Don't move,* but no words came out.

"Lie still," he said, fanning her with her baseball cap. "You had the wind knocked out of you." He reached down and raised her arms above her head. "Take shallow breaths."

Trina followed her dad's instructions, breathing so lightly her chest barely moved.

He put her baseball cap in her hand and pointed toward the trees. "There's an apple orchard on the edge of the property. A few more weeks and we should have a nice crop of apples."

Trina knew he was trying to distract her from the pain and it worked. She managed a deeper breath, got up on her hands and knees, and began to feel the ground around her.

Augustine had warned her to be careful, and now the little doll was lost somewhere in the vast yellow field. When her dad bent down to help her up, she cried, "Don't move, Poppo! She's very fragile."

"Who's very fragile?"

"Augustine!" Trina snapped, angry with herself, not her dad.

"Who on earth is Augustine?"

"The doll from the dollhouse, Poppo. I dropped her, so you have to be careful where you step or you'll break her."

"What's she doing out here?"

"She . . . We . . ." There was no way Trina could tell him that she and Augustine were on their first adventure together, a hunt for enchanted frogs. "It's a girl thing, Poppo. But you have to help me find her. Just be really careful."

Her dad looked at her for a moment, head tilted, then he nodded. He crouched down and started moving slowly away from Trina. Trina continued her search, crawling through the soggy weeds inch by inch, pushing aside stems and stalks, looking for a bit of white against the greens, browns, and yellows of the old garden. Just as her hand grazed a big chunk of rock that must have been what tripped her in the first place, her dad shouted, "Now that's what I call luck. Here she is."

Trina scrambled to her feet and ran to her dad as he lifted Augustine from the petals of a giant bowing chrysanthemum. "It's like the flower caught her in midair and lowered her to the ground." He pinched Augustine between his giant thumb and his forefinger and held her out to Trina.

Augustine's eyes were closed, her dress was askew, and her hair was flying every which way, but she was clean and whole. "She's okay," Trina said with huge relief, at which Augustine opened her eyes and winked.

"Don't do that," Trina said without thinking.

"What did I do?" her dad said. "I just found your doll!"

"Not you, Poppo. I mean the doll . . ." Trina took Augustine and shook her finger at her while faking a stern voice. "You must never get lost again."

"You better keep her inside from now on," he said.

"I'll put her in my pocket." Trina slipped Augustine into the front pocket of her jean shorts. "So she'll behave herself," she said. But her dad wasn't listening anymore. He had already shifted his attention to his own project.

"This stake here marks the old well," he said, pulling the biggest stake from the ground as he walked backward, his arms outstretched while he eyed the distance to the French doors as if a measuring tape ran from the house to his fingertips. "I think I'm safe putting the new septic system somewhere . . . about . . . here." He stopped and shoved the stake into the ground. "It has to be at least one hundred feet from the . . . Whoa!" he hollered.

In an instant he was gone, and all Trina could see was a ripple in the yellow tops of the goldenrod spreading in front of her like deep water. "Poppo!" Trina shouted as she ran toward him, but the whipping stalks seemed to hold her back. What if he had fallen into the old well? What if . . . ? And then he popped up right in front of her like an old-fashioned jack-in-the-box, scaring the wits out of her.

"Poppo!" she wheezed.

"No wonder they never farmed this land," he said, brushing off his pants. "It's full of rocks."

"No kidding," Trina said. She bent down and picked up a chunk of broken stone, took a good look at it, and held it up for her dad to see. "Look, Poppo. It's not a rock; it's cement." She pushed back the stalks of goldenrod and tracked the chunks of cement in a straight line for several feet. "And there's a ton of it."

When Trina looked at her dad and saw that they were nearly the same height, she figured out he was standing in a sunken part of the field. The answer to the riddle clicked in her head. "This is where the carriage house was." She picked up another chunk of cement. "And this is the foundation."

"I'm impressed," he said. "Maybe you'll grow up to be an archaeologist someday."

Trina was too busy analyzing the foundation to think about what she wanted to be when she grew up. "But where did the carriage house go, Poppo?"

"Who knows? I think we'll leave that up to the next carpenter who passes through," he said as he pulled his notebook from his pocket.

But Trina wasn't going to give up that easily. *Could the mystery of the carriage house be what Goldenrod wanted her to know?* For the first time since they arrived in New Royal, Trina was curious about where they lived. "Did Mr. Sheg-stad tell you anything else about the house and the people who lived here?"

"Just that it was built in 1904 by a Mr. Harlan M. Roy. And how the light fixtures were from England and the fireplace tiles came from Italy. Stuff like that. Mr. Roy was a millionaire and he left everything he owned to his nephew because he didn't have any children of his own."

Trina felt a nerve spark inside her. "But that's not true, Poppo. He had a little girl. She slept in my room and played with the dollhouse, remember?" Trina touched her pocket and gave the very quiet Augustine a little pat.

"Hm. Maybe you should become a detective instead," he said, but he wasn't the least bit interested in the Roys or the carriage house. He was completely lost in thought as he scribbled in his notebook. "I'm headed into town. Hank said my order should be here. Want to come along?"

"I sure do," Trina said, surprising herself that she had any interest in going back to New Royal, but now she planned to learn as much about Mr. Harlan M. Roy as she could. "You can drop me at the library. I kind of like that detective idea."

Her dad nodded, and as he tucked the notepad back in his pocket, they heard something. The noise came from the front of the house, and soon it became clear it was a truck engine rumbling.

"Maybe Mr. Hank is delivering your spindles," Trina said.

"Not likely," her dad replied, setting off at a run.

Trina followed. They ran toward the house, weeds slapping at their legs. The rumbling got deeper as the truck shifted gears and by the time they rounded the corner of the front of the house, all they could see was the back end of a pickup truck hightailing it out of the Land of Goldenrod.

"What in the world . . . ?" her dad said, and then he and Trina both spotted an enormous antique rocking chair sitting by the steps.

"I think someone else just returned some stolen merchandise," Trina said.

The chair was plain, with tall slatted sides. Despite its thick green leather cushion, it looked like nothing more than a big wooden box on rockers. "Sure is in great condition," her dad said. He gave the chair a push, but it was so heavy it barely moved. "I think a big chair like this belongs in the library."

He groaned as he picked up the chair and his muscles bulged in his arms. All Trina could do to help was run ahead of him and open both front doors. Once inside, she helped push the chair across the foyer floor and into the library. When they finally placed the chair in front of the fireplace, she was out of breath too.

But as she stood back and admired it, she had to admit it was worth the effort. The chair made it easy to imagine the library filled with books and desks and old-fashioned lamps. The dining room had its table and now the library had its reading chair. A sense of peace and contentment seemed to float through Goldenrod.

Trina's dad plopped into the chair and the leather seat gave out a poof of air, like a sigh of relief, as if glad to be sat in after so many years. "Maybe I'll take up smoking again," he said.

"Oh, no, you won't," Trina said, squeezing into the chair next to him. The chair rocked in a comforting way, her dad's long legs making it go back and forth. "It's not good for you. Besides, the library is not the smoking room."

"Then bring me a book."

"One of those books?" Trina said, playfully, pointing at the towering, empty bookshelves.

Her dad frowned. "Then bring me my slippers!"

"Don't be so silly, Poppo. We have servants who take care of such things."

"Servants, huh? Did you eat the oatmeal the cook left for you this morning?"

"Yes, I did, but I think we're out of milk. When the chauffeur takes me into the city, perhaps he could get a few groceries."

"I'm sure he will if the maid folds all that laundry she washed."

"Of course she will. As soon as she gets that raise she was promised."

Her dad slapped the wide arm of the rocker. "Then bring the chauffeur his keys. A trip to the bank is in order!"

Trina giggled. "They're in your pocket, Poppo, where they usually are." She wriggled out of the chair and started making a mental list of all the things she wanted to research at the library: Queen Anne houses, New Royal, the Harlan M. Roy family, and carriage houses. Anything that might help her understand the mysterious old house she was supposed to call home.

Chapter Eight

"I shouldn't be more than thirty minutes," Trina's dad said as the truck pulled up to the front of the New Royal Public Library.

Trina looked up at the stately building, which stood nearly as tall as the treetops, and then up and down Main Street. She could see as far as the Cat's Meow Diner and beyond the city park. Once again, the streets were completely empty. Did anyone besides Miss Kitty live in this town?

"What if I need more time than that to become a detective?" Trina said as she jumped from the truck's running board and slammed the door. Hearing a hissing sound near her feet, she looked down cautiously, half expecting to see a snake like the ones that slithered through their yard in New Mexico. "Do you hear that, Poppo?" Trina bent close to the front tire. "This tire's going flat."

Her dad hopped out of the truck and wiggled free a spike of metal. "They don't make nails like this anymore. Must've picked it up in the yard," he said. "Better give me at least an hour so I can get this tire fixed."

Trina waved good-bye to her dad, ran up the broad stone steps, and used every muscle she had to open the heavy, polished brass door. The door closed soundlessly behind her as the snap, snap, snap of her flip-flops echoed beneath a rounded ceiling two stories high.

Afraid of making any noise in this lifeless library, Trina put one hand over the pocket that contained Augustine and carefully slid her feet across the black and white marble floor all the way to a large desk made of dark wood that matched the woodwork at Goldenrod. A domed bell, like the bells she'd seen in motels, sat on one corner of the desk. She tapped it and listened as the tinkling sound softly reverberated around her. A tall elderly gentleman with perfectly combed white hair stepped from behind an enormous bookshelf. He moved so elegantly in his bright white shirt and black bow tie, Trina pictured him greeting guests at Goldenrod—wearing a tuxedo.

"Good day. I am the librarian, Mr. Peter Kinghorn. And you are?"

Trina looked up in the dim light. The old gentleman's voice was serious, but his face was kind. "I'm Citrine Maxwell," she said, impressed by how studious her name sounded in a library. "Do you have a computer I could use for some research I'm doing?"

Mr. Kinghorn tipped his head toward a clunky computer on the big desk. "I do, but the Internet is down and there is no telling when it will be up again." He sighed a little. "Truth is, New Royal has been quite overlooked by the modern world, so we are frequently required to do things the old-fashioned way. With books." Almost smiling he added, "However, if you ask me, nothing electronic surpasses a book." He picked up a pencil and notepad. "You just tell me what you need and I'll help you find it."

"I'm looking for information on Goldenrod," Trina said stoutly, wondering if he too would back away at the mention of the house's name.

To the contrary, Mr. Kinghorn perked up. "That's an easy one." He set down his pencil and notepad. Trina's heart skipped with excitement as he leaned forward, pointing to a low bookcase on the far side of the library. "Goldenrod is from the genus *Solidago*, so you'll want to look under *S* in those big white encyclopedias."

Trina's expectations sank lower and lower with every word Mr. Kinghorn uttered. "You'll never find pictures on a computer as exquisite as the ones in those books," Mr. Kinghorn said proudly. "You can make tea from the flowers, you know."

"I didn't mean the flower," Trina said as politely as possible. "I meant the house."

Mr. Kinghorn gripped the desk, as if he needed it to keep himself upright. "*That* Goldenrod? How do you know about *that* Goldenrod?"

"I live there," Trina said.

Mr. Kinghorn eyed Trina thoughtfully. "I heard there was a little girl. Your father must be the carpenter Mr. Hank told me about."

Trina nodded.

"Miss Lincoln said you didn't register for school. She was certain you and your father had left town."

News sure traveled fast in New Royal—even without the Internet. Trina could feel her face turning red as she pondered what other rumors might be going around New Royal. And she wondered if Charlotte had anything to do with them.

"I am afraid we are a very small community, Miss Citrine," Mr. Kinghorn continued, seeming to guess what she was thinking. "We all keep each other's secrets, if you know what I mean."

Keeping secrets in New Royal obviously meant poking your nose into everyone else's business. Trina wanted to turn around and walk out the door so there would be nothing more to say about her, but she steeled herself. She couldn't leave empty-handed. "So, do you have information about the old house? I'd like to see anything you have."

Mr. Kinghorn's bony hands shook slightly as he straightened his already perfectly straightened bow tie. "I do, but I have never kept it in the main library, child. I keep it downstairs. Locked in the vault." He scanned the empty library before he leaned his head over the desk toward her and lowered his voice. "I'll retrieve it for you." He turned from the desk, strode through an arched doorway made of stone, and disappeared.

The thought of information so secret it had to be locked away made Trina jittery, so it took her a moment to feel a poke in her side. She pulled Augustine from her pocket. "I'm so sorry, Augustine, I forgot you were in there."

Augustine opened her eyes and brushed her hair back from her face. "I am not sure what is worse: to be catapulted across the Land of Goldenrod or to be forgotten in a deep, dark pocket. Where are we? We are supposed to be looking for my prince."

"We're in the New Royal Public Library." Trina held Augustine up to see the giant shelves stuffed with books, the big-paned windows, and the balcony on the second floor, which had to be the equivalent of at least half a mile overhead to the little doll. "The library is also known as the Land of Books," Trina said.

Augustine's mood changed from angry to a little bit shy. "Does my prince live in the Land of Books?"

Mr. Kinghorn's footsteps sounded in the stairwell.

"I'm sorry, Augustine, but I have to do this to you." Trina hurriedly stuffed Augustine back in her pocket, feet first.

"But my prince—"

"Shh!" Trina said, shoving the doll deeper into her pocket.

Mr. Kinghorn was panting as he emerged, carrying an old wooden apple crate. What looked like a dish towel was draped over his arm. "I found these papers in my father's desk after he passed away. Some belonged to my great-grandfather."

"Are you related to the Roys, then?" asked Trina as she followed Mr. Kinghorn to a large table with carved lions' heads for feet.

"No, no, child," Mr. Kinghorn said without further elaboration. "Would you lay the linen cloth on the table, please, Miss Citrine," he said. "I don't want to scratch it."

Trina took the cloth from Mr. Kinghorn's arm and smoothed it across the table. As he set down the crate, the scent of the wet fields at Goldenrod wafted through the air. Then Mr. Kinghorn pulled out one of the fancy chairs that matched the fancy table and nodded his head at Trina. She sat down and watched anxiously as he reached into the crate. His trembling hands withdrew a large flat book with a brown leather cover and black pages. "Wow, that's a really old book," Trina said.

"A scrapbook," Mr. Kinghorn said, drawing her attention to the word "Scrapbook" etched in the leather cover. After he sat down, he took a moment to put on a pair of reading glasses and get comfortable. "A lot of people kept scrapbooks back then. And the Roys were kind of like celebrities." He opened the cover of the scrapbook to a yellowed newspaper clipping. "Here we go. Front page of the *New Royal Register*, Sunday, May 28, 1905," he said, squinting despite his glasses.

Trina leaned in for a closer look at the blurry black-and-white photograph of a garden in full bloom. It had cobblestone paths and a fountain and was filled with fancily dressed people. The caption read: "*Mr. and Mrs. Harlan M. Roy host the first annual flower gala in the East Garden at Goldenrod.*" Trina couldn't tell among all those fancy people who Mr. Harlan M. Roy was, and she didn't see any children running around.

"The Roys are the ones who built Goldenrod, right?" Trina asked eagerly.

Mr. Kinghorn shook his head. "Not exactly. The

Roys paid for everything, of course, but my great-grandfather designed and built it, as he did everything in town. He was the architect for Mr. Roy's construction company. My great-grandfather could build anything and everything." Mr. Kinghorn sounded proud, and no wonder. His ancestor was responsible for all the grand buildings in New Royal.

Mr. Kinghorn pointed to a tiny head of a partygoer. "That's my great-grandfather right there."

"But why did they build their house way out here?" Trina wished she had kept her mouth shut, knowing she had just insulted Mr. Kinghorn and the town he lived in. "I mean, so far away from town."

"You mean, in the middle of nowhere?"

When Mr. Kinghorn's serious face cracked a smile, Trina nodded, relieved.

Mr. Kinghorn cleared his throat. "Mr. Roy was an Iowa boy. He made his fortune in railroading, but he never took to the big city life. He built the house as a wedding present for his wife." Mr. Kinghorn crossed his arms and leaned back in his chair. "They say it was the only way he could convince her to leave New York City. He promised her that someday New Royal would have everything she loved about the city—shops, restaurants, theaters . . ." He peered at Trina over the tops of his glasses. "He had what you call a big ego. Even named the town after himself."

Mr. Roy. New Royal, of course. "I guess it didn't turn out like he planned," Trina said.

"Such are many promises," Mr. Kinghorn said.

"Mrs. Roy must have been very lonely."

"Indeed. I think that's why they had so many parties out there." He leaned forward and turned the page to another newspaper clipping with a similar photo of another party. "They had spring parties and fall parties . . . Every year." He kept turning the pages of the scrapbook, one party picture after another, until he came to a blank page. "Every year, that is, until the tragedy."

Trina stared at the empty black page. "What tragedy?"

"Diphtheria. The dreadful epidemic of 1912. Mr. Roy caught diphtheria on his travels and brought it home. He recovered and was traveling again, and all seemed well, but then his wife, Anne, and their little girl, Annie, became ill."

Goosebumps popped up on Trina's arms. *Annie.* Annie had to be Augustine's little girl. "What happened?" Trina said breathlessly.

"Mrs. Roy survived, but little Annie died." Trina put one hand to her mouth and the other over her pocket as if she could protect Augustine from the unbearable truth. She swallowed hard. "A few days later, they found Mrs. Roy wandering in the East Garden, calling for the dog. She said Annie had thrown a ball for him to fetch, but he never came back." Mr. Kinghorn took off his glasses and looked into Trina's eyes. "The dog—Toby, they called him—had died the winter before." Mr. Kinghorn shook his head sadly. "Pure grief. It unsettled her mind. She couldn't accept the fact that Annie was gone. Eventually she lost all sense of reality and Mr. Roy had to put Mrs. Roy in an institution. Different times, you know.

Mr. Roy never forgave himself for bringing the illness home to his family."

Mr. Kinghorn recounted the story as if it were ancient history, but to Trina, given the strange goings-on, whatever happened at Goldenrod mattered as much right now as it did a hundred years ago. "No wonder the house is so sad." Again, Trina wished she hadn't said anything. She didn't want Mr. Kinghorn to think she, too, had lost her sense of reality, believing a house had feelings.

But Mr. Kinghorn didn't even blink. "You mean, you can tell how the house feels?"

Trina nodded, relieved to talk to someone who might understand. "Yes," she said. "There's a loneliness in the house. Except for the dining room. And the library."

Mr. Kinghorn's eyes were bright with curiosity. "Why just those two rooms?"

"Because Mr. Hank brought the dining room table back last night, and today somebody else dropped off a big rocking chair. It seemed like a good chair to read in, so we put it in the library. I don't know how to explain it, but now those rooms feel . . . happier."

Mr. Kinghorn's nostrils twitched. "Hank's older brother, Jake, and a couple of his friends stole that table the summer before we all started high school. The next winter Hank's family lost a whole herd of cattle. Never really recovered after that. When Jake sold the family farm a few years back and moved to Des Moines, he gave the table to Hank. Hank's been wanting to return the table ever since, but I think he was just too scared to go into that house."

Mr. Kinghorn rubbed his chin. "Ever since he's had the table, business has been rough."

Mr. Kinghorn fell silent, which made Trina pretty sure he had a lot more to say about Goldenrod than he was willing to tell.

"I've heard a lot of people tried to sneak into the house over the years," Trina said, hoping for at least one more story.

Mr. Kinghorn looked up sheepishly. "You know about the Dare Club?"

Trina nodded. "Miss Kitty didn't say it was a club, but she told us all about it. She said the bets added up to more than $300."

"Ah, Katherine," Mr. Kinghorn said with a sly smile. "Miss Kitty to you, but she'll always be Katherine to me. She would be the one to remember the numbers, all right. Probably still has that can of money locked away somewhere—safe, sound, and counted to the penny." He shook his head. "Poor Katherine. She lost her daughter in an accident up on the highway several years back. At the exit that brings you right past Goldenrod and into New Royal from the west. For that reason, most everybody in town keeps using the old road. They'll drive five miles out of their way to avoid going anywhere near Goldenrod."

So it *was* a tear she saw in Miss Kitty's eye yesterday morning in the diner. No wonder she got so mad at her dad. He said you could blame everything on the interstate and he was right. "Was the daughter who died Charlotte's mother?" Trina asked, suddenly making the connection.

Mr. Kinghorn nodded so somberly, Trina was afraid he'd pack up the crate of stuff and put it away without another word. "But why did people steal from the house?" she blurted.

The somber look on Mr. Kinghorn's face changed into one of embarrassment. "I'm afraid it was all for a reason that made sense only when we were kids. If you couldn't spend the night at Goldenrod, you had to take something to prove you were there. Or else you'd be kicked out of the Dare Club."

"The Dare Club sure must have had a lot of members," Trina said, feeling like her detective work was beginning to pay off.

Mr. Kinghorn nodded. "If I were you, I'd expect many more deliveries. We were all told to stay away from that house, but you tell a child not to do something and that's exactly what makes him want to do it, scared or not." Mr. Kinghorn shook his head. "I think just about everybody's got something—afraid to throw it away and afraid to return it. I'd say the townsfolk are beginning to see your living at Goldenrod as a chance to ease their consciences."

"No wonder everyone I've met is scared to death of Goldenrod," Trina said. "They think the house is out to get them."

"I keep telling them it's all coincidence, but they won't hear it. The whole town blames every ounce of bad luck they ever had on that old place. Tornadoes, bad crops. Deaths. Even something as simple as a flat tire."

"A flat tire? Really?" Now Trina wondered if Goldenrod had something to do with a rusty nail puncturing a hole in her dad's tire, but she wasn't sure what it meant. Was a flat tire meant to trap them at Goldenrod or scare them away? And then the answer was obvious: Goldenrod wanted her to have more time at the library.

"That's how legends get handed down," Mr. Kinghorn continued. "One scary story leads to another." He looked around at the big stacks of books as if they contained all the legends and secrets of New Royal. "Some people say we're the town time forgot. I think we're the town *happiness* forgot."

Trina had been listening so intently to every word, with her elbows propped on the table and her chin resting on her hands, that her right arm had fallen asleep. She shook her tingling arm and stood up to see over the edge of the crate. "What else do you have in the box?"

"Books from Goldenrod. What else would a librarian have but books?"

A surge of excitement rippled through Trina. "Did you steal them?" But as soon as she asked the question she flushed with embarrassment. She was just like her dad, saying something without even thinking.

Mr. Kinghorn raised his eyebrows, shocked at first, but then he allowed a little smile. "I'm sure it would make a more interesting story if I had, but the boring truth is, I was the first and only one to be kicked out of the Dare Club. I'd made it into the house as far as the library, and I'll never forget its magnificence as long as I live. I was scared, but my conscience scared me even more. I couldn't bring myself to take anything." He looked down at the books in the crate. "My grandfather borrowed these books. Unfortunately, they were never given back."

Mr. Kinghorn laid the books on the table, reading their titles one by one: "*Great Expectations, The Jungle Book, The Thousand and One Nights,* and *Aesop's Fables.*" He stroked the cover of *Aesop's Fables* and its raised picture of a little red fox. "My grandfather read these to me when I was very young."

"Is that everything?" Trina asked, still a little disappointed.

"Everything except the blueprints." Mr. Kinghorn pulled two rolls of crisp, yellowed papers from the crate. "The main house and the carriage house, drawn by my great-grandfather himself."

Trina leaned in as Mr. Kinghorn carefully unrolled the blueprints for the carriage house. The carriage house had two bedrooms, a bathroom, and a balcony upstairs, and a parlor, dining room, kitchen, and stable downstairs. It was exactly like the dollhouse! Trina was giddy with excitement—and maybe a little fear, as she geared up to ask a question that might have a scary answer. "Do you know what happened to the carriage house? It's not there anymore."

"Yes. It's all right here." Mr. Kinghorn rolled up the blueprints and reached for the scrapbook again. Another newspaper clipping was folded up and tucked inside the back cover. He unfolded it and turned it toward Trina. This one was dated Wednesday, February 22, 1928.

Trina read the headline in a hushed voice. "*New Royal Founder, Mr. Harlan M. Roy, Dies in Fire. Carriage House a Total Loss. Goldenrod Survives.*"

"After Annie died," Mr. Kinghorn explained, "the Roys never set foot in the main house again. Mr. Roy had it boarded up and they moved into the carriage house. Left everything just as it was. After Mrs. Roy was sent away, he lived alone in the carriage house for fifteen more years until it burned down." Mr. Kinghorn tightened his lips and shook his head. "Fell asleep reading by the fire. They think he was smoking his pipe."

Annie had died of diphtheria, Mrs. Roy had lost her mind, and Mr. Roy had died in a fire. "Goldenrod sure has a sad history," Trina finally said. "And now the house is empty."

"Except all these things can go back home where they belong," Mr. Kinghorn said. With great reverence, he put the books back into the crate. "Might as well take this too," he said, setting the scrapbook on top of the books. "I have no use for it." He put the blueprints in last, stood up, and handed the crate to Trina. "Maybe luck will pick up again for New Royal, now that you're here."

Trina considered his words carefully. "But I thought you said all the bad luck was just coincidence."

"That I did, child. But sometimes the truth and what you believe are two different things."

Chapter Nine

On the way home, Trina told her dad all about Annie Roy and how she died in the diphtheria epidemic. "That's why they boarded up the house, Poppo. The Roys were too sad to go on living there."

He listened to the whole story. She caught him rolling his eyes when she got to the part about Goldenrod causing all the bad luck, but when she pulled the blueprints out of the crate, he hit the brakes. "Blueprints?"

"Yup! For Goldenrod and the carriage house."

He pulled to the side of the road, shifted into park, and unrolled the blueprints for Goldenrod across the steering wheel. "Miss Detective, I think you hit the jackpot!" He peeled back the first page. "Looks like once upon a time there was some kind of garden room off the dining room. And see? There's the elevation of the front porch." Whistling, he rerolled the blueprints, handed them back to Trina, and shifted gears. The truck lurched forward.

"And guess what, Poppo? The dollhouse is an exact replica of the carriage house."

"That tells me Goldenrod was yellow. Just like you

suggested." He tapped on the bill of her cap. "Must feel pretty good solving the mystery."

"I don't know, Poppo. I don't feel like I have the whole story." She couldn't tell him how the dining room and the library felt happy, but Goldenrod still felt sad.

Her stomach grumbled with hunger. She looked over her shoulder for a bag of groceries. "Did you get milk?"

"Dang it all," he said, pounding the steering wheel with his fist. "I got to talking with Hank and forgot all about it."

Typical Poppo. She sighed to herself. "Anything from Mom?"

He slapped his shirt pocket. "Nope. Nothing today. Didn't you just get one?"

Trina nodded. "Yeah, but she's been sending them more often, so I just wondered."

Silence followed as usual, which made Trina want to talk about something other than her mom. She glanced at the blueprints in the crate and said the first thing that came to her mind. "Wouldn't it be great if they hired you to build the carriage house too? Then Goldenrod would be perfect."

Her dad shrugged. "Don't go getting your hopes up." Then he turned to her with a look of surprise on his face. "Don't tell me you're starting to like it here."

"I'm not," she said quickly, but then she felt that poke in her hip again. She cupped her hand over the small lump of doll. She liked Augustine. If her mother ever did come for her, it would be hard to leave Augustine behind.

As the truck pulled through the gate, Trina could see something tall leaning against the cargo trailer. Mr. Kinghorn was right. Another delivery. This time it was all the pieces to a beautiful four-poster bed. It was just like Augustine's except that it was painted white. She beat her dad out of the truck to touch the elegant headboard. "Someone must have had an awful lot of bad luck to get rid of something so pretty."

"Now, Trina—I mean, Citrine—I'm sure people see our living here as a chance to clean out their basements and garages, and that's all." Then he scratched his stubbly beard. "On the other hand, their bad luck is our good luck. I say we put this princess bed in your room. Your mattress should work just fine."

Piece by piece they carried the bed upstairs. When her dad finished assembling it, they set Trina's mattress on the old frame. It wasn't a perfect fit, but it would do.

"Back to the porch," he sighed. Within seconds, his saw was whirring away.

Trina made a trip to the truck for the crate of books and papers and carried it to the kitchen counter. First, she pulled out the blueprints and put them on the buffet in the dining room. Then she stacked up the books and the scrapbook and carried that whole pile of stuff into the library. She placed the books side by side on a shelf and stepped back admiringly. With four books standing upright on the shelf and a chair that was big enough to curl up in and read, the library felt like a library.

But Trina felt something else, too. She felt as if she were

a giant balloon filling with air. She felt herself stand up straighter and taller—pleased with herself. She felt proud, but the funny thing was, she knew it wasn't her pride she was feeling. It was Goldenrod's. Goldenrod was proud to have a library.

She sat down in the big rocking chair, but when she felt Augustine poke her in the hip she popped right up again. Now Trina felt terrible. She freed Augustine from her pocket and set her on the bookshelf next to *Aesop's Fables*. "I'm so sorry, Augustine. I forgot again. Why didn't you say something?"

Augustine opened her eyes and shook her head. "Speak? In front of your father? And risk being thrown into the Land of TV? Forever? I think not. But now it is quiet." Augustine smoothed her messy hair with her hands. "Now I feel safe."

"I'll always keep you safe," Trina said gently. "And look, Augustine. Books have come back to Goldenrod."

Augustine's little head swiveled, but after one glimpse of the cover of *Aesop's Fables* she screamed, "A fox! A fox!" and ran to hide behind *Great Expectations*.

"It's only a picture, Augustine. It can't hurt you." Trina rescued Augustine from the fox and set her on an empty shelf.

Augustine was quick to assess her surroundings, and then she stomped her foot and put her hands on her hips. "Citrine, I have not enjoyed our adventure today in the least."

Trina leaned against the shelf, eye to eye with the angry doll, disappointed in herself for letting her down.

"I know." Trina held out her hand, pretending it was a carriage for a princess. "What if we look for your prince some more?"

Augustine shook her head as she stepped into Trina's cupped hand. "I believe it is too soon to search for him. If I go looking for him and he comes looking for me, we might never find each other. Perhaps you should take me to my home."

Augustine talked the whole way through the parlor and up the stairs. "I will try not to grow anxious, Citrine. Clearly he is traveling a great distance. Perhaps his steed needs rest."

"Perhaps it does," Trina said, not really knowing how to explain the difficulties of waiting for a fairy-tale prince.

Sitting on the floor, just outside her bedroom door, was a small bucket containing a bottle of glue, toothpicks, a handful of small rags, and a little jar of lemon oil. A gift from Poppo. "Look, Augustine, now I can fix up your house." She set Augustine down in her dining room and got right to work rubbing lemon oil on the dollhouse banister until it shined.

Augustine gave a sigh of relief to be home, but then she became very thoughtful. She walked into her parlor and fluffed a little pillow in one of the chairs by the hearth. "Shall we instead venture out to find my mother and father? My house is quite different without them sitting in their chairs."

"But Augustine," Trina began, holding out her hands helplessly, knowing she was going to disappoint the doll with bad news. "I am sorry to tell you this, but Goldenrod is empty. You and your house and this book," she said, pulling *Grimm's Fairy Tales* closer to the dollhouse, "are the only things that were left behind. Everything else was . . . stolen."

Augustine's little face crinkled. "But you said yourself books have come home to Goldenrod. And did we not sit in a chair and dine at a grand table? Perhaps my mother and father will—"

Trina shook her head.

Augustine put her arm to her forehead. "Are you saying my mother and father are lost to me forever? Please, Citrine, spare me the tragic news unless you are certain. Have you any proof?"

"Proof?" What in the world would a doll know about proof?

"Yes, proof," Augustine insisted. "The wicked queen demanded that the huntsman bring her Snow White's heart as proof. How can we be certain they are lost forever without proof?"

Trina was horrified by the idea of finding parts of Augustine's mother and father and showing them to her, even if they were just dolls. "No, I don't have any proof."

"Then my dear Citrine, we cannot be certain my mother and father are lost to me forever. And I cannot bear the uncertainty any longer. We shall leave no stone unturned. If you help me, then I shall help you."

"Help me do what?"

"I can only imagine how much you must miss your mother, so I will help you find her."

"But my mother isn't really lost to me. Not like that." Trina closed the jar of lemon oil and opened the bottle of glue while she came up with an explanation about her mother that the doll might understand. "Like your prince, my mother is traveling a great distance. My father says she is trying to find herself." Trina dipped a toothpick in the glue, dabbed it behind the curling wallpaper in Augustine's parlor, and pressed the paper to the wall.

"Your world is very confusing to me, Citrine. If your mother is not lost, how is it she does not know where she is?"

Trina took a deep breath. "My father means that some-day, when my mother is ready, she'll figure out what she wants and where she wants to be. And then she'll come home." Trina smoothed the wallpaper to make sure it would stick, and then she got up and pulled the hot-air balloon postcard from the top of the pile of postcards on the mantel. "Right now she's in New Zealand." Trina crouched again to Augustine's level. "See? She just sent me this postcard. It's like a letter."

Augustine peered at the words and touched the letter Z. The letters were the size of her hand. "What tidings does this letter bring you?"

"She says, '*Someday I will show you what the world looks like from way up here.*'" Trina turned the postcard around so Augustine could see the picture. "She spends a lot of time in one of those. It's a hot-air balloon."

"Her world is very small, so it will be easy to find her."

"Augustine, the real world is very, very big. This is

just a picture of a tiny fraction of it. Like the fox is just a picture."

Augustine frowned. "Still, you are fortunate, Citrine, to be spared the uncertainty of not knowing where your mother is. You know your mother is in a balloon in the Land of New Zealand. Do you have any notion what a misery it is *not* knowing?"

Trina was pretty sure she did have such a notion because she always knew where her mother was not, but she also understood that having a mother who loved to travel had to be better than having your mother lost to you forever. She put the balloon postcard back on the mantel.

"As I said, Citrine, if you promise to help me, then I will promise to help you, because helping each other is what friends do. Is that understood?"

Augustine had a way of making everything seem so simple. But more important than that, it felt good to have Augustine call her a friend. "Yes," Trina said. "It's more than understood."

Augustine clasped her porcelain hands together. "Then let us get started. Where should we begin?"

Trina had been in every room of the house except for the attic. She had vowed not to go up there, but now she had Augustine to go with her. "We'll start by looking for your mother and father in the Land of the Attic."

The first thing Trina did to prepare for the adventure was swap her flip-flops for tennis shoes. Then she grabbed her flashlight from her backpack. When Trina extended her hand to Augustine, the doll pulled herself into Trina's palm, but she didn't stop there. She crawled up Trina's arm, tickling her to the point of giggling, and settled in the crook of her neck.

With Augustine clinging to her earlobe, Trina walked down the hall to the attic door and put her hand on the cold brass doorknob. The door creaked as she opened it. "This hinge could use some oil," she said, thinking how much she sounded like her dad.

Trina turned on her flashlight and made her way up the narrow staircase one creaky step at a time. The air was stale and musty. "It's hard to see in this narrow stairway," she said to Augustine, but all she got in response was a faint little chuckle. "This is no time to laugh, Augustine. How can I look for your mother and father if I can't see anything?"

"I am not laughing," Augustine said directly into Trina's ear.

"But you did. I heard you."

"I did not."

"Then who did?"

"I did not hear anything," Augustine said firmly. "You must have imagined it."

There is no such thing as a haunted house, Trina began to recite in her head. *There is no such thing as a haunted house.* When a blast of wind rushed across the rooftop and something scraped the slate shingles, she could hear her dad telling her it was just the wind in the big oak tree.

At the top of the stairs, Trina made out a pale gray light coming through a curved row of small windows and figured she was at the top of the turret. The wind gusted again, and a hand-like branch of the tree brushed against the glass.

"Maybe my father is right," Trina said out loud, trying to stay calm. "Every time I think I hear something scary, there's a logical explanation. See, it's just a branch scraping against the window."

She glanced down at the windowsill. Dozens of dead flies were tangled in gauzy, dusty spiderwebs—one more sign that all the life had gone out of Goldenrod a long time ago. For a tiny second Trina hoped a prince would never kiss Augustine, or all the dead flies might wake up.

"Citrine?"

"Yes?"

"What is this word, *logical*?"

Trina kept her eyes on the floor in front of her while trying to figure out a way to explain the word *logical* to a doll who talked, which wasn't the least bit logical in the first place. "It means something makes so much sense you don't need any other reason for the idea to be true."

"What if something makes so much sense the idea is not true?"

Augustine's ideas always seemed to send Trina's mind in circles, so she had to think about that one for a moment. "I guess that works too," she said.

Now they were standing under the giant rafters of the attic. The air was hotter than the desert in New Mexico, and the attic floor appeared to be just as endless.

And dark.

Trina shined the flashlight in front of her. Thick beams crisscrossed the low ceiling, and rows and rows of black electric wires as thick as ropes ran along the beams, looping and coiling their way to white glass knobs. Her dad was right; it did look like Frankenstein's lab.

A hundred years of dust crept up Trina's nose, and she sneezed so hard that Augustine squealed and slipped from her perch. She grabbed Trina's hair and dangled like a mountain climber. Trina swept Augustine back to her shoulder before Augustine could fall, and sneezed again.

"Oh, Citrine! That sound—is it a dragon?" Augustine whispered, crouching desperately in the nape of her neck. "Is that what keeps me from my mother and father?"

"No, Augustine, there's no dragon." Trina would have thought Augustine's question was funny, except the deep corners where the eaves met the roof could easily hide a dragon. "I sneezed, that's all," she said, taking a careful step forward.

"Sneezed?" Augustine asked.

Before Trina could answer, something thin and cold brushed against her face. She swatted at it with the flashlight, missed, and then whatever it was reached out and touched her again.

She frantically swung the flashlight in the air until the beam showed a bare bulb on the ceiling. The wisp of cold was just the light chain. Trina pulled the chain, hoping for more light, but nothing happened.

"Nope. Nothing's here," Trina said, ready to go back downstairs. "I'm sure of it."

"Remember," Augustine whispered in her ear, "no stone unturned."

As much as she wanted to, Trina couldn't turn back. She couldn't let a three-inch doll be braver than she was. She crept forward, ducking under the rafters, sweeping the flashlight in front of her. She imagined it was the beam of the lighthouse she and her dad had seen on a cliff above Lake Superior, scanning the dark unknown as big as an ocean. Keeping everyone safe.

And they were safe. Trina saw nothing in the attic except posts and rafters. "Just like I thought, Augustine. There's nothing up here."

Crunch!

Nothing except for what crunched beneath her shoe.

Augustine crawled forward on Trina's shoulder as Trina lifted her shoe from what looked like a dried flower. She picked up the long sprig and twirled it in the flashlight's beam. Bits and pieces of the petals fell like dust to the attic floor, but slowly she recognized the flattened stalk as an ancient piece of goldenrod.

"It's a flower," Augustine said.

"Yeah, but it's been squished."

"Did you not step on it?"

"I mean it was squished long before we—or at least *I*—got here."

Just as she spoke, the wind slammed against the house. Trina quickly turned for the stairs.

"No, we cannot leave," protested Augustine. "We have not searched every corner. How can you be sure my mother and father are not here? Perhaps they are lost in this dark Land of the Attic." Augustine pulled Trina's hair, forcing her to look up. "Have you looked there? Have you—"

THUD!

Thud, thud.

Something had streaked past Trina's eyes and stopped at her feet.

Slowly she pointed the flashlight at the floor. A ball. A red and white striped ball with stitching on its side like a football. An old leather ball had dropped out of nowhere and landed right in front of her.

On instinct, Trina gave the ball a good kick and it rolled across the uneven floor until coming to rest in one of the dark corners.

Trina dragged the words from her mouth. "Where did that ball come from?"

"From that corner, up there, where I was pointing," Augustine said cheerfully.

"But . . . it . . . bounced. Right in front of me," Trina squeaked.

"That is what balls do. Unless they are rolling. Is that not logical?"

"That's not what I mean, Augustine. Balls don't just move by themselves."

And then.

From behind her.

Zaa-huh-zaa-huh.

"Did you hear that?" Trina asked, afraid to turn around.

"Is it not the tree branch scraping against the window?"

Zaa-huh-zaa-huh.

Trina reached up and clasped her fingers around Augustine and turned around. "There's no such thing as a haunted house," she recited as she looked at the attic window.

The spindly black tree branch outside wasn't moving.

"There is too such a thing!" Trina shouted, dropping the flashlight. She hurried down the attic stairs and ran down the hall and into her bedroom where she plastered herself against her closed door as she slid to the floor.

Safe and sound.

Outside, her dad's nail gun gasped and thunked. Eventually the rhythm calmed her and she caught her breath enough to speak. "Augustine," she said. "You have to tell me . . ." Her voice trembled. "Is Goldenrod haunted?"

Trina looked down at her right hand which was still clinging to the sprig of goldenrod.

And when she opened her left hand, bracing for Augustine's response, her hand was empty.

Chapter Ten

Trina stared helplessly at her empty hand. She remembered grabbing Augustine, but she must have dropped her on the way downstairs. She had to go back for her. She had to go back to the attic.

Alone.

And without her flashlight.

She headed back down the hall—afraid to return to the attic and afraid not to—and pulled open the attic door. If she was scared, she could only imagine how much more frightened Augustine was, and that made her take two steps upward into the pitch-black stairwell. Then two more. From the landing above her came a faint glow of light. Trina took two more steps—the flashlight was there, pointed at the wall.

She picked it up and searched the stairs, but Augustine was nowhere to be found. Trina filled with dread. "Augustine," she called.

No answer.

Slowly she continued up the attic steps. She turned away from the windowsills with the dead flies, ducked under a rafter, and shined the flashlight all around her.

There, in the distance, where the roof met the eave, was the ball. Trina froze. But then she saw something glimmer right next to it.

Augustine?

She had to keep going.

She made her way toward the faint glimmer on the floor, keeping one eye on the ball to make sure it didn't move. The ball remained still, and whatever was next to it was still too. But it didn't look like Augustine. The closer she got, the bigger the thing got until she could see that it was a large book with shiny gold letters on a very thick cover. The gold letters glimmered.

Trina bent down and brushed the dust away from the cover, and made out the word *Album*. More curious than afraid, Trina lifted the cover. On the first page was a black-and-white photograph of a woman holding a baby bundled in blankets. The baby's face was barely visible, but beneath the picture was written, *Little Annie, five days old*. Trina felt as if she had just uncovered a buried treasure.

The album was so heavy she needed both hands to pick it up. She set down her flashlight, lifted the album from the dusty floor, and spotted Augustine in the beam of light, lying on her side.

"Augustine!" Trina cried.

But Augustine's little eyes didn't open.

With a sinking feeling, Trina wondered if she had broken the doll when she dropped her. What if she had broken her beyond repair?

She closed the book, picked up Augustine and laid her

and the flashlight on top of it, and slowly navigated her way downstairs into the sunlit hall. Augustine's eyes fluttered and Trina's heart lightened.

"My prince?" Augustine said, barely moving her tiny lips.

"No, Augustine, it's just me. Citrine." Trina was about to explain how she had dropped her as she ran from the attic, was about to apologize for leaving the little doll behind, when Augustine's lips parted. "I ran, calling and calling for you. I was afraid the dragon got you," Augustine said weakly.

"I didn't hear you, Augustine."

"But you came back. You braved the dragon to rescue me, Citrine. You are a true friend." Augustine's eyes fluttered shut again.

"Oh, Augustine," Trina said, tears filling her eyes.

She carried the book and Augustine downstairs, as far away from the scary attic as she could get, and set them on the dining room table, side by side.

"I have a surprise for you," Trina said. "A book you might like very, very much."

"Is it a storybook?" the little doll asked, sitting up unsteadily.

"Kind of," Trina said, dusting off the album's cover with the hem of her T-shirt. "I think it tells the story of the family who once lived here."

Augustine's little mouth eased into a smile. "A story would be wonderful, Citrine."

Trina propped up the album so Augustine could see the pictures as she turned the pages. The first few pages were filled with pictures of Annie as a baby, wearing lacy dresses and bonnets, but Trina could tell Augustine wasn't very interested. "There are no words," Augustine said. "I would like to hear a different story." She ducked under Trina's hand and wandered the top of the dining room table.

Then Trina turned the page to a very large photograph of a man and a woman standing on the porch at Goldenrod. The woman wore a straight dress with a ruffle that fell just above her ankles, and a big brimmed hat. She had on long gloves and carried a frilly umbrella that matched her dress. The man looked much older than the woman. He had a black mustache and wore a round black hat and a black suit. And he carried a cane. Between them stood a little girl whose long blonde hair was pinned back with a large white bow. She wore a pretty white dress and looked a lot like Augustine. She was smiling at the camera. The caption beneath the picture read, *Welcoming home our dear Papa.*

"But, Augustine, this is the story of Annie Roy," Trina said.

Augustine turned around, her little feet pitter-pattering as fast as they could, until she crawled back under Trina's arm. "My Annie?" With a hopeful look, Augustine placed her tiny fingertips on Annie's cheek. "Annie? Have you come back to me?"

"She can't hear you, Augustine. What you see is just a picture."

"Does she live in a book now?" asked the puzzled little doll. "Is that why she is gone?" Trina ached with the truth.

"No, Augustine. She does not live in a book."

"Did she grow up, Citrine? Did she grow up and go away?" Augustine turned to Trina with a look of despair. "Will she ever come back to me?"

Trina's heart was crumbling with every question. As much as she didn't want to tell Augustine the truth, she knew she couldn't lie to her. "No, Augustine, Annie never had a chance to grow up." Trina shook her head, struggling with the words. "Annie died. A long time ago."

"Died? Is that all?" Augustine's worried little face relaxed. "Then a prince must kiss her and wake her up."

A huge lump caught in Trina's throat. "No, Augustine, there's a big difference between sleeping and dying. Dying means you never wake up. It means . . . it means Annie is lost to you forever."

Augustine's whole little body trembled. "Forever?"

"Forever," Trina said.

Augustine collapsed in a sad little heap.

Trina's mind raced as she tried to think of something to make Augustine feel better. "But at least you have memories."

Augustine lifted her head. "Memories? Please tell me, what are memories?"

"Memories are like stories," Trina said. "But they are true stories. They're not made up."

Augustine smiled. "Stories have happy endings."

"Some stories do," Trina said.

Augustine reached out and touched Annie's face again. "I remember when Annie went away. The house was very still. Annie's mother put me to bed and she put my house away. She did not read to us ever again. And then it became very, very dark and quiet and I went to sleep for a very long time."

Augustine placed her hand where her heart would be. "I feel broken, Citrine. I do not like this story. Could you please tell me a different story about Annie?"

"I wish I could, Augustine, but Annie's story isn't a fairy tale. If I change the ending, it won't be true."

"All stories are true, Citrine. You simply have to believe them."

"But," Trina started to say until she realized she was trying to make Augustine understand something that wouldn't make any difference in her little world. There was nothing wrong in letting Augustine believe whatever she needed to believe to make her happy.

"Please, Citrine, read me a different story." With all her might, Augustine tried to close the photo album, but ended up turning to another page: a photo of Annie and a small spotted dog. And a ball. A striped ball. The same ball that was in the attic. The caption read, *Annie and Toby playing in the East Garden.*

"I think you're right, Augustine." Trina picked up the doll and then she shut the album so hard dust flew. "We should definitely read a different book."

"Could you please read to me until nightfall?"

Trina glanced out the window. Nightfall was hours away, but after such a difficult day, Trina knew she owed it to Augustine to read to her as long as she wanted. "Yes, I will," she said.

She carried Augustine to the library, pulled *Aesop's Fables* from the shelf and climbed into the big rocking chair, leaning against one arm of the square chair with her feet hanging over the other and Augustine sitting on her chest. But Trina couldn't get comfortable. She couldn't get the striped ball out of her head. Or the photo album. Or the idea that she found the ball, the album, and Augustine together in one corner of the attic.

"Augustine," she said in a rush, terrified to learn the truth. "Is Goldenrod haunted?"

Augustine jumped to her feet and put her hands on her hips. "Goldenrod? Haunted?"

Trina nodded, but she wasn't sure if Augustine knew what the word meant.

"Does haunted not mean Goldenrod is full of ugly and evil things?" Augustine folded her arms, huffed, and looked away. "Why ever would you ask such a horrible question?"

"Because so many strange things keep happening. Because of the ball. And, well, because of you."

"Me?" Augustine turned back to Trina. Her eyes were wide with indignation.

"You're a doll who talks," Trina said.

Augustine was crestfallen. "But I am a good thing, am I not? Is talking not good? Does it not make you happy?"

"Yes, you are a good thing," Trina said, gently stroking Augustine's head. "But I don't know of any other dolls that talk, and I don't understand why you do. Or how that ball dropped right when it did. Or how you ended up by the book about Annie. People in my world like explanations for things they don't understand, and I don't understand what is happening here. Please, Augustine. I have to know. Is Goldenrod haunted?" Augustine tilted her head to one side and then to the other, so Trina continued. "Everyone is afraid of her, Augustine. They say she causes bad luck."

"I am not afraid of her," the doll said. "Are you?"

"I don't know what to think," Trina said.

Augustine shook her head, disappointedly. "You ask me many questions, Citrine, but you do not ask the most important one. Why would beautiful Goldenrod choose to be haunted?"

The answer was easy. "To scare people away," Trina said.

"Precisely," Augustine said.

But now Trina was really confused. "But why would she want to scare people away?"

Augustine put her dainty little forefinger to her daintier little brow, and a very wise look crossed her face. "How would you feel if people stole from you? Precious things that belonged to your family? What would you do?"

Trina had never thought about Goldenrod this way. "I suppose I'd try to keep the bad people away and then somehow try to get all my things back."

Augustine nodded smugly. "And, may I ask, has Goldenrod hurt you?"

Trina thought and thought, remembering how she had come to the conclusion that Goldenrod seemed to be crying wolf. She had been frightened and startled, but never hurt. And she had been afraid of Augustine only until they became friends. Trina couldn't argue with Augustine's logic. She shook her head slowly.

The doll raised her eyebrows. "So maybe you should take a very good look at Goldenrod and tell me what you see."

Trina looked around the library—at the few books on the shelves, the charred fireplace full of ashes and soot, and the faded walls with dark squares where the pictures once hung. "I see really old green wallpaper. And floors that need to be refinished. And a fireplace that needs to be scrubbed."

Augustine shook her head in frustration. "Citrine, have you no imagination? Perhaps you should look for what is not here, such as the laughter of children or a fire burning in the fireplace." Augustine's feistiness had all but faded away. She looked up at Trina with a pleading look on her face. "I believe the house longs for a family, Citrine. I believe Goldenrod simply wants someone to call her home."

Poppo had said the same thing. But Goldenrod was never going to be Trina's home. Goldenrod was going to be sold. Who knew what would happen to her next?

Being the new kid in school, or being bullied by Charlotte, or even looking at Annie in the photo with her mother and her father, hadn't made Trina feel as lost or alone as she felt at this minute, putting herself in Goldenrod's place.

Instead of being afraid of the house and its squeaks and groans and unreliable lights, Trina tried to listen to it the way someone might listen to a good friend's secrets.

"I think she feels alone," she finally said.

Without wind, and without the push of a switch, the sconces on the library wall dimmed to a sad, golden light.

Chapter Eleven

Trina read fable after fable to Augustine, and then she moved on to *Grimm's Fairy Tales* when Augustine insisted on hearing "The Frog Prince." "Imagine what she could have missed, Citrine," Augustine began very seriously, "if the princess had not kept her promise and allowed the hideous frog to live in her castle. She never would have found her true love."

An hour later, Trina was the one getting sleepy, but she kept her word and read to Augustine until the sun went down and it was time to tuck the doll into bed. As Augustine fell asleep, Trina began to fix the blue velvet doll chair with a dab of glue. She pinched its broken leg in place, holding it until hunger overcame her and she went downstairs in search of food.

She was making herself a big plate of cold pizza in the kitchen when she heard her dad finally come in from working on the porch. He walked into the kitchen carrying the photo album. "Where'd you get this?"

"I found it in the attic," Trina said. "It's a photo album of the Roys and their little girl."

He set it on the kitchen counter. "I hope you're

sharing," he said as he picked up a slice of pizza from her plate. "I forgot to eat lunch."

"Look," Trina said, turning the pages slowly so her dad could see Annie Roy as a baby, and Annie playing outside with the dog and the ball, and the Roys on the front steps. She felt safer looking at the album with her dad right next to her.

"Look at the background," he said. "I love seeing pictures of the house as it used to be. Look, there. It's a porch swing. We're going to make the porch look just like that again."

But Trina was mostly interested in the people. She turned the page to a picture of Annie in her playroom, and there was the dollhouse. Trina squinted hard, pretty sure she could see Augustine sitting on the horse in the stable.

The next page was blank.

The next one too.

The whole rest of the book was blank.

"Oh, Poppo. It's so sad."

"What is?"

"All these blank pages. Annie must have died right after the picture was taken of her in her room." She flipped back to the photo of the Roys on the porch. She liked to think of them as a whole and happy family, the way she wished her family was.

Her dad was very quiet, studying the photo. Maybe he was thinking about her mother, missing her just the way Trina was. Maybe now was a good time to ask about her, but Trina didn't know how to bring up the subject. "I think they loved each other very much," she said.

He put an arm around her shoulder. "Love is the easy part." Trina was about to ask what her dad meant, when he added, "Bath night."

"Poppo," she said, embarrassed. Just when she thought she was proving her independence, he managed to make her feel like a baby. "You don't have to remind me."

She turned a few more pages of the album, just in case she had missed something, and her heart plummeted all over again at the sight of the first blank one. But then she noticed a stain on the page, a faint outline of a stem and flowers. A shape that looked familiar. "I'll take a bath now," she said excitedly as she closed the cover and ran upstairs to her room with the album in her hands. Where had she put it? She looked around her room until she spotted the dried sprig of goldenrod lying on the floor next to the dollhouse. She placed it on the stained page of the album. What was left of the stem of goldenrod fit the outline perfectly. A sense of comfort filled Trina, happiness she knew was not her own. The flower was back where it belonged.

In the bathroom, she filled the claw-foot tub with hot water, squirted soap into the stream, and climbed into the froth. She scrubbed her dirty feet with a washcloth, leaned back, and buried herself in the bubbles, thinking about Annie Roy.

Annie Roy would have touched the banister and climbed the stairs. She would have slept in her room and she would have looked out the same windows. She would have played with Augustine.

And she would have taken a bath in the same tub.

Trina sat up quickly, climbed out of the tub, and pulled the plug. As the bathtub emptied, the drain made a great gulping noise and sucked down her white washcloth with a greedy swallow. Behind her, water started gurgling and rising in the toilet.

"Poppo!" Trina screamed. She pulled on her clothes over her wet, sticky skin as water spilled over the toilet's rim onto the floor. "Poppo, the toilet!" She ran down the hall and leaned over the railing. "It's overflowing!"

Taking the steps three at a time, her dad raced past her, splashing across the water on the bathroom floor. He pushed the plug back in the slowly draining tub and the toilet waterfall stopped. "What on earth happened?"

"My washcloth went down the drain," Trina said.

"That's it?"

Trina nodded. "I'm sorry, Poppo."

He looked from the bathtub to the toilet and back. "It's not your fault. There's no drain cover. But I still don't understand. These old drains are so big you could flush a boot down the toilet if you wanted to." Frowning at the mess, he said, "I'll get the snake."

Trina used up every bath towel they owned while she waited for her dad. "Good news," he said as he reappeared with his tools and a five-gallon paint bucket. "The kitchen sink drains just fine, so the clog shouldn't be too hard to reach."

Trina wrung the towels over the bucket as her dad knelt on the bathroom floor and cranked the plumber's snake, sending the long metal chain through the drain in the tub into the guts of the house, cranking and cranking and cranking.

"I can't seem to reach it," he said, standing up. "I guess that's what we get for tall ceilings. Looks like I'll have to open up the wall in the downstairs bath and go up from there. Think you can help?" Trina scowled. She wanted to go to bed. "Don't worry. I'll do the dirty work," he said.

They set up shop in the bathroom next to the kitchen. The job required a sledgehammer, a ladder, an electric saw, the emptied five-gallon paint bucket, two pairs of gloves, two pairs of safety glasses, earplugs, and a big plastic bag. As her dad bashed the wall near the ceiling, Trina stuffed the falling chunks of plaster and lath into the garbage bag. When the hole in the wall was almost as big as she was, and the big black cast-iron drainpipe was exposed, her dad picked up the saw and climbed the ladder.

Sparks flew and vibrations traveled through Trina's whole body as she tried to hold the ladder steady. Eventually the saw hummed to a stop and he climbed down from the ladder and stood on the floor to make the bottom cut. "Help me here," her dad said. He handed her the saw so he could heft the large section of pipe to the floor.

A clump of wet cloth hung from the open drain.

"That's pretty dirty to be your washcloth," he said. "Hand me the bucket."

Trina handed him the bucket.

"Bombs away," he warned. He gave the clump a tug, and sludge slopped into the bucket with a big splash. "Looks like a hundred years of clog."

"Gross," Trina said, trying not to breathe in the pungent smell of the ancient slime.

Her dad pulled a small flashlight from his hip pocket and shined it into the pipe. "And another hundred to go." He reached into the pipe, gave another little tug, and Trina's washcloth plopped into the bucket followed by a small torrent of water and a lot of soap bubbles. "Looks like your washcloth wasn't the culprit. That first clump of whatever-it-is caused the whole problem."

Pinching her nose, Trina peered closely at the muck in the bucket. "It looks like a dead animal."

"Could be," he said, grimacing. "Like maybe a rat." He picked up a piece of lath and poked at the soggy mass. Blobs of muck slid from the clump and then a fleck of something white flashed and disappeared.

"What was that?" Trina's heart raced. Could it be? She grabbed the bucket from her dad. Water splashed, mud washed away, and a face appeared. A little white face with sparkling eyes. And they were staring straight at her.

"Here, I'll dump it out back," he said, reaching for the bucket.

"You can't," Trina said, whirling around with the bucket tight in her arms. The mud sloshed again and the little face vanished. "Oh no, she's drowning!"

"Who's drowning?"

"Augustine's mother." Trina tilted the bucket until the doll's face appeared again. "Annie must have taken her into the bathtub and she went down the drain."

"Annie?"

"Annie Roy, Poppo," Trina said with exasperation. "The little girl who used to live here." Trina closed the stopper in the bathroom sink and turned on the hot water. "I can't believe it. Augustine has a mother again." With a piece of lath, she carefully scooped out the muddy doll and slid her into the sink. "She's so lucky."

"She looks pretty hopeless to me," her dad said. He wound up the cord of his saw and collapsed his ladder. "Don't worry, I'll fix the drainpipe tomorrow." And then he left with the bag of plaster and lath and the bucket of sludge. "Good luck trying to revive her."

Revive. Poppo had no idea how alive the mother doll might be. Trina squirted some hand soap into the sink and then she stirred the soapy water with the piece of lath like a gentle washing machine until the doll was clean enough to pick up.

The mother doll wasn't as lifelike as Augustine, but she was beautiful, just as Augustine had said. Her brown eyes didn't blink, and her dark brown hair and black shoes were painted porcelain, but her arms and legs moved. Her simple ruffled dress, which must have been much whiter once upon a time, was stitched into her soft body, and it was identical to the one Annie's mother wore in the photograph.

Trina wrapped paper towels around the doll and squeezed her gently, over and over again, until the mother was nearly dry, and then she took her upstairs and leaned her against the mantel in Augustine's bedroom.

Sitting cross-legged on the floor with her elbows on her knees and her chin in her hands, leaning as close to

Augustine as she could, Trina whispered, "Augustine, I don't know if you can hear me at night, but I have a wonderful story to tell you. Once upon a time, a mother was lost from her daughter. It seemed she was lost to her forever because she was gone for years and years without any explanation at all, but then she was found in a . . ."

Trina stopped. She could never tell Augustine that her mother had been trapped in a dark, slimy drain for a hundred years. She would have to make up a different story. A nice story. The kind of story Augustine would like to hear.

"Augustine, your mother left home to go on wondrous adventures to see the world, but she became trapped in a cave for many years until a golden bird found her and carried her back to the Land of Goldenrod. And now she is very happy to be home because she missed you very much. She loves you, Augustine."

Trina paused, then said, "You were right, Augustine. No stone unturned."

Chapter Twelve

As the sun came up, Trina was awakened by a faint hum. Like the buzzing of a bee around a flower. She sat up in bed and looked toward the dollhouse. Augustine was singing. "Good morning, Augustine," she said.

"Oh, Citrine. It is the most wonderful day!" Augustine had slipped from her bed and was twirling toward her mother, who still leaned against the miniature mantel. "My mother is no longer lost to me."

Trina climbed out of bed and knelt down by the dollhouse. "She came back to you, Augustine."

"Mother, this is my friend, Citrine. Her mother is traveling in a distant land just as you were, and soon she will come home to her as you have come home to me."

The Land of Smelly Sludge, thought Trina, tamping down a grin. "Welcome home," she said, nodding at Augustine's mother.

"She flew home on a golden bird, Citrine," Augustine continued. "The bird freed her from a great cave. She said it was a dreadful place and she prefers not to recall a single moment."

The mother doll said nothing.

"Does your mother talk?" Trina asked.

Augustine put her hand to her mouth to smother a little laugh. "Yes, but not so *you* can hear her."

Trina felt left out of the joke, but it was probably a good thing Augustine's mother didn't talk. Having to deal with one talking doll was hard enough.

"My dear Citrine," the little doll said, her feet skipping across the polished floor to the open edge of the dollhouse. "My mother and I would like very much to have a tea party today as a celebration of her homecoming." She ran downstairs and climbed into a velvet chair at the dining room table and folded her hands in her lap. "Would you be so kind as to set my mother at the table next to me? And then you must make us some goldenrod tea and bring us some cream and sugar, just as Annie did."

You can make tea from the flowers, you know, Mr. Kinghorn had said. No, Trina hadn't known, but she would try. She set the mother doll in a chair next to Augustine and then, pinching the edges of the tray, she carried the tiny tea set downstairs into the kitchen and put a pan of water on the stove to boil. By the screech of the saw outside, she could tell her dad was already working.

When she went out the front door to pick the goldenrod, she was surprised to step onto a section of cedar planking, and even more surprised to look up and see the framework for the porch roof. She breathed in the sweet cedar scent and admired her dad's work.

He stopped the saw instantly. "Good morning, Princess. Watch where you step."

"You sure have made a lot of progress," Trina said as she began to pick the goldenrod for the tea.

"Not enough," he said. "But Hank told me the *Farmer's Almanac* predicts the next several days should be nice and dry, so I need to finish the porch and get to the painting ASAP."

"Sounds like you need my help," Trina said. Proving to her dad that he needed her help would be a perfect way to get out of going to school.

"I sure do. If I don't finish the outside work by the time it freezes, I'll never meet the deadline. Pretty soon I'm going to wish they gave us two years to finish this project." Then he caught himself. "Not so fast," he said. "What about school?"

School. She had to come up with something. "It's almost the weekend, Poppo. And then it's Labor Day. We don't have school for days and days."

Her dad's eyes narrowed, reminding Trina of Miss Kitty's laser-beam glare when she wondered if they were telling the truth about living at Goldenrod. He pulled out his little notepad and flipped to the calendar. Trina crossed her fingers. "Hm," he said. "I guess I'm in luck. You're hired."

Trina turned away from her dad to hide her grin as she picked a big batch of goldenrod. Now she'd just have to figure out what to do to avoid going back after Labor Day.

Her dad followed her into the kitchen. He got a glass of water as Trina plucked the tiny flowers from their stems and dropped a handful of them into the boiling water. She stirred the tea with a spoon, poking the flowers under the water as fragrant steam filled the air.

"What are you making?" he asked. "It smells like licorice."

"Goldenrod tea," she said.

From the corner of her eye, she watched her dad pick up the tiny teapot, squinting as if it were covered in fine print he couldn't read. "I don't think I've ever seen you play like this before," he said.

"Poppo, I'm not playing," she said, insulted that he made her sound like a little girl and worried he might think she was. "I'm trying to make the dollhouse as authentic as it can be." She opened their one and only cupboard of kitchen supplies, pulled out one of her dad's gas station coffee mugs, and frowned. "Do we have a strainer?"

He seemed to give the question serious consideration. "I think I have just what you need," he said and hurried outside.

First, she filled the tiny sugar bowl with sugar. Then she filled the creamer with milk. She was placing the little pitcher back on the tray when her dad came in with a piece of window screen. "Hold this over the mug," he said, handing the screen to Trina. Then he picked up the pan and carefully filled the mug with goldenrod tea as the wet flowers collected on top of the screen.

Trina dipped the spoon in the mug and filled the tiny teapot drop by drop until it was full. She pushed the mug toward her dad and picked up the tea set. "Thanks, Poppo. You can have the rest."

"Yum," he said. "I'll sip it on my way into town. I have to order the paint and pick up about a hundred pounds of nails. And a couple other things I forgot."

As the kitchen door swung shut behind her, he hollered, "See you in an hour or so. And don't forget your tool belt."

"Okay," she called back.

Upstairs, Trina set the tray on a little side table in Augustine's dining room. She poured a tiny stream of tea into the mother doll's teacup as Augustine gave her mother a furtive glance and lowered her voice. "Citrine, my mother wonders if you know anything about my father."

"No, I don't," Trina said, filling Augustine's cup with tea and finally her own. "But tell her I won't give up hope."

"Hope? What is hope?" the doll asked.

Trina sat down on the floor and pondered the question, wondering how she could explain the wishful feeling of hope in a way Augustine would understand. "Hope is like waiting for the happy ending to a story," she finally said, sprinkling a few crystals of sugar into each cup followed by one drop of milk.

Augustine sighed wistfully. "You have many words for things in your world I cannot see or touch. But I like this word hope. My mother and I will spend our day hoping. Would you like to join us?"

"I wish I could," Trina said truthfully, "but I have to help my father today." She took a minuscule sip of tea, a mere drop on her lips, while Augustine held her cup in both hands like a big soup bowl. The tea tasted good. "This is delicious," Trina said, making small talk.

Just when Trina thought she might sneak away, Augustine said, "Can you please tell me of the weather?"

"The weather?" Surprised by the question, Trina said the first thing that popped into her mind. "The *Farmer's Almanac* says we're due for a dry spell."

"A dry spell, is that so?" Augustine pursed her lips, looked to her mother, and shook her head in dismay. "I imagine the flowers shall not fare well."

Trina almost laughed out loud. Augustine didn't sound like herself. She was playing make-believe. "Possibly," Trina said.

They chatted more about the weather and flowers until Trina heard her dad's truck coming through the cornfield. With the tip of her pinky, Trina wiped clean her teacup and then she dabbed the little napkin at the corner of her lip. "I'm afraid I have to run along now. Thank you very much for the hospitality," she said and stood up.

"But Citrine, you cannot leave."

Trina stopped. "What is it?"

"Annie always drank our tea for us," Augustine said matter-of-factly.

"Of course. What was I thinking?" Trina sat right back down and sipped first from the mother doll's cup and then from Augustine's. "I must be going now," Trina said, aware she was sounding like Augustine. She stood up and grabbed her tool belt and her Minnesota Twins baseball cap, and just as she was leaving, Augustine stopped her.

"Citrine?" The doll was holding her teacup in the air. "We would very much like to have more."

"More?" Trina said, amused because Augustine and her mother didn't drink the tea in the first place, and a bit frustrated because she was in a hurry. She refilled their cups and ducked out of her room before Augustine could say another word, leaving the two dolls alone to enjoy their first tea party together in a hundred years.

Trina met her dad's truck as he came through the gate. "I've got two surprises for you," he said. He parked and hopped out of the cab. "Come see."

She followed him to the cargo bed where something large was covered with a canvas tarp. He peeled back a corner of the tarp, uncovering a box of blue dishes. "First, real dishes."

Dishes! Trina was amazed. Poppo had actually listened to her.

And then, like a magician, he pulled back the rest of the tarp to reveal an antique porch swing. It was all beat up and the chains were rusty. "Al from the antique store stopped me on the street. Said a swing had mysteriously shown up outside his shop door with this note taped to it." Trina leaned in to read the note. "BELONGS TO GOLD-ENROD," it said.

Trina grinned. Goldenrod was working her magic, drawing her things back to her like a magnet.

"We'll hang it right there," her dad said, pointing at the nook by the bay window. "Right where it used to be. We just have to build the porch first. Ready to get to work?"

Trina nodded. She buckled her tool belt around her waist, and her dad filled the loops with a hammer and a pair of needle-nose pliers and the biggest of the pouches with a handful of nails. "We're going to finish the decking, which means I'll cut the boards and you can nail them in place." He handed her goggles and a pair of gloves, and the first thing they did was measure and cut a cedar board. Then he laid it across the support beams and showed her where to place the nails. "Pinch it like this, tap it gently to get it started, and then give it three solid whacks. Got it?"

"Got it," Trina said, suddenly realizing how many boards it would take to cover the whole floor. But she didn't want to give up before she got started. If Poppo trusted her to help him, she wouldn't let him down. She set the next nail, tapped it gently, and whacked the floor of the porch with a loud crack as she missed. She looked up at her dad, knowing her cheeks were bright pink.

"Just take your time," he said. "I'll cut more planks."

It was hard for Trina to keep up with her dad, and the boards started piling up. The work gloves made her hands feel clumsy, so she pulled them off. About the time Trina was ready to quit, her dad started nailing the planks too and they worked side by side. "We make a good team," he said, which gave Trina the encouragement she needed to keep going.

When they finished the section by the library, they broke for a late picnic lunch on the new porch—peanut butter sandwiches and chocolate milk—and watched the combines rolling through the amber-topped fields. "I like this time of year," her dad said, leaning back on his elbows. "Some people get sad because summer is coming to an end. I like to think the world is resting up for a new beginning."

A new beginning. Trina leaned back on her elbows too. If she could spend her days working with her dad like this and having adventures with Augustine, she wouldn't mind this new beginning. Especially since Goldenrod seemed to be behaving herself. But she knew she'd have to go back to school at some point. And then what?

Her dad hopped up and pulled her to her feet. "Let's get working." He picked up her tool belt and handed it to her.

The day was another hot one. She had a blister forming where her hand rubbed against the hammer, and her back hurt, but she didn't let on. If she could prove to her dad how big a help she could be, maybe she wouldn't ever have to go back to school.

They were rounding the corner by the bay window when her dad said, "I think we should call it a day." She had been working in the shade of the oak tree and had no clue so many hours had passed—except for the giant blister on the palm of her hand.

"One more," she announced. She hauled back her hammer to give the last nail a whack. The hammer missed and smacked her thumb. Pain instantly seized her. She dropped the hammer and jumped up and down, clutching her thumb and yelling, "It hurts! It really hurts!" She tried not to cry as her dad ran toward her.

He put his arm around her and gently bent her throbbing thumb. "It's not broken," he assured her. "Let's get some ice; that'll make it feel better," and they went inside.

Her thumb hurt like crazy, and so did the stupid blister, but she also felt embarrassed. And afraid. What if Poppo changed his mind and decided she was too young to help him with the real work? What if he sent her back to school?

He placed a bag of ice next to her thumb, wrapped her hand in a dish towel, and sat her down in the rocking chair. Then he made pancakes for dinner, just like he'd done when she was little. At bedtime, she let him tuck her into bed, even though she hadn't let him do that in almost a year. She closed her eyes, miserable that the day, which had started with such hope, had ended so badly.

The next morning, when her dad knocked on her door, Trina bolted up in bed, worried that Augustine might step out of her house or start singing.

"Can I see your thumb, Princess?" he asked.

Trina glanced first at Augustine, who smiled as she put one finger to her lips and sat as still as could be, and then at her thumb, which still throbbed inside the now soaking-wet towel. She opened the door, held out her bandaged hand, and let her dad unwrap it. Her thumb was a deep purple and almost twice its normal size. "Bruised but whole. Still up for helping me?"

Trina nodded, relieved. Glad her dad still wanted her to help.

"I'll be down soon, Poppo." As he shut the door behind him, she turned back to the dollhouse. Augustine gave her a little wink.

Trina hurried to get dressed. Before she left the room, it occurred to her she'd be leaving Augustine alone for another whole day. "Augustine, I wish I could stay and play with you today, but I have to work again. Would you like to come outside with me? Maybe you could look for your prince while I help my father. Just don't wander away."

Augustine shook her head. "I appreciate the invitation, but I believe I will keep my mother company today. However, if you please, we would like to sit together in your window and watch the great outdoors."

Trina set the mother doll and Augustine side by side in the window overlooking the front yard so they could watch the farmers harvesting the corn. "Fare thee well, Citrine," Augustine said, waving good-bye as if Trina were leaving to travel the world and not just heading outside to work.

Trina waved back, and in that moment she swore she saw lace curtains in her window billow in the late summer breeze and brush lightly against the dolls. But there were no curtains, which meant the memory wasn't her own. Somehow the memory belonged to the house. "Fare thee well, Augustine," she said.

Trina spent day two helping her dad finish the porch floor and building what he called a balustrade —the fancy railing that would edge the entire porch. Trina set the spindles in place and her dad followed her with the nail gun. By the end of the day, the balustrade was beginning to look like a lace ribbon running across the front of the house, but there were at least another hundred spindles to go.

After they finished the balustrade, Poppo seemed to forget all about school. Each day they worked on something new—the porch roof, the ceiling, the steps and the latticework. Trina was exhausted, but she could feel herself growing stronger and she loved how her dad treated her as an equal. Every morning started with oatmeal, and every hard day's work ended with dinner in the dining room, eating off the blue china plates. Even Trina lost track of the days.

One morning, when Trina woke up to Augustine's singing, she was filled with pangs of guilt. Except for an afternoon tea party when her dad went into town for more lumber, she hadn't been paying much attention to the doll. She got out of bed and immediately went over to the dollhouse. Augustine was busy sweeping her kitchen floor with a broom the size of a birthday candle. "Good morning, Augustine," she said.

"Good morning, Citrine."

Trina watched sleepily as Augustine swept bits of dust out her kitchen door and onto Trina's bedroom floor. She set the broom next to her stove and brushed off her hands. "That is quite enough work for now." And then Augustine looked up at Trina. "Are you off to work with your father again today?"

Trina nodded and started getting dressed.

"All you do is work, Citrine. Are there no good fairies or elves to help you?"

"Augustine, in my world we must do everything ourselves. Even if we don't want to."

"Very well, then. Perhaps when you return, you could bring with you a book from the library. My mother and I would very much enjoy a story."

Trina felt guiltier yet. She could barely remember the last time she read to Augustine. She thought about telling her dad she wanted to take the day off, but he had promised her a reward for all her hard work. A surprise just for her, he had said.

"How about I read to you this evening, Augustine?"

"I will look forward to it, Citrine," said the little doll earnestly. Augustine sounded so serious, Trina was about to get a book right then and start reading, but her dad called from downstairs and she dashed out of the room.

He had a long list of chores for her, from filling nail holes to sanding the railing. She worked all day and she wasn't even half done. In the late afternoon, he sent her to the grove of trees to see how the apples were coming along. When she returned, carrying one small green apple, he was standing on the back stoop outside the French doors. She held up the sad-looking apple. "They're not ready yet."

"Close your eyes," he said with a wink as she neared the door, and Trina knew checking on the apples was a trick and it was time for her surprise. He took her hand and led her through the dining room, across the parlor, and back outside again through the front doors and along the new porch, all the way to the bay window, as close as Trina could tell. "Now you can open them," he said.

Trina opened her eyes and there was the porch swing— a perfect porch swing hanging from shiny new chains.

Somehow, secretly, her dad had sanded it and painted it white. "It's beautiful," she said, and it really, truly was. Given everything she had learned from building the porch, she knew how hard her dad had worked, probably long after she had gone to bed, to make the swing perfect just for her. It was the best reward she could think of.

Standing there, worn out from working all day, they both had the same idea at the same time and practically fell into the porch swing, laughing. "Thank you, Poppo," she said, and she meant it with all her heart.

The evening sky was pink and the air had a tinge of fall to it. A yellow leaf fell from the big oak, twirled across the brand-new balustrade, and landed in Trina's lap.

"Red sky at night," her dad began.

"Sailor's delight," Trina finished, twirling the leaf in her fingers.

They sat there, swinging quietly until her dad crossed his arms and made a funny face. "Oh, I almost forgot. I picked this up the last time I was in town." He pulled a postcard from his pocket—a picture of a baby penguin tucked against its mother on an ice shelf.

"Dear Citrine, Antarctica . . ." was as far as Trina got when she heard an engine purring and they both looked up. A small blue car was winding its way through the cornfield toward the house.

"Maybe it's another special delivery," her dad said, his hand at his brow so he could see into the sun. "We could use some dining room chairs. Anyone you know?"

Chapter Thirteen

Trina heard the car rumble through the gate. She heard the engine shut off and the car door slam, but she didn't look up to see who the driver was. She was too busy reading the new postcard to herself for the third time.

Dear Citrine,

Antarctica reminds me of Wisconsin in the winter, except it's warmer here. Wait 'til you try battery-operated mittens. Someday I'll take you whale-watching in the snow.

Love from the ends of the Earth, Mom

Trina was looking at a picture of ice, but her heart was melting. There was something different about this postcard. First of all, it was a picture of a mother and a baby. And that part, *Love from the ends of the Earth*, sounded like her mother knew she was really far away. Like maybe she really missed her.

"I can't tell who that is," her dad said.

Trina finally looked up and when she recognized their visitor, her heart skipped way more than a beat. "It's

Miss Dale," she said under her breath.

"Miss Dale?" His eyebrows pulled together, trying to remember. "Miss Dale . . . You mean your teacher? Why is she—? Oh, Trina, we've really done it this time."

Citrine, she wanted to correct him as he jumped to his feet, but she could feel him getting anxious and she didn't want to make it any worse. Miss Dale walked toward them with an armload of books and papers and a small white box.

"Hello, Citrine," she said kindly as she came up the steps of the porch.

"Hi, Miss Dale," Trina said, slipping her postcard into her back pocket. And then, thinking good manners might help her out in this awkward situation, she said, "I'm sure you remember my father, Mr. Michael Maxwell."

"Mike," he said. "I mean, you can call me Mike." He held out his hand to shake Miss Dale's but dropped it when he saw her hands were full.

"Carrie," Miss Dale said.

"Oh," he said. "Of course, I can carry this." He took the stack of books and papers and the box labeled *Cat's Meow Diner* from her arms.

Trina thought she might die of embarrassment right then and there. "Carrie, Poppo," Trina whispered. "Miss Dale's *name* is Carrie."

His face flushed pinker than the sky. "Of course. Car-rie. I knew that. And what brings you way out here on this fine evening?"

"Mr. Kinghorn said he saw Citrine at the library several days ago and then Mr. Hank and Mr. Al said you had been in town, so I assured Miss Lincoln that if Citrine wasn't in school today, I'd pay you a visit." Miss Dale smiled. "Miss Lincoln is kind of the boss, you know," which made Trina smile too, despite her own nervousness.

"C'mon, tell the truth," Trina's dad said. "You all thought the house got us. WOO-HA-HA," he added in his scary voice just before he laughed.

Trina cringed as she saw Miss Dale's green eyes flash with fear. She knew her dad was trying to lighten the mood, but it wasn't working. "Don't, Poppo. Don't scare her."

"Oh, I'm sorry," he said, sheepishly. "I didn't mean—"

"That's okay," Miss Dale said. "Although I'll admit we were a little worried about the two of you way out here."

"We're getting along just fine. Come on in and see for yourself." He motioned her toward the front door, which was standing wide open. "Even Citrine has decided the house isn't haunted."

"Poppo," Trina said again, embarrassed for both of them this time.

Her dad hurried ahead and put the books and bakery box on the dining room table and disappeared into the kitchen while Trina showed Miss Dale the main floor. "This is the parlor," she said, watching the look of amazement on Miss Dale's face. Then she guided her across the foyer into the library and pointed out its four books from Mr. Kinghorn and told her all about the delivery of the rocking chair.

Next, she led Miss Dale through the smoking room. "The funny smell is from the tobacco," Trina said. "And this is the best part. Follow me." She opened the door to the secret passageway and led Miss Dale into the dining room. Trina wrapped up by explaining how they would repaint the entire exterior before winter came, then plaster the walls and the ceilings and order custom wallpapers to match the originals.

"Wow," Miss Dale said. "This is a really big project."

"And that's just the stuff you can see," Trina's dad said, walking into the dining room, drying his freshly washed hands on a paper towel. "Please, have a seat. Can I offer you a cup of coffee?"

"No, thank you," Miss Dale said as the downstairs toilet decided to flush itself with a great gush of water.

Miss Dale's head whipped around.

"Just one of our ghosts," Trina's dad said.

Trina wanted to sink under the table. "It's really a leaky valve," she said.

An awkward silence followed until Miss Dale pointed at the bakery box. "How about we eat the cupcakes I brought?" she said. "While we talk."

Trina jumped up and grabbed the box, glad to leave the room. She put the cupcakes on the new blue china platter from Al's Antiques and brought it into the dining room. Then she got three little matching plates. She even folded three paper towels to look like napkins. The table was nearly as welcoming as Augustine's—except for the folding chairs.

After they had enjoyed the cupcakes for a few moments in silence, Miss Dale got really serious and started talking about school and state laws, and Trina got more and more uneasy as she listened. "The bottom line is," Miss Dale concluded, "Citrine needs to return to school."

Trina shook her head.

"C'mon, Trina. I mean, Citrine." Her dad's face flushed again. "You know we talked about this. We agreed you would take a couple days off and then go back."

"But I changed my mind, Poppo. I can learn more from home than I can at school." Trina looked at Miss Dale, hoping she wasn't offending her. "Look at everything we've done. All the measuring and the planning and all the work. It's like math and art and gym all at once. Everything I need to know, you can teach me."

"We both know that's not true, Princess."

Trina hooked her feet on the rungs of the chair and wrapped her arms around herself. She would have curled into a ball if she could have. "I didn't go to school at all in Portland, and everything was fine."

Her dad looked to Miss Dale. "We weren't there very long." Then he turned back to Trina. "And you were a lot younger then. Now you have to go to school."

Trina knew this was an argument she couldn't win, not now that Miss Dale was there. If Goldenrod wasn't such a big house, they wouldn't have to stay for a whole year. She could look forward to moving soon and school wouldn't matter. Or if her mother would just come home and rescue her, but her mother seemed to be getting farther and farther away.

Trina looked down at her still-bruised thumb. On the verge of tears, she tried one last time. "But we're a team. Remember, Poppo?"

"Citrine," he said softly, and Trina looked up, right into his eyes, surprised he got her name right. Suddenly everything felt more serious. She was afraid she might cry, but if she cried she'd look like the baby she didn't want to be.

"What happened at school?" he said. "This isn't the first time you've been the new kid. Something must have happened."

Trina shifted in her chair. "I already told you, Poppo. The kids all know each other."

Miss Dale nodded. "That's true. It's a pretty close group."

"And they don't want anyone new," Trina continued. And then she couldn't help herself. "And they're mean."

"All of them?" her dad asked.

Trina looked down. She didn't want to say anything more. Tattling was worse than crying if you were trying to be grown-up.

"Are you talking about Charlotte?" Miss Dale asked.

Trina's head jerked up, her eyes alert.

"Who's Charlotte?" her dad asked, frowning.

"She's Miss Kitty's granddaughter, and a cousin of mine," Miss Dale said. "She's a bit of a handful. For everybody."

"Miss Kitty's granddaughter!" he repeated. "Huh." The frown on his face turned into a grin. "I guess that explains everything."

Trina snorted, a laugh mixed with almost crying. "Poppo," she said, trying to hush him, but then she noticed Miss Dale had her hand over her mouth, trying to hide her own smile.

"So it wasn't enough that I put her up front by me?" Miss Dale said, pulling her chair closer to Trina's.

Trina shook her head. Miss Dale didn't know about the name calling. Or how Charlotte had squeezed her hand so tightly she thought it might break after the dodgeball game. Or how she held up her big fist at the water fountain.

"Listen," Miss Dale said. "Let's start over tomorrow. It's Friday, so it will be just one day before the weekend. And it's the last of our 'One-Minute Me' days."

One-Minute Me? Really? Fifth grade still sounded like kindergarten. Trina shook her head slowly and looked at her dad, who was nodding along with Miss Dale's idea. How could he do this to her? How could he side with the teacher?

"I brought all your homework, but don't worry about catching up right now. Just come prepared to tell the class about someone, or something, that is special in your life and why. For one minute. You can bring pictures or souvenirs. Anything that will help you tell your story." Miss Dale looked around at the blank walls and the empty rooms. "Or you don't have to bring anything. You can just talk. And leave Charlotte up to me." She reached for Trina's hands and held them gently. "Are you willing to give it one day?"

Trina could feel her anger slipping away. Miss Dale not only had the kindest eyes she had ever seen, but the gentlest hands. And no matter what she hoped, Trina knew they would be living out the year at Goldenrod and that her mother wouldn't be rescuing her anytime soon.

"Okay," she said quietly, thinking everything would be easier if she could hang onto Miss Dale's hands forever. "I'll go for one day and see."

One more horrible day.

One more terrible woe to tell Augustine.

Augustine. She had to tell Augustine. Maybe Augustine would make her feel better.

Trina looked out the dining room window at the darkening sky. She needed to hurry if she was going to tell Augustine the news before the little doll fell asleep. "Can I please be excused?"

Her dad nodded. Trina raced out of the room, turned around to say a quick good-bye to Miss Dale, and then ran upstairs. Augustine was in bed, her eyes already half-closed.

"Augustine," Trina said. "Stay awake!"

Augustine sat right up. "Have you come to read us a story?"

Trina shook her head. She didn't have time to read a story and talk to Augustine before it got dark out. "No, I have a problem."

"Oh, dear, another woe." Augustine pulled up her knees and rested her chin in her hands, ready to listen.

"I have to go back to school, but I don't want to go."

"Ah, yes, I remember. The witch lives in the Land of School. You have stayed away many days, safe in the Land of Goldenrod. Are you afraid to return?"

Trina nodded, blinking away tears.

Augustine held out a little hand to her. "I understand. Still, I believe you must return. I know of no good story where the maiden gives up. You must simply be brave and valiant."

Augustine made it sound easy, but Trina knew it would be hard. "That's not all. My teacher says I'm supposed to tell a story about someone or bring something that is very important in my life and tell why, but I can't think of anything. I don't want to talk about Goldenrod because they all think it's haunted, and I don't want to talk about working on the house . . ."

Trina broke off, her voice wobbling.

"Can you not read the story of Briar Rose?"

Trina slouched against her bed. "That's not the kind of story she means. It has to be a story about me."

Augustine reached for her silver hairbrush and brushed her fine blonde hair as she stared toward the fireplace in Trina's room. Then she clasped the hairbrush in her other hand. "I have an idea!" she cried.

Trina followed Augustine's gaze to the fireplace mantel. "You're brilliant!" she said, standing up. "Why didn't I think of that? My mother's postcards! I can tell the class all about her adventures." Trina reached for the stack of postcards. "I'll take New Zealand and the one I just got from Antarctica," she said, pulling the new one from her pocket. When Trina turned around, Augustine was standing outside her house with her hands on her hips.

"Citrine, could it be that you are forgetting something?"

"What?" Trina could tell Augustine was mad, but she didn't know why. And then it hit her: Augustine expected to go to school with her. But just the thought of Augustine dropped on the playground or taken away by Miss Lincoln made Trina feel queasy. Trina shook her head firmly. "Augustine, I can't take you to school with me."

"Then tell me how you plan to push the witch into the oven all by yourself?"

Augustine's reply was such a surprise Trina couldn't help smiling. But her problem was a real problem, not a fairy-tale dilemma, and Augustine's plan of action would be of no use to her at school. "We're not allowed to push witches into ovens anymore, Augustine. The Land of School has new laws that say we can't hurt anybody."

"Must everyone follow these new laws?"

What a relief. For once Augustine understood what she was telling her about the human world. "Yes," Trina sighed. "Everyone."

"But you said the witch wants to eat you up."

"*Beat* me up. She wants to *beat* me up, Augustine."

"Would that not hurt you?"

Trina bit her lower lip. "Yes, it would."

"Citrine, I do not understand. Are you saying she may hurt you, but you may not hurt her?"

Trina sat down on the edge of her bed. "I guess so."

Augustine stomped her little foot. "Then she must be revenged upon."

Revenged upon? For a second the idea of getting revenge sounded good to Trina. Maybe there *was* a way to stop Charlotte. Give her a taste of her own medicine. But what would Miss Dale think of Trina then? Revenge wasn't part of their agreement. "No," Trina finally said. "Revenge is mean."

Augustine tapped her tiny chin, thinking. "Then we must teach her a lesson. Books are full of lessons, are they not? And the Land of School is full of books?"

Trina felt herself filling with hope despite Augustine's crazy idea. "Yes, it is."

"Because I have promised to help you, I will accompany you to the Land of School. There we will use one of the many books to find a lesson to free you from the perils of the evil witch. And that is that."

Augustine crawled back into her bed, put her head on her pillow, and yawned. "Now, if you please, put my mother to bed. She is quite stiff from sitting at the table day in and day out. I have explained that you have been very busy, but she feels terribly forgotten."

"I'm sorry," Trina said guiltily as she laid the mother doll in the four-poster bed in the room next to Augustine's. It was hard enough to feel bad about Augustine, but now she had to feel bad about her mother too. She should have been taking better care of Augustine's mother, especially since she had spent a hundred years in a disgusting drainpipe. She pulled the quilt over the mother doll and whispered, "I promise I'll take good care of your daughter in the Land of School. I won't let her out of my sight for a second."

Chapter Fourteen

Trina hardly slept a wink, worrying about school, and she woke up at sunrise just as Augustine stirred in her little bed. She dressed in her good shorts and her red T-shirt—the one with the extra-big pocket—and brushed her teeth.

"Good morning, Citrine," Augustine called as Trina returned to her room. The little doll had already changed into her dress and brushed her hair and was standing in a ray of sunshine. "I am ready for our great adventure in the Land of School."

"Me too, Augustine. And I'm glad you're coming with me. I don't like talking in front of a group. I get stage fright." Trina filled her backpack with her new school-books, a couple notebooks, and a few pens and pencils, and she zipped the two postcards from her mother into the front pouch. Then she picked up Augustine. "I'm going to put you in my pocket."

Augustine gasped. "Please, Citrine, not your pocket!"

"This pocket, see?" She lowered the little doll into her shirt pocket. "You can still peek out if you stand on your tiptoes, but you can't say a word."

"I understand very well the dangers of speaking, Citrine."

Augustine stayed low and quiet at breakfast as Trina ate her oatmeal. In the truck, too, on the way into town.

"Think you can manage?" Trina's dad said as they pulled up in front of the New Royal Public School.

"Yeah," she said, but she couldn't tell him why. She couldn't say she and Augustine had a plan, so instead she said, "It's just really weird. They still write on chalkboards and they don't have any computers."

"Sounds normal to me," he said.

"That's because you went to school in the Middle Ages." Trina hopped out of the truck. "Three thirty and not a second later, Poppo."

"Your lunch!" he hollered, handing Trina the paper bag stuffed with a PB&J sandwich, cookies, and potato chips through his window. Moments later she was walking cautiously into room 216. The kids were already there, but Miss Dale was nowhere in sight.

Nobody said a word. She took her seat behind Prissy Missy, who was wearing a green dress with puffy sleeves, and in front of Charlotte, who had her thick hair pulled into a ponytail. Her long bangs were held in place by a pink angel barrette.

"Ee-ew. Do I smell Latrine?"

An angel. Right. Where was Miss Dale when she needed her? Trina ignored Charlotte, faced the board, and read the agenda in a whisper, directing her voice at her pocket. "Math, Geography, Art Masterpiece, One-Minute Me, Lunch, Recess—"

"When do we read stories?" asked Augustine, doing her best to whisper.

"I don't see reading," Trina whispered to her pocket, which made Prissy Missy turn around.

"Do you always talk to yourself?" Missy asked, making an extra-prissy face.

Trina shook her head. "No. I mean, yes. I mean . . . sometimes."

Missy put her nose in the air. "We have *Silent* Reading in the afternoon. Right after Spelling. It says so on the board."

"Oh, I see it now." Trina gave Missy an overly friendly smile as she patted her shirt pocket, giving Augustine a gentle reminder to be on her best behavior. "Then we'll just have to be very patient and very quiet and do everything Miss Dale says, won't we?"

"Yes, we will," Missy said, copying Trina's singsong voice.

When Miss Dale finally walked into the classroom, all attention turned to her right arm, which was wrapped in a bandage from the tips of her fingers to her elbow and held close to her body in a sling. "What happened to you?" Edward asked.

"I fell down my basement stairs last night and sprained my wrist."

Ben raised his hand while he talked. "My dad says 77 percent of all accidents happen in the home."

"He's probably right, Ben. We should take it as a lesson to be careful."

Looking around the room, Miss Dale caught Trina's eye and smiled, which felt a lot better than a big "welcome back" in front of the whole class. "Everyone, please open your math books to the story problems on page forty-two."

At the mention of the word *story*, Augustine crept to the top of Trina's pocket and peered over its edge.

"Who would like to read story problem number three?" Miss Dale asked.

"I would!" Augustine shouted just as Missy raised her hand.

"You can't read," Trina scolded without thinking.

"Yes, I can!" Missy said, turning around in a huff.

Mortified, Trina shrank back in her chair, one hand clamped over her pocket.

Miss Dale smiled at Missy, but then she turned to Trina. "Would you like to read the question, Citrine?"

Trina sat up as properly as she could, trying to cover for Augustine's outburst. "Yes, Miss Dale."

"*Yes, Miss Dale,*" Charlotte mimicked behind Trina's back in a voice so quiet Miss Dale couldn't hear her, but that meant Miss Dale couldn't do anything to help either.

Trina flipped open her math book and frantically scanned the page to find problem number three and read it out loud. "*A farmer planted 850 acres of corn and 750 acres of beets. If 250 acres of beets died, how many successful acres did the farmer harvest?*"

Augustine harrumphed loudly in Trina's pocket, "What kind of a story is *that*?"

Again, Trina was so flustered she forgot to whisper. "It's not a story, it's a story *problem*."

"It's a story about a dead-beet farmer," Edward said. "Get it?"

The class laughed at Edward's joke, but Trina wanted to crawl under her desk and disappear. Augustine wasn't making things better; she was making them worse. Trina coughed once. Then she coughed again. Pretending she couldn't stop coughing, she raised her hand. "May I get a drink, Miss Dale?"

As soon as they were alone in the hallway, Trina pulled Augustine from her pocket. "Augustine, I told you. You have to be quiet."

"But I feel put away in your pocket and time is fleeting, and I do not like these stories of farmers and numbers and vegetables. Furthermore, I want to see the witch."

"The witch sits behind me. She has a pink angel clipped in her hair and her name is Charlotte. Now can you please be patient?"

"I will try, Citrine, but do tell me. Is Miss Dale the Queen or Snow White? For she is very beautiful."

"She is the queen of the classroom. But she's young, so she's more like a princess than a queen."

"Ah, then she is Snow White. She is the fairest in all the land. She, too, is waiting for her prince."

Trina rolled her eyes. "We have to go back to the classroom, Augustine. Promise me you'll be as quiet as a mouse."

"All right," sighed the little doll. "But mice are not very quiet."

Augustine behaved through the rest of Math. Geography, too. She was even a little sleepy when Miss Dale read to them about the famous art masterpiece, the Mona Lisa, painted by Leonardo Da Vinci. It was on display in the Louvre in Paris, France. Trina's mind wandered, wondering if her mother had been to the Louvre when she lived in Paris. And then her stomach clenched when Miss Dale said it was time for "One-Minute Me."

"Please move forward and fill in the empty desks so you can hear better," Miss Dale said. She looked at her list as everyone shuffled forward and took a different seat. "We're down to Charlotte, Edward, and . . . Citrine. Who'd like to go first?"

Edward waved his hand in the air.

"Great, Edward. We'll start with you."

Edward retrieved a small aquarium from under his desk and carried it to the front of the room. He removed its screened lid and took out a warty bullfrog about the size of a softball.

"You brought a stupid frog?"

Charlotte had barely uttered the word "frog" when Augustine peeked out from Trina's pocket and shouted excitedly, "A frog?"

"Shh!" Trina said loudly, putting her finger to her lips.

"I can talk if I want to," Charlotte said.

Great. Charlotte thought Trina was telling *her* to be quiet.

But Charlotte wasn't quiet, of course. "I want to know what's so special about a frog anyway. The world has millions of them."

"Charlotte," Miss Dale said. "Consider this your first warning."

Meanwhile Augustine had her hands on the top edge of Trina's pocket, trying to climb out, so Trina had to pinch her pocket shut.

"Go on, Edward," Miss Dale said.

"I found this frog near the creek that runs through our farm. He's an amphibian and he's special because Miss Dale said he gets to be our class mascot. If we take good care of him, he should live for seven to nine years." Edward rocked from one foot to the other. "And he's important to me because . . . because me and my dad caught him when we went fishing. He's a very special frog."

"My dad and I," Miss Dale corrected. "And what else?"

"Oh, yeah. Miss Dale said we get to name him."

"How about Fred?" Ben said.

"Or Buddy?" Charlotte said.

"Is that frog my prince?" Augustine asked in a muffled voice.

"Your prince?" Trina exclaimed, shaking her head at Augustine in amusement before she realized that everyone was looking at her and she had forgotten to whisper. "Prince," she said again, feigning a look of love. "I just love that name, Prince."

"All those in favor of naming the frog Prince, raise your hands." Trina watched as Miss Dale counted the hands in the air. Every hand but Charlotte's. "We have a majority. Our new class mascot is Prince, the frog."

"Prince!" Augustine shouted as she leaped from Trina's pocket and clattered onto her desktop.

"Oh, no!" Trina shouted.

Everyone stared at Trina.

"Never mind," Trina said, her heart thumping. She glanced at her desk. The doll was face down, motionless, with one arm sticking up in the air.

Before Trina had a chance to hide Augustine, Miss Dale stepped close to Trina's desk. "Is that what you brought to share, Citrine?" Miss Dale asked, leaning toward Trina for a better look at the doll.

Trina thought fast. "Um, yes. It's a doll I found in the playroom at Goldenrod. A doll left behind by the Roy family."

The classroom was instantly silent, frightened by the mere mention of Goldenrod.

"I'm sure everyone would like to hear about her. Why don't you go next," Miss Dale said.

Trina scooped up Augustine and took her place in front of the class next to Miss Dale's desk. She had planned to tell about her mother's adventures and hot-air balloons and penguins, not a talking doll. She took a deep breath. *Please be quiet, Augustine,* she wished, slowly opening her trembling fingers. Augustine lay perfectly still and then her eyes opened. Trina jumped, but the doll didn't make a sound. She just winked her little eye once, which made Trina's stage fright disappear. Besides, she knew Augustine would love being the center of attention.

Trina hooked her fingers under the doll's arms and held her up for the class to see. "She has a dollhouse, too. It's an exact replica of the carriage house that used to be on the grounds of Goldenrod."

"May we all see her?" Miss Dale asked.

Trina nodded and handed Augustine to Miss Dale. "Don't worry," Trina said, noticing that Miss Dale's good hand was shaking nervously. "She's an antique, but she's pretty sturdy."

Miss Dale examined Augustine as if she were a fine diamond. "She's a French doll, isn't she?" she said, passing the doll to Missy, who tried to hand it to Edward, but he was still holding the wriggly frog, so Missy quickly gave Augustine to Ben.

"She's from Paris, France," Trina said, smiling proudly until she saw Augustine land in Charlotte's big hands.

Charlotte made a snooty face. "She's French, all right. Look." Charlotte lifted up Augustine's dress and sang, "I see London, I see France . . ."

Everyone laughed except for Trina, who closed her eyes, embarrassed for Augustine.

"Charlotte," Miss Dale said sternly. "This is your second warning. Please be respectful."

"It's a stupid doll," Charlotte sneered.

"That's enough," Miss Dale said. "And your last chance. Please see me after school." She took the doll from Charlotte and handed her back to Trina.

Trina was relieved to have the doll back in her hands

and gently smoothed Augustine's ruffled hair and crumpled dress.

"Can you tell us why the doll is important in your life, Citrine?" asked Miss Dale.

Trina's mind went numb. She couldn't tell the class the doll could talk. And she couldn't tell them Augustine was the only friend she had in the whole world, or about how scared she was when she nearly lost her in the garden—and then again in the attic. And no way could she tell them how she tucked Augustine into bed at night and read her fairy tales.

Her minute had to be up. She looked at the clock, hoping she could sit down, when Miss Dale said, "Or maybe you'd just like to tell us a little more about living at Goldenrod."

Talking about Goldenrod wasn't any easier. "Daisies and chrysanthemums still come up in the yard," Trina said without thinking. "The same ones your great-grandparents planted, Miss Dale."

"Yeah, right," Charlotte said. "Like flowers live for a hundred years."

The whole class giggled, but Miss Dale said seriously, "Sometimes they do, Charlotte. Many species reseed themselves. It's quite amazing how such small things can take root and survive." Her tone made the class stop laughing, although Trina heard Charlotte give a little snort under her breath. "Is there anything else you want to say, Citrine?"

Yes, there was. Trina wanted to say something to put Charlotte in her place. In fact, Augustine's idea of revenge was sounding better and better. If only she could tell Charlotte she and Augustine had a plan . . . whatever it was. And then she had an idea. "There is an old legend, but I'm sure everyone knows it."

A hush fell over the entire classroom until Edward spoke up. "Nuh-uh. Tell it."

Trina leaned against the edge of Miss Dale's desk and spoke in a deep and scary whisper. "A hundred years ago, a little girl named Annie Roy lived at Goldenrod. She was the daughter of Mr. and Mrs. Harlan M. Roy, who built the mansion. She played with this doll." Trina held up Augustine so everyone could see her again, and Augustine could see her classmates, and then she put her back in her pocket for safekeeping. "But she died in the great Iowa diphtheria epidemic."

"So what?" Charlotte said. "Who cares about someone who died a hundred years ago?"

"Charlotte. One more outburst and you'll be meeting with Miss Lincoln," Miss Dale said.

Trina ignored Charlotte's glare and kept going with her story. "Mr. Kinghorn says that some kids started the Dare Club when Mr. Roy died. They broke into the house and tried to steal things. And everyone who went into the house uninvited had a spell cast upon them and was showered with bad luck." Trina paused, thinking about that word *uninvited*. Maybe that was the difference. She and her dad had been invited. Maybe that was why Goldenrod was trying to tell her something instead of trying to scare her away.

"And?" Ben said, urging her on.

"And the ones who actually stole something have had the worst luck of all."

"What kinds of things?" Missy asked with a quiver in her voice.

"Everything," Trina said. "Mr. Hank had the old dining room table. He didn't even steal it—his brother did. And then his business went downhill. He brought the table back the night of the big storm."

"I grew up with a lot of these stories," said Miss Dale. "You can't believe everything you hear."

Edward waved his hand in the air. "But Mith Dale, ith true. My dad thays Mither Hank hath had bad luck for yearth."

Miss Dale walked across the room, picked up the wastebasket, and held it out to Edward. "Edward. Gum."

"I'll thwallow it in-thead." Edward swallowed with an exaggerated gulp and swished his tongue from side to side to prove his mouth was empty. "See?"

"Hey, Citrine, why don't you tell us something we don't know," Charlotte said.

"Charlotte," Miss Dale said. "That's it. You'll be talking to Miss Lincoln after school."

"Well," Trina began again, fighting a grin as Charlotte's face contorted. "Very mysterious things happen in the house. Lights turn on and off by themselves. Strange noises fill the air. And steam comes out of the radiators like heavy breaths." She lowered her voice again. "Sometimes, at night, it sounds as if someone walks the halls."

"It's a ghost," said Ben. "I knew it."

Missy and the other kids gasped, but Charlotte held her eyes on Trina and didn't show an ounce of emotion. "Like a house would know if you took something."

"What if Annie Roy knew you took something?" Ben said.

"So what?" Charlotte said. "I don't believe in ghosts."

"Your grandma does," Edward said.

"Doesn't mean I do," Charlotte shot back. "It's all hogwash."

It was all hogwash unless you'd been in the house, Trina was thinking. And then she had another idea. She stared into Charlotte's mean, unblinking green eyes. "Have you ever been in the house?"

"Of course not," Charlotte said. "That would be trespassing."

Trina's trap had worked. "Then how would you know?" Trina said. "Only the people who are brave enough to enter Goldenrod know for sure."

"Good one," Edward said. Most of the kids dared to laugh, which made Trina feel as if the bases had been loaded against her and she'd just forced out the runner at home plate.

Charlotte made a mean face at Trina first, and then at Edward.

"Thank you, Citrine," Miss Dale said. "Charlotte, you're next."

"I saved the best for last, as usual," Charlotte said, carrying a large bakery box to the front of the room. She lifted the top to reveal squares of chocolate topped with gooey caramel. "Monster brownies from my grandmother's diner!" When the whole class oohed and ahhed, Charlotte reveled in the attention.

"And why are monster brownies important in your life?" Miss Dale asked.

"They are important because I helped my grandmother make them. And my grandmother is special because I have lived with her ever since my mother died."

As much as Trina didn't like Charlotte, she felt sorry for her. It didn't matter if Miss Kitty made delicious brownies if she was the meanest grandmother in the world.

"Can we eat them now?" Edward asked, climbing on top of his desk with Prince in his hands for an aerial view of the brownies.

Miss Dale frowned as she shook her head. "No, you may not. But you may take them to lunch with you. Edward, please get down. And put Prince away."

Edward jumped down from his desk as Charlotte picked up a stack of white paper napkins and handed out brownies as big as hands. "I get two," Edward announced. "One for me," he said, sneaking a big bite of brownie, "and one for Prinsh." And then he plunged the frog nose-first into the bakery box.

"Ee-ew!" Charlotte screamed, pushing Edward out of the way. Edward lost his balance and the frog flew from his hands and landed on Missy's shoulder. Missy screamed and ran across the room. The frog fell to the floor. Edward hollered. Missy screamed again. Everyone scrambled, first in one direction and then in another, as the frog leaped, landed, and leaped again.

"Dohn shep on Prinsh!" Edward yelled with his mouth full of brownie, and everyone stopped in their places.

Except for the frog.

In a grand leap, Prince landed at Trina's feet.

"Grab him!" Edward yelled.

Trina lunged to pick up the frog and nearly bumped heads with Charlotte, whose long fingers were closing in on Prince like claws. "I've got him!" Charlotte shouted, grasping one loose frog leg, but Trina already had the bulk of the frog in her hands. She was all set to stand up and announce her victory when Augustine slipped from her pocket and landed on Charlotte's foot.

Trina stood stock still with Prince in her hands. She knew she had to pick up Augustine so no one would step on her, but she didn't want Charlotte to end up with the frog.

"On second thought," Charlotte whispered with a gleam in her eye, "I'd rather have this." Before Trina could react, Charlotte bent toward the floor and clamped her hand around the fragile doll. Trina gulped.

Miss Dale blew her whistle. "Please get your lunches and line up at the door. And Citrine," Miss Dale called to her from the doorway, "would you please help Edward put Prince back where he belongs?"

Trina didn't know what to do. She wished she could tell Miss Dale what was really happening, but she knew better than to tattle on Charlotte. Her only choice was to leave Augustine behind and carry the frog to his aquarium.

As soon as Trina had placed Prince on a pile of leaves and grass, Edward set the screen on top. When Trina turned around, Charlotte was at her desk, zipping up her backpack. She had her lunch in hand, but there was no sign of Augustine.

As the class started lining up for lunch, Charlotte blocked Ben and Edward, who were pushing and shoving their way to the front of the line. And then Charlotte sneered at Trina, which made Trina more determined than ever to get back at Charlotte, but first she had to save Augustine.

Miss Dale blew her whistle again. "I want everyone to stand perfectly still and silent for the next sixty seconds." Preoccupied with Augustine's whereabouts, Trina felt as if she were watching her classmates in slow motion: Edward was chewing gum again, Ben was balancing his brownie on the back of his hand, Prissy Missy fidgeted with a bow on her dress, and Charlotte played with her ponytail.

In the fifty-ninth second, Edward blew a bubble as big as his head. In the same second, Charlotte pulled the rubber band from her ponytail. Trina watched, agog, as the bubble stretched and stretched from Edward's mouth toward Charlotte's shoulder.

And then, at the sixtieth second, Charlotte turned her head, the bubble popped, and Edward's wad of gum was left dangling from Charlotte's long red hair.

"Edward!" Charlotte screeched.

Trina covered her grin. She couldn't have imagined a better outcome for Charlotte.

"Shoot," Edward said, looking wide-eyed at Miss Dale. "That was my last piece."

Miss Dale couldn't contain her exasperation a moment longer. "Edward, you and I will be talking after school."

Sniveling, Charlotte pulled on the gum, but wisps of bubble stuck to her fingers and then to her cheek and then to more of her hair. Miss Dale tried to help, but she couldn't do much with one hand. And then Charlotte dropped her brownie and it slid, caramel side in, down the front of her shirt. And Edward managed to step on what was left of the brownie when it hit the floor.

"Charlotte, I think you should go see the nurse," Miss Dale said. "And Edward, please clean your shoe."

Amid snickers, Charlotte stormed to her desk, grabbed her backpack, and stormed out of the room, her red hair so tangled in pink gum it looked like cotton candy. "I'm being sabotaged," she hollered.

Trina was glad to see Charlotte go, but along with her went Augustine. How would she ever get the little doll back?

Chapter Fifteen

At recess, Trina sat on the bleachers, finishing the last of her potato chips while worrying about Augustine. What if Charlotte stuffed her in her backpack? What if she put her in her pocket and sat on her? It had just occurred to her that Charlotte might leave school early and take Augustine home with her when Edward tapped her on the shoulder with a butterfly net.

"Want to help me catch some fresh flies for Prince's dinner?"

Catching flies sounded disgusting, especially on such a hot day, but it was better than sitting on the bleachers all alone, worrying. "Sure," Trina said.

"I know the best place." He pointed to a big metal garbage can across the parking lot. "Race ya."

After a single stride, Trina knew she could beat Edward hands down, but she let him pass her when she caught a whiff of the garbage can, which was stuffed so full that the lid sat on top of the trash like a small hat. A cloud of black flies hovered there in a fury.

"You count to three and lift the lid, and I'll catch the flies with my net."

No way was Trina going to touch the garbage can. "*You* count to three," she said, pulling the net from Edward's hands.

"One, two, three," he said and grabbed the lid.

The stench of rotting garbage filled the air.

The flies buzzed madly.

Trina breathed though her mouth, gave the furious black cloud one quick swipe, and the butterfly net filled with flies. With her other hand, she pinched the net closed and handed it back to Edward.

"Wow!" Edward said. "You're not like other girls."

Trina wasn't sure whether that was a good thing. "Probably not," she said, trying not to gag on the smell of garbage.

"Let's take these to Prince," he said, waving the net full of flies.

When Trina and Edward walked into the classroom, Charlotte was sitting at her desk as if nothing had happened. As if no one would notice that she had changed her shirt. Or that her thick red hair barely brushed the tops of her shoulders. "Wow!" Edward said, carrying the flies toward Prince's cage. "Someone got a haircut."

"Someone better mind his own business," Charlotte snarled.

She didn't even look at Trina, but Trina was truly glad to see Charlotte. Now she had a chance to rescue Augustine before the end of the day.

Seconds later, as Miss Dale and the rest of the class returned from recess, Edward screeched from the back of the room. "Oh, no! Prince is gone! All that's left of him is a bunch of dead flies!" He waved the aquarium's lid in the air and then he shot such an angry glare at Charlotte, Trina thought steam might come out of his ears.

"What? I didn't do it," she said, looking up at Miss Dale pleadingly. "Really!"

Everyone gathered around Prince's aquarium as Edward shook the trapped flies from the butterfly net. A big black fly went buzzing by, but before any more could escape, Miss Dale reached down and repositioned the screen on top of the aquarium. "I have a feeling he just hopped out, Edward. And I think we'll need something more secure than this screen if we find him."

"If?" Edward said.

"When," Miss Dale corrected herself. "If we're really quiet, maybe Prince will croak—"

"Croak?"

"That's not what I mean, Edward. I think if we are very quiet, we'll hear him." She looked up at the clock as if searching for a way to fast-forward the day to three thirty. "Please take your seats. And take out a clean sheet of paper for your spelling test."

Moans and shuffles were drowned out by Charlotte shouting, "Someone stole Mr. Nubby!" Trina turned to look at Charlotte, confused. Something else was missing now? First Augustine and then Prince and now something called Mr. Nubby.

"Who is Mr. Nubby?" Miss Dale asked, as a group of kids swarmed Charlotte's desk for a glimpse of the crime scene.

"He's my little blue pencil. I've had him ever since first grade and I always keep him in my desk. I'm going to get whoever took him." Charlotte shot Trina an accusing look.

Miss Dale waved her good hand in the air. "Go back to your seats, everyone. Charlotte, let's keep everything in perspective. Please borrow a pencil from one of your classmates. We can look for—Mr. Nubby—later."

Trina zipped opened her backpack for a pencil and shut it instantly. In that split-second glance, she had spotted a little blue pencil sharpened down to the size of a paper clip. It had to be Mr. Nubby, which meant someone was framing her. But who? She caught Edward watching her, but he was the only one treating her like a friend. She slipped her hand inside the pouch and felt around for one of her pencils. "Here, Charlotte, you can borrow this one."

"Teacher's pet," Charlotte hissed at Trina beneath her fake smile. "I have my own pencils." And then, in a loud, polite voice she said, "I'm ready, Miss Dale."

"The first word is 'special.' Today is a special day," Miss Dale said. The room was silent as everyone wrote down the word.

"That's it!" Charlotte shouted behind Trina.

"What is it now, Charlotte?" Miss Dale said. She sounded seconds away from losing her temper as she walked down the aisle.

"I took out my barrette just before 'One-Minute Me' and I put it in my pencil tray. And now it's gone. See?" Charlotte opened her desk wide so Miss Dale could see for herself. "I bet two dollars the same person who stole Mr. Nubby stole my barrette," she said, scowling at Trina.

"Charlotte, please don't go jumping to conclusions."

Edward smiled slyly at Trina as he climbed up on his desktop for a better look. Clearly Edward thought Trina was the culprit, but he seemed to be happy with the idea.

"Edward, get down," Miss Dale said. "Charlotte, I think it's time to clean out your desk. It won't even shut. We'll keep an eye out for your barrette and pencil."

When the spelling test was over, Edward waved his hand in the air frantically. "Miss Dale, shouldn't we organize a search party for Prince?"

"Edward," Miss Dale said. "Frogs like water. Why don't you fill one of the art trays with water and set it on the floor. Right now it's time for Silent Reading."

Trina didn't have anything but her schoolbooks to read, so she pulled out her geography book and looked up all the cities and states she'd ever lived in. She was reading about the Santa Fe Trail when something tickled her ankle. A black fly was her first thought, until she remembered it might be Prince. Careful not to make any sudden movements, she sneaked a look beneath her desk.

No black fly. No warty bullfrog. But there, perched on the toe of her tennis shoe, was Augustine—leaning on a pink angel barrette half as tall as she was. The covert operation had been exposed. "So it's you!" Trina said out loud, forgetting all about Silent Reading.

"Is it Prince?" Edward shouted from his side of the room.

Trina shook her head and did her best to fake a sneeze. "Ah-choo!" And then she coughed. She reached under her desk, grabbed the pink barrette with one hand and Augustine with the other, faked the biggest, loudest coughing fit she could, and dashed out of the classroom, down the hall, and into the bathroom. She checked the stalls to make sure she was alone before she released her grip on the little doll.

Augustine stood up on Trina's palm with her hands on her hips, madder than a swatted bee. "You have ruined everything."

"Me?"

"Yes, you. You left my best treasure behind. It was very heavy. I needed your help."

"I have it right here," Trina said, waving the barrette at her before shoving it into her shorts pocket. She wasn't sure who made her angrier at the moment—Charlotte for stealing Augustine, or Augustine for stealing Charlotte's things. "This whole time I thought Charlotte had you. I thought she might take you home. And then what would happen? It's all been fun and games for you, but I've been worried sick."

Augustine fumed. "Fun and games?" The little doll was so mad that she shook to the point of rattling. "That witch nearly crushed me in her fist. And it was everything I could do to escape her big satchel." Augustine pinched her nose and shook her head in disgust. "I jumped from precipice to precipice. I climbed heavy ropes and slithered in and out of a vast, dark cave. I would not call my endeavors fun by any means," Augustine said, stamping her foot on Trina's thumb.

Trina flinched on instinct, but she barely felt a thing. She figured the precipices were desktops and the dark cave had to be Charlotte's desk. "That must have been horrible for you, I'm sure. But Augustine," Trina pleaded, "why are you taking Charlotte's things?"

"I am revenging upon her."

Trina slumped to the cool bathroom floor and set Augustine down in front of her. "Augustine, you don't understand. If anyone finds out I have Charlotte's things, I'll get in a lot of trouble."

Augustine folded her arms. "That is the problem with you, Citrine. You are just like Snow White. Snow White was too nice to everyone and that is why she choked on a poisonous apple."

Trina stifled a laugh. It was impossible to be mad at Augustine for more than a few seconds. "That's true, but in the end, Snow White lived happily ever after."

"Only because her prince rescued her and shortly thereafter they were married in great splendor." Augustine smiled her winsome little smile. "Dearest Citrine, may I tell you a secret?"

"Of course. Tell me your secret." Trina leaned her ear close to Augustine.

"I am also to be married."

"Married! You?"

Augustine placed both hands at her cheeks and nodded with pure joy. "It is true. As soon as I kiss my prince and free him from his wicked spell, we will be married."

It took Trina a few seconds to understand who Augustine meant. "You mean Prince? The frog?"

Augustine spun in a circle, the back of her hand at her forehead. "Oh, Citrine, my heart aches at your words. How he longs to be free."

"He *is* free. No one can find him anywhere. He's lost."

"No, Citrine, he is not lost." Augustine cupped her hands at her mouth and spoke very softly. "I freed him from his dungeon and now he is in hiding."

"You mean *you're* the one who let him go?"

Augustine smiled demurely. "Oh, Citrine. He leapt with great surprise at the sight of me and broke free from his prison. He waits for me now." She held her hand to her tiny brow, searching high and low. "Although I am unsure where he awaits me."

Just then there was the sound of high heels in the hallway. Trina put her finger to her lips and watched the large gap between the floor and the door as the toes of prim gray shoes approached the bathroom. Down the hall a teacher's voice said, "Miss Lincoln, may I speak to you?" and the shoes turned and the footsteps faded away. As soon as Trina removed her finger from her lips, Augustine picked right up where she had left off.

"We must find my prince, Citrine."

"Augustine, he's five times as big as you are. If you get close enough to kiss him, he'll swallow you whole."

"Please, Citrine. You do not see him as I do." Augustine knelt on one knee and held out her delicate white hands to Trina. "I beg of you to give us this chance."

"But there's no such thing as a—" From the corner of her eye, Trina saw something move. Without turning her head, she watched Prince land in a small puddle under the sink. He must have sneaked under the door in search of water. Trina stayed calm and whispered, "Be very quiet, Augustine, and turn around."

Augustine whirled around and swooned. "My prince! You have come for me!" Her little doll arms motioned urgently to Trina. "Hurry, Citrine. Help me kiss him and set him free."

Poor Augustine. How could Trina tell her there was no such thing as a frog prince? She couldn't. Besides, Augustine would never believe her. Trina grabbed Prince with both hands and held him steady as Augustine reached up and fearlessly took the frog's fat cheeks in her delicate hands. Trina took a deep breath and pointed his slimy green lips at Augustine's face. When she bumped them together . . .

Nothing happened.

"Again, Citrine. Again!"

This time, Trina held the frog like a bottle of ketchup and aimed him downward at the little doll, who was standing on her tiptoes, trembling. Augustine closed her eyes and kissed the frog smack on his lips.

Again, nothing happened.

Augustine looked up at Trina with a worry-stricken face. "Citrine, do you think he is ill?"

Trina set the frog on the floor and wiped her hands on her shorts. "No, I think he's just a frog. A regular old frog."

Augustine's face fell, and her eyes glistened as if she might cry.

"Don't worry, Augustine. There will be other frogs. We just have to find the right one." Trina picked up Augustine and stroked her cheek. "I am so glad to have you back," she said as she tucked the doll into her pocket. "Don't worry, school gets out soon and then we get to go home."

"Now, just one minute." Augustine leaned over the edge of Trina's pocket. "First of all, your witch is not truly a witch. She is a giant. And if there is one thing I know about giants, it is this: they all have their weaknesses. Secondly, the giant thinks I am among her belongings. What if she finds out I am no longer in her possession? What will she do then?"

Augustine had a good point. Simply having the doll back in her pocket was not the end of the battle. Even though Charlotte had taken Augustine in the first place, if Trina kept the little doll, it might prove to Charlotte that she had gone through her things and stolen Mr. Nubby and her barrette. "I never thought of that," Trina said with a sinking feeling. "But give me your word you won't steal from her anymore," she said, shaking her finger at the doll. "I don't want to get in trouble for something I didn't do."

"I do not have to steal from her. You told the giant yourself that bad luck comes to those who steal from Goldenrod, did you not? And I am from Goldenrod." Augustine winked at Trina. "Now put me on the floor. I will find my way to the giant's satchel."

Contrary to what Trina thought best, she set Augustine on the floor. "But how will I get you back?"

"It is quite simple, Citrine. You will convince the giant to return me to you." Without another word, Augustine scurried across the bathroom floor as fast as a mouse and ducked beneath the swinging door.

"No!" Trina called, but Augustine was gone again, leaving her alone with the ugly bullfrog. Twice Prince escaped her reach until she cornered him in one of the stalls. She picked him up, water dripping from his webbed feet, and carried him into the classroom. "Look what I found."

"Prince!" Edward shouted, grabbing the frog. "All hail Citrine!" The whole class circled around Trina, chanting, "All hail Citrine!"—except Charlotte, who glowered from her seat.

The rest of the afternoon was as normal as could be. No escaped frogs and no bubble gum. But normal also meant no Augustine. Trina still had no idea how she would convince Charlotte to give the doll back to her. She probably blamed Trina for everything that had gone wrong, including the unlucky moment she stood by Edward when the bubble gum bubble popped. All Trina knew was that she couldn't go home without Augustine.

The little doll's words rolled through Trina's head. *I know of no good story where the maiden gives up. I know of no good story where the maiden gives up.* Trina looked up at the clock. It was almost three thirty and she hadn't come up with a single idea to save the doll. Maybe it wasn't *her* lucky day, either.

Lucky? Story? That was it!

When the bell finally rang and the kids grabbed their things and headed for the door, Trina stood up in Charlotte's path.

"What do you think you're doing, Latrine?"

Trina did her best to keep a straight face. "I just wanted to say, I think your shorter hair looks really nice."

"You can't fool me," Charlotte sneered. "All you want is your precious doll."

Trina couldn't let on that Charlotte was right, so she pretended she didn't care about Augustine. "That's okay. She's just a stupid doll. Besides, the gum in your hair and the brownie falling on your shirt was just a little bad luck. I'm sure it had nothing to do with Goldenrod. I mean, if you don't believe the legend, it wouldn't matter if you kept something that belonged to the house."

Charlotte didn't respond, so Trina said as calmly as possible, "See you next week," and then she turned around and walked up the aisle. As she got to the door she looked over her shoulder and added, "Maybe."

With one ear on Charlotte, Trina walked very slowly. Augustine's life could be on the line. Every second mattered. But her plan didn't seem to be working.

Trina was headed down the steps when Charlotte shouted, "Not so fast, Latrine." Trina stopped cold and turned around. Her insides churned and bubbled as Charlotte caught up to her.

"Hold out your hand, Latrine."

Could her idea be working after all?

Faking confusion, Trina extended her hand and held it steady with all her might as she watched Charlotte unzip the pouch of her backpack.

"Dolls are for babies," Charlotte said with disgust as she pulled out a messy Augustine and dropped her into Trina's sweaty palm.

"Oh, thanks," Trina said as if she hadn't been the least bit worried. But she closed her hand around Augustine before she let herself relax. Then she watched Charlotte's eyes flicker—as if a fuse had popped in her brain from thinking so hard when she figured out that Trina had outsmarted her.

Chapter Sixteen

"Augustine, I was so scared my idea wouldn't work," Trina said, skipping down the steps of the school as the doll bobbed in her pocket. The wind was so strong that Trina clamped her hand around her pocket to keep Augustine safe. "I was afraid the giant would keep you."

"You gave her no choice. Now you are the heroine, Citrine, for you did not give up."

"But I'm sure she's madder than ever, now. If she wants revenge, I'll need an escape plan."

Still, every time Trina thought of the bubble gum in Charlotte's hair, she started to laugh. As she got into her dad's idling truck, glad to be out of the wind, she knew she couldn't say much about the best worst day ever, but she couldn't stop thinking about it. *Bubble gum, Mr. Nubby, and Prince and the frog kiss.*

"How was your day?" her dad asked.

"Great," Trina said, giggling.

"What's so funny?" he said.

"Nothing." How could she tell her dad about Augustine kissing Prince, or how Augustine revenged herself on Charlotte, or how Trina herself had tricked Charlotte into handing over Augustine, without telling him *everything* about the little doll?

"Look at that." Trina said, pointing at a big gray cloud hanging just above the cornfields. It *was* a really big cloud, but mostly she wanted to change the subject.

"And look at this," he said. He pulled a postcard from the stack of mail sitting next to him and sailed it into Trina's lap. Then he leaned forward for a better view of the bulging cloud. "Looks like another big storm."

Her mother's timing was perfect. Trina's escape plan had landed right in her lap. She hoped for a picture of the Statue of Liberty or the Golden Gate Bridge—anything in the United States, one short plane ride away, just in case Charlotte came after her and she needed to get out of New Royal fast.

But the stamp, a white tiger, was too fancy and too foreign to be from anywhere local, and the postcard was a picture of the Taj Mahal. *Shoot.* India was halfway around the globe. Her mother would never make it to New Royal in time. At least it was Friday. Maybe Charlotte would forget the whole thing over the weekend and Trina wouldn't need an escape plan.

"She sure gets around fast." Trina sighed and then read the postcard to herself.

Dear Citrine,

India is a swirl of colors and music and home to the world-famous Taj Mahal. Imagine living in a house like this someday.

Love, Mom

The wind whipped so hard the truck swayed. "Man, when this storm hits, it's really going to be something." Her dad rolled up his window. "Where is she now?"

"India, but it seems impossible. Last time she was in Antarctica." All Trina had to do was look at the stamp to know her mother was in Asia. But something about this postcard didn't feel right.

"Nothing's impossible if you . . ." her dad said, switching on his headlights. He raised his eyebrows, waiting for a response. And then he nudged her along, "put . . . your . . . mind . . ."

". . . to it." Trina finally finished his sentence, but she said it out of habit. She was thinking about all the other postcards her mother had sent her over the years—skydiving over the Pacific Ocean, walking a tightrope in Russia, and mountain climbing in Africa—and picturing their colorful stamps. Her mother had been writing to her about doing crazy things all over the world and Trina had believed every single word.

Until now.

Trina looked out on the cornfields swaying in the wind. The brewing storm was nothing compared to the tornado churning inside her. She could feel its force sucking her up and turning her inside out.

Her dad glanced in the mirror as he shifted lanes to pass a slow-moving cattle truck. "What does she have to say?"

His voice sounded a million miles away. When the words finally reached her, Trina turned the postcard so he could see the picture. "It's the Taj Mahal. She says, *Imagine living in a house like this someday.*"

"She's got us there." He slapped the steering wheel, chuckling. "We've lived in a lot of houses, but we've never lived in one like that!"

Trina bit down on her lower lip and tried to hold her hands steady in her lap. She had written a report on the Taj Mahal last year. She knew all about it. And she knew it wasn't a house. It had never been a house. If her mother had really visited the Taj Mahal, she would know that too.

"I know what you're thinking," her dad said. "Maybe someday we should take a job in Timbuktu and really see the world."

No, that wasn't what she was thinking. As far as she was concerned, they already lived in Timbuktu. "Sure," she said, trying to remember something else. Trying to picture the stamp on the first postcard she ever received from her mom. The one of the Eiffel Tower. The one she got when she was three years old.

The sky grew darker and darker as they got closer to home, and lightning shimmered on the gray-green horizon. As they pulled up to Goldenrod, a jagged vein of light cracked the sky and lit up something bright and shiny in the yard.

Her dad shifted into park. "Look, it's an old oil lamp. And a table! Help me get them inside before this storm cuts loose."

"I can't, Poppo. I have to use the bathroom." She got

out of the truck, tucked herself against the wind, and ran past the oil lamp and the fancy table it sat on and went straight into the house and up the stairs to her room. She slammed her door, dropped her backpack by her bed, set Augustine on the floor of her parlor, and gathered the postcards from the mantel.

She flicked through the thick pile as fast as she could: Beijing, Moscow, London, Lima, the rain forest in Costa Rica. Happy Birthday, Happy Birthday, Be My Valentine. One by one she tossed the postcards with postage stamps of exotic animals and flowers to the floor like playing cards until she found the picture of the Eiffel Tower and turned it over. The stamp had nothing to do with France. It was the Liberty Bell. A US stamp with a US postmark. The postcard she thought she got from France had been mailed from Wisconsin.

Dear Citrine,
    I wish you were here with me, chasing doves and eating pastries. Someday I'll teach you how to speak French.
    Love, Mom

Trina picked up the postcard from Costa Rica. And then the one from Antarctica. The handwriting on those postcards matched. But the handwriting on the postcard of the Eiffel Tower was different from the handwriting on all the others. That postcard, she now realized, was in her dad's printing. It looked just like his scribbles in his notebook. What did it all mean?

The storm surged inside her. She kicked the pile of postcards on the floor with the sudden realization that not a single one had come from her mother. All those promises . . . No wonder "someday" never happened. Someday was *never* going to happen. She had read the postcards hundreds of times, but now the real message was as plain as day: her mother was never coming home. And she had never, ever written to her. Not once in almost eight years.

But why?

And how could Poppo do this to her?

Trina's head filled with questions until her thoughts were tied up in knots. She flopped down on her bed, buried her head in her pillow, and let the tears come, crying and crying until she felt the gentlest brush of her hair.

"What are you doing?" Augustine asked, standing on Trina's pillow, reaching high over her head to touch Trina's forehead.

Trina sniffed. "I'm crying."

"So this is crying?" Augustine craned her neck, curious to see more.

"Yes, this is crying," Trina said harshly to the doll, growing tired of having to explain everything she did. "Please leave me alone. I'm sad."

Augustine nodded a very knowing nod. "Ah, yes. I remember sadness. Sadness is when your things are taken away and everything becomes dark and quiet. Have you lost something important to you?"

Trina hugged her pillow tight and rocked. "Just my mother."

"Did you not receive word from your mother moments ago? Is she not living in a grand house? Is that not the story I heard from your pocket?"

"It's a story, all right. All those things she was supposed to be doing. The hot-air ballooning. The mountain climbing. That's all they were. Just stories."

"Do they have happy endings, these stories?"

Trina shook her head.

"Perhaps your mother is locked away in a castle and cannot escape. You must rescue her."

"Trust me," Trina said, wiping her eyes. "She is not locked up in a castle."

"Until you are certain your mother is lost to you forever, you must search for her. Remember, no stone unturned. Think of my own mother's return to me."

"You don't understand, Augustine. Everything I thought I knew about my mother is a lie. My father lied to me."

Aghast, Augustine clutched her chest. "Do you mean to tell me he betrayed you?"

Trina's eyes burned with tears. "Yes. For years." Her voice cracked as she said the words.

Augustine crouched and whispered in Trina's ear, "He is a trickster who cannot be trusted." Then she stood tall and put her hands on her hips. "I know of only one thing you can do."

Trina looked up, desperate for help, desperate to hear what the doll would say. Maybe she could help her. For someone so little, sometimes she was awfully wise. "You must run. Run to escape. Run to find your mother. Run like the Gingerbread Man. Run, run, as fast as you can."

Trina sniffed hard and wiped the tears from her eyes. Augustine was right. How could she trust someone who had told her lies her whole life? She had to run away. It was the only option.

Augustine pointed at the window as lightning snapped across the cornfield. "Be brave and valiant! Go!"

Trina no longer felt sad. She felt determined. She grabbed her Brewers baseball cap and pulled it on tight. Then she picked up the postcard of the Taj Mahal and stormed downstairs into the parlor, past the new oil lamp glowing on top of the fancy new table, and into the dining room, where she found her dad sitting at the big table, writing on a pad of paper.

"We need groceries," he said without looking up. "I should have picked them up while we were in town, but I didn't think of it. You want anything?"

Trina didn't answer. As the parlor window hummed in the strong wind, she slapped the postcard of the Taj Mahal in front of him, picture-side up.

"Isn't it something?" He turned it over, read the note, and smiled. But when he looked up at Trina and saw her wet eyes and runny nose as she stood there, waiting for an explanation, his smile disappeared.

He set down his pencil and put head in his hands.

"No one has ever lived in the Taj Mahal, Poppo. The emperor built it for his wife after she died. The Taj

Mahal isn't a house. It's a tomb. Everyone knows that." She reached in front of him and jabbed the postcard in its corner. "It even says so." The tears welled again. "My mother wasn't there. She didn't write this. I don't understand." She choked on her words. "How——?"

Her dad didn't move a muscle. Eventually he took a deep breath. "I sent the first one. And then my buddy, Matt, the pilot, remember how he——"

"I don't mean how you mailed the postcards, Poppo. I mean, how could you do this to me? Why?"

"Because . . ." He looked down at his grocery list for the longest time before he raised his eyes to meet hers. "Because you missed her. And you loved to get mail. You were so little . . ."

He stood up, reaching for her.

But Trina stepped back. "All this time. You made me think she was coming home."

"I know. I've been meaning to tell you. I just didn't know——"

"You lied to me!" Trina shouted as the tears returned. "Is anything I know about my mother true? Is her name really Caroline? Is her favorite color yellow? Were you really going to build her a dollhouse?" She caught her breath and looked back at the picture of the Taj Mahal, the most famous tomb in the whole world.

All at once the room started to spin. She could feel her mouth open, but she was unable to form any words. Was her mother lost to her forever? She had to know. "Is she . . . dead?"

Her dad's face turned white. "Oh, no, Trina. No, she's not dead. I never meant for you to think . . ."

Trina shook with anger. "Then why skydiving over the ocean? Why hot-air ballooning in New Zealand? Why such crazy ideas?"

He closed his eyes and hung his head. "Because all I know is carpentry." When he finally looked up he was fighting his own tears. "I wanted you to grow up thinking you could do anything."

Her dad was a master carpenter who could fix broken things, but he could never fix any of the things she really wanted—a home and a whole family and friends and a mother. "But you lied to me. How could you lie to me?"

"I didn't look at it like that. You were little—"

"But I'm not little anymore!" Trina shouted. "And I want to know where she is!"

He ran his hand through his hair and shook his head again and again. "I don't know. I really don't know."

Trina glared at him. "Are you at least trying to find her? Is that why we keep moving?"

His shoulders slumped. "No, Trina. It's not like that. I was just used to moving around, I guess. But I'm trying to change that now. For you. That's why I took this job. For once we get to put down roots. Make it our own . . . at least for a while."

"Roots?" Trina screamed. She couldn't stop herself. "Who'd want to put down roots in the middle of nowhere? Besides, Goldenrod doesn't belong to us, remember?" She picked up the postcard of the Taj Mahal, ripped it into pieces, and threw them at her dad. Then she stomped to the front door and turned the knob.

But the door wouldn't open.

"Trina, where are you going?"

"I don't want to live here anymore." Trina jiggled the lock and twisted the knob again, but the door still wouldn't open.

"Trina, please," her dad said.

"And don't call me Trina," she said, gripping the doorknob with both hands and giving it everything she had. But it still wouldn't budge. Now she wasn't mad at just her dad—she was mad at the house too. "Goldenrod, if you want me to help you, open this door!"

The wind gusted outside and the house creaked. Air gasped in the chimney. And then all the lights went out except for the new oil lamp sitting in the parlor window. Trina jumped at the sudden darkness, but she wasn't going to give up. Not now. "Please, Goldenrod. Help me!" With one more jiggle and pull, the door finally opened. "Thank you," she whispered, stepping outside, and then she closed the door behind her until it clicked shut.

She stood on the front steps, clinging to the banister to stay upright in the wind. The porch swing rocked and squeaked. Leaves on the old oak tree turned their silvery sides to the wind as others fell like heavy rain. Behind her the doorknob twisted and clinked, and then the door thunked with the heavy clunk of her dad's boot. She knew he was trying to follow her, but the door wouldn't open for him. "Thank you, Goldenrod," she whispered again.

Run, run as fast as you can.

Trina dashed down the steps, across the yard, through the gate, and into the sliver of black dirt road that ran between the swaying cornfields, running straight into the oncoming storm. The heavy sky opened and cold rain slammed her skin. Cornstalks swished all around her, and her tennis shoes, instantly wet, squeaked with every slippery step. If she were racing Edward now, she'd lose for sure.

"Tree-nah!" she heard her dad call. And then, "Ci-tree-een!"

But she didn't turn back. She ran until Goldenrod was far behind her and the road was turning into mud. Panting as she neared the wooden bridge, she stopped to catch her breath. The creek was rising fast. Water was already pooling at the base of the bridge. When she took a step forward, her foot sank in the mud. When she pulled it out, the other pushed in deeper, and she sank nearly to her knee.

Afraid she'd sink to her waist with the next step, she sat down. As the sludge released her ankles, she crawled backward as fast as she could beyond the reach of the flooding creek. The dark sky flashed with spears of light and the ground rolled with thunder. She looked from the bridge to the swaying walls of corn. Maybe the Gingerbread Man could get away, but she was trapped. She had no choice but to turn around.

Reluctantly, she changed direction and headed for Goldenrod. The wind was now at her back as she stumbled along the rutted, muddy road, covering her eyes and then her ears. She was relieved when she finally caught sight of the yellow glow of the new oil lamp in the distance, but then she was mad all over again. She was mad at the storm for making the creek rise and stopping her from running away. She was mad at her dad for lying. And she was mad at herself for being so stupid. How could she have believed for even a second that her mother was traveling the world until she was ready to come home?

Suddenly the yellow glow from the oil lamp was gone. Trina slowed.

In the next second, Trina heard the slam of her dad's truck door. The engine revved and red taillights flicked on. Her dad was coming to look for her. But she was not ready to be found.

When the wind pushed her forward, she let herself fall between the cornstalks, out of sight. She stayed there, hidden, as her dad's truck raced by, headlights bobbing and the wipers flying across his windshield in the pouring rain. She waited until she heard the truck rumble across the bridge before she crawled out of the cornfield.

Eventually, if her dad didn't find her on the road, he would turn around and come back. What would she do then? He would want to talk to her, but she wanted to be alone. As she passed through the gate, she spotted the one place she could hide. She wiped the mud from her arms and legs, opened the back end of the trailer, and crawled inside, cold, wet, and defeated.

She nestled herself in some old packing blankets bundled in the corner and soon her hide-out became stuffy and warm. She didn't mind that it was pitch-black inside the trailer; it was safe and familiar. She swore she could smell all the places they had ever lived: spicy pine trees from Colorado; dry, dusty earth from New Mexico; and lots of salty breezes from Oregon.

The trailer was the closest thing she had to home.

Chapter Seventeen

Trina woke up with a start in the dark trailer, wondering if the voices she heard were from a dream, or if the whooshing of wind and rain was playing with her imagination. She had no idea how long she'd been asleep. She crawled out of her nest of blankets and cracked open the trailer door for a peek outside. The storm had ebbed and the moon was struggling to show itself between the dark clouds. But if it wasn't raining, then the voices she heard—

"See, I told you she doesn't live here." A girl's voice, deep but breathless. *Charlotte!* Trina put her hand to her mouth to keep from gasping. "The lights are off and there's no car," Charlotte said.

Metal clanked as wet tennis shoes sloshed and squeaked outside the trailer. "I think she's telling the truth." A boy's voice. *Edward!* But what in the world were Charlotte and Edward doing together after a day like today?

Charlotte said something else and Trina strained to hear, opening the trailer door a little more. It gave a rusty squeak.

"What was that?" Charlotte said.

Trina held her breath. Then she heard the porch swing creak.

"Just that old swing," Edward said. "Here, lean your bike against this tree. Next to mine." The porch swing creaked again. "Geez. You sure picked a great night for a bike ride. I bet you ten bucks the storm starts up again."

"Then what are you waiting for?" Charlotte said. "You have the flashlight. Go in."

"Me go in? What about you?" Trina was impressed by how Edward could stand up to Charlotte. But what were they doing here?

"I'm the one who dared you. Besides, you owe me," Charlotte said.

"You're too scared, aren't you? Charlotte's a scaredy cat. Charlotte's a scaredy—"

"I am not. It's just a stupid old house."

Trina cringed, hoping Goldenrod couldn't hear. As the voices faded, she stuck her head out the trailer door. The air was strangely warm and still. She looked toward the house and spotted Charlotte and Edward, a pair of black figures on the porch. Edward had his flashlight aimed at the front door. He turned the knob and to Trina's surprise, the door opened easily. Edward and Charlotte sneaked inside the dark house like cat burglars.

Trina had an idea. If the Dare Club was being resurrected, she could help Goldenrod scare them away. And what better way to get even with Charlotte?

Trina wrapped herself in one of the old packing blankets and climbed out of the trailer. Keeping low to the ground, she scurried across the yard, crept up the porch steps, and waited, crouching low outside the open front door.

Charlotte and Edward were in the foyer, talking in whispers. The flashlight beam moved from the stairway in the foyer to the dining room archway. As Charlotte and Edward neared the fireplace in the parlor, Trina sneaked into the foyer and kicked the front door shut.

SLAM!

Charlotte screamed.

"Shh!" Edward hushed her. "Do you want someone to hear us?"

"Yes," Charlotte's shaky voice answered. "I want someone to save us."

Their footsteps shuffled in the dark. The beam of light turned and bounced from the parlor floor to the banister to the baseboards, across their wet footprints toward the front door. Trina hid beneath the dark blanket and pressed herself flat against the wall, hoping she wouldn't be seen.

"See. The front door blew shut. That's all." Edward was spitting distance from Trina now, but he didn't see her.

"We did it. We made it inside. Now let's go home," Charlotte said.

"But we just got here," Edward scoffed as he pointed the light at the staircase. "Let's go upstairs."

"No!" Charlotte shrieked. "We already proved she doesn't live here. Nobody lives here. The house is empty."

"We should look for food in the refrigerator," Edward said, and Trina could hear his footsteps moving away from her. "C'mon. If they live here, they'll have food." He moved through the parlor toward the dining room. Charlotte's footsteps finally followed.

With Charlotte and Edward headed for the dining room, Trina knew it was the perfect chance to make her move. She tiptoed across the foyer and then she scurried all the way to the smoking room and felt the wall for the secret doorknob to the secret passageway. She wrapped the blanket tightly around her, made her way between the rooms in the dark, turned the knob as silently as possible, and opened the door to the dining room. The flashlight beam just missed her as it swept past the French doors.

"The kitchen must be somewhere over here," Edward said. And then their footsteps stopped and the massive mahogany table lit up. "Milk, sandpaper, bread, nails, oatmeal, and chocolate pudding," Edward read from a list. "And a picture of an igloo taped together. See, Charlotte? They do too live here."

"That's not an igloo, you dope. That's the Taj Mahal. You better sharpen up if you want Latrine to like you."

Latrine. Trina steamed beneath her blanket.

"So that's it," Edward said, shining the light in Charlotte's face. "You're jealous of her."

Charlotte put her hand over the flashlight, which made her face look incredibly creepy. "Why would I be jealous of a wimpy know-it-all?"

Revenge. It was sounding better than ever as Trina huddled in the dark, waiting to make her next move.

"I think she's nice. And she's not afraid of anything. She helped me catch a ton of flies for Prince's dinner."

Wow. Edward was sticking up for her. To Charlotte, of all people. But if he liked her, then what was he doing here? Was he planning to steal something?

"So what?" Charlotte said. "That doesn't mean—"

Trina shifted the blanket around her and the floor-board creaked beneath her feet.

Charlotte stopped in the middle of whatever she was saying.

"Let go of my arm," Edward yelled, yanking it free. In the tussle, the flashlight smacked to the floor and rolled away, blinking out when it came to a stop.

The house was pitch-black and silent.

No one moved.

No one breathed.

The time for revenge was now.

"WOO-HA-HA," Trina howled in her deepest, scari-est voice, waving her arms under the blanket like an enor-mous bat as she ran across the dining room and swooped around Charlotte and Edward, but mostly Charlotte. "WOO-HA-HA!"

"Help!" Charlotte screamed. "Help!" Trina chased Charlotte around and around in the dark. The wet floor squeaked. Charlotte fell. A yowl. She scrambled to her feet and ran through the parlor to the front door. The door-knob twisted and clinked.

"It won't open!" Charlotte screamed.

Edward went running after her.

Trina smiled to herself, pretty sure Goldenrod was holding the door shut.

"Let me try," Edward said.

Thumps and kicks resounded, and more twisting of

the doorknob, but Goldenrod wouldn't let them go.

"YOU BELONG TO ME!" Trina roared, sweeping into the foyer.

Charlotte screamed again. And then lightning flashed. In that millisecond, Trina could see them both cowering by the front door as thunder rumbled over the house. But if she could see them, they could see her. Lightning flashed again.

"Citrine, is that you?" Edward yelled.

"I AM THE MIGHTY CITRINE," Trina howled. And then she started to giggle.

"I'm telling my grandma!" Charlotte yelled.

"You can't or she'll know we were here," Edward shouted over the thunder.

"You shouldn't scare people like that, Citrine. It's mean!"

Trina could hear tears at the edge of Charlotte's voice, but that didn't stop her. She threw off the heavy wool blanket and said, "Then what are you doing sneaking into my house?"

"It's not your house. It belongs to the Roy family. You're just fixing it up so someone else can live here." Trina might have apologized for scaring Charlotte if Charlotte hadn't turned right back into her nasty self. Now she was glad she had given Charlotte a taste of her own medicine.

"At least I'm not afraid to live here," Trina said.

"That's different," Charlotte said. "You have to live here."

"Then why are *you* here?" Trina asked, even though she already knew.

"We're here because we had a bet," Charlotte said.

"Wait a minute," Edward said. "You mean *you* had a bet. You're the one who wants that old coffee can of money and you know it. And you didn't want Citrine to do something you couldn't."

"That's not true," Charlotte stammered. "My grandma has talked about this house my whole life. I wanted to see if it really was haunted."

The house lights flickered on the word *haunted*. In those few seconds of light, Trina spotted the flashlight on the floor across the room. "You could have asked to come in," she said. And then she couldn't resist taking her prank a little further. "Of course, if Goldenrod lets you stay, she'll want you to mind your manners."

"What does that mean?" Charlotte asked, sounding alarmed again.

"Goldenrod wouldn't want you to call her a stupid old house—or break in, uninvited."

"But I didn't mean it like that." Charlotte's voice was shaking again.

It was easy to stand up to Charlotte in the dark, so Trina kept going. "The truth is, she wouldn't want you to call anybody any names, like Latrine or wimpy know-it-all or dope." She looked toward the shadow of Edward.

"Yeah," Edward said.

"But I was just kidding," Charlotte said.

"Goldenrod didn't think it was very funny. That's why she held the door shut."

"Maybe we should go home now, Charlotte," Edward said. "Where's my flashlight?"

"I'll get it," Trina said. She hurried toward the dining room, found the flashlight on the floor, and was hitting it against her palm as she returned to the foyer. The bulb blinked on and then off, leaving them in the dark again, with the wind howling and thunder rolling in.

Squeak.

Creak.

Charlotte grabbed hold of Trina's arm. "What was that?"

"It sounded like it came from upstairs," Edward said.

"It sounded like the attic door," Trina said. "My dad says old houses creak with the weather and make all kinds of noises. That's why people think they're haunted. Right, Goldenrod?"

Charlotte tightened her squeeze on Trina's arm. "Are you talking to the house?"

"Yes," Trina said.

Bump . . .

Bump . . .

Bump . . .

"What's that noise?" Charlotte asked.

Trina didn't answer. She was concentrating on the noise; she had never it heard before.

"It sounds like someone coming down the stairs," Edward said, moving closer to Trina and Charlotte. "Someone really small."

The hair on Trina's arms began to stand on end, but she was more confused than she was scared. She had made up the story about a ghost walking the halls. Goldenrod hadn't scared her in a long time—not since the day in the library when Trina figured out Goldenrod was sad and frightened. And it couldn't be Augustine. It was night-time; she would be sound asleep. Besides, Augustine was too small to make that much noise. What in the world was coming down the stairs?

Bump . . .

Bump . . .

Bump . . .

Bump . . .

That mysterious feeling was back again. Trina wasn't afraid, but something was wrong. She had the feeling Goldenrod was urgently trying to show her something again, and she just couldn't understand.

Bump.

Bump-bumP-buMP-bUMP . . .

BUMP!

And then, whatever it was stopped.

Close enough to breathe on them.

Trina pounded the flashlight against her fist. She shook it and twisted the handle and finally its small bulb glimmered. She pointed it toward the sound. There, sitting at the bottom of the stairs, barely visible in the dimming light, was the striped red ball, the one that had been in the attic.

Why did Goldenrod want her to see the ball? And why now? She had found the ball days ago. And how did it get out of the attic anyway? Did Poppo leave the door open? Or was it possible Annie Roy really did walk the halls?

"It's just a ball," Edward said. "I'm not afraid of a ball." He ran up to it and kicked it into the dining room.

It bumped against one of the folding chairs, but it didn't roll back.

Zaa-huh-zaa-huh.

The breathing noise? What did it mean? Trina's mind was racing, trying to put all the pieces of the puzzle together. What was going on with Goldenrod?

"Is that the ghost?" Charlotte whispered.

"You mean you can hear that?" Trina asked. "My dad has never been able to hear it."

"It sounds like someone sighing really far away," Edward said. The sighing sound drifted through the house.

"You're just tricking us, aren't you?" Charlotte ran for the front door again and pulled on the doorknob. When the door didn't open, she kicked it.

Outside, the storm raged. Lightning flashed and thunder rumbled around them like a hundred combines.

"I'll open it," Trina said, but no matter how she fiddled with the knob, the door wouldn't open. Except this time she didn't understand why. Why would the house want Charlotte and Edward to stay?

"Goldenrod," she begged, as if she could actually see the dusty old lady she'd only sensed blocking her way when she entered the house the first time. "Please."

Zaa-huh-zah-huh, the air responded.

"What is it, Goldenrod? Tell me!" Trina asked desperately.

This time the air did not respond, but the French doors did. They burst open with a loud creak in a gust of wind. "I think she wants us out of the house. Follow me! This way!" Trina shouted. She ran through the parlor and into the dining room. The French doors were swinging wildly on their hinges, open and shut, open and shut, beckoning them outside.

Trina ran around the dining room table and out through the French doors, with Edward and Charlotte dashing after her.

Outside, Trina kept the lead, running through the sodden field, stalks of goldenrod grabbing at her legs. When she glanced back at Edward and Charlotte, she felt the hair on her head lift for the sky.

"Down!" Edward shouted. He charged for Trina's knees, tackling her as he grabbed Charlotte's hand and pulled her to the ground with them.

Down Trina went, slapping into the wet weeds. Charlotte landed on Trina and Edward landed on Charlotte, pushing all the air out of Trina's lungs. A second later, lightning burst from the menacing clouds and the field lit up like a sunny afternoon—and then a booming crash shook everything around them.

They lay there in a heap of legs and arms. Wedged under Charlotte, Trina wheezed, "I can't breathe."

"Edward, get off my leg," Charlotte said, and slowly they untangled themselves.

The lightning had struck so close, Trina was certain Goldenrod would be on fire. She sat up as quickly as she could and looked at the big old house. Between the shifting clouds, in a haze of moonlight, Goldenrod's majestic outline stood tall. No flames were licking at the roof. And the turret was still intact. Trina breathed a sigh of relief but she couldn't take her eyes off the grande dame. She hadn't been destroyed, but something about her was different. Something Trina couldn't explain.

"Is that all the thanks I get for saving your lives? We almost got struck by lightning," Edward complained.

"I had no idea what was happening," Trina said, finally catching her breath. She used a big rock next to her to push herself up and stopped when she noticed it was a flat slab of stone. She immediately knew what it was Goldenrod had been trying to tell her. "Of course," she said. She saw the flashlight glowing in the weeds near her foot. She reached for it and shined the light on the stone.

Charlotte crouched next to Trina, and Edward leaned over her shoulder. "Of course, what?" Edward said.

"It's a gravestone," Trina said.

Chapter Eighteen

"Whose grave?" Charlotte muttered, gripping Trina so tightly Trina could hardly move.

"Her grave," Trina whispered, wiping the tombstone with the palm of her hand, reading the worn inscription. "Annie Roy's."

Charlotte squeezed Trina's arm even tighter. "You mean we're in a graveyard?"

"No, we're in the East Garden," Trina said. "Listen to this: *Annie Roy, darling daughter, aged six years.*"

Trina ran her fingers in the curves of the letters. "Now it all makes perfect sense."

Edward stood up, brushing mud and leaves from his knees. "Who in the world is Annie Roy?"

Charlotte gave Edward a shove. "Don't you ever listen? Annie Roy was the little girl who used to live here." She turned to Trina. "She's the ghost, isn't she? That's who we heard breathing."

Trina felt a calmness sweep through her. "I don't think so," Trina said. "My dad says there's no such thing. And I think he's right. All the scary noises have logical explanations like radiators heating up or pipes rattling." An image flashed through her mind—of gates and paths and partygoers—but instead the field was dotted with stakes for the new septic system. She could see them in the shadows. No wonder Goldenrod was scared. If they had never found Annie's grave, it would have been dug up by the septic company and Annie would have been lost forever.

"Explain why she's buried out here," Edward demanded. "Why isn't she in the Roy family plot at the cemetery with everybody else?"

Trina thought back to Mr. Kinghorn's story about how they found Mrs. Roy wandering in the garden after Annie died. "I bet her parents couldn't bear to have her so far away from them." For the first time all night, since she ran from the house into the storm, Trina felt guilty. Her own dad was still out looking for her.

"She sure is a long way from them now," Edward said.

"I bet she's lonely without them," Charlotte said.

Trina was surprised to think she might have loneliness in common with the meanest girl in fifth grade. "I bet you're right."

"Girls are crazy," Edward said.

"I think you're crazy." Charlotte lunged for Edward again, but this time, as he ducked out of the way, he lost his balance and tumbled backward into the tall weeds.

A loud "Ow" was followed by a frantic rustle. When he sat up, he was holding the striped ball.

Charlotte gasped.

Before Trina could react, Edward had put down the ball and was yanking a handful of weeds from the ground.

"Hey! Give me the flashlight. I think I found another grave." Edward shined the flashlight on another flat slab of stone. *"Toby, our eternal best friend."*

"Toby was Annie's dog!" Trina cried, leaning in to see better.

"Then that's why she's buried here. They must have buried her by her dog so she wouldn't be all alone." Edward handed the flashlight back to Trina and picked up the ball. "Mystery solved."

"But what about the ball? How'd it get out here? How do you explain that?" Charlotte asked.

Trina knew the ball was Goldenrod's way of leading her to the graves, but she also knew Charlotte and Edward would never believe her if she said it out loud. "Maybe Annie wanted to play with us? Maybe she felt left out."

"Maybe," Charlotte said.

Edward snorted and dropped the ball into the weeds. "We better get home, Charlotte, before your grandma—"

Thunder rolled in the distance, followed by a streak of lightning. "You can't go anywhere in this weather," Trina said. "You'll have to spend the night." She stood up and headed for the French doors.

"Do you think it's safe?" Charlotte asked.

"I know it's safe." But Trina didn't want to let her off the hook too easily. "That is, as long as you follow Goldenrod's rules." Trina tried not to sound too gleeful.

But Charlotte seemed to have gotten over her fear. "Edward." Her voice brimmed with excitement. "Think about it. We'll be the first kids in something like . . . four generations to spend the whole night at Goldenrod. We'll win the dare!"

"Yeah, right," Edward said. "Until your grandma finds your pillows in your bed and comes looking for you."

"How did you even get out here, anyway?" Trina asked. "The creek flooded the road."

Edward pointed toward the apple trees. "The old path there. Through the cornfields. Goes all the way into town."

"We didn't want anyone to see us," Charlotte said.

A secret path. Of course there would be a secret path. There was secret everything in New Royal. How else would the Dare Club's members have come and gone from Goldenrod without a secret path?

As the rain started coming down again, the three of them hurried into the dark house. Trina shut the French doors and made sure the lock was secure.

"I'll get a light," she said. She got a match from the kitchen cupboard, lit the wick on the oil lamp, and carried it to the dining room table. The lamp lit up the wall in a semicircle, like a warm, yellow smile.

"Wait 'til you see all the stuff I have on the house," Trina said. "I'll be back in a second." She left the oil lamp with them and picked up Edward's flashlight. In its fading beam she made her way to the library where she kept the photo album and Mr. Kinghorn's scrapbook and brought them to the dining room table.

Edward opened up the album and flipped through the pages. "Look, there's Toby," he said.

Trina pointed at the picture. "Look what he's chasing."

"The ball," Edward said. "In the East Garden."

"That's creepy," Charlotte said as she unfolded a newspaper clipping. A newspaper clipping Trina had somehow missed. "Listen to this: *The annual Harvest Moon Masquerade Ball will be held at Goldenrod Saturday evening, the seventh of October. Mr. and Mrs. Roy request that guests dress as their favorite literary characters in honor of the new library.*"

"What's a harvest moon?" Trina asked.

"It's a full moon . . . at harvest time . . . when the corn is ready." Edward looked up from the photos. "This year it's the last week of September. Duh. Everybody knows that."

"You mean, everybody who isn't a city kid," Charlotte said with a sneer, although it was a friendlier sneer than usual.

"Look," Trina said, reaching in front of Edward to turn the page of the photo album. "From here on, all the pages are blank."

"Why?" Edward asked.

"Because Annie died," Trina said.

"That's sad," Charlotte said, just as footsteps sounded on the porch. Charlotte and Edward didn't move, but Trina headed instantly for the foyer, wondering why she hadn't seen headlights coming though the cornfield. When the front door pushed open, her dad stepped in. Wide-eyed and covered in mud, he was squeezing her baseball cap so tightly water dripped on the floor. Trina touched her head, trying to remember where she would have lost her hat.

As soon as he saw her, his frantic look changed to a look of tremendous relief. He rushed to Trina and lifted her off the floor, nearly crushing her with his muddy hug as he twirled her around the room. "Thank God you're okay," he said. "Thank God." Trina could hear the worry in his voice, which made her feel guilty again, and his hug felt safe and good. Still, she was glad Charlotte and Edward couldn't see her all the way from the dining room as her dad twirled her around and around.

When he finally set her down, he went to the front door and hollered out, "You were right! She's in here!" Then to Trina, "I drove all the way into town and couldn't find you anywhere. On my way back, I found Carrie—I mean, Miss Dale—and Miss Kitty stuck in the mud on their way out here. They assured me they hadn't passed you on the road. I hauled their car out of the mud with the truck and they followed me here, sure that this is where you'd be."

Miss Kitty came up the porch steps and stepped across the threshold, clearly too afraid to go any deeper into the darkened house. She looked nervously around the foyer as if she might need to make a quick getaway. For some reason she was carrying an old flour sack, which seemed to weigh a ton.

Miss Dale followed, clutching her purse with her good arm. The two of them huddled together under the chandelier in the foyer until Trina's dad lit the gas sconce on the wall. Then he led them through the parlor and into the dining room.

Trina was anticipating the moment Miss Kitty would spot Charlotte, when Edward sneezed. Miss Kitty yelped and dropped her flour sack. It clanged so loudly it sounded like a bag full of chains. She reeled around and around, like a scared cat on the lookout, until she recognized Charlotte lurking in the shadows of the dining room.

"Just what do you think you're doing way out here on a night like this, Miss Charlotte?" Miss Kitty took a step forward, waggling her finger at Charlotte. "You took your bike out here, didn't you? In this terrible weather, no less! And you were snooping around, weren't you? Did you take anything? Because we sure don't need any more bad luck than what we've already got."

Charlotte shook her head so hard her red hair flew straight out from her head.

Miss Kitty put her hands on her hips and huffed. "I thought you went to bed awfully early." Miss Kitty paused. The shadowy light did nothing to hide the angry look on her face. "You stuffed your bed with pillows, didn't you?"

Miss Dale put her arm around Miss Kitty as if to corral her anger. "Charlotte, what your grandma is trying to say is she was worried about you because she did the same thing when she was your age. Aren't you, Aunt Kitty? That's all you talked about the whole way out here."

When Edward snickered, Miss Kitty pointed her finger at him. "Just because I did it doesn't mean it's okay. You understand me?" Miss Kitty glared at him. "Do your parents know you're out here?" Edward's snicker disappeared and he shook his head.

"They weren't snooping around, Miss Kitty." The lie came out of nowhere, but Trina couldn't think of any other way to calm her down.

"Then tell me what they were doing that they had to sneak out here to do it. Why couldn't Charlotte come right out and tell me?"

Trina looked at Charlotte and Edward, then at Miss Dale and Miss Kitty and lastly at her dad, trying to concoct a story to keep Charlotte and Edward, and maybe herself, out of trouble. "Poppo," she said, "this is Edward. And this is Charlotte." She looked her dad straight in the face, hoping he would remember. "Charlotte is Miss Kitty's granddaughter," she emphasized. "I asked them to come over to help me solve a mystery."

"Ah," he said, nodding, and Trina could tell he was trying to put the pieces together. "Nice to meet you." He let it sink in for a moment and added, "How about we all sit down so we can have a good talk about what's going on."

Miss Kitty plopped down in one of the folding chairs at the dining room table. She ran her hand across the polished top as though she recognized it, and then said, "A mystery? Really? I'm all ears. And it better be a good one."

"Just a minute," Trina's dad said. "Let's get some coffee on and let me wash up a bit."

"Do you have any tea?" Miss Dale asked, taking a seat next to Miss Kitty.

"I can make goldenrod tea," Trina said, suddenly glad she had picked such a big batch for Augustine's tea parties.

"That would be lovely," Miss Dale said.

As the rest of the group sat quietly in the dining room, Trina rushed around the kitchen by the light of her dad's flashlight, and her dad washed up in the bathroom in the dark. She put a big pan of water on the stove to boil and got out six of their new blue coffee cups, six plastic spoons, and the pretty tray, and she arranged a plate of vanilla wafers. She was glad to have a house full of company; that way she didn't have to talk to her dad about her mom, or about running away, or about their big fight. And the last thing she wanted to do was talk to her dad without talking to Augustine first. She wondered what Augustine would say when she learned Trina had come back home.

When the water had boiled, her dad made a pot of instant coffee, and Trina made the goldenrod tea. She poured the tea into the new blue teapot, refilled the sugar bowl, and poured milk into a little blue pitcher. Together they carried everything to the dining room. It was almost like having a real party, except Trina and her dad had to stand because there weren't enough chairs.

Edward was the first to try the tea with a big slurp. "This is good. It tastes like a dandelion smells."

Miss Kitty held her coffee cup with both hands and took a sip. Trina noticed her hands were shaking a little, but her voice was strong when she said, "So, Miss Citrine, let's hear about this mystery of yours."

Trina had so much to tell, she didn't know where to begin, so she started with day one. She described what had happened with the fireplace flue and the furnace. She told them about finding Augustine and her dollhouse in the secret turret room—although she didn't mention that Augustine could talk—and finding Augustine's mother in the drain, and all about finding the album and ball in the attic. She told them about Mr. Kinghorn and the scrapbook and the original house plans, and she told them about Annie Roy dying so young. "I told Edward and Charlotte that the house made strange noises and they could come over any time they wanted to help me figure out why."

Charlotte's eyes were practically bugging out at the story, especially the part about the invitation to come over whenever she wanted, but Edward jumped to his feet and started reenacting the whole scene.

"We got here and it was pitch-black and we couldn't see anything," Edward said, leaving the dining room and gesturing for everyone to come with him. His audience steered clear of the flour sack in the middle of the floor and followed him into the foyer, spellbound. "Something went bump on the stairs and a ball bounced down the steps all by itself and rolled to a stop. Right here." He stood a few feet away from the bottom step of the staircase.

"Was it a striped ball?" Trina's dad asked.

"Yes," Charlotte said. "It came down the stairs like someone had pushed it." She sounded scared all over again and Trina saw her step closer to Miss Kitty.

"The only strange thing about that ball is that it's still full of air," Trina's dad said. "I found it in the attic and stuck it up in the rafters the first time I went up there. The wind must have dislodged it."

Maybe the wind had knocked the ball free and blown open the attic door, but Trina knew there was more to the story. After all, something helped her find the album and

Augustine in the attic, and the ball *had* rolled outside and into the East Garden and stopped right next to Annie's and Toby's graves.

Miss Kitty looked around the foyer as if something might jump out at her. "Where's the ball now?"

"Outside!" Edward led the group back into the dining room and pointed through the French doors. "Out there. Right by the graves."

"Graves?" Miss Kitty plopped back down in a folding chair as if her legs had given out from under her. "You mean dead bodies are all around us?" Even Miss Dale's eyes flashed wider than usual.

"No," Trina said. "Just Annie's. And her dog's." Trina turned to her dad. "Annie is buried in the East Garden, Poppo. Right where you're thinking of putting the new septic system."

Her dad walked to the French doors and cupped his hands to the glass. He shook his head. "Wow. We're really lucky you found them when you did. The workmen come next Tuesday, but the graves will have to be moved first."

Lucky, Trina thought to herself. There wasn't a single bit of luck involved. It was all Goldenrod's doing. Goldenrod had led her right to the graves. She looked around the dimly lit room. Not one thing about Goldenrod scared her anymore, because in that moment Trina knew the answers to her questions. *If Goldenrod wasn't haunted, why would she scare people away?* Because she was protecting Annie Roy. *And why were Trina and her dad allowed to stay?* Because Goldenrod needed their help.

"So Annie Roy is a ghost. And that's why you hear things in the night," Miss Kitty said.

"Yup," Edward chimed in. "That's why the house is haunted."

Trina's dad put his hand on Edward's shoulder. "If I've said it once, I've said it a million times. There's no such thing as a haunted house."

Right on cue, the downstairs toilet flushed itself. Edward jumped as Miss Kitty gripped the table. Charlotte flung herself into Miss Dale's arms. "It's just a leaky valve," Trina said. She figured Goldenrod was trying to agree with her dad when Miss Kitty spoke up.

"There are 397 people in this town who think there is such a thing as a haunted house, Mr. Mike. As one of them, I'm not going to take any chances." She slapped the dining room table. "Charlotte, I have half a mind to ground you 'til the cows come home, but . . ."

Trina was so afraid of what Miss Kitty might say next, she couldn't help coming to Charlotte's rescue. "Wait a minute, Miss Kitty. If you thought Charlotte was home in her bed, why are you here?"

Miss Dale gulped, but then she smiled at Trina.

"Because . . . I . . . uh . . ." Miss Kitty looked around the room nervously. She glanced at her flour sack sitting in the middle of the floor and up at Trina. And then she turned to Miss Dale for help.

"Aunt Kitty and I were talking about all the stories about the house over the years—"

"And Carrie," Miss Kitty interrupted, "she got so

scared, she decided she couldn't wait another minute to make amends and bring back something that belongs to this house. Right, Carrie?"

"Right, Aunt Kitty," Miss Dale said, winking at Trina. "So I guess I'll go first." Miss Kitty helped Miss Dale open her purse, and then Miss Dale reached inside and brought out a bundle of worn cloth tied with a thin white ribbon and laid it on the dining room table. Her pink fingernails peeked from her bandage as she untied the ribbon with both hands. Everyone huddled around her. "My mother gave this to me—"

"Because her grandmother gave it to your grandmother," Miss Kitty interjected. "She didn't steal it, mind you. She found it in the garden when her mother came to dig up a few daisies." Trina covered her mouth to keep from gasping. Even the flowers had been stolen, but Miss Kitty didn't seem to realize that as she talked. "Go on now, Carrie. Don't be so shy," Miss Kitty said.

"When you brought the doll to school, Citrine, I knew I needed to give this one back. I knew they belonged together." Miss Dale peeled back the last corner of cloth to reveal a small porcelain doll dressed in black trousers and a white shirt. The doll had a dark brown mustache to match his dark hair.

"Augustine's father," Trina whispered. Augustine had a whole family again. Just like that.

Miss Dale handed the doll to Trina. "I kept him in a drawer and never played with him. I was afraid he might break." Miss Dale placed her hand on her chest as if to slow down her heart. "I have to admit, I feel a lot better now that I know he's home where he belongs."

Trina cradled the fine gentleman in her hands as if he were a soap bubble that might pop and vanish into thin air, and then she set him down safely in the middle of the dining room table.

"Have you had a lot of bad luck, Miss Dale?" Edward asked.

"Just with basement steps, apparently," Miss Kitty said, patting Miss Dale's bandaged arm ever so gently. "And boyfriends."

Miss Dale's face turned pinker than her nail polish. Charlotte giggled, Edward gave a little snicker, and Trina's dad looked down at his feet. But Trina felt embarrassed for the nicest teacher she had ever known.

Before Miss Kitty could say anything more, Miss Dale jumped in. "Aunt Kitty, why don't you take your turn, and then we should get going. The storm seems to be over."

Miss Kitty pointed across the room. "Edward, grab me that flour sack." Then she patted her knees. "Put it right here."

Edward jumped up to obey Miss Kitty. "This is heavy," he said, lugging it across the room and hoisting it into Miss Kitty's lap. He tried to open the drawstring.

"Don't go peeking in it," Miss Kitty said. "It's not yours." She opened up the flour sack and reached inside. "I didn't take this, I'll have you know," she said as she pulled a book from the sack. "Jerry Binty did, rest his soul. He gave it to me for my sixteenth birthday, but I know it came from here. Got Annie Roy's name right inside the cover."

Trina leaned in and read the title: *Andersen's Fairy Tales.* Augustine would be thrilled.

"And then there's this," Miss Kitty said, pulling out a red coffee can with both hands. "Me and Hank and Evvie and Pete and those of us who are left from the Dare Club, we got to talking." She looked at the coffee can fondly. "We figured you're the first kid ever to spend a whole night here." With a deep breath, she stood up and held the coffee can out to Trina. "That's $329 even. And it's all yours, Miss Citrine, fair and square."

Trina didn't know what to do. She didn't feel right accepting the money, but Miss Kitty stepped forward and practically shoved it in her arms. The can was so heavy, Trina almost dropped it, and as soon it was in Trina's hands, Miss Kitty exhaled mightily and plopped back down in her chair.

"Wow," Edward said, scooping a handful of coins and letting them clink back into the can. "Look at all this loot, Charlotte."

But Charlotte hung back.

Trina could feel Charlotte's anger growing as heavy and as stifling as the old packing blanket. Of course Charlotte was mad. Trina didn't grow up in New Royal. She had no right to the prize. But Trina also knew Charlotte couldn't argue with her grandmother.

"All that? Just for her?" Trina's dad asked.

"Yeah," Charlotte said smiling her familiar mean smile.

"Fair and square." And then she sneered at Trina when no one was watching and mouthed the word *Latrine.*

But Charlotte's insult didn't bother Trina this time. Not now that guilt was eating at her. The money didn't belong to Trina. She and her dad had moved into Goldenrod because they signed a contract. She *had* to sleep there. And she didn't know a thing about the Dare Club. But the money didn't belong to Charlotte either. If it belonged to anybody, it belonged to Goldenrod. But what would Goldenrod do with a coffee can full of money? She set the can of money on the floor and rubbed the creases it had left in her palms.

Miss Kitty pushed back in her chair and stood up. "Now that we've made amends, we'd better go. Don't want to wear out our welcome," she said. "Saturdays are my busiest days at the diner and they start plenty early." She waggled her finger at Edward. "Don't worry. I'll do the talking for you."

"That's it?" Trina's dad shook his head, bewildered. "That's what I pulled the two of you out of the mud for? An old doll, a book, and a can of money?" He took a few paces around the dining room. "I darn near yanked the transmission right out of my truck."

Miss Kitty was already ushering Charlotte and Edward to the foyer. Miss Dale gave Trina and her dad a helpless look. Miss Kitty laughed a little shakily as she reached the front door. "Don't tell me you thought we came for a cup of tea." She turned the knob, pulled open the front door, and marched onto the porch. Charlotte, Edward, and Miss

Dale followed behind her. Trina was sad to see Miss Dale and Edward go. She was even sorry to see Charlotte and Miss Kitty go. She liked having company.

"Wow!" Edward said from the porch, followed by a huge whistle. "I knew that big bolt of lightning would get something. Just think if we'd run out this door. We would have been killed for sure."

Trina hurried onto the porch to see what Edward was talking about. The old oak tree was sprawled across the yard, its limbs reaching for the porch like a monstrous hand. Leaves and branches blocked the parlor windows like a black curtain. No wonder she had never seen her dad's headlights. And no wonder Goldenrod had looked so eerily different in the moonlight when they found Annie's grave. "Poppo, look," she said sadly as he stepped next her. "It was here forever."

He put his arm around her and hugged her close. "I know," he said.

"Thank you for your hospitality, Mr. Mike," Miss Kitty said, as though they really had just come for a social visit.

From the top of the steps, Miss Dale looked over her shoulder and gave a little wave. "Thank you," she said to Trina's dad.

"My pleasure," he said.

"And, Citrine, we'll see you in school on Monday, right?"

"That's right," her dad said before Trina could answer. "And you be careful going down any stairs, okay?"

Miss Dale nodded as she grabbed the railing. It was too dark to see the color of her cheeks, but Trina was pretty sure they had flushed bright pink again.

"And, Miss Kitty, you take my advice and stay on the road next time you come for a visit."

"There won't be a next time. I've had my fill of haunted houses, Mr. Mike. We came to settle up. That's all." Miss Kitty had to lead the group to the far end of the house to circle the tree, and then they all disappeared. Four car doors slammed shut, a motor started, and the rumble of an engine faded into the distance.

Trina plucked a leaf from a tree branch that hung within an inch of the new balustrade and twirled it between her fingers as the realization sank in: she and Charlotte and Edward had been just moments away from being hit by a falling tree. *And* they were nearly struck by lightning. Now she was surer than ever that Goldenrod was looking out for her. And Mr. Kinghorn was wrong: what happened this night had nothing to do with coincidence. But he was right too: luck did seem to be coming back to New Royal little by little.

When Trina closed the front door, the house lights popped on and the refrigerator whirred. Goldenrod hummed with electricity. Trina recognized this feeling that made the house seem so alive. The feeling was hope. She walked into the dining room and picked up the father doll, hopeful for Goldenrod and hopeful for Augustine. Even a little hopeful for herself. But when Trina entered the foyer and there was her dad, standing at the bottom of the stairs with a we-need-to-talk look on his face, hope was no longer what Trina felt.

"Citrine," he began.

"In the morning," Trina said. "I have to take the father doll upstairs so they can all be together again." She circled around her dad and went up the steps, wincing at how serious he sounded when he called her Citrine. As if he knew she wasn't a little girl anymore, and that things between them had changed forever.

She closed her bedroom door and tiptoed to the dollhouse. Augustine was sound asleep in bed, but the mother doll was sitting alone in the parlor in one of the blue velvet chairs by the hearth.

Trina walked the father doll into the little parlor and helped him stroll up to the fireplace so the mother doll could see him. She imagined the mother doll leaping from her chair with joy and throwing her arms around the father doll and him hugging her so tightly she would be afraid she might break. "I've missed you so much," she would say. "I'm never leaving your side again," he would say. Moments later he would ask, "How is our daughter?" And the mother would say, "Wonderfully happy. She is all grown-up. And she has made a new friend."

And then Trina sat the father down next to the mother in the biggest of the blue velvet chairs and placed his porcelain hand on hers. Augustine's family was back together again.

Chapter Nineteen

Trina woke up before it was light out. She couldn't wait for Augustine to wake up and find her father sitting by the hearth, so she sat on the floor and watched as the morning sun lit up the dollhouse, window by window, until it made Augustine's face sparkle. Her eyes opened, her quilt rippled, and then her tiny porcelain hand slipped from under the covers and reached for her silver hairbrush on the bedside table.

"Good morning, Augustine," Trina whispered, startling the little doll.

The silver hairbrush fell to the dollhouse floor with a tiny *tat*.

"Augustine," Trina said a bit louder, "I have a surprise for you."

Augustine sat right up. "Oh, Citrine! It's you! You have returned from your great adventure. Tell me, did you find your mother? Is that the surprise you speak of?"

Trina picked up the hairbrush, handed it to Augustine, and shook her head. "I think I'll just have to wait for the golden bird to bring my mother home too," she said, keeping her sudden tears at bay. She didn't want her own woes to ruin Augustine's real surprise.

Augustine brushed her hair. "Is it my prince? Has he come for me? Is that the surprise?"

"I think it's better than a prince, Augustine. But you must close your eyes. Here, take my finger." The doll's cool hand was as gentle as a butterfly leg on Trina's fingertip. Trina guided her from her bedroom down the staircase and into her parlor.

Augustine danced on her bare tiptoes. "When may I open my eyes, Citrine?"

Trina let go of her hand when they arrived at the hearth. "Now."

When Augustine spotted her father, her smile glistened from one porcelain ear to the other. "My father is no longer lost to me. Look, Mother. Father is home!"

Trina's breath clutched in her chest. Her happiness for Augustine was overwhelming, but so was the ache in her heart. Augustine had something Trina didn't. "You're a whole family again," Trina said, trying to sound happy for Augustine. Trying not to be jealous of a doll. "Now you can live happily ever after."

Augustine placed one of the little newspapers in her father's stiff hand. "Tell me, Citrine, wherever did you find him?"

"Remember Miss Dale? My teacher? She's had him for years. But don't worry. She kept him wrapped up and safe in a drawer. She never played with him."

"In a drawer? Never played with him?" Augustine covered her ears in horror. "What an indignity! A doll should be played with. Please, do not speak of this again."

She knelt by her father's chair and clasped his hand in both of hers.

"But you said you didn't like it when Annie played with you. You said she put you places you didn't want to be."

"That is true, Citrine." Augustine got up from the floor and slipped out the front door in her nightgown. She strolled along a thin strip of wood flooring in Trina's room as if it were a sidewalk. "Sometimes I long for Annie to play with me now." She gave a little sigh.

Trina felt a twinge of regret. She wasn't very good at playing with the doll. And except for taking her to school, she hadn't had much time for their adventures. "Would you like to have a tea party? We could celebrate your father's homecoming. Would that make you feel better?"

Augustine chortled. "Oh, no. My father does not think much of ladies' tea parties." Then she put her forefinger to her temple and her eyes lit up. "Perhaps you would place me on my pony. I think I should enjoy such a diversion on this fine sunny day. I believe my mother and father would like to watch."

Trina wished her mother were there to watch her do something—anything. But her mother was gone. And the hope of someday was gone too. And things would never be the same with her dad.

"I can see you still long for your mother," said Augustine, patting Trina's hand. "Tell me, how is it you found my father but not your mother?"

Trina looked down at Augustine, wondering how in the world she could explain that it was easier to find a doll mother stuck in a bathtub drain, or a doll father hidden away in a drawer for a hundred years, than it was to find a real mother who wasn't really missing. "It's a long story, Augustine."

Augustine sat down cross-legged and rested her pointy little chin in her hands. "You know how I love stories."

Of course Trina would tell Augustine the whole story. She was her best friend.

Trina started with the postcards. She told Augustine that her father's friend, who flew golden birds all over the world, had sent the postcards, and her father only pretended they were from her mother. When she told Augustine her mother was never coming back, Augustine covered her ears. "But, Augustine, listen. There's more," Trina said.

She told Augustine about running away but getting only as far as the flooding creek and having to turn around, and how Charlotte and Edward sneaked into the house. "I'll tell you later how I revenged upon Charlotte," she said. And then she told Augustine about finding Annie's grave and how it would have to be moved before the workmen came, and finished up with how her dad had driven off to find her and had come home filthy after pulling Miss Dale and Miss Kitty's car out of the mud. "I'm afraid he's going to be really mad at me for running away," she concluded, dreading the moment they would have their serious talk.

Augustine, who had barely blinked through the whole story, said very purposefully, "I trust you are right, Citrine, for fear and anger can be very confusing. But mostly I believe your father was worried about you, much like the woodcutter worried about his Hansel and Gretel. I no longer believe your father is a trickster."

"But he lied to me," Trina said. "How do you explain that?"

"So you are still angry with him?"

Trina nodded, feeling herself heat up with anger all over again.

"Is it possible you blame him for something he did not do?" asked Augustine.

Trina didn't like this question. She felt as if Augustine didn't believe her, as if she were the one who had done something wrong. And she knew her anger showed in her face.

"Please, Citrine, tell me again what your father did."

"He told me stories about my mother. He lied to me. He made me think she was going to come home."

"To make you happy?"

"Yes," Trina said. "But it didn't work."

"But it did," said Augustine.

"Not after I found out the truth."

Augustine became pensive. Trina wondered what the doll knew that she didn't. And she was getting more and more frustrated waiting in the silence. "I don't understand, Augustine. How am I blaming him for something he didn't do?"

Augustine raised one porcelain eyebrow. "Tell me, where is your father now?"

Trina turned her head toward the door of her room. "I think I heard him go downstairs."

Augustine tapped Trina on her fingernail until she turned her head. "My dear Citrine, if your father is still here with you, and your mother is not, perhaps it is your mother who is the trickster."

It took a few minutes for Augustine's words to make sense. As they did, a new storm surged inside her. "How can you say that? You don't even know her."

"Nor do you," the little doll said.

Trina didn't want to talk to Augustine anymore. What kind of friend would be so mean? She scooped up the doll and stomped around her room. Maybe she would put the doll back in her dollhouse and lock her up in the turret room and never let her out. And then she'd run away again. As far away from her dad as she could get.

"Help! Help!" The little muffled voice called Trina to her senses. Trina opened her fist and looked at the doll trembling in her hand. Trina was shaking now too, beginning to understand what Augustine had meant about fear and anger being confusing.

"I'm so sorry, Augustine. I don't know what came over me. It's not your fault."

"It is quite understandable," the doll said breathlessly. "You thought you were angry with me."

Trina had never been more grateful for Augustine than she was at this moment. Grateful for a friend to tell her secrets to. And grateful for someone who really understood her. But mostly she was grateful that Augustine had pointed out the truth. A terrible truth Trina didn't want to believe: Her father wasn't the only one who had betrayed her. Her mother had betrayed her too. At least her father had tried to make her happy. In Augustine's own way, she made Trina realize there might be two sides to the story. And then a new worry set in.

"But why, Augustine? Why did my mother leave me?"

"I do not know why, Citrine. I believe you will have to ask your father."

Only now, holding onto Augustine, could Trina muster the courage to admit what had been on her mind since she ripped up the postcard of the Taj Mahal the night before. "Augustine, I'm scared to hear the rest of the story. I'm afraid this one won't have a happy ending."

"Oh, Citrine, how you amuse me. If the story does not have a happy ending, you simply make up a new one."

Trina set Augustine on the floor and wiped her eyes. Maybe it was too much to expect the doll to understand everything, but her silly sense of the real world sure came in handy when Trina was feeling unhappy.

"That reminds me . . ." Augustine glanced sideways and whispered, "Is the giant dead? Is that how you revenged upon her?"

"Charlotte? No, she's not dead." Trina laughed. "In fact, you'd be proud of me, Augustine. I stood up for myself and told her she has to be nice to people."

Augustine crossed her arms and pursed her lips. "Do you mean to tell me you have made friends with the angry giant?"

"I wouldn't exactly call us friends. Now she thinks I have something that belongs to *her*."

Trina didn't get very far recounting the saga of bets and dares when Augustine waved her hands in the air. "I already know this story of giants and coins. Is there not a beanstalk you can chop down?"

"No, Augustine. There is no beanstalk."

"Then I suggest you give the money to the giant and all will be well."

Trina shook her head. "I'd give the money to Goldenrod if I could, but in a way it really belongs to the whole town."

"Then you must find a way to repay the whole town."

Trina frowned. "That would be, like, one dollar apiece, Augustine."

Augustine held her hands to her ears. "I do not like these stories of numbers. I like stories about surprises and fair maidens and grand parties." Her blue eyes twinkled. "Therein resides the answer, Citrine. We must have a party and invite the whole town!" Augustine twirled like a ballerina and her little nightgown fluttered like moth wings in the sunshine. "We were always the happiest when there were parties."

A party! Images of Goldenrod all dressed up with streamers and flowers and filled with happy people flashed through Trina's mind. A party would be something wonderful to look forward to. "Augustine, that's the best idea you've ever had." She stared out her window into the morning sun, thinking how happy Goldenrod would feel to be all dressed up at her own party. "We could have a costume party. It will be the first Harvest Moon Masquerade Ball in more than a century," she said.

"Yes, it will be the merriest of times," Augustine said. "But for now, Citrine, would you mind putting me back in my house? There are many things I would like to tell my mother and father."

"Sure," Trina said absently, but she was thinking of everything she had to do to prepare for the party. The first thing she needed to do was make invitations. Three hundred ninety-seven of them, to be exact.

"Citrine?" Augustine tapped her foot impatiently. "Citrine!"

"What?" Trina said without looking up. She was trying to figure out how she'd make all the invitations when the harvest moon was only two weeks away.

"My goodness, Citrine." The doll reached out and pinched Trina's big toe. It didn't hurt, but it made her look up.

"What?"

"It is as if you are under a spell. I said, please put me back in my house. I do not have all day to wait for you."

"You sure are bossy today," Trina said. She placed Augustine in her parlor next to her mother and father. Then she pulled a notebook and pencil out of her backpack and sat back down to create a list of things she needed for the party. *Invitations, decorations, flowers, costume,* she wrote before she was distracted again by Augustine's unusually high-pitched voice.

"Mother, Father, I have the best news. We are going to have a party. After all this time, Goldenrod will once again open her doors to the people of the town."

A terrible thought crossed Trina's mind. She looked up from her notebook. "Augustine, what if no one comes to the party?"

Augustine turned around and looked at Trina. "Whatever do you mean?"

"If people are afraid of Goldenrod, they'll never come to a party here."

"But they have no reason to be afraid," Augustine said. "I have told you this already."

"Yes, they do. Miss Kitty will tell everyone in town that Goldenrod has been sitting in a graveyard for a hundred years, haunted by the ghost of a little girl."

First, Augustine's mouth made a perfect little O. Then she motioned for Trina to come closer. "Citrine, you said people in your world like logical explanations for things they do not understand, did you not?" Trina crawled closer to the dollhouse, nodding. "Perhaps sometimes they try so hard to understand, they believe things that are not true."

Trina's brain felt as twisted up as a pretzel. "Are you trying to say people believe what they want to believe?"

Augustine smiled her ever-winsome smile. "I am trying to say you must give them an explanation that makes so much sense the idea must be true."

A warmth filled Trina from the inside out. All mixed up between "There's no such thing as a haunted house" and "logical explanations," the answer was clear: "So, if we let people believe that Annie was the ghost haunting Goldenrod, and then we make them believe the ghost is gone, no one will be afraid of Goldenrod anymore." As convoluted as it was, the story made perfect sense. Trina cheered up. "I think it might work."

"Of course it will work. And then we shall have a party and you will invite your mother."

"My mother?" Trina gasped. "But you called her a trickster."

"I said *perhaps* she is a trickster. Or perhaps there is a logical explanation. You must always hear the whole of the story before you know its truth." Augustine twirled through her dining room, humming her favorite song as she straightened the silverware at each place. "A party is a wonderful reason for a mother to come home." The little doll waltzed into her parlor and put her hand on her mother's chair. "Now all the lost mothers will be found."

Trina's head was spinning faster than one of her dad's drill bits. Her father, a trickster. Her mother, a trickster. What was the true story? What if her mother had made a mistake when she left them and didn't know how to say she was sorry? What if she had been the one waiting all this time for Trina to find her?

"But I don't know where to send the invitation. My father says he doesn't know where she is."

Augustine looked at Trina the way a mother might look at a child. "Then you must try to find out. Remember, no stone unturned."

Trina was afraid to let herself get too excited. But what if her mother could come to the party? Maybe she could stay in the pretty white room with the window seat. Trina drew a delicate sprig of goldenrod at the top of a blank page in her notebook.

Beneath it she wrote, *You're invited . . .*

Chapter Twenty

Trina was so lost in her daydream about the Harvest Moon Masquerade Ball and making an invitation for her mother, she jumped when her dad knocked on the door.

"Okay if I come in?" he asked quietly.

"Sure," she said, feeling herself getting all jumbled up inside. She was still mad at her dad for lying to her, mad at her mom for leaving, and mad at herself for running away, but she was also scared to hear the whole story about her mother. She looked to Augustine for advice, but Augustine was already sitting stiffly in her chair—just like the mother and father dolls.

I can do this, Trina said to herself. She had braved her fear of Goldenrod and a new school and even Charlotte, and now she would brave the truth about her mother.

"Think you can open the door?" he said.

Trina opened the door and her dad stepped in with a glass of milk in one hand and his other arm wrapped around the red coffee can of Dare Club money. The peace offering he brought with him this time was bigger than usual: balanced on top of the coffee can was a blue plate bearing a fried egg sandwich, which oozed with melted yellow cheese. "I thought you might be hungry," he said.

"Not really," she said, afraid she'd throw up anything she ate.

Without spilling a drop, he managed to set the can, the plate, and the glass on the floor, right next to the dollhouse. "You're doing a really nice job with this place," he said, peering inside it.

"I've been fixing up houses my whole life," Trina said. She could tell he needed time to warm up to the real subject on his mind, but so did she. She sat back down on the floor next to her notebook.

"Kind of a crazy night, huh?" he said, pacing in a small circle near the dollhouse.

"Sure was," she said, feeling as if all the questions she had about her mother had lodged in her dry throat. "Now all we have to do is prove to everyone in New Royal that Goldenrod isn't haunted and then everything can go back to normal."

"Trina . . . Citrine . . . Princess, don't you think you've taken this haunted house stuff a little too far?"

"I think you can believe anything you want, if it works," she said. As her dad walked over to the big mirror, she decided she was hungry after all, so she took a big bite of egg sandwich. She watched him pull her dirty, wadded-up baseball cap from his pocket and hang it on one of the mirror's fancy hooks. Then he picked up her softball glove. "I've missed our games of catch," he said.

Trina shrugged, already certain she couldn't get through the conversation without crying.

"I know it's hard for you to live here," he said.

Hard? He had no idea. And then her heart seemed to stop beating when he reached for the postcards and fanned through the pile.

She knew what she was about to say would hurt his feelings, but she had to say it anyway. Augustine had forgotten to point out there was her side to the story too. "They're all I ever had of her, and now they don't mean a thing," she said.

He nodded sadly. "Someday I'm going to make it up to you. All of it. Okay?"

Someday. Trina didn't like that word anymore. She didn't want to nod her head and let him think that someday was okay with her. Someday was full of empty promises. Gone were the stories of her mother's adventures. "You made me hope for something that could never be true," she said.

His shoulders dropped as he set the postcards back on the mantel. "Oh, Trina." He walked toward her, but she quickly looked down at her drawing of the sprig of goldenrod in her notebook and kept working on the invitation for her mother. Her bed creaked as he sat down behind her. "I'll admit I've made a lot of mistakes over the years, but this one . . ." When his voice trailed off, Trina turned around. He was staring at the floor.

"I promised myself, no matter what, I'd always keep you safe." He shook his head. "Last night, I thought you'd cool off and come right back home, but you didn't. When I found your hat in the mud by the bridge, I . . ." He looked up at Trina, tears welling in his tired eyes. "Do you know what it's like, even for a split second, to think . . . ?" But then his voice cracked and he looked away. "When you're older, you'll understand." He stood up and paced the floor.

Trina was listening, but there was only one thing on her mind: the truth. "But why did you lie to me? Why didn't you tell me the truth?"

Her dad sat down on the floor across from her and pulled a bit of cheese from her chin. "I didn't mean to lie to you. I didn't think of it that way. All I wanted was for you to stay my happy little girl." He reached out and squeezed her small fists in his big calloused hands and looked her in the eyes. "I love you. And I promise I'll never lie to you again."

Trina blinked back tears. "I love you too, Poppo. And I'm sorry I ran away. I just wasn't thinking for myself." She glanced over at Augustine. "But I'm not a little girl anymore."

"I know. I just didn't think you would grow up so fast." He smiled faintly.

"And I'm old enough to know the truth about my mother." Trina tried to sound strong. "Is she ever coming home?"

His grip on her hands tightened. "You have to understand, Trina. Your mom and I . . . You . . ." He shook his head. "We're never going to be a family like your dolls or the Roys."

Trina's anger eased. Poppo *had* been listening. He had listened to everything she ever said about whole families.

"Then at least tell me what happened. And tell me the truth." She took her hands out of his. "I need to know what happened."

Her dad swallowed. Hard. "She . . ." He gripped his knees. "Left."

"I know that, but why?"

His face reddened as he continued. "I'd taken a big job on Lake Michigan building a log cabin." He shifted his eyes to the fireplace, as if he were watching a sad movie on TV. "Turns out she hated the woods. And then one day she went into town to get groceries . . ."

Trina leaned forward. "And?"

"She didn't come back."

Her mother had run away. Just as she had. But Trina came back; her mother didn't. "Why? Didn't she love me? Did I do something wrong?"

"No, Princess." He looked down and picked at a chunk of mud on his jeans. "It was what I didn't do." Raising his eyes to hers, he said, "It was nothing you did. You were only six months old the first time she left." He shook his head. "I had no idea how I was going to take care of a baby all by myself."

A baby? The first time? "I thought I was three years old when she left."

"That was the fourth time and the last time she left." When he swallowed, his eyes welled with tears. "That's when she wanted to take you with her."

Trina felt a glimmer of hope. "You mean she wanted me?"

The question clearly took her dad by surprise. "Of course she did. But she talked about moving to New York. She talked about making it big." He shrugged his shoulders. "She had lots of ideas, but I don't think she knew what she wanted out of life." He took a deep breath and let it out slowly. "But I knew what I wanted. I fought hard and I won. Once the divorce was final and I had custody of you, I packed us into the truck and kept moving."

There it was. The truth. Like a cement wall in the middle of an obstacle course. She either had to climb over it or give up. And she couldn't give up now. "You didn't want her to find us again, did you?"

He looked down at the floor as if he'd been caught in another lie. "I fell for her every time she came back, and I knew I couldn't do it again. I couldn't handle her walking out and then coming back a few months later like nothing ever happened. And I couldn't bear what it did to you."

Now Trina was the one standing up and pacing. She walked to the mantel and looked at her souvenirs. She gave her snow globe a good shake and watched the fake snow drift around the fake mountains. She picked up her sea glass, which was just broken glass tumbled smooth by lake water. Everything she had was fake. She picked up the stack of postcards, wondering what her mother would say if she really sent her a postcard.

She thought of the party. "What if I wanted her to come back? Would she?"

Her dad shrugged. "I don't know."

Trina stared out her window at the fallen tree. Its leaves were already drooping. She turned away and caught a glimpse of herself in the tall mirror. Her knees and her face were still covered in mud. "Does she have another family? Is that why?"

"I doubt it. She didn't want to be tied down. She wanted her freedom and fancy things. Things I'd never be able to give her. Cars, clothes, jewelry, houses . . ."

Trina ran her hand along the carvings in the tall mirror. "Would Goldenrod be fancy enough?"

"Oh, Princess, I'm not sure anything could ever be good enough for her."

Trina was reeling. If only she could live in Augustine's fantasy world, she would make up a new story and skip all the hard parts. She didn't want to hear another word about her mother, but at the same time she wanted to know everything. "Where is she? And I mean for real this time." She watched her dad in the mirror. He was standing up, staring into the dollhouse.

He shrugged again. "I don't know. New York, Los Angeles. I'm not sure. Last I heard she was some kind of TV producer."

"Really?" Trina gasped excitedly. "In the United States?" Compared to Antarctica, New York and Los Angeles were practically right next door. But in a way, knowing her mother had been living close by was worse. One visit, even a hundred visits would have been easy for her to make. But she had never visited. Not even once. Trina crawled up on her bed. Her stomach hurt and she wanted to hide under her covers. "You mean I could've known her all these years?"

"Oh, Trina. This is what I was afraid of." He sat down next to her and pulled her close. "It wouldn't have been like that. She was so . . . unpredictable."

Trina pulled away. "But people can change, can't they? Look at Miss Kitty. She was almost nice last night."

Her dad stood up. "Miss Kitty was scared."

"Maybe Mom was scared. Maybe if she met me now, she'd change her mind. I'm all grown-up." Trina got down from her bed and picked up her notebook. She ripped out the page that had her mother's invitation on it and folded the frilly-edged paper in half and finally into eighths. "We're having a costume party at Goldenrod to celebrate the harvest moon. I'm going to invite the whole town, so I decided to invite Mom too. I made her this invitation."

Her dad was pacing again. "Since when do we celebrate the harvest moon?"

"Since forever. It's a tradition at Goldenrod. The old newspaper said so." She kicked her foot against the coffee can. "I think this money belongs to the whole town, not just me, so I'm going to use it to pay for the party." For Goldenrod, but she didn't tell him that part.

The floor squeaked a little and the room was quiet. Her dad had wandered to the window and stood gazing down at the tree. He reached into his pocket and pulled out his bandana and wiped his face. "I can't believe the tree missed the house. Not even a scratch. Missed your friends' bikes too."

"Poppo, you're not listening to me."

"Yes, I am. I'm just not sure it's a good idea."

"Don't worry. I'll do all the work. I'm going to make caramel apples and—"

"Citrine," he said, interrupting her. "I mean the invitation for your mother."

"But why? Why can't I try to find her? Please, Poppo. I want to try." She looked at Augustine again and could hear her words of wisdom: *I know of no good story where the maiden gives up.* "You can do anything if you put your mind to it, right?" She marched across the room and pushed the invitation into his hand. "You have to know someone who knows where she is. Promise me you'll try."

He nervously creased the folds of the invitation. "I'll give it my best shot. On one condition."

"What?" Trina said.

"You have to promise me you won't get your hopes up."

"I promise," Trina said, but her hopes were already up. Way up.

Chapter Twenty-one

Clink. Clink. Clink. Trina was standing at her bed, counting out fifty dollars in quarters and even a couple old fifty-cent pieces. Enough, she hoped, to make posters instead of invitations, and buy decorations and other stuff for the masquerade ball. The rest of the money she would leave in the can and give to Miss Kitty for food. *Clink. Clink. Clink.*

"Citree-een! Citree-een!" Augustine called at the top of her little lungs. Trina turned around as Augustine stumbled out through her front door with her hands over her ears.

When Trina stopped counting the money, Augustine released her ears. "What is the news of the day? I heard the bell tolling."

Trina turned toward her window. Poppo was working to clear the big tree, but his chain saw sounded more like a distant truck than a bell. "I don't hear a bell. All I hear is my dad's chain saw." *Clink. Clink.*

"There it is again," Augustine said, looking a little faint.

"Oh," Trina said, about to drop another quarter in the pile. She bent down and showed Augustine her handful of coins. "It's not a bell. I'm counting money for the party. I'm going into town today, on a bike. All by myself."

"Unescorted?" The little doll sounded worried.

Trina nodded. "I'll be okay, Augustine. It's how we do things in my world."

"Then all is well with your father?"

Trina nodded again. "He promised to send my mother the invitation to the party." She counted out the last two dollars without making a sound. "Do you want to come with me? You can ride in the basket."

Augustine shook her head. "I think not today. While living in your world, I have learned many things about myself I did not know. I find I am quite content right here."

"But what about adventure? I thought you wanted a life full of adventure?"

"My dear Citrine, the Land of School has too many rules. And a frog who is not a prince. And the Land of Goldenrod is far too big for me. They are grand places to visit, but they are not home." Augustine glanced back at the dollhouse. "That is my home, Citrine. That is where I am meant to be."

"I understand completely, Augustine. You're lucky to know where your home is." Trina filled her pockets with twenty-five dollars in coins. "Would you like to ride your pony now?"

"I would indeed."

Trina placed Augustine on her pony and handed her the reins. Then she picked up the mother and father dolls and leaned them against the door of the stable for a perfect view of Augustine riding her horse in the sunshine. "I'll see you later," she called to Augustine as she carried the coffee can out of her room.

The front door was wide open. The yard was strewn with branches and leaves, but already Trina could see a cleared path from the porch to the gate and a mound of sawn logs. Edward and Charlotte's bikes were leaning safely against the trailer and her dad was wielding the chain saw, wearing his goggles and bright yellow earmuffs. When she waved her hands in the air to get his attention, he cut the motor and uncovered his ears. "Plan on picking me up in a few hours at Miss Kitty's diner," Trina said, strapping Charlotte's pink helmet to her head. "And don't forget to bring Edward's bike."

"I lowered the seat for you. I'll fix it when I'm in town. And be careful," he said. He watched as she put the coffee can of money in the pink basket hooked to the handlebars of Charlotte's pink bike. And she knew he continued to watch as she walked the bike toward the East Garden. Just as Trina rounded the corner of the house, she turned and waved and he waved back, and then she heard the grinding whir of the chain saw resume. Poppo was letting her grow up.

Trina pushed the bike through the field of goldenrod, past Annie's grave, and all the way to the apple orchard. She could smell the ripening apples before she got there. She found the path between the cornfields where Edward said it would be and hopped on Charlotte's bike.

She stood up on the pedals and ground her way along the rutted path. Bumping along for six point four miles, the coins jingling in the coffee can, she pretended she had lived in New Royal her whole life and riding her bike into town all by herself was an everyday thing to do.

Her first stop was Hank's Tool and Lumber for a box of colored markers and a package of eight sheets of heavy paper for posters. Her dad was right. The hardware store was a mess and it smelled like sawdust, but it had everything—towers of paint cans, scrap wood, buckets of tools, crates of old plumbing. The paper was in a section marked "Toys." A teenage boy named Tyler rang her up as Mr. Hank walked into the store. "Tell your dad the paint should be here next week." And then he handed Trina a baby sucker.

"I'll save it for later," she said, to be polite. She popped it into her T-shirt pocket and went out the door.

With the markers in Charlotte's basket and the paper rolled up under her arm, she rode the bike down the sidewalk. She saw Mr. Kinghorn coming out of the bank and nodded to him when he waved. Maybe, if she had her own bike, she might like living in New Royal.

When she arrived at the Cat's Meow Diner, she leaned the bike against the flower box, put the poster paper in the basket, and grabbed the coffee can. Even before she pushed open the door, she could hear the chatter of voices and the clink of silverware. When the little tin cats chimed overhead, Miss Kitty looked up from wiping the counter. "Charlotte," she hollered over her shoulder. "You got company."

Every seat in the diner was taken and a few people were standing in a corner waiting to be seated. "You're so busy!" Trina said, amazed at the number of customers.

"You should have seen the breakfast crowd," Miss Kitty said. "Everyone wants to hear about last night."

Trina set the coffee can on the end of the counter with a loud clang, which caused the customers to stop chewing and turn their heads. "I told you," Miss Kitty said. "That's yours and I want nothing more to do with it." Miss Kitty stepped back as Charlotte pushed through the swinging doors, carrying a bucket of water. Edward followed with a mop.

"What are you doing here?" Trina asked Edward.

"Working off his punishment, what do you think?" Charlotte snarled before Edward had a chance to open his mouth. "What are you doing here?" Charlotte's eyes were on the coffee can.

"I want to place an order for as many monster brownies and cupcakes and whatever else I can afford with this money." Trina carried the coffee can to the cash register, where Miss Kitty was ringing up a customer. "For the first Harvest Moon Masquerade Ball to be held at Goldenrod in more than a hundred years." She spoke in a loud voice, making sure everyone could hear her. "It's in two weeks and the whole town is invited."

The conversations in the booths fell to murmurs. Hesitant, grumbling murmurs. Trina felt as if she'd just invited everybody to help paint Goldenrod, not come to a party there.

Except for Edward.

"Wow!" Edward said, glancing up at Miss Kitty. "How many do we get?"

"None, if you don't get your work done," Miss Kitty said, looking at the coffee can as if it contained worms instead of money. She looked around the diner before she pulled the can to her side of the counter.

"I kept fifty dollars for decorations and miscellaneous things, but you get the rest," Trina said to Miss Kitty.

"Seems mighty equitable to me." Miss Kitty had a tinge of excitement in her voice until she looked up and realized all the customers' eyes were on her. "But I don't know. I just don't know."

The murmurs got louder, but Trina didn't pay any attention to them. She was concentrating on Charlotte, who hadn't said a word. Charlotte looked at the coffee can and back at Trina. Trina held her breath, expecting the word *Latrine* to cross Charlotte's lips at any moment. She and Charlotte had a stare-down, beady eye to beady eye.

When Charlotte squinted, Trina squinted.

When Charlotte blinked, Trina blinked.

When Charlotte breathed, Trina didn't.

"Can I be Princess Leia?" Charlotte asked.

Trina exhaled, relieved. Maybe she and Charlotte had a chance at becoming friends. A small chance. "You can be anyone you want. I already decided there isn't enough time to make 397 invitations, so I wondered if you could help me make posters and then we can put them up all over town."

"Can I help too?" Edward asked.

"Of course. I have everything we need," Trina said.

Charlotte and Edward looked up at Miss Kitty and both of them cowered in her firm glare. "Pretty please,

Miss Kitty," Edward said as the tin cats chimed again and the place started to clear out.

"I guess there isn't any harm in making posters," Miss Kitty said. She grabbed the mop from him and gave his feet a nudge with the mop head. "But get to it before I change my mind."

Trina got the supplies from the bike basket while Charlotte and Edward pushed two tables together, and then the three of them sat down and got to work. They decided to make posters for the library, the school, the diner, and all the businesses, like the bank and Mr. Hank's store.

In the middle of her second poster, Trina said, "I invited my mom too."

"Why do you have to invite her?" Charlotte asked. "Where is she?"

As strange as it was to talk about her mother so openly, Trina knew she had to get used to it. But it took her a minute to figure out the best way to answer Charlotte's questions. "She's in the process of moving," she said, which seemed to satisfy Charlotte's curiosity. She had an urge to tell them her mother was a big TV producer, living a fancy life, but the last thing she wanted to do was give Charlotte and her mean fist the idea that she thought she was better than anyone else. The fancy things didn't matter, anyway. She just wanted to see her mom.

"It'll be the first time I've seen her since I was really little."

"Wow!" Edward said, sitting back to admire his picture of a sharp-fanged bat. "Are your mom and dad divorced?"

Charlotte kicked Edward under the table.

"Ow," he yelped. "What'd you do that for?"

"Geez, Edward, you don't ask personal questions." Trina thought Charlotte was sticking up for her until she added, "You wait until they tell you." Charlotte turned to Trina with a sneaky smile. "You can tell if you want."

Trina had stopped drawing. She was thinking about that word, *divorced*. It sounded final, but it sounded better than *maybe* or *someday*. It was easier to know the truth, even a hard truth, than it was to wonder. "Yeah. Divorced. It happened a long time ago," she said. And now she felt satisfied with all the answers, too. She looked down at Edward's picture, finally paying attention to what he was drawing. "Why are you drawing a bat?"

"Because Goldenrod is a haunted house. Duh."

"No, it's not," Charlotte said, reaching for the yellow marker to color what looked like a field of daisies. "We broke the spell, right, Citrine? By finding Annie's grave?"

Trina felt a great weight lift from somewhere deep inside her. Augustine's logical idea was working. Trina nodded happily. "Yup. Now all we have to do is get Annie and Toby buried in the cemetery where they belong before my dad puts in the new septic system."

Edward frowned at his poster. Then he scribbled over his bat and turned it into what looked like a monster brownie. "I think we should bob for apples like they did in the olden days."

"I think we should have a piñata," Charlotte said.

"I like both ideas," Trina said.

Edward put his finished poster aside and started on another one. "Do we really have to be characters from a book like it said in the newspaper?"

"Yes. Or a movie," Charlotte said before Trina could answer.

"Well, if you get to be Princess Leia, then I'm going to be Obi-Wan Kenobi." Edward held his marker like the handle of an imaginary light saber and waved it across the table.

Charlotte twirled her hair to the sides of her head, imitating Princess Leia's hair-do. "Who are you going to be, Citrine?"

Trina was shocked. Twice now Charlotte had called her by her real name, Citrine. "I'm thinking about being Briar Rose," she said. She wanted to wear a fancy dress and look grown-up for her mom. Just in case she came. And she kind of liked it that her dad had been calling her Princess ever since they arrived at Goldenrod. But Edward looked like he had no clue what she was talking about.

"You know, Sleeping Beauty. Except I can't sew."

"Make room," Miss Kitty said, waiting for Charlotte to move the markers before she set a plate of warm chocolate chip cookies on the table. When Edward grabbed three cookies, Miss Kitty swatted his hand. "One at a time, buster."

And then the little metal cats clinked above the door and in walked Miss Dale.

"Hey, Mith Thale," Edward said with his mouth full of cookie.

Miss Dale walked right up to their table. "Hey, Aunt

Kitty. I'm ready for all the tin cans you've been saving for me."

"What for?" Edward asked as he swallowed.

"For a surprise art project coming up at school."

"Oooo," Charlotte said. Then Charlotte held up her finished poster. "Look. The whole town is invited to a masquerade ball."

Miss Dale read the poster and nodded happily. "So we have to dress up as one of our favorite characters, huh? Sounds like a lot of fun."

Miss Kitty shook her head. "That's some mighty high pie-in-the-sky thinking, if you ask me. You can make the prettiest posters in the world, but I don't think it's going to be enough to convince the town to go to a party at Goldenrod."

"But you'll come, won't you, Miss Kitty?" Trina asked. If Miss Kitty wouldn't come after surviving a visit to Goldenrod, then no one would come.

Miss Kitty looked as if she were literally biting her tongue. Miss Dale put her arm around her. "Aunt Kitty, you were there last night and nothing happened."

"Nothing? You call driving off the road and getting stuck in the mud nothing? And that big tree just about smashed these kids to smithereens. That isn't nothing."

Miss Dale winked a wink that only Trina, Charlotte, and Edward could see. "You can count on my being there, Citrine. I just have to come up with a costume."

"Me too," Trina said, adding leaves to a sprig of goldenrod at the top of her poster. "I'm thinking about being Briar Rose—"

"But she doesn't know how to sew," Charlotte said.

"Carrie can teach you how to sew," Miss Kitty said, nibbling a cookie with her front teeth. "She can't cook worth a pickle, but she can sew rings around any seamstress I ever met."

Miss Dale rolled her eyes behind Miss Kitty's back as the tin cats sounded again. This time Trina's dad came through the door.

"Poppo, what are you doing here so early?" Trina scolded. Trina didn't want to go home. She was just beginning to feel a part of something. And she'd only finished two posters. But deep down inside she knew why he was there. He couldn't let her grow up all at once.

"Hey," he said, but he didn't step any farther than the doorway. "I've got frozen pizzas and ice cream in the truck, so you need to hurry. Edward, your bike is out here. Next to Charlotte's."

"But Miss Dale's going to teach me how to sew," Trina said.

"Now?" he asked.

Trina looked at Miss Dale with hopeful eyes.

"Sure, we can start today. But I'll need a lift home." Miss Dale tapped Miss Kitty on the shoulder. "Are the cans out back?" When Miss Kitty nodded, Miss Dale turned to Trina's dad. "Would you mind grabbing the big box of tin cans by the back door? I was going to ask Mr. Hank, but if you don't mind . . ." She held her bandaged arm in the air. "No sling, but still no heavy lifting."

"Sure, no problem," he said, following Miss Kitty's

pointed finger to the back of the diner. Miss Dale followed him.

Trina helped Charlotte tape up her poster in the diner's window—in the middle of the blinking lights. "I'll take mine to the library and Mr. Hank's on our way home." They hurried outside to see how the poster looked. Edward came racing out too, and the three of them stood on the sidewalk facing the window. Charlotte had spelled the word "masquerade" with a *k*, but Trina knew better than to point out the mistake to her. Instead she said, "You draw really nice flowers."

"Thank you," Charlotte said. "I can't wait until the party." *This is how friendships begin*, Trina thought. Little by little. "Edward and I'll make more posters. We'll get the gas station and Millie's Grocery Store."

"And Shegstad's Funeral Home," Edward said.

Trina and Charlotte frowned at him in unison.

"What?" he said.

"Geez, Edward," Charlotte said.

"Maybe you should skip Shegstad's," Trina said.

When they finished dividing up poster duty, Trina climbed into the back seat of the truck's cab and sat next to the big box of miscellaneous tin cans so Miss Dale could sit in the front. First they stopped at Mr. Hank's. Trina was stuck next to the tin cans, so her dad delivered the poster. When they stopped at the library, Miss Dale delivered the poster.

Afterward, Miss Dale pointed the way to her house. They wound through the back streets of New Royal, under a canopy of trees just beginning to turn color, and arrived at a white cottage with blue shutters and yellow window boxes, which were overflowing with pink flowers. A white picket fence bordered the yard and a brick sidewalk led to a quaint front porch.

"Here we are," Miss Dale said.

When they got out of the truck, Trina's dad grabbed the box of tin cans. But when he set it down and opened the screen door for Miss Dale, the door came off its hinges. Trina cringed, embarrassed for her dad, who turned a million shades of red.

"I usually go in the back," Miss Dale said. Her cheeks were turning pink too.

He leaned the door against a window box. "Lucky for you, I know how to fix it," he said in his know-it-all voice, which made Trina feel even more embarrassed.

"Where do you want these?" he asked, pointing at the box of cans.

"In the garage, if it isn't too much trouble."

"See you later, Poppo," Trina said.

"Give us about two hours," Miss Dale said.

Trina followed Miss Dale into her cozy house, through the living room and dining room and into a tiny sewing room. Rolls and rolls of material leaned against the walls—crunchy fabrics and shiny gold ones and silky blues. Ribbons hung on a wire suspended from the ceiling and a glass bowl of many-colored buttons looked like it was full of candy. The sewing machine sat on a table, which was piled high with pillow stuffing. The mess reminded her of

Mr. Hank's hardware store. And just like Mr. Hank, Miss Dale knew where everything was.

"Halloween is my favorite holiday," Miss Dale said, opening a closet in the room, "so I have a lot of costumes." The closet was jammed full of costumes. "Maybe we'll find something for you here." Miss Dale pulled out what looked like a big red balloon. "It's a tomato," she said.

"But we're supposed to dress as a character from a book. Or a movie," Trina said, trying to be polite.

"I know," Miss Dale said. "No tomatoes." She pushed some more costumes aside. "Ah, here it is. Sleeping Beauty." She pulled from the closet a blue gown with puffy sleeves and a layer of silky fabric over layers and layers of crunchy fabric. "Maybe we can take this in to fit you."

The dress was perfect for Briar Rose. But as much as Trina wanted to try wearing a dress, the frills and ruffles were too much. And it would be impossible to sit down in. Trina shook her head. "It's a little too fancy for me. Maybe I should go as someone else."

Miss Dale pulled out a Snow White dress followed by a Pinocchio costume, but Trina shook her head again. For all the fairy tales she had read to Augustine, she couldn't think of a single fairy-tale character she wanted to be. Snow White was too nice. Cinderella was too prissy. She didn't want to wear something that made her feel silly.

The next costume Miss Dale selected was a pioneer dress, something Laura Ingalls Wilder would wear. Another one looked like a Pilgrim dress, and a green tunic was perfect for Robin Hood, but Trina kept shaking her head.

Then Trina spotted something black and had a whole new idea. "How about that one?" she said.

Miss Dale pulled it from the closet and held it up. It was a cape, just as she had hoped, but it was way too long. Maybe Miss Dale would help her shorten it.

"This is a witch's cloak," said Miss Dale, looking a little puzzled. "Are you sure you don't want something more cheerful?"

"Nope," Trina said. "I want to be Hermione Granger from *Harry Potter.*"

Miss Dale nodded instant approval. "She's the perfect heroine. She works magic to make things better. And she's brave. All you need is a white shirt and tie—can you borrow those from your dad?"

"My dad?" Trina had never seen her dad wear anything but blue jeans and work boots. She shook her head, pretty sure he didn't even own a tie.

Miss Dale didn't miss a beat. "That's no problem. I'll lend you a shirt and a skirt too, and we'll make a tie. How about that? And then we'll raise the hem on this cape about six inches. And you can make a wand when you get home."

Miss Dale opened a cabinet full of spools of thread and selected a black one. Then she picked up a small wicker basket and sat Trina at her dining room table. "This is really my favorite place to sew," she said. "The light is better."

The basket held rulers and scissors and needles and pins. Miss Dale showed Trina how to fold the hem up six inches and pin it in place. "I'm still a little clumsy," she said, wiggling the fingers of her bandaged arm. "Maybe you can thread the needle." Trina made several stabs at the tiny eye and finally succeeded. Then, leaning over Trina, Miss Dale showed her how to catch just a few threads of fabric to make invisible stitches.

Miss Dale sat down and measured one long section of gold fabric and another one of maroon fabric for Hermione's tie. Then she measured again. "Measure twice, cut once," she said. While Trina watched, she cut, folded, ironed, and pinned, and then she disappeared into her sewing room for a few minutes. When the hum of the sewing machine stopped, Miss Dale emerged with a perfectly knotted striped tie complete with an elastic band to go around Trina's neck and a snap to hold it tight. Together they sat at the dining room table, chatting, while Trina hemmed her cloak.

"Maybe now I can make curtains for the dollhouse," Trina said.

Miss Dale looked up, bright-eyed. "That's right." She held her good hand out to Trina, ready to shake hands. "I tell you what," Miss Dale said. "I'll send you home with some fabric scraps for curtains if you show me the dollhouse sometime."

"It's a deal," Trina said, shaking her hand.

Trina stood up and put on the cloak. Then Miss Dale popped a pointy witch's hat on her head, and together they snapped Trina's tie in place. "Go take a look in the mirror by the front door," Miss Dale said. "I'll clean up."

The front door was wide open, and Trina forgot all about looking at herself in the mirror when she spotted her dad's truck still sitting in front of Miss Dale's house. She opened the screen door, which didn't fall off its hinges, as her dad came around the corner.

"Poppo! What are you still doing here?"

He gave her a funny look and then he waved his screwdriver in the air. "Well, Miss Hermione Granger, so far I've fixed the screen door, the back railing, and the garage door—with my own two hands, mind you, not magic. By the way, have you seen my daughter anywhere?"

Miss Dale came up behind Trina and opened and shut the screen door. "It's perfect. And it doesn't even squeak anymore," she said. "Now I can use my front door again. Thank you."

"Still got a fence to look into out back. Already got the wood for it from Hank's."

"Thank you again," Miss Dale said. "It went down in the storm last night. I didn't think it was fixable."

Trina waited for her dad to say something in his know-it-all voice, but fortunately all he said was, "I'm happy to help."

The sun was so low, it had to be late afternoon. No wonder Trina was starving. "Oh, Poppo, what about the pizzas and the ice cream?"

His face fell as he remembered. "I suppose the ice cream's all melted by now."

"Nothing to worry about," Miss Dale said, heading down the sidewalk to the truck. "We'll bake the pizzas for dinner and make raspberry smoothies out of the ice cream for dessert. You can stay, can't you?"

"Yes!" said Trina and her dad at the same time.

After dinner, Trina helped Miss Dale pick raspberries from her garden. Soon Trina was slurping her second raspberry-chocolate smoothie while she and Miss Dale watched her dad repair the fence.

When it was starting to get dark out and time to go home, Miss Dale gave Trina two grocery bags. One held her Hermione Granger costume and the other bag was full of fabric scraps, ribbons, and lace. "I'm sure you'll find what you need for your dollhouse curtains in there. Needles and thread, too."

Trina wanted to hug Miss Dale but didn't know if fifth graders hugged their teachers. Instead she said thank you as heartily as she could. As she and her dad got into the truck, all three waved good-bye. But Trina turned in her seat and she and Miss Dale continued to wave until they couldn't see each other anymore.

With the truck windows wide open, Trina and her dad sang along to a golden-oldies tune that faded in and out until the radio turned to the usual static and her dad shut it off. In the distance, Trina could see a few dots of light like oversized lightning bugs. It had to be Goldenrod. "Look, Poppo, I didn't know you could see her from here."

"I didn't either. I must have left some lights on."

Despite all the comings and goings lately, Trina thought Goldenrod still looked forlorn sitting all by herself in the field. "What if no one comes to our party? I think Goldenrod's feelings will be hurt," Trina said.

"You really think a house would have its feelings hurt?"

Trina didn't think—she *knew*. But she figured her dad would laugh at her if she said so, so she said the one thing that would keep him from asking any more questions. "It's a girl thing, Poppo."

Her dad was quiet until they slowed at the red barn to turn right onto the muddy road that led to Goldenrod. "I know of at least two people who will be coming to your party."

Trina sighed. "Yeah. You and me."

"What about your friends?"

"That won't be much of a party," Trina said.

"What about Miss Dale? She says she's coming and she has the perfect costume for me. How does that sound?"

As they bounced over first one big rut and then the other, Trina imagined her dad dressed as a big red tomato and started to giggle. "Depends on the costume," she said. She was still laughing at her own joke when they pulled through the gate and parked next to the huge pile of wood her dad had chopped and stacked—and he still had the enormous trunk left to go.

"I sure miss the tree," she said.

"I do too," he said. "But I'm thinking, before we go, I'll make a big table or a bookcase from it. That way we'll always have a souvenir of our time at Goldenrod."

Trina loved the idea of making furniture from the big old oak tree. And it made sense to have a really big souvenir from the biggest place they ever lived. Of course, the only souvenir Trina really wanted was Augustine, but she knew that Augustine belonged to Goldenrod.

Augustine! She had so much to tell her and so little time before the sun would set. She grabbed the grocery bags and ran up the steps to the porch, nearly tripping over another special delivery of stolen goods. This time, a tall pink vase with a swirl of raised yellow flowers and a copper lamp with a stained glass shade sat right by the front door. "Can you get these, Poppo? I'm in a hurry," she called, and then she ran up the stairs to her room.

"Augustine," she said, putting the bags down and peering into Augustine's bedroom. Augustine wasn't there. For a second, Trina was scared the little doll had wandered off on her own adventure after all, but then she spotted her sitting on her pony. "I'm glad you're still up."

"Citrine, where have you been? I have waited and waited for you to come home and put me to bed. I cannot climb down from this pony by myself and I am quite stiff from sitting so very long in one position. I dread the long walk up the staircase and I have grown weary of doing everything myself."

"I'm sorry, Augustine, I didn't know we'd be home so late. But I had the best day ever." Trina knew she was responsible for all of Augustine's woes, but she also knew how to cheer her up. "And I have a surprise for you."

Augustine smiled. "A surprise?"

Trina pulled a lacy fabric from the bag and waved it in the air. "Look. Now I can make new curtains for your house." She spotted a little sewing ruler in the bag and immediately pulled it out and measured the windows in Augustine's bedroom, and then she measured the mother and father dolls' windows, too. "All exactly two inches by five inches. And guess what? My father said Miss Dale is definitely coming to the party. And I'm sure Edward and Charlotte will come too, and maybe Miss Kitty, even though she says she won't. So that makes six people!" As she spoke, she lifted the little doll from her pony and helped her change into her nightgown.

Augustine climbed awkwardly into bed and leaned back against her pillow. "Tell me again, when is the party?"

"Two weeks from today," Trina said, pulling the quilt to Augustine's chin.

"I cannot wait to hear all the stories of this grand party."

Grand party. Trina hoped it would be a grand party. She hoped everyone in town would come. Most of all, she hoped her mother would come. And then she understood what Augustine had just said. "Augustine, don't be so silly. I'll bring you to the party with me. You can wear a costume and pretend to be someone from one of your favorite stories."

"Tell me, Citrine. Who should I pretend to be?"

Trina glanced into the bag of scraps at a piece of shimmering, silky blue fabric and gave Augustine a wink. "I have the perfect costume in mind for you."

Chapter Twenty-two

Ever since Trina, Edward, and Charlotte made the posters, Trina felt like she belonged in New Royal, which meant almost a whole week of belonging. The occasional people on the street recognized her dad's truck and waved to them on their way to school. And when Trina raised her hand in class and answered questions, no one whispered or made funny faces. Prissy Missy even picked Trina to be her partner on a geography project.

Miss Lincoln was as cantankerous as ever, and Miss Kitty was pretty much her same old self, but Charlotte was almost nice. And the townspeople seemed to know at least two things about Trina that were kind of like secrets: her mom and dad were divorced, and she liked softball.

It was Edward's idea to combine forces with the fourth and sixth grade classes and create a league of two coed softball teams. Miss Dale said she would help with a fundraiser to buy team T-shirts and caps, so Trina, Charlotte, and Edward headed to the diner Friday after school for a milkshake meeting to come up with names for the teams.

"I've got one," Edward said as they squeezed into a booth. "The Goldenrod Ghosts."

"Ooo," Charlotte said excitedly. Trina had the same reaction and wrote it down.

"I don't know about that," Miss Kitty said, carrying three chocolate milkshakes to their table. "If I'm going to sponsor a team, I think I should have a say in the name. 'Cat's Meow something' sounds good to me."

They were quiet for a moment until Edward said, "How about the Diner Dogs for the other team? Get it? Dogs chase cats."

Trina and Charlotte just looked at each other until they burst out laughing.

"How about the Corn Cats?" Charlotte said.

"Definite possibilities," Trina said. She was thinking back to naming Augustine. "But I think Miss Kitty is right. The team names should have meaning."

"The New Royal Raiders versus the Ferocious Felines," Edward said.

"Now we're onto something," Trina said, nodding approval and writing down the names. Edward bobbed his head smugly. They brainstormed, laughing and sipping milkshakes, until it was time to go home.

The next day was Saturday. Exactly one week until the party. Trina had stayed up late and had hoped to sleep in, but instead she was awakened when it was still dark by the sound of engines groaning through the cornfields. She figured they were more combines harvesting more corn, but the engines got closer and closer until she knew they had come through the gate. She got out of bed, opened her window, and leaned far enough into the cool morning air to glimpse the star of a county sheriff's car as it rounded the side of the house. She pulled on a pair of jeans, a T-shirt, and her Minnesota Twins baseball cap and ran downstairs into the dining room to see what was happening.

The French doors were open, swinging slightly in a breeze, and Poppo was outside sipping coffee from one of the blue cups, nodding seriously while a stout bald man in a suit waved his hands in the air as he talked. Wisps of breath visible in the chilly air swirled between them.

The sheriff's car had stopped behind a large truck and a black hearse, which were already parked in the East Garden, motors running, headlights aimed toward the apple orchard in the morning mist. Two men, hulking shadows in the gray light, got out of the truck and walked up to the sheriff's car. Then they walked back to the truck and grabbed two shovels.

They had come for Annie Roy.

When the workmen drove their shovels into the dirt, Trina shivered and rubbed her arms.

"Sorry it's so early," her dad said, stepping inside. "Turns out we needed a permit. I couldn't reschedule the septic company, so I had to lean on Mr. Shegstad for emergency help to get it done on schedule." He sipped his coffee and looked toward the garden. "Mr. Shegstad arrived with the burial permit and signatures in the nick of time."

Trina sat down on the stoop and watched the men shovel the earth into two piles as they dug up the graves: Annie Roy's and her beloved dog Toby's. Poppo, Mr. Shegstad, and the sheriff watched, too. Nobody said a word. The soft thud of a shovel striking wood broke the silence and the workers put down their shovels. One of the workmen climbed into the shallow hole and handed up a small, plain wooden box the size of her dad's toolbox. It had to be Toby. The other workman slid it into the hearse.

The men worked side by side on the other hole and eventually put down their shovels. Together they lifted out a casket—a white casket not much bigger than Toby's. Annie, who had been Augustine's little girl a hundred years ago, was still a little girl.

Trina could feel Goldenrod's relief that Annie would be safe now, but she also felt her deep grief at letting Annie go. Goldenrod had watched over Annie for more than a century. Saying good-bye to her, even if it meant Annie would be reunited with her parents, was breaking her heart. Annie wouldn't be lonely anymore, but what would Goldenrod do without her?

As one workman walked over and whispered something to Mr. Shegstad, the other workman pried up the old gravestones and put them both in the back of the truck.

"Poppo," Trina said quietly, getting up from the stoop. "We can't let Annie go like this. Not alone. Goldenrod needs to know I'm going with her."

For once the look her dad gave her didn't question what she was thinking. He pulled her into the warmest, tightest hug and rested his chin on the top of her head. "Whatever you need, Princess."

As the sun began to light up the East Garden, the truck revved its engine. "Tell the men we're coming with them," Trina said as she ran up the stairs to her room.

"I'll be in the truck," he said.

"Augustine," she called. She wanted Augustine to go with her. "Augustine, wake up."

Augustine didn't answer. Trina peered into the bedroom of the dollhouse and waited a few moments for the sun to touch Augustine's cheek and wake her.

"Augustine? Augustine, Annie and Toby are to be buried in the cemetery today, and I want you to come with me to say good-bye to them."

Augustine sat up in bed, a thin ray of light glowing around her head like a halo. "Tell me, Citrine, what is a cemetery?"

Sometimes Augustine was like a grown-up, but sometimes she was like a child. This time she was like a child and it was hard to explain things to her in a way she could understand. "It's a place to keep people after they have died."

"Died. I remember, you told me this word. Died is when people become pictures and stories, is that true?"

"Yes," Trina nodded. She had found the right words to explain after all. "When they have become pictures and stories."

"Will Annie be safe there? Will this be her happily-ever-after place?"

"Oh, yes," said Trina. "Annie will finally be with her mother and father. And Toby too."

Augustine pushed back the covers and stretched out her porcelain arms. "I am happy for Annie, but I believe I shall wait for you here. I have vowed to my mother and father I will stay by their sides so that we will not be separated again."

Trina was desperate to find a way to change Augustine's mind when one of the workmen leaned on his horn. Both she and Augustine jumped.

"What kind of animal makes that dreadful noise?" Augustine said, pulling up her quilt so that only her eyes showed.

"It's not an animal; it's a truck horn, Augustine. It means I have to go." Trina didn't mean to sound frustrated with the little doll, but she was in a hurry. "Right now."

As Trina ran from her room, she heard Augustine's little voice say, "Take her with you."

Take her with you? Trina raced down the stairs with no idea what the little doll meant. She wanted to take Augustine with her, but Augustine hadn't wanted to go. As Trina headed for the front door, the wind whistled through the bay window like a wail of sorrow that made Trina put her hand to her heart and stop running. Suddenly, Trina sensed the dusty old lady standing there, but this time there were tears in her eyes. "I know, Goldenrod," she said out loud. "I know you'll miss her. So will I. But Annie will be happy, and that will make us happy too. And she will always belong to Goldenrod."

And then Trina understood what Augustine had meant.

Trina hurried out the front door and into the yard, where she gathered an armful of the tall yellow goldenrod, roots and all. "A part of you is coming with me and will stay with Annie," she said out loud to the house, and then she climbed into her dad's truck.

The sheriff's car led the way through the cornfields under a blue sky with hazy clouds. The hearse followed the sheriff's car and the workmen's truck followed the hearse. Trina and her dad brought up the rear for the somber six-point-four-mile drive into town. They didn't talk, but her dad glanced in her direction and seemed to understand why she was holding the bouquet of goldenrod.

By the time they got to New Royal, the sun was well up and the town was wide awake, waiting as the modest funeral procession passed the population sign and rolled into town. It seemed the little town expected them. Of course it did. Mr. Shegstad probably told Miss Kitty about the burial and then word would have spread to each and every one of the 397 citizens.

For once Trina was glad New Royal didn't mind its own business. She was happy that the townspeople were paying their respects to Annie. But Trina had never seen so many of the New Royal residents out and about. Some stood and watched. Some waved, while others bowed their heads at the solemn parade.

Mr. Kinghorn was standing on the library steps and nodded at Trina. She nodded back. She saw people streaming out of Miss Kitty's diner to watch. Even Mr. Hank stopped unloading his truck in front of Millie's Grocery Store and tipped his head.

They drove single-file up the hill toward the school but then made a sharp left turn into the drive to the New Royal Cemetery. Mr. Shegstad got out of the sheriff's car and unlocked the gate. He motioned the sheriff, the hearse, and the big truck to continue inside the cemetery, but he held up his hand for Trina's dad to stop, pointing at a place to park just outside the cemetery's gate. Then another car parked behind them. And another. When Trina got out of the truck and looked down the hill toward town, she could see dozens of people heading for the cemetery on foot, on bikes, and in cars. Halfway down the hill she spotted Miss Kitty, Miss Dale, and Charlotte walking together. Edward was riding his bike in zig-zags, occasionally circling the threesome as they came up the hill.

"Oh my," Mr. Shegstad murmured at the growing crowd.

Trina and her dad followed Mr. Shegstad across the immaculate green lawn of the cemetery to two deep rectangles perfectly cut into the ground, one small and one slightly smaller, next to a large monument of pink granite. The monument said nothing but ROY in big block letters, but below the family name, engraved in the pink stone, was a single sprig of goldenrod. Just like the sprig in the album.

The workmen were quick with their task, and soon Annie and Toby were buried, but poor Mr. Shegstad was flustered by all the activity. As the crowd gathered, he showed everyone where to stand around the big monument, but then it was clear he didn't know what to do next. "I didn't expect this. I'm not prepared," he muttered so low that only Trina could hear him.

"Isn't there a minister?" Trina asked.

"No," Mr. Shegstad said. And then, "Yes." And then, "I mean, he travels town to town. He won't be here until tomorrow. Do you think you could say something?"

"Me?"

Mr. Shegstad nodded.

Without even thinking, Trina climbed up and stood on the big granite base of the Roy monument, holding tight to the bouquet of goldenrod. But one look at the big crowd made Trina tremble with stage fright. If only she had Augustine in her pocket, maybe she could do it.

Trina was about to step down when a hush fell over the cemetery. Then she spotted Mr. Kinghorn. And Prissy Missy was standing there with an older couple—probably her mom and dad. Miss Lincoln and Mr. Bert, the school custodian, were in the crowd too. And of course, Miss Dale and Miss Kitty. They were all counting on her. If she didn't speak, who would? Nobody knew Annie and Goldenrod the way she did.

Trina took off her baseball hat, trying to think about Annie Roy instead of the few hundred strangers staring at her. In the biggest voice she had, she said, "Thank you all for coming. It means a lot to . . ." Goldenrod was what she wanted to say, but as she looked into the faces of the townspeople, old and young, she knew they wouldn't understand. "I'm sure it means a lot to the Roy family. Annie was the beloved daughter of the Roys. Now they are finally a whole family again." And then she didn't know what to say next. Nothing came to mind except the truth. *The truth.* The thought of telling the truth made her stand up straight and tall.

"I know for a long time people have been afraid of Goldenrod. But I think they were afraid because they didn't understand. I was scared at first, too. But my dad will tell you there's no such thing as a haunted house." The silent hush turned into murmurs and whispers. Trina looked for her dad and caught his eye. Just as she had hoped, his wink gave her all the confidence she needed to continue. "And he's right. Goldenrod isn't haunted. At least not anymore. Not now that Annie is buried here in the cemetery where she belongs. Goldenrod is just a big old empty house." Trina paused. She knew this moment, standing in front of the whole town, was her one and only chance. "She isn't done yet, but it would really make her happy, I mean us, happy, if you all come to the party next Saturday night so you can see for yourselves how beautiful Goldenrod really is."

Then Trina knelt down at the base of the monument, dug a hole with her hands, and buried the roots of the goldenrod in the fresh, wet dirt of Annie's grave. Over time, she knew it would grow and spread just as it had grown beyond the gates of the East Garden.

"There you go, Goldenrod," she whispered. "A part of you will always be with Annie."

When she stood up, the townspeople were silent. She figured there were Dare Club members in the group she hadn't met, and probably a lot of people who still blamed their bad luck on Goldenrod. Trina hoped that they were taking in what she had said and maybe even beginning to think of the old house in a new way.

One by one the townspeople left, saying good-bye to neighbors and waving at Trina and her dad. A few even stopped by to introduce themselves. One man in overalls said, "Thank you," although for what, Trina didn't know.

Charlotte grabbed Edward's hand and dragged him over to where Trina was standing. "I just want you to know," Charlotte began. "We're going to come early next Saturday and help you decorate."

"Yeah," Edward said. "And my dad's going to deliver a brand-new horse trough so we can bob for apples."

"Cool," Trina said. "I'll pick the apples."

"Hey, there's Ben," Edward said, and ran off.

And then Miss Kitty came up and took Charlotte by the arm and led her deep into the cemetery. To visit Charlotte's mother, Trina thought sadly. Trina's own mother wasn't with her, but at least she was somewhere in the world, alive. Not like Charlotte's mother.

"That was a nice speech," Trina's dad said, appearing next to her. He put his hand on her shoulder. "It's not easy to get up in front of a big group like that. I'm proud of you."

Miss Dale was standing next to him, nodding, but she was more intent on watching the crowd. "Seems a funeral is about the only thing that brings this town together any-more," she said softly.

Her dad and Miss Dale turned and headed down the hill toward the truck. Trina hurried to catch up. "But what about the party?" Trina asked. "Do you think they understood what I was saying—that Goldenrod is a happy place now and that whatever ghost they thought was there is gone? Do you think they got that part? Do you think they'll come?"

"I don't know," Miss Dale said. "A lot of folks here are set in their ways. But what you said might change a mind or two. I wouldn't give up."

"See you in school," Edward said, sailing past on his bike, riding no-handed.

"Yeah, see you in school," Trina called after Edward as Miss Kitty and Charlotte reappeared arm in arm.

"We'll be riding back with you, if that's okay, Mr. Mike," Miss Kitty said, opening the truck's door. She let Charlotte and Trina and Miss Dale climb into the back seat first and then she climbed into the front seat. "Park in front of my place, Mr. Mike, and don't any of you dare leave until I tell you."

Charlotte, Trina, and Miss Dale looked at each other. "What is it, Aunt Kitty?" Miss Dale asked, her voice quavering.

"Just got something gnawing at my conscience worse than ants on sugar," Miss Kitty said. "Never you mind."

After that, nobody said a word. The quiet was excru-ciating and so was the slow ride down Main Street. The crowd from the cemetery filled the street and they had to drive behind them at a speed of about one block per hour. All Trina could figure was that she had really upset Miss Kitty with her speech. Her knees began to wobble worse than they ever had with stage fright.

When Trina's dad finally parked, they all climbed out of the truck and followed Miss Kitty through the crowd to the front of the diner, where she reached up and clanged the rusty dinner bell with everything she had. Trina swore she felt the ground shake. Soon most of the town was standing around Miss Kitty in complete silence.

Miss Kitty cleared her throat before she shouted, "Seems mighty fitting that we would come together for a meal after such a special morning. So I'm going to cook up some eggs and bacon. Pancakes, too. All you can eat and it's on me."

Charlotte gave Trina a sudden hug before Trina knew what hit her. The crowd hooted and hollered until Miss Kitty rang the bell again and all the commotion came to a screeching halt. "But listen up," Miss Kitty shouted and the crowd went silent again. Miss Kitty reached out and pulled Trina's dad to stand next to her. Trina gulped. What did Miss Kitty want with her dad?

"We've all had our share of bad luck, but I'd say Mr. Mike here and his daughter, Citrine, are about the two luckiest things to happen to this town in years. They're good, honest, hardworking people. The kind of people who make me proud to live in New Royal. If we can't trust 'em, we can't trust anybody. So let's eat breakfast and then I expect every single one of you—" She stopped talking and looked behind her at the poster in the diner's window. "To be at the party at Goldenrod, next Saturday night at 6:30 p.m. sharp. If I can do it, you can do it."

She snapped her mouth shut, gave the crowd an emphatic nod, and pushed open the door of the diner. The crowd was still so quiet you could hear the little tin cats tinkle above her head. "And don't forget your costumes," she hollered over her shoulder.

As if an "on" button had been pressed, the whole town resumed its hooting and hollering. Happiness bubbled up in Trina, bringing with it uncontrollable laughter. Charlotte was dancing around, her red hair flying, so Trina danced too. The two of them laughed so hard they doubled themselves over, gasping and holding their stomachs.

Trina was laughing at the shock that Miss Kitty had something nice to say, but she was also laughing for a reason Charlotte might not have thought of: she was pretty sure the town was more afraid of Miss Kitty than it had ever been of Goldenrod.

A joyful town also meant Augustine was right. The Harvest Moon Masquerade Ball would be a very grand party.

Chapter Twenty-three

On Friday morning, the day before the masquerade ball, Trina was up early. Miss Dale had told her she had a surprise for her and she could stay home from school to get ready for the party. But Trina wasn't sure how to break the news to her dad—except for getting right to work. She brought an empty laundry basket outside and then she grabbed a packing blanket from the cargo trailer and carried it across the field to the orchard.

The apples were so ripe they practically fell off the trees. She tossed the wormy ones with little black holes in them to the ground for the birds; the good ones she tossed onto the blanket. And one she wiped on her shorts and ate for breakfast. She picked every apple she could reach and then she towed them back across the field to Goldenrod and filled the laundry basket with them. She couldn't budge the basket by herself, so she left it for her dad.

He still wasn't up, so she made his coffee and a big batch of oatmeal for both of them. She filled the new-old blue sugar bowl up to its brim with sugar and the new-old creamer with milk. Using dish towels as place mats, she set her dad's place at one end of the table and set hers at the other, as if they were the grand owners of Goldenrod who always dined this formally. She topped off all the elegance by filling the new pink vase with a big bouquet of golden- rod and set it in the center of the table.

"You're up early," he said, coming into the dining room and looking around, pleased to see breakfast ready and a cup of coffee waiting for him. And then he noticed the flowers and gave Trina a dubious look. "Is there some- thing else you've got cooking?"

"Poppo," she said, trying to sound especially sure of herself, "I've been meaning to tell you something since last night. Miss Dale said I could stay home today and work on the party. She said she cleared the whole thing with Miss Lincoln. It has to do with a surprise."

"What kind of a surprise?" he asked as he sat down at the table.

"I don't know, Poppo. All she said was it's a big surprise."

He took a sip of his coffee. "So it's just one day off from school and then it's business as usual, right?"

Trina nodded.

"Probably for the best, I guess." He sprinkled a big spoonful of sugar over his oatmeal and tipped another into his coffee. "I'm going to pick up the paint and get to work. My goal is to get a coat of paint on the front of the house by party-time tomorrow. That'll be Goldenrod's costume. She's going to the party as a yellow house."

Trina was glad her dad was taking the party seriously, but she worried he was trying to do too much in one day.

She didn't say anything, though. She didn't want to do anything to jinx the excitement.

She sat down and took a bite of her oatmeal. The vase of flowers in the middle of the table was so big she couldn't see her dad. As they ate, he kept peeking around the vase, making goofy faces at her, and then hiding again. Trina was embarrassed by his silliness, but it made her laugh.

When he left the table to get more coffee, Trina thought she heard the sound of a truck nearing the house and got up to look out the parlor window. As she stared across the tops of the cornfields, a huge cloud of dust rose up on the dirt road. It was rolling toward Goldenrod and it was getting closer by the second. "Poppo," she hollered. "Come here."

Her dad was instantly at her side, staring out the window with her. "It's a truck," he said. "Or two. Or three." Stunned, they went out onto the front porch. Now it looked like an entire train of trucks and cars, and Mr. Hank's truck was like the steam engine pulling them all toward Goldenrod. There were so many vehicles they couldn't all park in the yard, so they lined up alongside the road—and then what seemed like the whole town spilled into the yard.

Mr. Hank jumped down from his truck and walked right up to Trina's dad. "One good deed deserves another, Mr. Mike, heh-heh," he said, bouncing on his toes. He handed him a paintbrush and waved the crowd forward. "A little birdie told me you need some help out here."

"But I don't have the paint yet," Trina's dad said.

"Got it all in my truck, heh–heh," Mr. Hank said.

Trina watched her dad's shocked expression slowly turn into the biggest grin she'd ever seen, except maybe when she played first base for the Santa Fe Vipers and caught that pop fly and threw it home for a double play. But whatever was happening at this moment felt even more magical to Trina than winning a softball tournament. Miss Dale was right. It was a really big surprise. But the biggest surprise was that the town could keep it a secret. No one had breathed a word to Trina or her dad.

"She's taped off and ready to go," her dad said. Soon paint cans were popped open and ladders leaned up against all the sides of the house, and not just the front. Some people were standing on the ladders; others were standing on the ground. And everyone was painting with the prettiest buttery yellow paint imaginable. Without a doubt, Goldenrod would be all dressed up for the party by the end of the day.

But that wasn't all. More people were unloading their cars and trucks with furniture and household items and boxes full of stuff Trina couldn't see. It was as if they were moving in. "Where does this go?" one man asked. He was carrying a coat tree taller than he was. "Um," Trina's dad said, completely overwhelmed.

"In the foyer," Trina said, taking over.

"I'm Ben's dad, by the way," the man said on his way out as more people came through the open front doors. Trina sent people with boxes into the basement and up the stairs to the empty rooms, so the boxes could be unpacked later. Nearly a century's worth of Dare Club goods, Trina figured. No wonder there was so much stuff.

Miss Dale pushed through the crowd, her arm around Miss Lincoln's shoulders. Trina was surprised to see both of them. What if Miss Lincoln had changed her mind and come for her? "Miss Dale, what are you doing here?" she asked warily.

Miss Dale waved her bandage-free arm in the air. "I'm all better, so I took the day off to help."

"Only because Mrs. Harold agreed to take your class today," Miss Lincoln said matter-of-factly.

"Yes, thank you, Miss Lincoln," Miss Dale said. "That way I could deliver all the sandwiches and cookies Miss Kitty insisted on sending for the workers. And I brought some decorations we can work on." Miss Dale gave Trina a knowing little wink and turned to Miss Lincoln. "It's okay," she said, patting Miss Lincoln on the back. "It's okay, Miss Evelyn," she said again, softly. "You just give it back. You won't get in any trouble."

In a funny twist, Trina felt as if *she* were the principal and she had called Miss Lincoln into *her* office. "I didn't take this," Miss Lincoln said shyly, holding out a large teapot with a blue and white flowered pattern. She paused, looking at Miss Dale with desperation, and then she turned back to Trina nervously. "My brother did."

"But you took these, Aunt Evvie," the teenager from Mr. Hank's store said. He was coming up the steps behind Miss Lincoln with a box of matching teacups. *Evvie!* So she was the "Evvie" Miss Kitty had mentioned. Trina wondered if she would ever get over the shock: Miss Evelyn Lincoln, the prim and proper principal-secretary, was a member of the Dare Club.

Miss Lincoln's thin face blanched as white as the background of the china teapot. "This is Tyler, my great-nephew."

Trina smiled at Tyler, but her heart went out to Miss Lincoln. "Thank you, Miss Lincoln. Thank you for bringing it back. We can put the tea set in the dining room on the buffet. I think that's exactly where it belongs."

"I'll set up the food in the kitchen," Miss Dale said as Trina led Miss Lincoln and Tyler into the dining room. Trina waited patiently as Tyler handed Miss Lincoln the teacups and saucers one at a time and Miss Lincoln arranged them in a perfect circle. Trina offered to show Tyler and Miss Lincoln around the house, but Miss Lincoln insisted on getting back to school immediately.

As Tyler and Miss Lincoln went down the porch steps, two men came up, carrying a tall wooden cabinet with a crank and what looked like a big metal morning glory coming out of its top. "That's an old wind-up record player," Trina's dad said, looking down from his perch on a ladder outside the turret. "For old-fashioned music," he added, turning back to his painting.

"Then put that in the parlor," Trina said. "In the bay window."

"And records to go with it," another man said, following the old phonograph with a big box in his arms. Trina peered into the box. The records were as big as dinner plates. "Remember me?" the man asked. Trina did. He was the man in the overalls who had thanked her after Annie's funeral. She could tell he was glad for the chance to bring the stolen records back to Goldenrod—no questions asked.

At the tail end of the parked cars, two more men were unloading the back of a big truck. As they walked up the drive, Trina recognized them as the workmen from Mr. Shegstad's funeral home. Each of them was carrying a dining room chair tufted in blue velvet—just like the chairs in Augustine's dollhouse. Not until they came through the gate did Trina spot Mr. Shegstad, who was nervously directing the men toward the house. "Be careful, now," he said. "Don't scratch anything."

As Trina propped open the front door with a piece of wood from the oak tree, Mr. Shegstad just about walked into her. He had a ghostly look on his face. "My father . . . we . . . very comfortable . . ." he stammered, and Trina figured she had the whole story. Mr. Shegstad didn't take the chairs; his father did. And people at Shegstad's Funeral Home had been sitting in the elegant velvet chairs from Goldenrod for decades and didn't even know it.

"They're beautiful," Trina said. "You must have had them redone."

Mr. Shegstad nodded, looking relieved now that he had unburdened himself. "My wife, my wife," he said.

The two men made five more trips to the truck before all twelve chairs were in the dining room. "Right here, right here," Mr. Shegstad said, directing where each chair should go and adjusting the space between them so they fit perfectly around the huge table.

The dining room was now fit for kings and queens. "Thank you, Mr. Shegstad," Trina said. "We really appreciate it."

The house filled up with side tables and more chairs and rugs and lamps as Trina guided the furnishings to the most appropriate rooms. A big rolltop desk was placed in the library, along with a plant stand and dozens more books. Brass fireplace tools were set at the hearths, and a large portrait of Mr. Roy in his derby hat fit perfectly in the darkened outline above the library mantel. When two huge fancy beds arrived, Trina guided the guilty parties, carrying the beds piece by piece, to the master bedrooms, making sure no one went anywhere near Augustine and her dollhouse.

Within a matter of minutes, the job was done. The crowd thinned, motors revved, and the dust floated down the road in the other direction. The only people left were the paint crew and Miss Dale.

"What else can I help you with?" Miss Dale asked.

Trina didn't answer right away. She was too puzzled by an odd change she was noticing in the house. Filled with her belongings, Goldenrod didn't echo anymore. She no longer sounded hollow and empty.

"We could make the caramel apples," Trina finally said. She took Miss Dale into the kitchen and showed her the bags of caramels she bought at Millie's Grocery Store and the carton of sticks she got from Mr. Hank's hardware store—in the art department. "But first we have to bring in the apples and wash them."

Trina bribed her dad with one of Miss Kitty's sandwiches and got him to carry the basket of apples into the kitchen, while Miss Dale emptied the caramels into the spaghetti pot. Then Trina rinsed the apples and Miss Dale dried them until Trina's fingers started to shrivel in the water and they switched places. Some of the apples were saved for bobbing, but the rest of the apples they dipped in the melted caramel, which Miss Dale kept a close eye on so it wouldn't burn. "See," Miss Dale said, "I can cook more than my Aunt Kitty thinks."

Trina liked being alone with Miss Dale. It didn't feel like being with a teacher, except Miss Dale was always teaching her something, it seemed, like setting the caramel apples on a piece of painter's plastic instead of using up all the plates.

"Did you make your wand yet?" Miss Dale asked as Trina set the last apple on the plastic tarp.

Trina made a face, feeling as forgetful as her dad. "No, I forgot all about it." She still had the wand *and* Augustine's costume to make. "Maybe I can just use a stick from the old tree."

"Don't feel bad," Miss Dale said. "I'll be up late too, putting last-minute touches on your dad's costume."

"Who's he going to be?" Trina asked.

With a gleam in her eye, Miss Dale shook her head. "I think it should be a surprise."

Ever since she pictured her dad as a big red tomato,

Trina was dying to see him in his costume. But if the look on Miss Dale's face was any indication, Trina had a feeling his costume was going to be something better than a big red tomato.

"And now for the decorations," Miss Dale said. "Follow me." She climbed into Mr. Hank's truck and brought out the box of tin cans from Miss Kitty's diner. "We can make lanterns with these. I have a bunch of stubby candles we can stick inside them."

"And we can poke holes in the sides with a hammer and nails. I'm good with a hammer," Trina said, quietly checking out her pale green thumb. "Pretty good, anyway."

They spent the rest of the afternoon making lanterns. Lanterns for the edge of the porch and lanterns to line the path from the gate to the steps.

It was late afternoon when the paint crew started to clean up and the air filled with the smell of turpentine. Miss Dale shouted at Mr. Hank, "How long 'til we head back?"

"Ten minutes, heh-heh," Mr. Hank shouted back.

Miss Dale nodded at Mr. Hank and turned back to Trina. "Citrine, do you think you could show me your dollhouse?" She said it shyly, the way Augustine asked about her prince.

Trina said yes before she realized it was still light out and Augustine would be wide awake. What if she opened her bedroom door and caught Augustine cleaning her house? Or singing? How would she explain that to Miss Dale? But how could she say no to Miss Dale without explaining the situation? She had to take her chances. She led Miss Dale upstairs.

"This is my room," she said loudly when she arrived at her closed door. She opened her door just a crack and peeked her head in. Augustine was standing outside her dollhouse, dancing and humming in a ray of sunshine. "Oh, Miss Dale, I am so excited to show you the dollhouse," Trina said, hoping Augustine would get the message. When Trina opened the door a little bit wider, Augustine dropped to the floor with barely a clink. She was lying there as stiff as a board by the time Miss Dale noticed her.

"Oh," was all Miss Dale said as she sank to her knees. She picked up Augustine as if she'd just gotten her for her birthday. She smoothed the doll's hair and straightened her dress while holding her very, very gently. "It's all so perfect," she said. She touched the copper weather vane and the shingled roof and the brass doorknob on the front door. "Just perfect." Miss Dale sat Augustine down at the dining room table and put a tiny fork in her hand. "I always wanted a dollhouse."

"Really?" Trina knelt down by Miss Dale. "So did my mom." It felt safe to talk about her mother with Miss Dale.

"How about you?" Miss Dale looked at Trina with her kind green eyes.

Trina shook her head. "Not me. I like softball and fixing houses with my dad. But it's been fun to work on this house by myself." She didn't mention that talking to Augustine was the best part.

"That makes perfect sense," Miss Dale said. "I can see you're a lot like your father."

"Maybe," Trina said. And maybe she was a lot like her mother too. And then, because she was so excited and the party was only a day away, she had to say it out loud. "I invited my mom to the party tomorrow."

Miss Dale opened and shut the cupboards in Augustine's tiny kitchen. "Has it been a long time since you've seen your mother?"

"Yup. Not since I was three," Trina said.

"I know what it's like to have your mom live far away." Miss Dale spoke very softly. "My dad died about ten years ago and my mom got remarried. She lives in Mason City. It's only a few hours from here, but I don't get to see her very often. She has a different life now." Miss Dale brushed the bangs out of Trina's eyes. "I hope your mother can come to the party." She stood up to leave.

"I'll go downstairs with you," Trina said. On her way out the door, she grabbed the bag of fabric scraps and Augustine's little nightgown, which was hanging on the tiniest hook in her room. When she caught Augustine's eye, the little doll flashed a huge smile just for Trina.

By the time she and Miss Dale got downstairs, her dad was outside in the yard, waving good-bye to Mr. Hank as he pulled away in his truck. He stood for a moment, looking up at Goldenrod with the same awe that showed on his face the very first time he saw her.

"What an amazing day," he said as he came up the steps.

"There have been a lot of amazing days lately," Miss Dale

said. And then she got an anxious look on her face. "Wait a minute. Hank was supposed to give me a ride home."

"I'll take you," Trina's dad said.

"Are you sure it's not too much trouble? I can always call—"

"No trouble at all," he interrupted. "And then I'll get the cider and pop for tomorrow too." Trina couldn't believe it. For once in his life her dad was planning ahead. "Do you want to come with us?" he asked her.

"No thanks, Poppo. I have an important sewing project to finish."

"Okay. I'll be home for dinner."

Trina said good-bye to Miss Dale and as the truck drove away from Goldenrod, she set up her sewing station at the dining room table. She got out a needle and thread and scrounged through the bag of scraps looking for the shimmery piece of blue fabric for Augustine's costume, but when she came across the piece of lace, she couldn't resist making the curtains first. She cut the lace into four long strips, rolled their edges, one by one, and hemmed them with tiny invisible stitches. Dollhouse curtains were so easy to make, she decided to make curtains for Augustine's parents' room too.

Next she laid Augustine's nightgown on the dining room table as a pattern. *Measure twice, cut once*, Miss Dale had said. She measured and measured again, allowing for a tiny seam. Then she cut the shimmery blue fabric, a front and a back, and stitched and hemmed as the afternoon slipped toward evening. Sewing was as magical as building the porch—making something out of nothing.

In the middle of stitching the hem, a giddy feeling swept through Trina out of nowhere. It was as if someone had run up to her, whispered the most wonderful secret in her ear, and skipped away laughing. She couldn't help responding. "I feel the same way, Goldenrod. Something very special is going to happen."

It wasn't just the party, or that she was certain the whole town was coming. All that was special enough, but the feeling that Goldenrod had told her something *extra-special* was going to happen could mean only one thing: her mother was coming to the party. She just knew it.

She was nearly finished with the hem of Augustine's party dress when her dad returned from his trip into town. He carried jug after jug of apple cider into the kitchen. "I got paper cups too," he said in passing. On one of his trips from the kitchen to the truck he paused at Trina's chair just as she tied a knot and broke the thread between her teeth.

When she looked up, he reached into his shirt pocket. "This was in the P.O. box," he said. He pulled out a small cream-colored envelope and placed it on the table in front of her.

Trina set down her needle and searched the little envelope for a return address. It was on the back, printed on a gold label: *Caroline Adams. Los Angeles, California.*

"Adams," Trina said. "Is that her real name?"

Her dad nodded. "It's her maiden name. I looked her up on the Internet at the library and found out where she works."

Trina flipped the envelope over again and ran her finger along the beautiful script of her mother's name, and then she looked up at her dad. "Poppo, did you . . . ?"

He shook his head. "This one's for real."

Trina's whole body trembled with anticipation as she opened the envelope and pulled out a note card with an elegant, raised gold *C* on the front.

Dear Citrine,

Thank you for the invitation. What a coincidence. My crew is wrapping up a shoot in St. Louis, Missouri. If all goes as planned, I'll swing through New Royal on the way home. Looking forward to it.

Fondly, C.

"Oh, Poppo," Trina said, jumping from her chair and hopping in a little circle. "I knew it! I knew she'd come!" She didn't even mind that her mother hadn't said "Love, Mom," like the postcards always did. What mattered was that she was coming to the party.

Her dad read the card. "You mean she'll try. St. Louis is a long way—"

"No, Poppo," Trina said as she felt a huge unstoppable grin spreading across her face. "She says she's looking forward to it. She's coming. I can feel it." She knew Goldenrod could feel it too, had even told her about it, but she didn't say that part.

Trina couldn't wait to tell Augustine. *No stone unturned.* She left Augustine's costume on the table with her sewing supplies, but she grabbed the note and the lace curtains and ran upstairs to her room.

"Augustine," she said, bursting through the door and kneeling in front of the dollhouse. "I have the most wonderful surprises!"

Augustine ran to her window and peered up at Trina with her bright doll smile. "First, here is your nightgown." She hung Augustine's nightgown on the post of her bed. "Second, a letter from my mother," Trina said. She held out the card so Augustine could see the gold *C* and then she read the note to Augustine. "I know she says she'll try, but if she's looking forward to it and if she's going to be that close, she'll have to come to the party."

"It is a beautiful letter, Citrine. What a wonderful surprise for you." Augustine leaned farther out her window, straining to see around Trina's back. "And is there also a surprise for me? Is it my costume? Should I close my eyes and wait patiently?"

Trina shook her head. "No, it's not your costume. I have a few finishing touches left to do on that. But yes, Augustine, close your eyes."

As soon as Augustine's eyes were closed, Trina lifted the tiny brown wire curtain rods from Augustine's bedroom windows, wove them in and out of the tops of the lace curtains, and set them back in place in their tiny brackets. "Now you can open your eyes and turn around."

Augustine spun around and cried out, "Thank you, Citrine!" When she pulled her new curtains across the window, dots of light speckled the floor. "They are beautiful."

Trina hung the other pair in the other bedroom. "Miss Dale taught me how to sew."

Augustine clasped her hands together, overcome with joy. "Ah, yes, Miss Dale. Did you see how she put the fork in my hand?"

Trina nodded.

"That made me very, very happy."

"Augustine, you're so funny," Trina said. "The littlest things make you happy."

"As the littlest things should," Augustine said. "If all the little things make for happiness, there is more happiness, is there not?"

"Yes," Trina said. "There is."

And Augustine really was right. It was the little things. Little by little, Goldenrod had come back to life. Little by little, luck was coming back to New Royal. Little by little, Trina had made friends. And little by little, Trina had found out about her mother. And now, after all these years, she was going to see her mother in real life.

Trina placed the note card from her mother on top of the postcards on the mantel. Little things like hopes and dreams really could turn into big happy things.

Chapter Twenty-four

"Citree-een, Citree-een." At first Trina thought her mother was calling to her, but then she realized there was only one being in the whole world who sang her name that way. She opened her eyes to see Augustine sitting on her pillow at the end of her nose.

"Today's the day, Citrine. Today's the party."

Trina sat up so quickly, Augustine tumbled from Trina's pillow into the covers.

"I overslept. How in the world did I oversleep? Of all days!"

Augustine righted herself and straightened her nightgown. "I have waited anxiously for this day, Citrine. I cannot believe it has come. Is my costume ready for me?"

"Almost," Trina said. She had so much to do she didn't know where to begin. "A list. I need a list." She grabbed a pencil and a sheet of paper and made a list of the final preparations. Then she set Augustine in her bedroom. "I'll finish your costume this morning, and then I have to decorate the house. I'll be back later to help you get dressed." She pulled on her shorts and T-shirt and shoved the list in her pocket.

"Citrine," Augustine said before Trina could get out the door. "I would prefer to sit at my table with my mother and father so we may talk about the party."

Trina hastily set Augustine at the dining room table with her parents. Then she raced downstairs and ate her oatmeal in seconds flat and ran outside to pick the last of the daisies, several giant bouquets of chrysanthemums, and armfuls of goldenrod. She was putting all the flowers in a big bucket of water when she noticed what looked like a shiny steel bathtub sitting by the stump of the old oak tree. It was another special delivery, but this one wasn't a mystery. Edward's dad must have delivered the horse trough before she woke up.

"Good morning, Princess," her dad said as she came into the house.

"Today's the day," she said with a big grin on her face.

"You're right." He hooked his tool belt around his waist. "Today's the day I fix the downstairs toilet. I figure the last thing we need is for the darn thing to flush itself and scare away all our guests. Especially after all your hard work. What's on your agenda?"

Trina pulled the list from her pocket. "Pick flowers, hang streamers, finish lanterns, and make wand." She skipped the part about finishing Augustine's costume.

"I think I'll be painting trim most of the day."

"Except when you help with the streamers."

While her dad fixed the toilet valve, Trina made the little doll a pointy hat by stitching a stiff piece of blue ribbon into a cone shape. Then she attached long, thin strips of a sheer white fabric to the point with a dab of glue and stuck a sequin on the very tip.

Lastly, she grabbed a long, slender stick from the woodpile. She sanded its rough spots and tied lots of colored ribbons to it. It didn't look like a wand Hermione would have used, but it was pretty.

She cleaned up her sewing station and was about to take Augustine's dress to her room, but she was afraid Augustine would demand something else. And she didn't want her dad to find the costume, so she folded up the dress and the little hat and carefully put them in her pocket.

Trina spent the rest of the morning outside, punching holes in a few more tin cans for the last of the lanterns. The biggest of the tin cans she saved to use as vases for the flowers.

But the day was already getting away from her. "Poppo," she called up to her dad. He was painting the trim on one of the turret windows. "We'd better put up the streamers."

She made them a couple of peanut butter sandwiches while she waited for him to clean up and put away all his tools. They gobbled down the sandwiches standing in the kitchen, and then her dad carried his two tallest ladders into the foyer and set one under the chandelier and one against the wall.

"Look," he said, pointing through the front door as Mr. Hank's flatbed truck came rolling through the gate. "Hank and Miss Kitty are here. Perfect timing. We need all the help we can get."

"And Miss Dale is right behind them," Trina said. She ran to outside to greet everyone.

Miss Kitty bulldozed past her, carrying a tray of cookies. "Be careful with those brownie boxes, Hank," she hollered over her shoulder. "They could use your help out there," she said to Trina, and then to her dad as she went up the stairs, "Lots more dishes and extra chairs to bring in."

"I'll get the chairs," her dad said.

Charlotte and Edward hopped out of the backseat of Miss Dale's car. It took both of them to pull out a rainbow piñata. "We filled it with candy and a bunch of toys and things we got at the dollar store out on the highway," Edward said.

"I paid for it with my own money. Except my grandmother helped," Charlotte said.

Trina was awestruck. "Wow, Charlotte. That's really generous."

"Hi, Citrine," Miss Dale said as she popped open her trunk. It was full of boxes with various fabrics poking out of them. "Costumes," she said excitedly, but then she frowned, counting them. "One for your dad, one for Charlotte, . . . Edward, Aunt Kitty, and me. Oh, thank goodness. For a second I thought I missed one."

"I'll help you," Trina said, reaching for a box that clinked when she picked it up.

"That's your dad's," Miss Dale said mysteriously. "Don't peek."

"I won't," Trina said, and she meant it too, even though she was desperate to know what it was.

"How can we help?" Charlotte asked.

Trina looked around the yard at the trough and the bucket of flowers. "Edward, why don't you fill the trough with water? And then fill it with apples. They're in the kitchen. Charlotte, could you put candles in the lanterns? And then can you fill some of the bigger cans with flowers and set them along the porch and walkway?"

As Trina passed through the foyer on her way upstairs, Mr. Hank and her dad were standing on the ladders, twisting the yellow streamers from the chandelier and taping them to the crown molding. The foyer was beginning to look like a giant pinwheel. "It's exactly as I pictured," she said, twirling around and around like Augustine to take it all in.

When Trina came back downstairs, she helped Miss Dale and Miss Kitty set up the food. She found a big white tablecloth among the stolen goods and laid it across the dining room table. Soon the table was covered with trays of wrapped sandwiches and brownies. Vats of hot dogs and baked beans were plugged in to get cooking. Bags of buns and chips were set out, along with stacks and stacks of white plates from Miss Kitty's diner.

Mr. Hank and her dad moved into the parlor and strung more streamers. And then Mr. Hank hung the piñata from a hook on the porch ceiling and tied the rope to the railing before he went home to get his wife.

The party would begin in less than an hour.

Now it was time for everyone to put on their costumes. Luckily, Trina could offer everyone a private dressing room. She grabbed her wand and showed Miss Dale and Edward and Charlotte upstairs to the other bedrooms.

"I'll be in here," she said, ducking into her own room. "Augustine," Trina called softly, holding the costume behind her back as the little doll ran to her window. Without being told, Augustine closed her eyes.

Trina draped the little blue gown across Augustine's bed and placed the tiny veiled hat next to it. "There. Now you can open your eyes."

Augustine opened her eyes and put her hand to her chest as if she couldn't breathe. "Oh, Citrine! I shall be the princess Briar Rose. How did you know? Please, dress me at once!"

Trina, familiar with Augustine's bossiness, obeyed happily.

The dress fit perfectly—almost. It was a bit bumpy at the waist, and the hem was a little uneven, but Augustine didn't seem to mind. And the pointed hat, with its fluttery veil, was perfect. Delighted by her princess costume, Augustine floated down her staircase, twirled up to the dining room table where her mother and father waited proudly, and swayed as if she were dancing in the arms of her prince. "I believe I shall wear this dress forever and ever."

"I'm glad you like it, but forever and ever is a very long time, Augustine. You can wear it to the party, but then I think you should save it for special occasions."

"You make no sense to me, Citrine. What is more special than forever and ever?"

Augustine was right. For someone who loved fairy

tales, there was nothing better than forever and ever. "You win," Trina said. "And now it's my turn to get dressed."

Augustine twirled around the room as Trina pulled her Hermione Granger costume out of the grocery bag. Both the skirt and the blouse were so big that Trina decided to wear them over her own shorts and T-shirt. She snapped the tie around her neck, slipped her arms into the black cloak, plopped the witch hat on her head, and picked up her wand.

Trina looked at herself in the mirror, pleased with her costume. She was waving her wand in the air when she heard a little noise at her feet. Augustine had tripped and was creeping backward on her hands and knees, escaping Trina's shadow with a frightened look on her face.

"What's the matter, Augustine?"

"Are you a witch?" Augustine asked.

"Yes," said Trina, before it dawned on her why the little doll was now cowering by the door to her house. "But I'm a good witch. I bring houses back to life and I reunite little dolls with their parents," she said.

"How can I be certain?" whispered Augustine.

"Because I do good deeds and cast good spells." Trina cupped her hands around Augustine and said in her kindest, most magical voice, "Apples and candy make me glad, but Augustine's the best friend I ever had." Trina pulled off her witch hat and dropped it to the floor. "See? It's just me."

Augustine's fearful look disappeared. She stood up again and pirouetted at Trina's feet, humming sweetly. "Will there be music at the party, Citrine?"

Trina hadn't thought of music. The only hope was the old record player. "Yes," she said, just to make Augustine happy.

Augustine stopped dancing and peered up at Trina. "Then I must ask a favor of you, Citrine. Would you please stand my mother and father together in the parlor? They would very much like to dance during the party this evening. Could you assist them?"

"Sure," Trina said, reaching to pick up her witch's hat.

"I mean now," the little doll said. "I do not want them to be forgotten."

Trina was surprised by how demanding Augustine was being, but then again, if her own mother and father had a chance to dance for the first time in a hundred years, she would be anxious to see it happen too. She picked up the father doll, straightened his legs, brushed a bit of lint from his trousers, and walked him over to the mother doll.

"May I have this dance?" Trina said in a deep voice, to which the mother doll answered in a lady's voice, "I would love to," and then Trina laughed, but it felt as if the mother doll were laughing happily inside her.

Trina leaned the father doll against the mantel as she stood the mother on her pretty porcelain shoes and raised her delicate arms. Then she matched the mother's right hand in the air with the father's left hand. With two fingers on each doll, Trina glided the pair across their polished parlor floor, humming along with Augustine. She didn't know the words, but she had learned the melody. The song sounded old and romantic.

Before she let go of the dolls, she made sure they were balanced, each holding the other up. A perfect couple. Trina stood and curtsied.

"Thank you, Citrine. Thank you! That was absolutely grand," Augustine said, clapping giddily. "Soon Goldenrod will be once again full of friends and laughter and joy, is that not true?"

"Yes," Trina said. "That is true."

"And you no longer need to be afraid of the evil giant?" The little doll was standing on her tiptoes, trying to see herself in the mirror.

"No, I don't have to be afraid of her any longer."

"And Annie is safe?"

"Yes, Annie is safe, the town is happy, I'm a good witch, and you're driving me crazy with all these questions." Trina turned sideways to look at herself one more time in the mirror.

Augustine didn't seem to mind Trina's exasperated tone and smiled contentedly. "Oh, Citrine. It is all quite perfect then. With my beautiful house, my mother and father found at last, and knowing that I have helped you, our story has a perfect ending."

"Ending?" Trina glanced down at the little doll.

"Yes, ending. Everything is how it is supposed to be. Except for one more thing." Augustine held up her index finger. "Because I have helped you, you must now help me."

Trina leaned down and straightened Augustine's little hat. She had helped the little doll quite a bit, she thought, but she knew she hadn't yet helped her with her most important mission. "Don't worry, Augustine. I haven't forgotten about helping you find your prince."

Augustine shook her head. "No, that is not what I speak of. I am afraid I will have to wait for my prince to find me. After all, that is the proper way in my world. But I do know of another way you can help me." Augustine looked toward the fireplace in Trina's room and became unusually thoughtful.

Trina stopped looking at herself in the mirror. A sad tone in Augustine's voice worried her. Something had changed. Trina couldn't imagine what Augustine wanted her to do now, but something about her request made Trina feel uneasy. "What is it?" she asked.

"Will you read to me again the story of Briar Rose?"

Trina was relieved that the problem was a small one. But no wonder Augustine was sad. They hadn't read a story in ages.

"Of course," Trina said.

"That is so very kind of you, Citrine, but please listen carefully. I should like you to lay me in my bed where I will let myself fall asleep while you read. My mother and father shall stay as they are. When you are finished reading, please return our house to the little room where you first found me. Lastly, before you go, please secure the shutters of that room. And then close the door."

Trina sat down on the floor, not sure she had heard the doll correctly. "What?"

"And promise me you will never open the door again."

"What are you saying, Augustine? I don't understand." Trina felt a wave of sadness go through her. What was happening?

"Is that not what children do in your world? Do they not grow up and put their toys away?" Augustine looked at Trina earnestly. "I am very glad I awakened when I did, or you might have outgrown my world before I had a chance to wake up in yours. I will never forget our tea parties and our wonderful adventures. I particularly enjoyed the Land of School, Citrine. And I am glad to think I may have helped you, at least a little, to find your own family."

"You mean—?" As much as she didn't want to, Trina understood what Augustine was saying. "No, Augustine, I can't. I can't do that."

"But you promised. Think of 'The Frog Prince,' Citrine. Think of the perils of a broken promise. The most horrible things can happen if you do not keep a promise. I kept my promise, and now you must keep yours."

Trina couldn't remember making any promise that meant giving up Augustine. And she wanted to tell the little doll that "The Frog Prince" meant nothing. That it was just a story. But how could she expect Augustine to understand, when stories were everything to the little doll?

A flurry of feet and laughter resounded in the hallway. Pound, pound, pound across the hall. Pound, pound, pound at her door. Trina held as still and silent as Augustine, hoping no one would come barging in.

"Hurry up, Citrine!" Edward yelled. "Everyone will be here soon."

"What's taking you so long?" Charlotte shouted.

Augustine raised one fine eyebrow. "The giant. I would know her voice anywhere."

Trina put her finger to her lips to hush Augustine. "I'm almost ready," she hollered. "I'll be there in a minute."

"Okay!" Edward yelled before his feet and Charlotte's pounded down the stairs.

"Should you not hurry, Citrine? Do they not need you?"

Trina didn't care about Charlotte or Edward or anybody else. All she cared about right now was Augustine. She cradled the little doll close to her face. "I don't want to put you away," Trina said as tears welled in her eyes. "I need you."

Augustine cocked her little head. "But do you, Citrine? You have friends now. Real friends, just as you wished. It is time to put me away. You are ready, and so am I. I belong in my world, and you belong in yours."

A single tear slipped down Trina's cheek. Augustine reached out and caught the tear in her hands. "This is sadness I am touching, is it not?"

Trina's voice cracked. "Yes."

"I feel this sadness too. It is very heavy and I cannot bear it another moment. Please, Citrine." She squeezed Trina's finger with one hand and gestured toward the dollhouse with the other.

Trina looked into Augustine's trusting eyes. She had no choice but to keep her promise. She laid Augustine, in her elegant dress, on top of her covers so her prince would see she was a princess. She made sure the little pointed hat was sitting on her head, tucked the veil beneath her, and laid her hair over her shoulders just so.

"I will never forget you," Trina said.

"I know you will never forget me, Citrine, for I will always be part of your memories and stories. And someday a little girl will find me and I will be played with again."

Someday. It was a word Trina had clung to until she couldn't trust it, but now she heard the hope in it again. Someday.

"Now, please, the story. It is my favorite."

Trina picked up *Grimm's Fairy Tales* and sat down on the floor outside Augustine's bedroom.

"Citrine?"

Trina leaned forward. "Yes?"

"Promise me you will always believe in happy endings."

Trina wanted to make the promise, but she couldn't. She couldn't imagine the sun coming up without it waking Augustine. What would she do tomorrow morning? And the day after that? She was too sad thinking she would never hear the little doll's voice ever again to believe in happy endings.

"Promise me," Augustine insisted as she sank into her little white pillow.

"I promise to try." That was as much as Trina could say, but it seemed to please the little doll.

"Citrine," she whispered, "I feel something more. Something I do not understand."

Trina leaned in closer. "What is it?"

"It is right . . . here." Augustine placed her hand on the center of her chest. "But I do not feel broken. I believe I have felt it before. A long time ago."

Trina placed her hand over her own heart. "It's love, Augustine. I feel it too. I love you, Augustine."

Augustine kept her hand at her heart. "So this is love. I am glad to have known love in your world once more. I also love you, Citrine."

With those words on her tiny lips, Augustine closed her eyes. There was nothing more Trina could say, so she opened the book to page fifty-seven and began to read. *"Once upon a time there lived in a distant kingdom a very lonesome king and queen. 'If only we had a child,' they wished, but for many years they remained alone."*

Trina read on and on, pausing at the point when Briar Rose pricked her finger on the spindle and fell asleep. No wonder Augustine loved this story. It was the story of a very happy house until the house fell under a wicked spell. Then it became a very sad house that went to sleep with everything in it. And its princess, who lay as still as a doll, waited a hundred years for a prince to kiss her and wake her and for all happiness to return. It was a story about love and patience. But most of all, it was a story about hope.

Trina finished reading the story, and when she looked up, Augustine was fast asleep.

Trina closed the book.

Slowly and carefully, she dragged the dollhouse from her bedroom into the turret room. She couldn't bear to shove the dollhouse deep beneath the shelf, dark and hidden, so she pushed the dollhouse to a stop in the center of the playroom, certain a prince would find Augustine more easily if she weren't tucked away.

Then she shut the shutters one by one and the room became as dark and as still as the day Trina discovered it. As she pulled the mirrored door closed behind her and heard the latch click, it was as if the princess had pricked her finger on the spindle one more time.

If Trina could believe in a happy ending, she hoped Augustine wouldn't have to wait another hundred years for a little girl to open the door and play with her.

Chapter Twenty-five

Trina wiped her eyes and stared at herself in the tall mirror. A sad Hermione Granger stared back at her. She would need nothing short of magic to look happy.

When a car honked outside, Trina pushed open her bedroom window to chaos. The road leading up to the house was filled with parked cars and strangely dressed people. She swore she heard someone say, "Be brave and valiant," just as Augustine would say. But all she saw was Ben, running through the gate dressed as Luke Skywalker, waving his light saber. "What?" he hollered at his mother, who was a few yards behind him.

"I said, behave and help out," she shouted.

The idea that she might always hear Augustine's words of wisdom made Trina feel better about joining the party without her. She put her witch hat back on her head, waved good-bye to the mirrored door with her wand, and arrived at the bottom of the stairs just as Miss Kitty, in a black witch costume, barged through the foyer on her way to the kitchen. "I'm the Wicked Witch of the East. The nice one," she cackled.

"I'm a witch too," Trina said, waving her wand at

Miss Kitty's back, thinking a little good magic wouldn't hurt her.

Miss Dale came down the stairs and stopped on the landing. Her hair was in braids and she was wearing a blue gingham dress. On her right arm she carried a wicker basket with a little stuffed dog in it. Charlotte followed with her red hair in braids too, braids that stuck straight out from her head. Her striped leggings clashed with her plaid dress.

"Guess who?" Charlotte said.

"Miss Dale is Dorothy and you are *not* Princess Leia," Trina said.

"You're Pippi Longstocking!" Prissy Missy shouted, coming in the front door dressed as Little Bo Peep—just in time to scream when a gorilla bounded out of the library into the foyer, pounding its chest.

"Who are you?" Prissy Missy asked the big gorilla.

"King Kong," the low, gruff voice answered. The gorilla removed its furry head to reveal Edward. He scratched his scalp, looking at Trina in her skirt, blouse, and cloak. "You should dress like a girl more often," he said.

Trina pointed her wand at Edward. "And you, Master Obi-Wan Kenobi, are now a gorilla."

Upstairs something clanged.

Charlotte gasped, "What was that?"

Whatever it was clanged again.

Trina had no idea what the sound was, but she knew it was nothing to be afraid of. And so did Miss Dale, it seemed, because she was doing everything possible not to laugh.

A door creaked open in the upstairs hallway and the clangs got louder. "I can't walk in this thing," Trina's dad shouted. A clang was followed by a stomp, followed by another clang. Slowly Poppo clanged and stomped down the stairs and appeared on the landing next to Miss Dale. He was wearing stacks of coffee cans wired together as pants and sleeves, most of a garbage can for a shirt, and a funnel as a hat.

The cans were sprayed with sparkling silver paint and his hands and face were smeared with creamy silver makeup. A black rubber washer was stuck to the end of his nose, which made his costume perfect. Trina laughed so hard at her Tin-Man dad that tears came back to her eyes. But this time they were happy tears.

Right then Mr. Kinghorn strode through the front door wearing a tuxedo. "Every British novel of any worth has a butler," he explained. He had draped a white dish towel across his arm and insisted on answering the door the rest of the night.

When Mr. Hank arrived with his wife, wearing matching plaid shirts and carrying inflatable plastic axes, Mr. Kinghorn said, "May I present to you Mr. and Mrs. Paul Bunyan." Trina had to laugh again because, at least for Mr. Hank, a plaid shirt wasn't much of a costume.

Mr. Shegstad came alone, dressed as an angel with a foil halo taped to his shiny bald head. "May I present to you the angel Clarence." Trina had no idea who Clarence was, but Mr. Shegstad made a perfect angel anyway.

Miss Lincoln and Mr. Bert stepped in behind

Mr. Shegstad. Miss Lincoln was wearing a tattered dress and a big hat, and Mr. Bert was dressed in a cape and top hat. "May I present to you Mrs. Whatsit and the honorable Sherlock Holmes," Mr. Kinghorn said.

Every time the door opened, Trina was on pins and needles, waiting for Mr. Kinghorn to announce the arrival of her mother, Caroline Adams, who probably didn't have time to find a costume. But that was okay. Maybe she was famous enough to come as herself.

Goldenrod filled with vampires, villains, sci-fi monsters, cowboys, and gentlemen and ladies in old-fashioned clothes, so fast that soon it was hard to move from room to room. People laughed and talked and told stories. More than once Trina overheard someone say, "The night I snuck in here . . ."

All the sandwiches had been unwrapped and the hot dogs, baked beans, and apple cider were piping hot. Miss Kitty's cookies and brownies were arranged around a giant bouquet of mums and goldenrod and a big tray of caramel apples sat at each end of the table. Everything was perfect . . . except something was missing. Not just her mother, of course, but something else. The music!

Trina remembered the old record player. She ran into the parlor, opened the top, and recognized the turntable because she had seen a record player once at a school party. She gave the crank a few turns and the turntable went around and around. She picked out a record and laughed at how big and heavy it was. The record held only one song, and no song she had ever heard of had such a strange name: "Believe Me If All Those Endearing Young Charms."

She placed the record on the turntable and lowered the needle. The raspy music crackled through the metal morning glory, sounding at first like radio static. Trina's heart sank. And then the noise evened out and a man with an Irish accent, accompanied by a violin, slowly sang the words in the title.

As the music filled the house, older men took the hands of older women and waltzed them from the parlor into the foyer, twirling them and occasionally bumping into another couple, causing shouts of laughter. Some of the teenagers slow-danced and most of the younger kids danced in groups.

Even tall Mr. Kinghorn took a break from answering the door to dance with stout Miss Kitty. They looked at each other with love in their eyes and Trina was certain she saw Miss Kitty smile. No wonder Mr. Kinghorn called her Katherine. Trina figured their romance was another secret everyone knew about and no one mentioned.

Trina found herself humming along to the lilting melody and then a crazy feeling of déjà vu swept through her. Everything was wonderfully new and yet strangely familiar at the same time. Hadn't she thought Mr. Kinghorn looked like a butler when she first met him? And didn't she picture the dining room table set with white dishes and flowers and the parlor filled with people all dressed up and laughing and talking? And this song, this ancient song she shouldn't know—but she did. It was the song Augustine was always humming. Trina closed her eyes and imagined the music floating up through the floor and into the turret room, just the way it would have a hundred years ago. She pictured Augustine's mother and father dancing in their parlor while Augustine dreamed of her prince.

Edward took off his gorilla head and came up to Trina shyly. It seemed like he wanted to ask her something—to dance?—when the song crackled to a stop and Trina's dad shouted, "Everyone to the porch! It's time for the piñata."

"Next time," Trina said, so Edward wouldn't be embarrassed and then they hurried outside together. Naturally, Edward managed to be first in line.

Charlotte's lanterns were glowing, warm, and welcoming, but the temperature had dropped so far the flowers were drooping. Trina pulled her cloak around her. "It's freezing out here, Poppo."

"Looks like I'll have to turn the furnace on tonight," he said.

"Get ready for an early winter, heh-heh," Mr. Hank said as he untied the piñata and gave it a yank. "*Farmer's Almanac* predicts lots of snow too."

"I can see my breath," Charlotte said, standing next to Trina for a turn at the piñata. "I guess summer is really over," she sighed, but then she added brightly, "At least we can look forward to big snowball fights!"

"And we can go sledding," Edward said. "And ice skating."

Trina was glad to be included in Charlotte's plans, but she liked Edward's ideas best.

Miss Dale tied an old scarf around Edward's eyes. He took a swing at the rainbow piñata with one of Trina's softball bats, and bumped it, but then Mr. Hank made the rainbow swing high and out of reach. Charlotte was next. She swung the bat and spun around in a full circle, missing the piñata completely. And just before it was Trina's turn, a little boy from one of the younger grades cracked it open.

Candy and trinkets fell like rain and all the kids lunged across the porch to grab the goodies. Trina ended up with a bunch of baby suckers—just what she wanted—and a plastic packet labeled "Exotic Sea Creatures." The little bag contained a whale, a jellyfish, a shark, and a green frog. "Charlotte," she said, laughing about the dollar-store purchase, "frogs aren't sea creatures!" And then she shoved the packet into the front pocket of her shorts for safekeeping.

Most of the guests went back into the house except for Tyler, Miss Lincoln's great-nephew, and a bunch of his friends. They hung around the water trough, bobbing for apples and sitting on the tree stump talking.

Trina wandered from room to room, savoring every moment of the party. In the parlor, voices blended into a chorus of excitement about how beautiful the house was. Edward was trying to juggle apples in the kitchen, Miss Dale and her dad were standing in the bay window, talking and eating caramel apples, and Mr. Kinghorn was carrying a tray of brownies from guest to guest.

Trina cranked up the music again and the party went on and on until the food was almost gone. No wonder Augustine said Goldenrod was the happiest when there were parties. Parties made happiness feel as if it could last forever—until people started to leave. Edward's big ape paw waved at Trina all the way from the foyer as his mother pulled him out the door. "See you Monday, Citrine."

Trina waved to Edward, but as more and more guests said good-bye, she started to get worried. Couldn't everyone please stay a little longer? Her mother might be here any second. She walked through the emptying rooms, on the lookout for any character she might have missed. A lost Cinderella or a Mary Poppins. What if her mother really *was* lost? What if she took a wrong turn? What if she had veered off the road and was stuck in a cornfield?

Trina arrived in the kitchen just as Miss Kitty took off her witch hat and rolled up her black sleeves to start washing the dishes. In the parlor, Mr. Kinghorn reached up and pulled down a handful of streamers. Then her dad slipped out of his tin cans and washed the silver paint off his hands so he could help reload Mr. Hank's truck. The whole place was cleaned up in one of Mr. Hank's quick jiffies.

"C'mon, Charlotte, you're riding home with us," Miss Kitty said, following Mr. Hank and his wife down the path carrying a box of clean plates. The candles had mostly burned out, which made Trina even sadder.

"Hey, where's your mom?" Charlotte asked, hanging behind as Trina held the door open.

Trina glanced around, pretending she hadn't noticed her mother's absence, and hoped Charlotte wouldn't see the quiver in her lips. "Something must have come up."

"Maybe next time," Charlotte said.

"For sure," Trina said as sturdily as she could. When she closed the door behind Charlotte, she knew the party was officially over and her mother had officially not come. Poppo had told her not to count on her mother coming, but she hadn't listened. All the happiness Trina had felt during the party had drained out of her. She felt like the flowers in the vases outside, wilting in the cold.

She walked slowly into the dining room where she could hear a murmur of voices. Mr. Kinghorn, Mr. Sheg-stad, and Miss Dale were sitting at the dining room table. Except for their costumes, and a few leftovers Miss Kitty had set on the blue plates, and her dad's silver face, it looked like the party had never happened.

"Come join us," her dad said, spreading out the old blueprints on the dining room table. "I thought I'd build a fire. Carrie wants to see the drawings, and Peter and Jerry have agreed to tell a few old stories before we call it a night."

Everything had gone perfectly for her dad. *Carrie, Peter, Jerry.* Trina felt like giving him one of Charlotte's mean old sneers. He had made new friends, but her own mother hadn't bothered to come to the party.

"No, thanks," Trina said and left the room.

She took the stairs one slow step at a time and went into her bedroom. "Be brave and valiant," she whispered to her reflection as she threw her wand on the bed and hung the cloak and hat on a hook next to her baseball caps, followed by Miss Dale's white shirt and skirt. Now she was down to her same old tomboy self in her shorts and a T-shirt. Shivering, she pulled on a sweatshirt and sat on the edge of her bed. Without the dollhouse, her room felt empty and lonely. If only she could talk to Augustine and tell her how her mother hadn't come to the party. It was her biggest woe yet.

Why did Augustine tell her she couldn't open the door to the turret room? Why couldn't she talk to the little doll one last time? She crossed her room and put her hand on the lever of the mirrored door. As she started to push down, she remembered she would be breaking a promise if she opened the door. She let go of the lever as Augustine's words came to mind: *I know of no good story where the maiden gives up.*

Trina glanced up at the mantel where her mother's note sat on top of the postcards. Why give up now? She had her mother's address. She could write her a letter and tell her all about herself and then her mother would write back and tell her all about her fancy life. By the time they met in person, they would be all caught up.

Trina grabbed a notebook and pen from her backpack and flopped on her bed.

And stared at the blank page.

Her mother had every chance to come to the party and she had decided not to, so a letter wasn't going to make a bit of difference. Besides, her mother had signed her note "Fondly, C." Her mother didn't want to be a mother. Trina knew that now in her heart. She wasn't giving up; she was just finally accepting the truth.

KNOCK!

Trina jumped.

"The Tin Man has come to see the wizard," her dad said.

"You mean witch, Poppo," she said.

"Not a wizard?"

Trina got off her bed and opened her door, shaking her head. "It's a girl thing, Poppo."

Her dad was standing there with a gooey monster brownie on one of the blue plates. "It's the last one. We're lucky Edward didn't see it."

Trina gave a half-hearted smile. "Did Miss Dale and everyone go home?" Trina asked.

"No, the three of them are still downstairs. I'm getting the inside scoop on the whole town."

Trina followed his eyes around her room. There wasn't a stick of furniture in it except for the four-poster bed. After all the special deliveries, it had become the emptiest room at Goldenrod. "Hey, where's the dollhouse?" he asked.

"I'm done playing with it, so I put it away," she fibbed, sitting down on the edge of her bed. "Fifth graders are too big to play with dolls anyway," she said. It crushed her that no one would ever know the truth about Augustine, or how much Augustine had helped her since they had arrived at Goldenrod. Or how she had lost her mother and her best friend in the same night.

Her dad sat down next to her on the bed and set the monster brownie between them. Trina didn't feel like eating, so she stared at the brownie. He stared at the floor.

"It's okay if you go back downstairs," Trina said, but he didn't move.

"I think I belong right here with you." Then he put his arm around her and said, "I'm sorry she didn't come to the party."

"It's okay," Trina said, picking up the brownie. But it wasn't. It really wasn't. And she couldn't pretend it was for another second. She dropped the brownie back on the plate and pushed it across her bed. "I even told Charlotte and Edward she was coming."

As she started to cry, her dad pulled her close with both arms, hugging her tighter and tighter. When her breathing calmed, he took her face in his hands and wiped her tears with his big, clumsy, loving hands. "You have no idea how much I wanted her to come tonight."

"Really, Poppo?" Trina was surprised. After all, her mother had run out on both of them.

He nodded. "For your sake. And I thought this time she would, after she sent you that note. I just didn't want you to get your hopes up."

"I don't think she ever wanted to come," said Trina. The words hurt like crazy, but she knew they were true. She trembled with her next breath. "Growing up is hard, isn't it, Poppo?"

"It sure is," he said. "That's why I'm here for you." He took her hand and squeezed it in his big grip. "I know how much it hurts to hope for something that doesn't come true. I hoped for a long time too."

"It's terrible, Poppo. How do I make it go away?"

He thought for a few seconds. "By hoping for something else, I guess. Maybe start with something small and work your way up. Tell me one little thing you hope for and I'll see what I can do."

Augustine had said it was the little things that led to happiness, and now her dad was saying the same thing, but Trina couldn't come up with anything small. Her mother hadn't come to the party. And the only other thing she wanted was a real home to live in forever. A home and a mother were pretty big things.

"You go first," she said.

Her dad shrugged. "Well, I'm a pretty simple guy. A lot of things make me happy." He reached for the blue plate. "I'd be happy if you let me eat this brownie."

"Poppo," Trina giggled, and then she picked up the brownie, broke it in half, and took a big bite from the biggest half. She held the other—smaller—half out to her dad. "You have to thtart thmall," she said to him, trying to talk around the mouthful of gooey caramel and chocolate.

Trina was still chewing her giant bite of brownie when a splash of bright light ricocheted off the mirror and lit up their faces.

"Look at that," her dad said, getting up and looking out the window. "Someone's coming."

Their playfulness had stopped in an instant. "But who would come at this hour?" Trina wondered out loud. Feeling uneasy, she followed her dad to the window. A pair of headlights was bouncing on the dark road that cut through the cornfields and heading straight for Golden-rod. The house lights dimmed as Trina cupped her eyes to the cool glass.

"It's a limousine," her dad said.

"How do you know?"

"Because the taillights are a long way from the headlights."

Standing at the window, Trina had never felt so cold. Not even when they were snowed in up in northern Minnesota. That day had been the best day of her life. She didn't know what to think of this day.

Trina couldn't read her dad's face. He wasn't happy or sad or excited or anything when he put his arm around her shoulder and spoke very calmly. "I've been thinking about this possibility a lot lately. And I'm pretty sure the future holds a ton of girl things I won't understand, so I want you to know . . ." Trina studied his reflection in the glass. There was no sign of that faraway look in his eyes. "If your mother ever invites you to live with her, it will be okay with me as long as it's okay with you."

What was Poppo saying? Was her mother really coming for her? The monster brownie did a full flip in her stomach as Trina watched the car roll through the field, moonlight reflecting off its chrome trim like sparkling diamonds. She wondered what it would be like to live in a place like Hollywood and wear expensive clothes. She wondered what kind of a mother her fancy mom would be. What would a fancy mom do to make her laugh?

Not only that, what would her dad do without her? And what would she do without him? They were a team. Poppo always knew when something was bothering her. He was grubby and absentminded, and he had a lot of trouble letting her grow up, but he was funny and kind. She always knew he loved her, but now she knew he loved her so much he would do anything for her. Even let her go.

Running away from New Royal was one thing, but actually living with her mom would be another. After saying good-bye to Augustine, Trina didn't think her heart could sink any lower in one night until she imagined her mother falling from the sky and plucking her from Goldenrod and the one place she really belonged: with her dad.

Staying with her dad would be the happy ending to her story.

"Poppo, I don't want to live with her," Trina finally said as the long, dark car approached the gate. "I want to stay right here with you."

"But I thought—"

Trina shook her head. "Sometimes what you think you want and what you really want are two different things."

Her dad turned from the window with a big smile on his face. But there was more to his smile than happiness and relief. She could tell he was proud of her, and that made her feel more grown-up than anything else she could wish for.

"Well, Citrine, it looks like we better get downstairs."

She raised her eyebrows at him. "On one condition," she said.

"What?" he asked, a little uncertainly.

"You have to call me Trina. Forever. No matter how grown-up I get."

Chapter Twenty-Six

The limousine's high beams lit up the parlor as Trina and her dad hurried down the stairs, hand in hand. Mr. Kinghorn, Mr. Shegstad, and Miss Dale were standing at the bay window, watching the car's arrival.

"Leave this to me," Mr. Kinghorn said. He strolled into the foyer, opened the front door, letting in a sweep of cold air, and walked across the porch and down the steps to meet the sleek black car as it rolled to a stop inside the gate. Trina and her dad followed him as far as the porch, while Miss Dale and Mr. Shegstad stayed in the doorway.

A chauffeur got out of the limousine and spoke to Mr. Kinghorn before he opened the rear door. A parasol appeared first, followed by a woman in a long white dress, holding its handle. *She* is *Mary Poppins*, Trina thought, trying to take in every inch of the woman half-hidden in the shadows. A man got out of the other side, carrying a cane. He wore a dark suit and a round hat, and his white collar and cuffs glowed in the moonlight. Most surprising of all, a little girl popped out of the back seat, wearing a white ruffled dress.

"Poppo, I thought you said she didn't want to be tied down," Trina said, grabbing hold of his hand.

"I did," he said anxiously, "but that was a long time ago. Maybe she remarried." Trina squeezed his hand. Hard.

Mr. Kinghorn shook hands with the couple, straightened his bow tie, and slowly turned to face the porch. "May I present to you Mr. and Mrs. Harlan M. Roy the Second of New York."

"The Roys?" Trina let go of her dad's hand and reached for the railing to keep from falling over. She was so relieved the surprise guests had nothing to do with her mother that she let her dad lift her up and swing her through the air, and she wasn't the least bit embarrassed.

But, the *Roys*?

"Oh, yes, yes, the Roys!" Mr. Shegstad exclaimed, hurrying down the steps and across the yard, his white angel wings flapping behind him. "I'm Gerald Shegstad, the funeral director. I invited you. So happy you are finally here." He shook their hands vigorously.

Mrs. Roy took her husband's arm and looked up at Goldenrod, who was all aglow with firelight. "Harlan, look. The house is far more beautiful than the pictures. More beautiful than I ever imagined."

"This is the man you have to thank for that," Mr. Shegstad said, accompanying Mr. and Mrs. Roy to the porch. He gestured to Trina's dad, who was still in such shock that he descended the steps as stiffly as if he still wore his Tin-Man costume. "This is Mr. Michael Maxwell."

Her dad's silver-sprinkled arm glittered in the

moonlight as he extended it toward Mr. Roy, and Trina could see the puzzled look on Mr. Roy's face. "He was the Tin Man tonight," Trina said, stepping up next to her dad.

"Ah, yes. A clever idea," Mr. Roy said, finally shaking her dad's hand.

"And this is my daughter, Ci—I mean, Trina," her dad said.

With absolute pleasure, Trina shook Mrs. Roy's hand and then Mr. Roy's hand. She was glad to meet them, glad they weren't her mother, but even gladder to hear her dad call her Trina.

"And up there," Mr. Shegstad said, pointing to Miss Dale whose teeth were chattering as she stood on the porch in her gingham Dorothy dress, "is Miss Carrie Dale. Her great-grandparents were gardeners here."

Mr. Harlan M. Roy the Second tipped his round black hat. "We had intended to arrive for the interment of my great-aunt at the behest of Mr. Shegstad here, but I couldn't get away at the time. Then Mr. Shegstad informed us of this costume party in honor of my great-relatives, and here we are. Seems a fine time to see how the remodeling is progressing." He tugged on his white cuffs. "I hope we are dressed appropriately."

"You're dressed just like the Roy family is dressed in a picture we have," Trina said.

"We must have that same picture," Mrs. Roy said.

"Ahem," said a little voice. When all heads turned, the little girl who had popped out of the backseat pushed her way to the center of the group. "And I'm Annie."

A shiver ran up Trina's spine. "You're Annie Roy?"

The little girl nodded with certainty. "I'm named after my great, great, great, great, great, great, great—" Mrs. Roy pressed one gloved finger to Annie's lips. "Aunt," Annie said as soon as her mother removed her hand. "And I'm almost this many years old." She held up all five fingers of one hand and her other thumb.

"Six?" Trina's stomach got ready for another backflip. She looked up at Mrs. Roy. "Is your name Anne, too?"

"Oh, no, please call me Maggie," Mrs. Roy said, twirling her parasol.

"Welcome to Goldenrod," Trina's dad said. "Let's go in. It's chilly out here."

The group hadn't gotten any farther than the foyer when Mrs. Roy gasped. "Oh, Harlan, the woodwork is gorgeous."

"The whole house is trimmed in mahogany," Trina said. "Follow me. I'll give you a tour."

"Please, let me take your things," Mr. Kinghorn said.

Mr. Kinghorn hung Mrs. Roy's parasol and Mr. Roy's hat and cane on the coat rack in the foyer.

"Take my sweater," Annie insisted. "I'm going to slide down the banister."

"Oh, no, you're not," Mrs. Roy said.

Annie stomped her foot and frowned as all the adults followed Trina into the parlor.

Trina was excited to show the Roys around the house, but it was Goldenrod who really welcomed her guests. For the first time since Trina and her dad had arrived, she looked lived-in, but mostly she looked loved. Two chairs sat on a fringed rug facing the roaring fire, a big bouquet of mums decorated the mantel, and the oil lamp glowed on the fancy little table.

"Harlan, listen to this," Mrs. Roy said, cranking up the phonograph. When she set the needle on the record, the Irish voice sang the sweet song about endearing charms and Trina was thrilled to hear the melody filling the house again—all the way to the turret room.

"I know that song," Mr. Roy said. "My grandmother used to sing it to me."

"Mine, too," Mrs. Roy said. The two of them hummed along as Trina led the group into the dining room, where Mrs. Roy raved again. "Harlan, just imagine the dinner parties we could host here!"

"Yes, yes. Seats twelve," Mr. Shegstad said.

From the dining room they pushed through the swinging door into the butler's pantry and on into the kitchen. Mr. Roy was in and out in a second, but Mrs. Roy lingered and Trina could tell she imagined cooking at the giant stove. Or maybe she imagined a cook cooking at the stove, because Trina had a hard time believing she did any kind of cooking herself.

From the dining room, Trina led them into the library—the long way. "Look," she said, pulling out one of the carved panels and pushing it back into place. "It has pocket doors."

"Lovely," Mrs. Roy said, but she wasn't really listening. She wandered the room, running her hand first along the rolltop desk and then along the bookshelves, pausing to read a title or two whenever she bumped into a book.

"As you can see, Mr. Roy was very generous with his books," Mr. Kinghorn said.

Mr. Roy sat down in the big rocking chair by the fireplace and held his chin in deep thought as he stared up at the portrait of his great-great-uncle, Harlan M. Roy. "I had understood the house was empty," he said.

Trina caught Mr. Shegstad's eye first. Nervous Mr. Shegstad rubbed his hands together and his lips moved, but he didn't say a word. Then she looked to Miss Dale and Mr. Kinghorn and finally her dad. Everyone was speechless. No way could they ever tell the Roys about the Dare Club.

"It was all in storage," Trina said.

"In town," her dad added.

"In a big shed," Mr. Kinghorn said.

"Under lock and key," Miss Dale said.

Mr. Roy stood up and carefully admired the chair he sat in. "Good to know it was well cared for all these years. It's probably worth a small fortune."

"Is the house drafty?" Mrs. Roy asked. She was standing by the windows.

Trina's dad shook his head. "She's got steam—" he began, but Goldenrod interrupted him with a gentle *psst, psst* from the library radiator, answering for herself.

Right then Annie came running into the room. "Come play with me, Trina." And then she found the pocket doors to the smoking room and opened and shut them and opened them again as if it were a game.

Mrs. Roy sailed out of the library and into the smoking room with a look of determination. Annie ran into the smoking room right behind her mother. As if she'd been there before, she instantly spotted the door to the secret passageway beneath the stairs. "Let's all go on a treasure hunt," she said, holding the door open for the entire group. They all followed Annie single-file into the dining room, and soon they were standing in a group in the parlor.

"Is there a school nearby?" Mrs. Roy asked.

"New Royal Public School," Trina said. "Miss Dale teaches there."

Miss Dale smiled and Mrs. Roy beamed, but Mr. Roy's eyes were as big as his derby hat. "Honey, sweetheart, you aren't thinking about living here, are you?"

The music crackled to a stop, but Mrs. Roy continued to hum and didn't answer. She simply wandered from the parlor to the dining room and back again with a tight-lipped smile. Finally, she turned to her husband with a warm and loving look. "Harlan, you can't sell it. I'd just die if you sold it."

"Maggie, my dear. It would cost a fortune to heat." He held his hands in the air as he spoke. "And the kitchen is from another century."

"Harlan, please, we have servants. And I'm sure Mr. Maxwell—"

"Margaret, we can't live here. It's impossible. There's no garage. Where would I store my car collection?"

"My dad could build you a garage," Trina said, startling not only Mr. Roy but also herself. "He can build anything." She took Mr. Roy's hand and guided him to the dining room table, winking at her dad. "Look. We have the blueprints for the original carriage house right here."

Trina flattened the plans on the dining room table for Mr. Roy as Mrs. Roy leaned over her husband's shoulder.

"The stable could easily be turned into a modern garage," Trina's dad said.

"Oh, Harlan, no. We must leave the stable as is. Don't you see? Annie could learn to ride. She could have her own pony."

"I get my own pony! I get my own pony!" Annie shouted, jumping up and down as Mr. Roy paced in frantic circles. Then Annie tapped Trina on her arm and motioned her to bend down. She put her arm around Trina's neck and whispered in her ear, "My father says my mother always gets everything she wants."

Trina nodded, pretty sure little Annie Roy got everything she wanted too, but suddenly she felt as if someone else had tapped her on the shoulder to get her attention. She turned around. No one was there. No one except Goldenrod.

Now what did Goldenrod want her to do?

Mr. Harlan M. Roy the Second stopped pacing. "My dear, we have too many houses as it is. And we travel constantly. Who would take care of this house in our absence?"

Trina felt as if she'd been pushed forward by a powerful hand. "We would."

All eyes were on Trina.

"If my dad builds the carriage house, we could live in it and take care of Goldenrod when you're gone."

No one said a word. Trina figured Mr. Harlan M. Roy the Second was trying to come up with another reason it wouldn't work, while Mrs. Roy was dreaming up more reasons why it should. The only thing Trina knew for sure was how she felt. Even though the house was in the middle of nowhere and filled with unfinished projects, she couldn't leave Goldenrod. The grande dame had begun to feel like home. Which meant the biggest question was, *What did her dad think?* "Maybe we could put down roots for a little while. What do you say, Poppo?"

Now all eyes were on her dad—particularly Mrs. Roy's eyes.

His face flushed through the silver makeup as he looked slowly from face to face, finally stopping at Trina's. "It's worth considering," he said. "It might be nice to settle down."

"The town would love to have you," Mr. Kinghorn said.

"Yes, yes," Mr. Shegstad said.

Trina looked up at Miss Dale. Her green eyes practically twinkled as she looked to Trina's dad and then back at Trina. "I would like it very much if you stayed."

"But, Maggie, my dear, what if—?"

"It's decided then," Mrs. Roy said, patting her husband's hand. "Annie, what do you think of your new home?"

Annie folded her arms. "If this is our house, where's my room?"

"Upstairs," Trina said. "I'll show you." She took Annie's hand and led her up the staircase into her own room. "Once upon a time, a little girl just like you lived in this room. She was your great, great, great . . ."

Annie wasn't paying any attention. She had let go of Trina's hand and was running around the room touching everything in sight. "She had her own bed and her own fireplace and her own mirror . . ." Annie scrunched up her face as she reached for Trina's Brewers cap. "And she had her own icky baseball cap—"

"That baseball cap is mine," Trina said, and then she froze in place. Annie had put one hand on the lever so she could reach for the baseball cap with the other.

"Hey, this wiggles," Annie said. She grabbed the lever with both hands and wiggled it again. Then she pushed on the lever until the latch clicked. "This is a door," Annie cried as the mirrored door creaked open. "To a secret room."

"But you can't go in there!"

"Who says?" Annie made a mad face at Trina and disappeared into the turret room. "Don't touch anything," Trina shouted as Augustine's words came rushing back to her. But she had told *Trina* never to open the door again, not Annie.

Annie was kneeling on the floor in a sliver of harvest moonlight that sneaked through a crack in one of the shutters, peering into the dollhouse. When Trina flipped on the light, Annie shook with excitement. "Look, Trina. There's a girl doll and a mommy doll and a daddy doll. Just like my family." Annie reached up and tugged on Trina's hand. "Why can't I touch it, Trina? How can I play with it if I can't touch it?"

Trina crouched next to Annie. Cleaned and polished, with its whole family under its roof, the dollhouse looked as lived-in and loved as Goldenrod. Sugar crystals still sparkled in the teacups, but to Trina it already seemed as if the tea parties had taken place a lifetime ago.

Seeing Augustine dressed as Briar Rose, lying lifeless in her four-poster bed, put away in the turret room, made Trina terribly sad until she realized the little doll wasn't forgotten—she was waiting. Her prince might never arrive, but here was a little girl who wanted to play with her—a wish come true.

Trina lifted Augustine from her bed. When the doll's eyes blinked open, Trina's heart gave a skip, but her blink was that of an ordinary doll. There was no wink, no glimmer of life. Trina smoothed the little doll's hair one last time and placed her in Annie's eager hands. "Don't ever leave her in the yard or she might get scared."

"She can't get scared, Trina. She's just a doll," Annie said.

"But she's not just any doll. Her name is Augustine."

Trina sat down on the floor and felt a sharp jab in her thigh. She reached into her pocket and pulled out the packet of sea creatures. Now the little frog didn't seem so silly. She opened the package and set the frog on Augustine's bedside table next to her silver hairbrush.

"What's that for?" Annie asked.

"That's her prince."

"No, it's not. It's a frog."

"It's an enchanted frog, like the ones they have in fairy tales."

"Fairy tales aren't true," Annie said, reaching for the pony.

"Fairy tales are true if you believe in them," Trina said. "Would you like me to tell you a story? Augustine loves stories."

"Yes, but only if it's true," Annie said.

"All stories are true if you believe them," Trina said.

Trina leaned back on her elbows as Annie made the pony gallop around the floor of the playroom with Augustine bouncing on its back, arms flopping and hair flying. "Once upon a time there was a little doll."

Psst, psst, the radiator hissed gently.

Annie's eyes widened and she sat right down in Trina's lap. "What was that?"

"The radiator," Trina said. "It does that once in a while, but you'll get used to it." But really, she knew it was Goldenrod whispering in her ear, saying thank you for the fire in her hearth and the music and laughter within her walls. And a new family. The same things that made Goldenrod happy made Trina happy too. For the first time Trina could ever remember, she had a real place to call home.

"Once upon a time," Annie said, bouncing in Trina's lap. "Keep going."

"Once upon a time," Trina continued, "there was a little doll. She was made of white porcelain and she had fine little jointed arms and legs. She was French, and one amazing thing about her made her different from all other dolls."

"What?" Annie asked, holding very, very still.

"She could talk."

"That's not true. Dolls don't talk."

Trina looked into Annie's sparkling blue eyes and smiled. "They do if you're lucky enough to hear them."

Acknowledgments

The route to Goldenrod has been quite an adventure, but clearly it was a path sprinkled with magic—the magic of love, friendship, family, and story. I have many people to thank for reading early drafts, for listening, or for simply believing in me. I thank them here for all of the above and then some:

Al Sicherman, for steadfast support, both technical and emotional, and for teaching me to make chocolate ganache in the middle of everything; Andy Cochran, for talking stories and for reading over and over and over again; Anne Budroe Benda, for being a great friend and an ardent fan ever since seventh grade; Ashley Tourville, for literally making it possible; Catherine Watson, for being the best lifelong mentor imaginable; Cindy Rogers and Jane St. Anthony and the rest of the gang at the Johnson Home, for sustaining me; Elizabeth Haukaas, for asking one heck of a question and also for that weekend of healing in New York; John Watson, for the extra magic; Larry Lavercombe, for terrific notes as usual; Liliana Becker, via Cindy Evensen, for wanting to know more about Trina's mother; Maggie Morris, for the paper wishes and Steven Watson, for imparting a love of history and books.

Deepest gratitude goes to Jane Resh Thomas for teaching me to write stories, to Anne Ursu and Phyllis Root for teaching me to play, and to the wonderful Hamline MFAC program—faculty and friends—for pointing the way.

Heartfelt thanks goes to my indefatigable agent, Sarah Davies, and my incredibly insightful editor, Alix Reid, both of whom loved Goldenrod before she knew who she really was and therefore guided me to a better story.

The humblest of thanks goes to my children, John O'Reilly, Helen O'Reilly, and William O'Reilly, my biggest champions, who grew up behind the scenes, but are always center-stage in my heart. (And a special thank you to Will for some of the best writing advice I have ever received.)

The ultimate thank you goes to my husband, John, for just about everything.

About the Author

Jane O'Reilly grew up in a very old house on a Mississippi River bluff in Fort Snelling, Minnesota. The youngest of five children, she enjoyed the family's annual, month-long camping trips, crisscrossing North America from Circle, Alaska, to the tip of the Yucatán Peninsula. Those trips sparked a love of travel, adventure, cultures, language—and coming home. Jane is the recipient of a McKnight Fellowship in Screenwriting and holds an MFA in Writing for Children and Young Adults from Hamline University. She lives in Minneapolis with her husband, dog, and cat in a hundred-year-old house that creaks in the night. *The Secret of Goldenrod* is her debut novel.